WHAT HARRY SAW

WHAT HARRY SAW

THOMAS MORAN

RIVERHEAD BOOKS

a member of Penguin Putnam Inc.

New York

2002

RIVERHEAD BOOKS
a member of
Penguin Putnam Inc.
375 Hudson Street
New York, NY 10014

Library of Congress Cataloging-in-Publication Data

Moran, Thomas.
What Harry saw / Thomas Moran.
p.   cm.
ISBN 1-57322-224-0
1. Men—Australia—Fiction.   2. Australia—Fiction.
I. Title.
PS3563.O7714W48   2002   2002016945
813′.54—dc21

Printed in the United States of America

1   3   5   7   9   10   8   6   4   2

This book is printed on acid-free paper. ∞

ACKNOWLEDGMENTS

With thanks to Miriam Goderich and Chris Knutsen. And with grati-tude to Wyatt Prunty and the University of the South for the gift of time in that house on Clara's Point Road.

For Jane

Now I know what Jesus had meant when he said,
"After me, it's the straight action and no more dressing up."

RUSSELL HOBAN

WHAT HARRY SAW

Here's a fair one: Born blind.

Give that beauty half a moment, see where it takes you. If it isn't near to tears, if you reckon it's just a tragic turn that sometimes happens to somebody else's kid, if you don't damn it as a scabby betrayal of life's promise, then I've grave doubts you deserve the air you're breathing.

Give it another moment. Imagine, if you're able, that you've been struck blind this very instant. Shocking, yeah? You're feeling really sorry for yourself.

But you've had your go, haven't you? You are not facing a total blank. You possess images of everyone and everything you ever cared for. You can put together a nice mental video, play it forward or backward just as you please, even freeze-frame the best bits. That should help you keep your grip on the world and where you once stood in it, where you might still stand.

Blind from birth? Could you ever be truly sure you were anywhere real at all? Or would you feel you were wandering in Dreamtime—as the Aboriginals who haven't gone urban still conceive—yet with none of the ancient abo prehension to compass you through it? Not that any of us fully understand this Dreamtime. It's only a word. Some people here like to drop it casually into cocktail chatter, as if that proves they've some spiritual depth within their Prada-sheathed, tennis-toned bodies.

Quite a rant I suppose, from a perfect stranger. It's shame, actually. Of the bitterest sort. A long time back in a place I never should have gone I saw a blind baby naked and crawling loose and aimless on the beaten earth floor of a hut. And I laughed.

I thought of a grub. Couldn't help it. A soft, squirmy grub, that's what the pitiful little creature first brought to mind. I laughed, right in front of the poor kid's mother. I cringe over the reflex still. I expect I'll always regret that cruelty I can never undo or make good.

So I tell myself there are more terrible fates. Born with half a brain, born with heart valves that won't close properly, born with cystic fibrosis or spina bifida, born with that almost inconceivable disease that makes a child look sixty at four and die of old age by nine or ten. Dozens of horrible afflictions.

For kids whose brains and bodies are perfect except for those sightless eyes, I've convinced myself life would be difficult but far from hopeless. It really couldn't be as if you weren't in the world, could it? As you grew, everything would eventually make itself known. You'd feel the ferocious summer sun on your face, the cool relieving winds and fat rain of the westerlies. You'd gradually learn to navigate your immediate geography, and the shapes and textures of objects there, by touch. You'd come to relish flavors: grilled king prawns, maybe, or a perfectly ripe banana, or a nice cold beer. Every day you'd be awash in aromas, from sweet-blooming jacarandas to reeking traffic exhaust, and know the messages they carry. You'd come to recognize tones of affection, or irritation, or joy, or sarcasm, or sincerity, or pity (which you would almost certainly

2

resent) in people's voices. You'd get the news of the day from radio, some ease and enjoyment from Mozart or Górecki, from Midnight Oil or Hunters & Collectors. You'd discover books and the beauty of stories through your fingertips, or the audio versions. No reason you couldn't master any number of trades or professions, up to and including the law or quantum physics, if you were clever enough and inclined that way.

You would never, ever have to dread the coming of night.

And if you struck it really lucky, you might even get to know the lovely intimate smoothness of someone's skin, someone whose body is rich with amazing possibilities, someone whose presence envelopes you with love. Someone with whom you might very well have babies of your own one day.

Someone like Lucy, who gave those gifts to me.

Beyond all that, I've the strongest intimation that not having had a single glimpse of this bloody world would give you the rarest sort of innocence and a wonderful state of grace, for all your life.

Proof? Well, it's pretty bloody funny, isn't it, how many of us with perfect vision would give almost anything never to have seen some of the stuff we've seen. It's hilarious how we go on and on trying any anodyne—from drink and drugs to the Dalai Lama—that might exile certain memories to an area of permanent darkness. If you know anyone at all who wouldn't love to erase a few bits of his life, who doesn't dearly wish certain scenes had never been played, your circle of acquaintances must include a saint.

My personal shortlist for total oblivion? Easy enough. Besides my heartless reaction to one blind infant, there are about three hundred days of my dad's final year of life. Lucy's eyes flashing cold and hard as a diamond for an instant when she told me she was pregnant. A beautiful old violin that never should have been lifted from its case. And a young girl's fall. Falling in a way that never looked like a fall, holding a dancer's line with her body even as a fucking dry-rotted fence slat suddenly snapped under her slight weight high on South Head. Even as she plunged down that sheer cliff, combers hard as the hands of God rising up to crush her.

MY NAME'S HARRY, by the bye. I'm just on the wrong side of forty now. I've lived in just one place since I was born, which I don't regret though it seems to be a negative distinction in my generation.

Where, exactly? Down under. The Antipodes, the end of the earth—which suits me, because I reckon being so far from anywhere is the chief reason Australia's remained as pleasant and lovely as it has. When we call the place Oz, and we frequently do, it isn't entirely a joke.

My dad lived all his life as well in this same ordinary brick house in a western suburb of central Sydney called Ashfield. His dad had bought the place when he returned from the Great War minus a proper digestive system (thanks to some serious dysentery) and an eye gouged out entire by a Turk grenade fragment.

Dad's own war souvenir was a hole in his left cheek. Nothing really disgusting but still a hole about the size of a bottle cap. You could see a bit of gum and false teeth through it. He was fine eating anything solid, so long as he remembered to take small bites and chew carefully on the right side of his mouth. But liquids were a problem. He had to drink his beer through a straw, which was the worst of it as far as he was concerned.

He acquired that little decoration in a truly pestilential place: the Kokoda Track, New Guinea, 1942. The Japs were battling their way up over the Owen Stanley Range to take Port Moresby. From there it would have been a hop to Queensland, and not a lot to prevent them from raging through Australia like the rabid dogs they'd shown themselves to be in China, Malaya, Hong Kong and everywhere else they'd come calling.

So the Aussie troops were shipped back from the Western Desert to stop the Short Ones on that lone bloody trail over those formidable mountains. What Dad stopped was a pointy little bullet from a Nambu light machine gun that put a cute dimple in his right cheek going in, and made a ragged wreck of the other, coming out sideways with most of his teeth in tow and blowing away so much tissue the field surgeons couldn't close the hole. They just debrided the rough edges 'til they got it fairly smooth, and stretched the skin to make it a bit smaller. Back home, they offered reconstructive grafts to seal up the thing, but Dad said no, he'd enough of army hospitals—a Nambu bullet from the same burst had smashed his hip and kept him in one for a year. And though he would never admit it, to him that hole was what he had instead of a medal. Something to be proud of, something that meant a great deal to all Aussies in those days, though no one cares anymore.

Lucky for him he'd got married before the war, what with that ugly phiz he came home with. No, I'll take that back. I don't think a hole—or a missing arm or leg—would have mattered one bit to that lovely young woman. Even if she'd met him for the first time already mutilated, after his return. For I believe my mother and he were made for each other in every way. Except maybe one, which is why I didn't come wailing into the world until six or seven years after the war ended, their first and last child.

Mum and Dad were a matched pair, as close and understanding a couple as any. That's what everyone said, anyway. Of course I'm likely idealizing a bit. I have no idea how many images of our early days as a family are only received memories. But the abiding feeling I've retained down all these years is a sort of brightly optimistic fifties snapshot: Dad grasping one of my hands, Mum holding the other, me toddling happily along between them, occasionally swung up off my feet, both of them laughing. And both of them smiling down at me, arms around each other's waists, after they'd tucked me in bed nights. The two of them doting on each other, doting on me.

And when I was five or six—old enough so that most recollections of the time can be trusted as my own—they were still that way. First thing

Dad would do after returning from work each evening was come up be-hind my mother, who was always aproned and concentrated on whatever she was fixing for supper, and wrap his arms around her, holding her snug to him until she'd turn to be kissed. That done, he'd pretend he'd just noticed me peering shyly from around the door, stomp over like an ogre, change his grimace to a grin and pick me up, his laughter matching my giggles. Then, while Mum finished the cooking, he'd hold me on his lap and ask about my day. Even when I'd grown a bit too big for that sort of thing, he would always sit me down next to him, offer me one tiny sip of his beer, and listen with genuine interest to what I'd been up to at school or at play.

The only time voices were ever raised in our home was when a few of Dad's mates dropped by. Dad was a pressman at the *Herald*, a big goer for the trade unions and Labour politics, and so were his friends. Often they'd get excited and very loud about some change the newspaper's management was proposing. On many of those nights I'd have my hair ruffled by the big rough hand of one or another of these men, and be told something like "Your Dad's game, Harry. He's one hell of a battler."

Dad must have reserved his fighting spirit for politics and picket lines. There was never any obvious strife between him and Mum. Not that things were always perfect. They did have their spats, their little disagreements, but they kept them fairly quiet, fairly civil. At the very worst (it happened rarely enough that I remember most every occa-sion), Dad would simply slip out and come home late, with one or two too many pints under his belt. Whatever dispute had caused him to go seemed forgiven and forgotten as soon as he returned.

Then came one departure that sent everything we had to hell.

Mum, with scarely a single sign of feeling ill to warn us, went very quickly, very painfully. It was a cancer so nasty and so intimately feminine that Dad decided I was too young to be told any details about it. And for a while—I was fourteen—it seemed to me it had just about killed Dad as well. That buoyant, energetic man went flat as a blown-out tire.

He kept on with his work and the union and politics, he made some effort each evening to seem interested in my doings, he always managed to throw together something for supper. But I could see he'd gone all hollow, that his mind was someplace I could not fathom or follow.

And some nights, very late, I'd awake to a wracked and wretched sobbing from the bedroom he had always shared with Mum. The most horrible sound I'd ever heard. I never got used to it. Whenever it started I'd cram the pillow tight against my ears, and spend the rest of the night shivering.

Presently Dad took heavily to drink. Alcohol never made him mean or aggressive, just dull and careless. And I turned morose and sullen, moping about, falling behind in school. Soon enough I found my own antidote: using rage to stifle grief. First time I tried that on, getting really furious at Mum for having abandoned me, guilt hit me as sharp and shocky as if I'd stuck a key in an electric socket. So I bypassed her and let anger pour over the world and the way everyone lived in it. Not exactly an original response—certainly not a wise one as things turned out—but it seemed clever enough to me at the time.

Dad drunk and me venomous in the ever bitter air of the house made our home in Ashfield not exactly a place you would enjoy coming back to at the end of your day. So we both kept away as much as we could. Dad began loitering around the pub or the Returned Servicemen's League club 'til they threw him out. I ran a bit wild with a couple of bad boys from school I hadn't wanted to know before, sniffing glue in brown paper bags. We moved on to various uppers and downers, some grass or hash once in a while. Our tastes eventually centered on the rush of crystal meth, and the speedy aggro it fueled.

Dad was either too drunk or too numbed to notice the hours I started keeping and the condition I'd stagger home in. My new mates and I got deeply into petty thievery, vandalism, devilry of all sorts. Wired on meth, we'd hang on some of the busier street corners, pick fights with boys almost at random. Never hesitating to put the boot in once we'd beaten a bloke to the pavement. And we'd make ourselves as obnoxious as possible to any girl past puberty who wandered by. It was so easy. We never had to say a word—just a really exaggerated lick in the air.

No love beads, acid highs, mellow opium dreams or maundering hippie shit for me, though there were lots of kids into that stuff at the time. I liked to play rough.

Or thought I did, until I found out what rough really is. Phuoc Tuy Province, Republic of Vietnam, 1971—the very arse-end of yet another war, my battalion of the Royal Australian Regiment gradually withdrawing along with most of the American troops. Hardly any serious fighting at all, just some very short and vicious skirmishes from time to time.

But then I got a beaut of a "so long, mate" from Mr. Charles in the form of an RPG as I was sneaking through the camp perimeter one night after a social call on a girl named Phong down at the local ville. Red-hot shrapnel shredded my flesh.

My right side and back from neck to hip still looks like it's been chewed by a mob of starving goannas. Or a couple of really big dingos.

Phuoc Tuy. Fuck Toy. Pretty funny, yeah? May as well add that to my shortlist for oblivion, too.

8

2

MIND IF WE HIT the fast-forward button now? Won't go too far past my illuminating rendezvous with NVA ordnance. Just a hop to 1973 and a key scene that defines the arc of my entire story.

A close-up. Here's young Harry Hull, lean-faced and looking (he hopes) maybe a bit like that great new Aussie actor, Bryan Brown. Tie loose at the neck of his starched white shirt, sleeves rolled up, cigarette pasted to his lower lip, leaning back in his swivel chair with a self-satisfied smirk on his face while a new IBM Selectric purrs in neutral on his desk.

Pull back: He's in a bustling newsroom, phones jangling everywhere, dozens of other Selectrics tap-tap-tapping in a hell of a hurry, a couple of editors at the far end of the room frowning at sheaves of paper in their hands and then shouting out someone's last name in tones only an asylum escapee might consider polite. Urgency is palpable. But no worries,

Harry's thinking. He's just sent his first story to the desk and he's sure it's all right.

Then a white paper plane comes spiraling down and augers into his desk. He grabs it, unfolds it. It's his story, more blue lines and editing symbols on it than he can count. And written in all caps at the top: "ENGLISH YOUR SECOND LANGUAGE?" A funny expression appears on his face. Not, sad to say, one of Bryan's patented ironic Aussie grins.

He is being invited by someone unknown—but clearly at least a couple of ranks above him, he understands instantly—to feel deeply embarrassed about his effort.

He smells her before he sees her. Just a light, clean scent that reminds him of Centennial Park in full spring. All fresh, green, pleasant. "Get the message, cobber?" he hears a voice clear as new rain. "You've just come on, so I'll forgive you this time."

Harry spins in his chair and there's a woman to look twice at standing quite close. She's as long and sleek as one of those single-masted racers moored in Double Bay, almost a proto–Nicole Kidman but without that haughty vanity. And she's having a serious problem trying to keep a grin from spoiling the stern expression she's put on her face. Not a drop-dead beauty. Just neat, even features. But a mouth rich with indecent promise she's clearly unaware it possesses. She's one of the subeditors, Harry realizes, though he doesn't know her name or a thing about her. Or how in hell he missed noticing her all week even in this stockpen of a newsroom.

"As bad as that, is it?" Best he can manage, our bold boy, bothered in a most unfamiliar way by green eyes as directly appraising as any he's ever encountered.

"Very bad if the managing editor has a bash at your story in its present shoddy condition," she says. "If I were you, I'd commit the stylebook to heart fast as I could, and spend my nights with a grammar text. As well as learning how to make use of the dictionary I see there on your desk, Mister Cadet."

She leans over Harry and taps that virginal, never-opened book just once with a lovely, long forefinger. Then she walks away.

Rather spend a night or two with you, personal instruction and all, Harry whispers to himself, watching her perfect bum for the moment or two it takes her to disappear among the maze of desks. That fresh spring greening smell stays around awhile as he gets to work cleaning up his story.

Hello, Lucy.

NOW IF WE REWIND, let the tape spin back a bit, and then press Play, we'll see the perfect continuity. Harry is in the right place at the right time for Lucy to stroll into his life only because some years previously the little retard committed a felony, was caught, had his bum run ragged in army training camps, then arrantly got himself shipped off to Fuck Toy and was blown to bits.

This peculiar odyssey began with Harry ricocheting around Sydney one night way too high on speed, convinced he was unloved, unwanted and misunderstood. And concluding, in the wealthy suburb of Vaucluse, that he was owed one of the lovely Mercs or Jags in the driveways there. But he was so chemically addled he made off with a ratbag Toyota. Went racing down the Eastern Highway, squealed through Double Bay and all the way over to Bondi Junction before the police managed to bag him.

But there was an even bigger shock than the snap of steel handcuffs around his wrists in store for this lad.

After posting bail and dragging me home, Dad strapped the hell out me. It was the first time in my life he'd raised voice or hand to me, and he did it thoroughly, using a thick leather garrison belt, stone sober the whole time. I was too weak and woozy to resist, couldn't feel much in the way of pain anyway because I'd swallowed the two ludes I'd had in my pocket when the coppers pulled me over. But the rage Dad displayed left me weeping.

The judge was more even-tempered. Very calm, very dignified, no rancor at all in his voice when he offered me the choice of six months in prison or what he termed, as I recall, "a character-building and quite educational" period of service in the Australian Army. I was nineteen. For two years I'd been loading lorries starting at 4 A.M. each day, a job Dad had wrangled for me after I left school. I failed to see how the army could be any worse than that, and it had to be better than gaol—everyone knew what happened to fresh youngsters there. So I became Private Hull.

Dad, naturally, would have been proud if I'd joined under my own power, military service being such a part of the family tradition. But he was scarcely recognizable when we walked out of court, my enlistment papers signed and sealed. His face was all mottled, and not, for a change, from drink.

"You give me the shits, Harry," were his parting words, after I'd packed and was ready to leave Ashfield. "You're a bloody disgrace. You're on your own after the army's done with you."

"Well, see ya when I see ya, then," I said, wanting to sound cocky and uncaring but feeling most unsettled at the sureness of his tone.

"Don't dream you'll be welcome at the house again."

"Ah, get stuffed!" I said, walking away with a pressure rising in my skull that only just failed to make me turn and beg the geezer to tell me that he hadn't fully meant it. But instead I fell back on my now habitual antidote to grief I couldn't otherwise bear: anger. At the world, at everything and everyone in it.

Conveniently excluding myself, of course.

I stayed ever on the borders of rage, though I had enough sense left to step very lightly when the potential object of aggression was an ignorant bellowing NCO instead of some hapless civilian in a pub with no clue what was about to hit him. On duty, I was a model soldier—properly cringing and subservient but crisp and keen as could be in all my training and tasks. I even made corporal in double-quick time, naturally took great delight then in bellowing at new trainees.

I bellowed in quite another way entirely when the RPG hit, you can be sure of that. As sure as I am that a couple of my former charges stood around laughing as they watched me writhe and bleed.

"Smarts a bit, does it, Corporal Hull?" said one. "Fetch you a beer then, shall I, Corporal?" another chimed in during a brief lull in my screaming.

When I was evacuated back to Sydney, my few friends from before the army who weren't either in prison or vanished on the hippie trail didn't want to know me. Seemed everyone except the old-soldier RSL types like Dad thought Vietnam vets were shits at best and more probably murderous psychos, the war there being so "indisputably morally abhorrent," as the prevailing sentiment went.

So it was Dad who showed up the first day and every day I was in hospital, almost as if the criminal circumstances of my going military had changed in his mind into a simple accident, with me an innocent injured passenger. He even smuggled in two cans of Toohey's that first morning, and most times after.

"Reckoned you'd have a hell of a thirst," he said, popping one and putting it into my good hand. "Easily fixed."

A long, very awkward silence followed—except for the sucking sound from Dad's straw sunk deep in the can.

Dad was so shy and shuffly at first I almost felt sorry for him. I was well past the dreadful feeling I'd had when he'd disowned and exiled me, but I reckoned he was probably still a hapless drunk, and I took little pleasure in his presence. He had to have felt this, but he bore it. After gabbing a bit about what was up with the Paramatta Rugby League, or who the Australian Labour Party had pinned their hopes on for next elections—as if I gave a fuck—he started in on what he was about.

"Harry, there's something I . . . how the hell can I explain it," he began. He sucked his straw too hard, and beer leaked down his cheek. "A real odd thing, coming back. Reckon it's as if those who never went to war are on the other side of some great plate-glass window from the likes of us. They see us, but they look away. They don't want to know anything about what we know."

"I've no urge to enlighten anyone," I said.

"Yeah, I felt the same. At first. But eventually you get to feeling so cut off, so bloody frustrated by the fact that nobody gives a damn."

"Can't say I care much what anyone thinks."

"I'm not wishing this on you, understand. But you will."

"Doubt it."

THERE WAS PLENTY of time to revise my opinion. It took an even dozen operations to mine all the metal out of me, with fairly long recuperation periods between each cutting. After the last, when I was starting to seriously ponder where and how I might live when they turned me out, Dad announced that of course I'd be coming home. My old room was waiting, everything just as I'd left it. He got a bit upset when I indicated I was not keen on that.

"And just where will you go, then? It'll be months before you're fit for any sort of work," he said. "And it'll be hard then, the way all these shits are treating your lot like criminals. We were considered bloody heroes, and still it was difficult to find a home and a living, because the bludgers who'd dodged the show resented us."

"I'll manage," I said, feeling none too sure of that.

"Know you're not real fond of me, Harry. Reckon you've your reasons, too," Dad said. "But come on home. At least you'll have a roof over your head 'til you heal up."

I was and am a very poor hand at forgiveness, even when there's really nothing to forgive. But I hadn't many options. A plummy-voiced army officer had made it clear to me before my discharge that there was no way

I qualified for any sort of disability pension, since the damage, terrible as it looked, was only superficial by military standards. I was inclined to simply drift back into the delinquent life I'd led before, especially to the crystal meth, in its field as distinctive and ubiquitous an American export as the 5.56mm M-16A1 assault rifle. There was, however, a strong deterrent: next time I got caught, no calm, rational judge would offer me a choice. He'd just tell me how many years I was going to be a convict.

So I went back to the house in Ashfield with Dad, and spent my days considering how I might get away.

University? Pure wanking, if you'd no particular arena of ambition— say medicine, engineering or law. Banking or any sort of business? You simply started right in at whatever the lowest level was. Journalists began as cadets straight from school, at seventeen or so. But you could not simply stroll into a bank or newspaper and say, "Here I am." It all depended on who you knew: tops was being a schoolmate of a proprietor's son, or the son of a friend of an owner. Or maybe your uncle sailed or played tennis with a shinybum executive of some concern or other. Of course that presumed somebody in your family was already in the top tier. Which in my case greatly limited the field. A fine school record (mine was surprisingly strong, considering I'd been absent in mind if not body quite often) was not enough.

The outlook seemed bleak as I hobbled around the garden each day, a self-directed physical therapy for my atrophied muscles. Dad mentioned the *Herald* once, but I didn't fancy another go at loading trucks, and I wasn't insensible to the tides of the time: the baby boomers, in which generally unlovely group I found myself, were moving into the economy in great greedy waves. The scions and the strivers headed for law, banking, manufacturing, the stock exchange. The flash profession for the morally challenged but madly ambitious was advertising. Those who fancied themselves truly creative were drawn to cinema and theater—pretty much a no-hope proposition, but then there was always advertising to fall back on after a few years of poverty and frustration.

Nothing there for me.

Media careers shone brightest for would-be yuppies with little or no money behind them. There was the glamour attached to it, the illusion of power, social respectability (unless you scribbled for a truly sleazy tab), and quite decent salaries. With lots of room for advancement, the acquisition of easily fiddled expense accounts, and travel as well. The Prime Minister himself would even stop in his tracks and answer any question you asked, provided it wasn't one he'd never thought of a good lie for. The more I hobbled around our garden, the more I realized journalism might be my only decent ticket. But Dad, I thought, had no means of helping me into anything but the scut part of the game.

I was wrong. Dad had already been giving his all for me outside the hospital the entire time I was in. Calling in every favor he was even vaguely owed. All his working life, he'd been slaving for the trade unions. He never rose in his union, never sought or achieved any power or position in it. He preferred behind-the-scenes work. There was no union task too petty for Dad to take on, and none too tough for him to have a go at, up to beating the hell out of anyone dumb enough to try to cross a picket line during a strike. Everyone who ever had ambitions wanted Dad on his side, knowing he was reliable, loyal and stubborn as a Blue Heeler. I guess that was why, when I was little, I used to get those pats on the head and those comments about him from his mates.

By the time I got home from the hospital, Dad had already taken the trouble to refresh the union president's recollection of just how much of his eminence he owed to the efforts of one Joe Hull, and put out the notion that Joe Hull's son, Harry, a wounded veteran, wanted very much to be a cadet. The union president then took the trouble to remind the editor in chief of the *Herald* how tractable the pressmen had been during the last contract negotiations, and had helped the paper get through a bad patch when circulation and advertising revenues were falling. The editor in chief remembered, and swore he'd remember a young man named Harry Hull, if this young man applied to be a cadet.

And one day, when I was fit again, Dad simply handed me a card with a phone number scribbled on it, smiled, and said it might be worth my while to ring up. I'd no clue what he was on about, but reckoned I might as well dial. I was stunned to find myself speaking to the personal assistant to the top man at the *Herald*, shocked when he invited me to appear at his office at my earliest convenience, and bludgeoned almost silly when, at the end of our little meeting there, he offered me a cadetship. Within days I was sitting before that Selectric, tie loose and cigarette pasted to my lower lip, newsroom style.

Since the editors in charge of my training were uncannily similar to my army NCOs, except that they wore suits instead of uniforms, I knew well enough how to make a good initial impression, though I had never written a line except for school essays.

And I even got a bonus my very first week: lovely Lucy Whitmoor and her paper plane.

LET'S FAST-FORWARD AGAIN.
No, let's drop the video conceit entirely. This is about people, how we lived, how we came together, formed bonds that seemed solid as Ayers Rock. How those connections eventually shifted, or suddenly sheared off. How some of us kept on after the shocks. How we had no idea what might come next, never mind how things would end. After all, lives aren't scripted, are they?

It all just happens.

I WAITED TWO YEARS for Lucy. Two orbits round the sun.

Ever tried waiting that long? Two hopeful springs, two blistering summers, two melancholy autumns, two dank winters, all for someone you found so desirable you could hardly believe in her existence whenever she was out of your sight? Two springs, summers, autumns and winters, anxiously wondering each day if that day she'd simply fail to walk back into it?

You bloody well haven't. Bet my bank balance on it.

From the moment I saw Lucy I was gone. Every day after, I found some reason or other to exchange a few words with her, some plausible excuse to pass by her desk and give her a smile and some banter. I extended some casual invitations, too, and made a point of being casually gracious when she declined.

After about six months of what I presumed was a fairly sophisticated display of charm on my part, she turned around and invited me to have a beer at her local pub. Where she cheerfully informed me that my performance had been the most extraordinarily pitiful begging she'd ever inspired.

"No offense, Harry, but no hope," she grinned. "Don't suppose you'd settle for just being friends? I'd be glad if you would. Because I do like you."

I gave her my best smile, hoping like hell she wouldn't sense how crushed I felt. "Love it," I said. "Never had a true female friend before."

"Don't know any men who have," Lucy said. "That's the way men are here. If you won't sleep with them, they don't want to know you. A bloody shame."

She was dead on about Aussie males, there was no denying it. It was part of the culture, quite firmly embedded. My very first instinct that night had been to say so long. But some powerful feelings—and some lingering hopes, I'll admit—beat that back. I nodded.

"So you'd be a first for me, too," she went on. "Reckon it might be fun, don't you?"

Wasn't entirely sure of that. But it was either give it a go or watch her walk out of my life.

"Well, it'd certainly be different," I said. "And bound to be pretty interesting."

She cocked her head, gave me a sly smile. "Damn, I'm good. Just knew you'd have a better attitude than the drongos I usually run into, Harry. Saw it in the way you've been handling yourself at the paper."

She raised her glass, clinked it lightly against mine. "So cheers, mate!" she said.

From then on, we'd meet for a beer or a bite to eat two or three evenings a week, always in places where we weren't likely to be spotted by other journos, who would never have understood what was really going on and would have delightedly spread the rumor: Hull and Whitmoor are rooting. I had a difficult time at first, because rooting was exactly what I most wanted. The great challenge was keeping all that desire damped down so low Lucy would never have cause to think I was just one more bloody shame.

So I did what you do with new friends: bitched about the bosses, retailed office gossip, shared some heavily edited bits of my history that put me in the best light, later told a secret or two that did not, hinted at a dream or two I harbored. And Lucy gave the same back. Soon enough we had built a base of affection and trust. Then we were as free as longtime pals to tease and taunt in the most personal way with no offense given or taken, though I skittered off instantly from anything that seemed even remotely close to taboo sexual territory.

It was new and interesting, all right. Felt to me we were learning each other in much more honest and intimate ways than you ever seem to manage when the hormones are zinging, when the main objective of every encounter is to get past the small talk as quickly as politeness permits and get on with the sex.

Very nice, but a heartbreaker, too. For the clearer her mind and spirit became to me, the closer we grew, the more I developed the unwanted notion—then the sure conviction—that Lucy was the love of my life. The woman I'd always cherish and want. The woman I'd always be thinking of even if I eventually married some girl I'd yet to meet and had a half-dozen kids with her.

—————

RECKON I ONLY ESCAPED plunging into a real deep funk when my feelings for Lucy came clear because I was still heavily engaged in learning what I needed to know in so many other sectors of my life.

First off, I'd no natural talent as a journalist. None at all. Clear from the moment my first story crashed and burned. So I set to work like a demon to master the craft, to acquire every skill that could help me not make a mess of it. I memorized word for word the *Herald*'s style manual by the end of my second week there. I did not mix at all with the other cadets—they were just kids with nothing to offer. Didn't chuff off with the mob to The Drowned Man for a beer minutes after we'd made deadline each evening, unless I had a specific invitation from an experienced reporter or editor who liked to talk serious shop. I gave even the most basic and boring cadet assignments—Woollahra council meetings that dragged for hours over riveting issues like the sewer system; the Pymble Bowling Club's annual jumble sale; the almost daily, deadly prang-ups on the Coathanger, Sydney's creaky and dangerous excuse for a Harbour bridge—my best effort. I took on as much overtime as they'd let me have.

All this enthusiasm didn't endear me with the rank-and-file journos, who in typical Aussie fashion deeply resented anyone who did more than the bare minimum required to keep his place. Well, they could go fuck themselves as far as I was concerned.

I went further. I got some books on reporting and writing, studied them thoroughly. Bought a little Olivetti, too, and practiced on it every evening until Dad couldn't take the clatter anymore and told me to give it a rest. I enrolled in night classes on writing at Sydney Uni. I was mulishly determined not to bugger this chance and wind up like a few of my ex-army acquaintances, whingeing that the reason they couldn't even tie their shoelaces right most mornings, let alone get on with a job or a life, was because they'd been too traumatized by Nam. I made myself so busy

THOMAS MORAN

it was sometimes difficult to keep track of the month, never mind weeks
or days.

When I could fit it in, I'd reward myself with a quick rooting of this
bouncy little sales clerk I'd discovered at a nearby Woolworth's in the
garden shed behind her parents' house. Or the occasional rebellious
Sydney Uni student. All very relieving, though most of the time I'd be
fantasizing it was Lucy I was with.

In the midst of this mad scrum but most absorbing of all, Dad and I
were meeting on more or less equal terms for the first time in my life.
The potential for misunderstandings seemed enormous to me at the
start. I underestimated the man.

He was wise enough, for instance, not to question me much about my
war. He listened carefully to the few bits I volunteered, saw how it was
with me, and let it go. And I imagined the war had let me go. No bad
dreams, no depression or any of the other stuff all the up-to-the-minute
psychologists and shrinks have turned into the cottage industry called
post-traumatic stress disorder. Maybe it exists and maybe not, I won't
presume to judge. It does make a fine excuse for not standing straight
under your burdens.

Dad left me in no doubt that he was standing straight under his.
Though he still liked his pint, he was no drunk. Many an evening he and
I would sit on the verandah and have just one together. Sometimes we'd
simply watch the fading of the light, keeping whatever thoughts we had
to ourselves (mine usually drifted to the disturbing notion that Lucy
might very well have her own version of a Woolies' girl to hand). Or I'd
tell him something about a story I'd done that day, and he'd fill me in on
the latest from his pressroom.

I LEARNED TOO that Dad had been right about war putting a sort of
glass wall between you and everyone who'd never had a taste of it. I
found it difficult not to laugh in the faces of people who got all bothered

22

about inevitable daily irritations: how their car had a dead battery that morning and wasn't that a pisser; how the wife was driving a man mental by demanding a new dishwasher; what a real fucking tragedy it was that their tax rates had just gone up a half-percent.

I had to squelch a lot just to tolerate most men day to day, and work like hell to keep up pleasant relations. Concerns that loomed large for them seemed petty, ridiculous. Their rabid interest in sports, for instance. Their half-baked politics, really nothing more than selfish concern over what party or policy was going to make them richer and more comfortable, and fuck anyone else. And their crude attitudes about women. All tits and asses. Whether or not a woman was worth rooting was far more important than the unmentionable speculation that she might be interesting enough to have a good long talk with.

The only time you could drop that mucker pose, as I believe Chesterton or some English writer called it, was with intelligent women, out of earshot of other men. Lucy'd been proving that to me. So most of the friends I made were the smart girls, though it was difficult to get past the distrust they naturally wore like armor, the ever-present suspicion that, as a male, all I was really interested in was a fuck.

For mates, besides Lucy, it was mainly Dad and his RSL lot. Because they were on my side of the glass.

THE BEST OF DAD'S MOB was Frank Rourke, a Tobruk and Kokoda man, who, despite living in Bondi mainly on a disability pension, spent most of his time and got most of his income from shark fishing. He called it a hobby to the pension bureaucrats who found his lifestyle pretty fucking active for a disabled veteran, but Frank had enough verbal guile—and an almost boyish innocence left in his deeply creased and sun-darkened face—to carry it off somehow. "Bloody genius," Dad said of him, in the same tone he used when he spoke of Pete Higby, top scorer on Sydney's Australian Rules Football Club.

"Still need your jugs?" Frank asked very early one fine, calm Sunday when Dad had taken me down to Bondi for a bit of fishing.

"You remember Frank, Harry," Dad had said just before that odd question. I looked at both of them like they were cracked. I'd no recollection of the man. Or any jugs.

"Ha ha," Frank cackled, turning toward my father. "Knew the little drongo wouldn't recall, Joe. Fried his brains with drugs, that's what he's done."

Dad just smiled.

"What's to remember?" I asked.

"Oh, maybe sixty or seventy Sundays, starting when you were about four, I reckon, and ending when you were getting pimples and an attitude just as ugly as your face," Frank said evenly. "Your dad would bring you down here to go fishing with us. 'Course you couldn't swim. So we'd tie a gallon plastic water jug, empty but sealed at the top with wax, to each of your arms, and one or two around your waist. Just in case you went over."

"Bloody hell!" I said. It was a total blank.

Frank and Dad were grinning at each other as we launched and headed slowly out over the swells. The motor sounded like it was going to die every time we just about topped one and were facing a slide down into the trough. We were at least a mile from the beach, well past the shark nets, when Frank cut the engine and let us bob, a somewhat leaky aluminum shell on the great, blue deep. We began to fish, Frank absently scooping up water from the bottom of the boat every once in a while with an old paint can. A huge disk of sun had risen almost completely clear of the vague horizon far to the east, beginning the slow arc that would peak directly overhead and then slide down behind the city at our backs. I was relieved to see a big Esky, that essential Aussie cooler, full of ice and bottles of beer amidships.

"Reckon there's something else young Harry here definitely doesn't recall, Joe," Frank said.

"Wish I didn't," my Dad laughed.

"Gave us a fright, the little bastard, didn't he?"

"Too right."

"What are you on about?" I asked. I was starting to pay real close attention to my line, waiting for the electric moment when you get that sharp tug of a fish hitting the bait.

"What was he, Joe? Maybe six?"

"And all jugged up, 'cause he still couldn't swim."

"There's a man here intent on his fishing, if you geezers don't mind," I said.

"You didn't give a damn about fishin' that day, Harry," Frank laughed. "Me and your dad had each hooked on, damn big ones from the way they were bending the rods and stripping line off the reels. We were fighting 'em, careful to keep the lines tight so they'd tire, but not too tight so they'd break 'em and get away. Total concentration. Reel in a bit, let 'em run a bit, reel in a little bit more. A lot of skill in the thing."

"G'day!" Dad shouted suddenly, and I saw his rod bend almost double as he set the hook in the mouth of whatever had just taken his bait. Then he was doing exactly what Frank had just been describing.

"Anyway, Harry," Frank said, "we were both deep into it when all of a sudden there's this tremendous splash behind me. I thought maybe it's a shark going after one of the hooked fish. Then I look around and see it's only a cheeky little larrikin with jugs tied all over him who's decided to jump overboard for a dip."

"Laughing his fool head off, too," Dad said, still working on his fish.

"The boat's drifting shoreward, and this comical midget is paddling toward Fiji. Not ideal," Frank went on. "Joe and I cut our lines—oh, I hated doing that, I knew I had a record setter. Then I started the motor and went after you."

"And damn you, Harry," Dad burst out, "if every time we got close enough to grab you, you didn't somehow manage to slither away, jugs and all. You were slippery as a stinger. A bloody jellyfish with a kid's face, mocking us. Finally, I had to steer the boat and Frank had to gaff you aboard, being real careful not to cut you or the jug strings."

"Dicey, it was," Frank said. "You were a mad little bloke, Harry."

"Tall tales. I never did any such thing, though I may have gone a bit mad some years later," I said, trying to exhale a swelling that was filling my chest, a racking feeling that I'd had times like that with Dad and had somehow lost them. It seemed some things could be exiled to an area of permanent darkness after all—you just don't get to choose which ones.

"Yeah, I'll believe you if you tell me I went pretty fast downhill later on," I said.

"No fear," Frank said. "You did."

HIT A NERVE, Frank had. After the first jolt, though, I managed to suppress any conscious reaction. It never surfaced again until Lucy and I were sipping beers at her local on a chill, misty evening maybe half an orbit past that day off Bondi.

"Ah, very early signs of antisocial tendencies," Lucy laughed when out of nowhere I found myself telling her the tale. She had been briefed on my criminal history long before, of course, though not what it had led to. "Explains why you turned into an outlaw, a regular Ned Kelly, the terror of Vaucluse."

"Feeling a bit afraid of myself, actually," I said.

"Because some old bloke reminded you of your brief foray into juvenile delinquency?" she said. "Being just a bit too touchy, don't you think?"

"Nothing to do with that," I said.

"Well, what then?" Lucy went serious.

"Not recognizing Frank. Not remembering things that should have been quite memorable. Sixty or seventy Sundays?"

"It was a long time ago, Harry," Lucy said. "A hell of a lot's gone on in your life since then. I don't think it's anything worth fretting over, that some childhood stuff got pushed down so deep it didn't instantly pop up."

"Neither do I, if it was just that," I said. "Problem is, it felt more like a fairly sizeable chunk of my life'd been surgically removed. Just cut out somehow. And thrown away."

"Ah, Harry," she said. "You might have told me about this a bit closer to the fact. We could have talked it through."

"Not sure I understood the feeling until now."

"But please remember it's just a feeling. Nothing gets cut out and thrown away. Everything we've ever done or seen is filed away in our minds. Sometimes we have trouble accessing it, that's all."

"Maybe you're right."

"I am. You've lost nothing. Believe me?"

"Suppose so. It's a crook sensation, though."

"But you're getting okay about it?"

"Suppose so. What you've said has helped."

"Good. Because—shitty timing, I know—I'm afraid I've got some bad news," Lucy said solemnly.

My scarred side instantly tightened, painful as tetanus.

"Don't know any easy way to break it," she went on, watching my face intently. "So I'll do it straight. It's time to say so long, mate. I'm leaving."

My heart went butterflying down about a foot below where it should have been pumping the regulation seventy-two beats a minute and fluttered frantically in the region of my stomach.

"Oh Jesus, Lucy. For where? And why?"

"For *The Bulletin!*" that mad girl grinned, hugging herself. "'Cause they've offered me a terrific job. I gave the *Herald* my notice today. It was wonderful, walking straight into that lecher McGuire's office and telling him he could bugger off, because I was."

"Christ, Lucy," I said. I couldn't stop the tremor in my right hand, the tremor I'd developed after a few too many near misses in Fuck Toy. "How'd he take it?"

"He was shocked. Which I'm getting a sense you seem to be. Any reason for that you'd care to share?"

"Hell, it's bonzer. A great break, well earned." I was trying hard to recover. She'd be working just a few blocks away. I wouldn't be seeing her every day anymore, but no reason anything else had to change between us, was there? "Couldn't be more pleased for you. It's just that you gave it such an ominous lead-in. Then this wonderful surprise."

"I'm having trouble handling it myself. Imagine this: 'Lucy Whitmoor, assistant foreign editor' on the masthead of the bloody *Bulletin*! Don't think I'll truly believe it 'til I see it in print."

"No need to wait for that. I believe it," I said. "I believe we ought to celebrate right now. Dinner on me. My shout. Won't hear a no."

"Dinner's exactly what I was angling for, Harry."

Lucy slung her arm around my shoulder as we walked a few streets east to a nice little Italian place I knew, talking happily about her good fortune. But some sense of vague unease, of impending loss, wouldn't quite leave me. It lingered through all three courses and the bottle of French—not Aussie—champagne I splurged on. Lucy remained vibrant, vocal, excited. Bubbly as the wine.

I'd taken care of the tariff and we were ready to leave when she touched the back of my hand with her fingertips, sought my eyes with hers, met them, then lowered her head.

"Would you come home with me tonight?" she asked softly, seemingly suddenly as shy and unsure as a young girl, all her bright, brash confidence gone. Now I was truly stunned. Completely paralyzed. She must have read something into that. She began to lift her fingers from my hand, saying, "Oh well, maybe that wouldn't . . ."

I grabbed her hand in both of mine, more roughly than I meant to in my haste, and kissed each of her fingertips.

"Been hoping for two years to hear that, love."

"Liar! You gave up on me a long time ago, or you wouldn't have been such a great mate," she smiled into my eyes, the brightness flooding back.

"No hints, no subtle pressures. For such a long time? Give me an honest answer, don't let me make a fool of myself. You sure I'm not offside now, and you're just too polite to say so?"

"Lucy, I never gave up. Not for a day. I've always wanted you. Just kept it dark—and it was real difficult to manage—because I thought you weren't at all interested in me that way."

She laughed. "Harry, I had all sorts of wicked intentions towards you from the start. But I was scared to get involved, since we worked together."

"You're having me on!"

"Am not." She leaned across the table and, first time ever, gave me a long, deep kiss.

Then Lucy took me home, proved to me as conclusively as any woman could that what she'd said was true, and gently sent me reeling off to Ashfield well after midnight wondering whether I'd hallucinated my own great good fortune.

4

OUR LOVEMAKING DIDN'T BECOME a regular event straight-away. Lucy would call when she was in the mood, never much minding mine. I wasn't exactly allowed reciprocal privileges for a while. If any of my friends had known that when Lucy whistled I came loping to her like a poodle with my tongue lolling, they'd have laughed me out of the country. But I couldn't have cared less.

Lucy was a couple of years older than me. I was patently eager to please but perhaps, given my history, in need of some remedial educa-tion. I was a dedicated pupil. That's part of why I soon seemed to fit her like a fine Italian calfskin glove, the incredibly soft and supple sort that shapes itself to your hand like a second skin, available for a small fortune at the Gucci counter in David Jones Department Store. My rough edges—manners, clothes, a couple of lingering attitudes—she smoothed out quite neatly. Very shortly I was up to standard; she could take me anywhere with no fear.

I'm sure, though, it took a large percentage of her will to dominate shock the first time our clothes came off. She'd hesitated—but so briefly I scarcely noticed—before touching and stroking my chewed-up bits exactly the way she was handling the rest of me. No woman before or since managed that. Some never could bring themselves to behave as if the right side of me above the waist existed at all, which made for some very awkward maneuvers in bed. And at least a couple had given me a miss entirely, once they'd seen the damage.

"Sorry, Harry, no offense, but I can't do it," said a lovely Polish migrant girl, badly shaken the instant I'd pulled off my shirt, yanking her skirt back on and frantically re-buttoning the blouse that had opened an intoxicating vista only moments before. Made me a bit mental for a while about having all the lights off, that little episode did.

But Lucy didn't care if it was high noon at the beach. I doubted her, naturally. Until she proved the truth of it more than once.

And she didn't mock me when I offered, in the tranquil aftermath of our first joining, a fluent but pretty transparent yarn of a bad accident hunting crocs in Queensland to explain my gruesome bodily state.

"East side of Cape York, round Lockhart River, was it? Christ, those salties terrify me," she said, cool as could be. "I had wondered why you were so much older than every other cadet when you started. I asked you about that, remember? When you said you'd been working in Queensland, I never imagined that sort of work!"

She had the grace not to probe my lame fiction for the longest time.

IT WASN'T UNTIL WE were well and truly on, one winter and one spring behind us and welcoming our first summer as lovers, that she finally did. We were having a delicious weekend at a small hotel above Whale Beach, a small cove tucked away on the Barrenjoey Peninsula.

"Harry, care to say what on earth you were doing in Vietnam?"

"Package tour," I said. "Won it in a raffle."

"That bad, was it?" The very gentlest reproval of my flip, defensive response.

I must have looked stricken anyway, because she kissed one of her own fingertips, touched my lips with it, and then tenderly kissed a dead-white excavation in what once had been a well-tanned and fairly impressive deltoid.

"It's all right, love," she murmured. And she never said another word about Nam. She let it rest, content that I knew that she knew, silently making a more important point: she'd be sympathetic if I ever cared to speak of it.

That particular night she just eased me straight on to a second lovely go.

An hour or so later, Lucy lost in dreams and breathing easily next to me, I stared at moonlight through the latticed shutters crosshatching her pale flank and the long leg she'd laid over mine. Down below, the surf was building, its hiss and rush deepening into muted but perfectly regular booms. A thousand miles east, a typhoon was smacking Fiji hard, we'd heard of it on the radio driving up from Sydney. That would account for the rambunctious ocean. It would be quite a sight in the morning, I knew, twenty-footers foaming pure white against a royal blue sky as they broke. The lifesavers would have to ban bathing, of course. Not because of the waves, which scads of surfies would be riding with delight, but because of the undertow and riptides, which could snatch you and sweep you to mangled death among the blade-edged rocks of the headland so swiftly even the lifesavers' speedy Zodiaks couldn't save you.

No matter. We could sun. Lucy always loved to slip through the surf like a dolphin, strong and sleek, but she'd be content to roll her Speedo off her shoulders and down below her navel, sun-baking back and front. I always wore a long-sleeved T-shirt with my trunks. Wore a big straw hat and smeared zinc oxide on my nose and cheekbones, too, so people would think I was just extra sun-sensitive. If it got too hot, I'd go for a little knee-deep splash with my T-shirt on. Or else we'd move our blanket back from the water to the edge of the beach, where a single row of tall Norfolk pines made a mottled bit of shade.

Lucy may have been ready for me in broad daylight on the beach, but I wasn't ready to inflict myself on anyone else. Experience caused me to be cautious about that.

But it wasn't self-pity or any sort of anxiety that kept sleep out of reach that night. My thoughts on balance were much more pleasant than disturbing; they just wouldn't stop flowing. The latticework of moon-light and shadow on Lucy's skin brightened into a sort of even, pearly sheen. I began to hear the birds bestirring themselves in the bush around the hotel, and one crazed kookaburra started cackling insane defiance at the thumping waves. Junglee noises, except for the sea. A Kipling sort of word, *junglee*. Had Dad read *The Jungle Book* to me when I was small? Or had it been Mum? One of them, I was sure, must have sat on the edge of my bed and read me off to sleep with it. Parts of the tale stayed with me, popping up at odd moments like this. Kipling's jungle never scared me. I felt no apprehension about the jungle at all when I finally got deep into a real one. The nightly riot of creatures known and unknown meant things were as they should be. It was any sudden silence in the leafy black that stopped your heart for a moment.

In Fuck Toy, anyway.

It was the going there that had surprised me, not the place. At that point the army was only sending in replacements for casualties in dribs and drabs to keep troop levels from dropping faster than the withdrawal schedule called for. I'd developed the conviction that I couldn't possibly be one of the dribs. Brilliant, right?

Fuck Toy was a lark at first. We were all big, strapping kids having a laugh at the little people moving earnestly through the rubber plantation and mucking about in the paddies trying to scrape out a living. In our dim-witted myopia, we only saw about two differences between the ancient Buddhist culture we were trampling through and the silly, jangling Aussie Hare Krishnas babbling and begging on Sydney street corners.

The one lot were real Asiatics who mainly wore black and worked like dogs and truly believed what they believed. And the other were blue-eyed, fair Anglo-Celts draped in colors that made lorikeets look drab, clutching a religion they only half-understood to escape a world they couldn't deal with.

We didn't bunker up like the Americans, more or less inviting the slopes to have a slap at a sitting target. We blackened our faces, taped our gear, and slithered out most nights into the bush like snakes—exactly as Charlie did. A major rush, that, but both us and them praying, I rather think, that we wouldn't slither into each other.

For a short while at the beginning I was dumb enough, or more likely bored enough, to actually hope for just one clear picture of some little fuck with a weapon through my rifle sights. One squeeze of the trigger and I'd knock the bastard flopping face down in buffalo shit. No luck, which was good luck. For four or five months I didn't get a glimpse of Mr. Charles. Didn't spot any figures flitting along the tree lines even those few times AK rounds were snapping past and mortars were making shit-black geysers all around us. Didn't see a dead NVA one of my mates had shot up.

Coming back to our tents in the slow, dappled dawns, we got a charge out of emptying twenty-round magazines at any slight stirring in the bush—never busting anything but leaves, twigs, lianas, mud and one poor little potbellied pig that I did feel bad about.

The truth is I felt worse about the pig than the slopes I greased later on. We'd set up an L-shaped ambush one night about five kilometers from camp, not really expecting any action. The jungle was raucous and roisterous in its familiar way. Just after three, every sound ceased. For about fifteen seconds. Then a brilliant white glare tore a rent in the pitchy blackness when a slope tripped one of our flares. My long L1A1 seemed to rise to my shoulder of its own accord, I zeroed on a black silhouette through the peep, squeezed off three rounds rapid, zeroed on another, squeezed off three more. Blokes all around me were blasting away at red muzzle flashes coming at us as the white flare light faded. It couldn't have lasted more than three minutes, start to finish.

We waited in place, rifles at the ready, until the first hint of dawn. Then the sergeant and I snaked over to the trail we'd shot up. Only two bodies, both near the flare. I was certain they'd been my silhouettes. Three holes in each, when we looked closer. The sergeant rolled over one of the bodies with the toe of his boot. I started when I saw two long pigtails. Full NVA uniform though, AK still cocked and locked in her little hands.

We didn't empty any mags into the bush on the way back to our tents that morning. We were carrying three body bags: Griffith had taken a round through the throat, Packer two in the center of his chest, and Maitland had a small hole in his forehead and no skull behind.

"Au-see numbah one, GI numbah five and VC numbah ten," I remembered Phong saying one night a few weeks later. On the other side of the beaded curtain that split her hut, I heard a baby cry, and some shrill gibberish from the old mama-san as she shut it up. "Two dollah, mate," Phong said when she'd done with me.

Phong asking for money was nearly the last thing I heard in Fuck Toy—besides the usual junglee noise, besides the startling whoosh and crack of an RPG, and then my own screaming.

A scream from that mad kookaburra jerked me back. It was full light now at Whale Beach, the surf really booming below. Lucy stirred a bit, slid her leg off mine. I ran my hand across my face. It came away wet with sweat.

5

G'DAY, COBBER," Lucy said, pressing up against me, her skin gone from pearly to golden in the early sun. "Love me as much as I love you? Maybe almost as much?"

I kissed her. She pressed closer. "Ah, Harry. A beautiful morning. Let's do it."

I felt wrung out. I hadn't had a night like that before. I was thinking of a graceful way to put her off when she rolled out of bed, stood up and stepped into her shorts.

"I'm starved. And once that's been well and truly dealt with, I'm dying for some beach," Lucy said, pulling a T-shirt on over her head, then shaking her hair into place and brushing it back with her fingers. "Wonder if they'll think I've gone bush if I ask for steak and eggs for brekkie?"

Let 'em think whatever the hell they like, I said to myself, a sweet tide of relief washing over me. I yawned hugely, stretched, felt taut muscles in my back and neck slacken. "Wonder if I could convince you what you really need is a sweet half-hour or so back in bed with me?" I said, not meaning a word of it.

Lucy grinned, but shook her head and patted her belly. So I got up, went to the bathroom, splashed cold water on my face and chest, and gave myself a brisk rub with a terry towel. She was leaning against the open door of our room when I came out, tapping her foot. I pulled on my khaki shorts fast, but took my time unfolding and donning a beautiful long-sleeved linen shirt the color of the sky. Lucy had bought it for me.

"Right then," I said, ready to step out into a fresh new day. "Lead the way."

"I'VE A CONFESSION, HARRY," Lucy said in the hotel dining room, prodding the golden egg yolks atop a well-charred steak with her fork and looking fairly gleeful when they popped. "I've been up to something really wicked."

"Such as?" I asked.

"Such as giving a great deal of thought to our future, love."

"God, you haven't, have you? Deeply disappointed in you, Luce," I said. "Thought it was only me doing something so perverse."

"Lying ratbag!" she laughed. "Your time horizon's about bedtime to bedtime, tops. While I've been gazing down the years. Well, perhaps not years. But longish-term at least."

"And?"

"Blue sky all the way out. Except there're two small clouds on the far horizon. Getting bigger."

"Yeah?"

"Yeah. One's named Bruce. The other's named Joe."

"Do they look like sheep? Or wombats or dingos or anything?" I grinned.

"Nah. Just like bother."

Lucy and I were sliding—joyously, it's true—toward penury with those expensive Whale Beach weekenders not only because we enjoyed them so much, but because of Bruce and Joe. Her brother and my dad made it a bit awkward for us to spend as many nights together as we wanted. Not that either of them did anything deliberate to thwart us. They were just there.

Lucy shied at the notion of staying over in Ashfield, though Dad wouldn't have objected. He was mad for her. That came clear the very first time he met her, which was some months before we actually became lovers.

I'd told him I was bringing a mate home for dinner. Fine by him, he'd said. But as soon as we walked through the door, Dad instantly went stiff and formal, behaving with a politeness so exaggerated that Lucy cracked up. When Dad looked puzzled at this, Lucy simply said to him in her best Oz accent, "Fuck all, mate. I'm not Lady Fairfax come for tea or anything. Wouldn't say no to a beer on the verandah, though."

Dad just grinned like a lunatic, and they were off. Before they finished their first bottles, they were thick as old union mates, cheerfully slagging *Herald* management and laughing at each other's colorful invective and off-color insults.

So the problem wasn't how Luce and Dad got on. It was the house. Any place inhabited only by men develops a certain pong. Not an actual odor (Dad and I were a tidy couple), but an overbearing male atmosphere, like an army barrack. I had no trouble understanding how Lucy would find that unappealing.

Our only private moments there came on the nights Dad would go down to the RSL or some union function. There was never any telling whether he'd roll home early or late, so at first we'd fumble and pant on the sofa like teenagers having an urgent grope while the parents were out—always poised to rearrange our clothes fast and put on an innocent look the instant we heard footfalls on the verandah. The absurdity kept us laughing for a while. We felt like naughty kids, getting away with something. But that game soon grew tiresome.

It was tiresome at Lucy's, too. She'd inherited a very nice old terrace house in Paddington jointly with her brother, and we had to work to get Bruce to go out at night at all. He'd object in his dull, whiney way, but he'd go. He was more terrified of Lucy than he was of me, and I did scare him. He'd been stupid enough to mutter something about Aussie army "baby killers" once when I first started visiting. I put my left hand under his chin, pushed him against the wall, and lifted, so that his feet were dangling a few inches from the floor. I let him hang, staring hard into his eyes, for maybe half a minute, then dropped him. "Got something to say, mate?" I asked him then. "Any little thing you'd care to sort out?" He just goggled at me, twitching his groin as if he had to take a leak real bad, and slid out of the room.

I found it almost impossible to believe that Bruce and Lucy had come from the same gene pool. Never would have, in fact, except for the stunning reality that physically they were almost twins, so alike it was uncanny. Otherwise, they shared nothing. Lucy was strong-willed, bright as the sun, quick in every way, full of wit and humor, fearless. Bruce was a slug. I wouldn't have put it past him to peek through the keyhole of Lucy's bedroom door while we were doing it.

The simple solution would have been for us to throw in together and get our own place. Or for me to take a flat of my own somewhere. But we weren't quite ready yet, for reasons that had nothing to do with the way we felt about each other.

Paddo had all sorts of hooks into Lucy, for one thing.

The Paddington terrace houses had been built for workingmen back before the first war. As neighborhoods will, Paddo had declined in latter years, starting during the Great Depression. As those with pride of ownership moved on or died off, their houses got sold to speculators who broke them up into apartments and then stopped caring about anything beyond the regular payments of rents. A sad shabbiness spread.

But in the mid-seventies gentrification had started. You'd now see a couple of BMWs, Volvos, or an occasional Jag parked out front in the evenings, and every day the streets were clogged with the trucks and vans of plumbers, carpenters, roofers, painters. The young Sydney comers, having decided Paddo was the new new place, were snatching up derelict houses and renovating like mad. Property agents kept leaving cards in Lucy's mail slot, promising her the moon if she'd let them put her house on the market.

She wouldn't. She'd grown up there, kept the place very decently maintained. There were deep, compelling attachments.

Her dad, an ex-Guards lieutenant with a solid English family behind him when he'd come out to Australia just after the war, could have afforded a better address. But he was above that sort of snobbery, Lucy told me. He settled on the place because the previous owner, a carpenter, had lovingly and artfully added room after room, so the place was sprawling. Her dad and mum dreamed of filling it with kids. Lucy came first, then Bruce. And then, over the next eight years, three miscarriages and one stillbirth ended hopes for a crowded, lively house—though her dad wouldn't hear of moving to a smaller home in a more fashionable neighborhood.

Lucy had to battle like hell to keep the place after her parents died together in an accident. She was twenty at the time, which caused some scary legal clashes, not because the will wasn't clear but because she was underage, and Bruce two years younger still. She'd faced down the court, which was inclined to put her and Bruce and the house under some sort of guardianship. To meet the taxes and the expenses, not to mention the fees of a couple of slick lawyers, she had to drop out of Uni, abandoning her dream of studying history all the way to a Ph.D., and an academic career. That's how she wound up as a cadet at the *Herald*, and nobody made it easy for her there, either.

"Just as well," she shrugged when she told me all this, though there was a hitch in her voice that hinted at keen regrets. "I'd been living in a dreamworld, protected and pampered. Uni suited me, I was a bit of a slut with the cutest boys and loving it. It was time I toughened up. Anyway, I'd have made a terrible professor. No patience at all with ignorant little snots."

My story was simpler: I just wasn't ready to abandon Dad in Ashfield. Not while I was enjoying him, and still in the middle of what felt like making up for the lost years.

So, as people will, we more or less ignored the issue, enjoyed our furtive hours at Dad's or at Paddo, and luxuriated in our weekenders.

IGNORING ANYTHING that didn't need immediate attention was easy for me then. The future had arrived in perfect nick so far as I was concerned. A very pleasing world it was; I had no complaints to lodge about a thing. I was happy in my work; I was delighted with Lucy. And with Dad.

The best of it with him came on so quietly and naturally I scarcely noticed what was happening. Lots of time on the verandah with cold ones, casually nattering about this or that, the affairs of the day, whatever.

"Bush telegraph says you're doing okay, Harry," Dad started in one night. "Not a natural to be appointed foreign editor by thirty, but a real good city reporter."

"That's what you hear, is it?"

"It's a good sign, Harry. You're giving this your best go, aren't you?"

"Yeah, suppose I am."

"Bloody selfish of me, but I'm real relieved. After you stole that car, and the drug stuff you'd been into—yeah, I knew very well about those mates of yours and the shit you were doing..."

Dad paused, sucked his straw too vigorously. Beer squirted from his cheek as usual. So I said something I'd been wanting to since I was about

41

twelve. "Why don't you put a cork in that hole so you can have a proper drink, for Christ's sake, you stubborn bludger?"

"Bugger off," he laughed. Then he went silent for a while.

"I'm so ashamed," he said.

"Why should you be?"

"You know very well. When your mother died . . . hell, you were only a kid, you needed me. But I was weak. I didn't hold up my end."

"Reckon I didn't make it any easier for you," I said.

"She and you were my whole world. Suddenly half that world vanished. I felt so bloody sorry for myself that I forgot about the half that was left. Fucking inexcusable."

"Suppose that's exactly what happened to me, as well."

"Except you were just a kid, and the half you had left was a useless drunk. So you lost everything. I'll always regret that."

"Don't. It all came right in the end."

"Harry, when I think of you at fourteen or fifteen, in all that pain . . ."

"Don't flog yourself, Dad. Lots of it was self-inflicted," I said, rising and walking into the kitchen, where I rummaged through a drawer until I found an old cork. Then I went back to the verandah, handed it and a fresh beer to Dad.

"Persistent little bugger. Always were," he smiled, rolling the cork around in his palm and then, to my surprise, pressing it into his hole. He put the can to his lips, poured in a mouthful, and swallowed.

"Fuck me stupid!" he cried. "That was great. Best drink I've had in thirty years."

"Clever of you to've thought of it," I grinned.

"That's right. Kick a man when he's down," Dad laughed. He took another great swig, swallowed, then sighed. "Harry, if at some point in your life, something hard and heavy should come down on you, take a lesson from me. Stay off the booze, forget yourself entirely, and give all you've got to whoever's next to you. And if you must get drunk, never go home that night to your loved ones. Sleep it off in a gutter somewhere."

"Know any choice spots?" I said lightly.

"Wish I had, back then," Dad replied, dead serious. "I can promise you that if you heed what I've said, you and yours'll have a hell of a lot better life than I managed to make for you."

"That's a real beaut," I said.

"Yeah. Disgusting, isn't it? But it's the fucking truth."

"FACE IT, you two perves are finally falling in love with each other again," Lucy laughed when I tried to describe what was going on between me and Dad. I blushed. She caught me.

"The way Aussie men do with other men, but would rather die than admit," she said. "'Mates,' you call each other, and woe to anyone who points out the preferred definition of *that* word in a Pom dictionary like the *Oxford*. You're so scared people'll think you're poofters or something, you all are. That runs real deep. But it's love, Harry."

The woman was right, of course. She was always right.

And whatever you care to call it, it was a gift I never expected to get, and a comfort and a pleasure, too.

6

LUGGING JUST A BIT MORE than my standard light ruck of
mental baggage, I made it home very late Sunday night, that Whale
Beach weekend when Lucy named a couple of clouds "Bruce" and "Joe."
Dad was already snoring vigorously in his bed, dreaming whatever he did
dream. And soon enough I was out, too.

But I was up brightly, dressed for work, and brewing tea next morning when I heard him clumping down the stairs slow and heavy. He
looked more tousled than usual when he came into the kitchen, and
glanced around almost as if he wasn't quite sure he knew where he was.

"Here's a man who clearly downed too many last night," I laughed.
"Murderous hangover, right?"

"Christ, Harry," he muttered. "Something's changed."

"Yeah, the world made half a turn like it does every night, and the sun
decided to report for duty instead of giving it a miss, so it's another damn
Monday again," I said, flinging some eggs around in the frying pan.

"No, no. First off, I wasn't drunk. One pint only. But something in my sleep like I never had before. And now everything seems off somehow."

"Aw, you just haven't woken up properly yet. Drink this," I said, sliding him a cup of black tea across the kitchen table when he'd flopped down in his usual chair.

"Oh, I'm wide awake. I see my son, Harry, cheeky as ever, doing his pathetic best on breakfast in the same kitchen we've always had. Same plates, same knives and forks, same tea mugs. Same dripping faucet 'cause you still never bother to turn it off tight. But everything's a little skewed."

"Kokoda dreams?"

"Nah. They're rare, and I know well enough when I've had one."

"Eye trouble?"

"Eyes're fine. It's like I'm the same man in the same place as always, but everything's slid sideways an inch or so in my mind. Feel like I'm a bit off true."

"Probably just dreams of some sort. Or more likely the weather," I said. "Reckon a westerly'll be coming in today. I always feel a bit odd before one hits."

"Maybe," Dad said, but he didn't sound convinced.

"Have another cuppa," I said.

He drank it fast, picked at his eggs a bit, then went back upstairs to dress for work. He seemed right enough that evening on the verandah, watching the rain. He didn't mention the morning or anything more about feeling off.

I'D COMPLETELY FORGOTTEN all about it when I walked into the house after work some weeks later only to find Dad sputtering into his beer at the kitchen table, glaring out the window at Jack Clarke's old house, right next door.

"Claim what you will, they ain't Australians and never will be," Dad growled, a finger plugging the hole in his cheek so the smoke from his cigarette would get down into his lungs instead of drifting sideways out of his face. He was flushed in a way I'd not seen since the day we'd parted angrily and I'd headed off on my way to becoming a fucked toy.

"Christ, Dad. Bit early to be so far into the beer, isn't it?" I said cheerfully, helping myself to an XXXX from the icebox. "What's got you so cranky?"

"Them, what else? Bloody migrants displaced poor old Jack."

"Right. You are drunk. So I'll say it nice and slow. Jack retired six months ago and moved up to Port Macquarie, as you well know. If he managed to rent that shack of his, he's lucky."

"Nah, the government kicked him out some way or other. To make room for more bloody reffos."

I took a look out the window then and saw two bruisers making a scene over a few pieces of furniture and a couple of clothes trunks. You'd have thought they were burdened with the contents of a twenty-room Point Piper mansion. A lot of show in the hopes of extorting more money than the contract called for. Watching these thespians was a very spruce couple who might have been in their mid-thirties, with a little kid whose face was round as a pie standing between them on the skinniest legs I'd ever seen on a child. All at once those twigs started flying and the kid was racing in big circles round Jack's back garden, which wasn't anything more than tufts of weeds and a couple scraggly hydrangeas. The woman, her mum I supposed, called out to her.

"Hell, Dad," I said. "They're just Italians."

"The ethnics are taking over the country, Harry," he said bitterly. "There's more of them than us by now, dammit."

Dad was totally polluted, I concluded. Must have had a hell of a bad day at work, for he almost never drank more than he could comfortably handle.

"Now why don't you just crawl upstairs and pass out gracefully in your bed? Saving me the trouble of having to carry you up?" I said. "You clearly guzzled more than you should have at The Drowned Man today. Even forgot what decade it is."

"Bugger off, I only had a quick one," he said.

"Dad," I said, starting to feel impatient with this nonsense, "Jack's only let his house to a nice Italian family. That's all. They're moving in today."

The flush made a fast fade. Dad looked like he'd just been shaken awake from a nap. He blinked hard a few times, rubbed his temples. He tried on a grin, seemed to find it fairly comfortable, so he kept it. "Jesus, lost it there for a moment. Gettin' old, I reckon." All rancor and tension gone from his voice, so completely it was almost as if they'd never been there.

He shook his head, then laughed. "Imagine that. What the fuck was I babbling about? Christ, I bloody *love* Italians. Plenty of them are great union men, have been for years. Let's step over and give 'em a hand."

"Let's not," I said. I was pretty sure he could barely walk. "We'd only be in the way. They've already got one more man than they need to handle their stuff. Doesn't look like they've all that much."

"Well, we've got to shout 'em a beer," Dad said. "Give 'em a little welcome."

I noticed his left hand was trembling slightly, but didn't think much of it.

"Be the right thing to do," I said.

"Couldn't do less," Dad said. "It wouldn't be neighborly, would it?"

So I went out on our verandah and called over to them. "G'day! I'm Harry Hull. Pleased to know ya. My dad and I wondered if you'd like a beer or something."

The man and his wife turned to each other and nattered a moment. Then the man smiled at me. "Many thanks," he said, accent heavy. Then he sort of shrugged and waved his arms about as if to point out the luggage and the thespians. "Now we moving in . . . *scusa*, no?"

I reckoned that meant another time, maybe.

———

TO UNDERSTAND WHAT DAD was on about, suppose I'll have to spill some things the Tourism Ministry's public loudmouth, Paul Hogan, will never tell. Unsavory titbits everyone these days would love to forget. I'll keep the rant brief as I can.

For ages the government enforced a "White Australia" immigration policy, "white" meaning mainly Anglo-Celts: English, Irish, Welsh and Scots. Only after World War II did a lot of other Europeans receive the dubious privilege of being considered white, and we opened the door to Balts, Italians, Yugoslavs, Greeks, even Turks under what was called "assisted migration." This was not a universally popular influx among Australians.

And not a great deal more civilized than the original convict transportation that settled Sydney Cove more than two hundred years ago. To get to Oz right after the war, a Displaced Person from Europe had to agree to work wherever the government cared to send him for two years. Two years. That was the price of admission. More like a gaol term if you ask me. We sent brilliantly educated men, doctors and professors and scientists even, out to the Snowy River Water Project or down into New South Wales coal mines as common laborers. What a hope. And if they were assigned to men-only camps like Snowy River, they had to leave their wives and kids behind in Sydney. For two fucking years.

Enough decent people felt embarrassed about this policy that after a few years European migrants could settle right in wherever they chose and get on with building fresh lives. "New Australians," they were called officially. "Ethnics," to most Aussies. "Coloureds" were still automatically rejected, though. When I came back from junglee time, the immigration law still in force was White Australia. You were barred if you were yellow, although the government had let a bit of slack into the regulations in the sixties and a few select Asians had begun to trickle in.

But we only got around to dumping White Australia as formal law in 1973.

It's a laugh, isn't it, how circles tend to close? There was a fairly broad public rant when the Central and Eastern European migrants started arriving in Dad's day. Faced with not so very many thousands of Czechs, Hungarians and similar exotics, some Aussies squawked so much you'd have thought the country was being invaded by hordes of Sarawak headhunters. They got past it, though. Now they were busy squawking about the newest migrants: from Vietnam, China, Cambodia, Laos, Indonesia, Korea. The funny bit is that some of the loudest were second-generation Italians, Balts and Greeks.

So Dad's mad minute when the Italians turned up next door was a shocker. It was already 1976, for Christ's sake. But what the hell. I'd had my fair share of mad minutes, too. We're all entitled to make fools of ourselves once and again. The truly odd thing, which came to me after Dad snapped back, was the unlikely fact that our little lane had been an utterly pure Aussie enclave all these years, each house passed from father to son. Maybe the only street in Ashfield, or in all of Sydney, to have never before had a migrant family at that late date.

THE KID NEXT DOOR was adorable. She must've been about five, though I wondered if she hadn't had some illness or other that left her so spindly. No worries about her spirit, though. Every time I'd step out the door and off the verandah and she was out front playing with her mum, she'd point at me the way kids do and call, "*Chow, chow,*" a big smile on her pie-face. Hello yourself, I thought, then chowed her right back, with one of those backward waves the Italians use sometimes, opening and closing a hand very rapidly with your palm facing you. The kid waved the same way and her mum nodded at me. It was a pretty nod.

That they were just off the boat—or the 747, rather—was clear, for the mum's skin was the ivory tone of piano keys. The dad and the kid hadn't yet been scorched either. Almost right away we were all saying "*chow*" whenever we saw one another. I thought they didn't know more than a word or two of English because that's as far as we got, and they seemed disinclined to drop over.

That Friday I had the morning off, and I heard the meter reader having a sort of monologue interrupted at intervals by this low, liquid sound. I stepped out and rounded the fence at the alley, and I saw the reader standing with the mum. He was pointing at the gas meter attached to the back of the house, and she was pointing to the kitchen door. The more she talked the louder and slower he responded. I sauntered over to see what I could do.

"A little trouble reading today, Mick?"

"I've got it read all right, but she won't let me go."

The mum looked at me with that pleading face you sometimes see on mutes who are dying to tell you something but can't. Then she spoke in a real urgent sort of way, and when Mick and I just looked blank, I got the feeling she wanted to take us by the shoulders and shake some sense into us.

"What do you think she's on about?" Mick said, backing away from her. The mum real quick reached out and grabbed my forearm.

"Oh ho," said Mick.

I let her pull me into the kitchen, wondering what would happen. Mick followed. The room smelled cleaner than most I'd been in lately, not a trace of grease or grime anywhere. Achieving that must have been a hell of task, considering old Jack's idea of housekeeping. She picked up a box of matches, struck one, turned on all three of the stove's gas rings, and moved the match toward them. "Uh oh," said Mick, sliding sideways so that I was between him and the stove. She touched that match to one burner after another. We were all about to get our eyebrows scorched off by a flare-up. But nothing happened. The gas wasn't turned on inside.

"Not my job," Mick shrugged. "My job's to read the meter."

"Which obviously isn't running, so you've nothing to read," I said.

50

"Reckon I can put down the same numbers I put down last month, and the month before that," he said, after pondering the complexity of the matter for a while. "She'll have to ring up the company to send out someone to turn it on. Then next month, they'll be different numbers."

"Ring up? So the gas company's got multilingual staff answering the phones now, has it?" I was growing a bit hostile toward Mick.

Then the kid came skittering in from the front room on a little homemade scooter, her skinny legs going every which way. She piped "*chow, chow*" when she saw me, and I chowed her back.

"Come on Mick, turn the lady's gas on, will you?" I said. Mick said he wasn't supposed to. I saw a little electric hotplate over by the sink.

"Mick, they've been here a week with no gas," I said. "Probably been cooking everything on that hotplate. She's got a little kid and a husband to feed. Just turn it on and I'll shout you a beer."

That did the trick. Mick got down behind the stove, took a small wrench out of his pocket and worked the valve. Then he lit a burner, just to show it was going all right. The mum relaxed; you could see a certain amount of tension go right out of her face and shoulders. The kid laughed.

Then Mick and I went over to my place and I got him a beer while he read my meter. I should have slipped a few grains of mouse poison into it, just enough to make him chunder. He was the sort who could copy down a string of numbers on his pad, but if you asked him how many houses were left on that day's route, he'd have to count on his fingers. Retards got fair play in Oz, sure enough. Bright lights often did not. The tall poppy syndrome, as it's known. Aussies don't like anyone who stands out. I hoped my new neighbor was a bit on the dim side, and not a renowned semiotician from the University of Padua or anything.

I THOUGHT THEY WERE a strange sort of family at first. The dad would be coming home from work somewhere between five and six most days, same as me, and his wife would leave immediately after he arrived. I didn't know what she did, but she was always beautifully dressed and didn't get home until quite late. It seemed like Sundays were the only days they had more than an hour or so together.

As for the welcome we'd discussed, Dad finally strolled across the garden one fine Sunday afternoon and insisted they come over for a beer after supper. No doubt he either baffled them or unknowingly intimidated them into it. Lucy was eating with us that night, and the neighbors tapped on our door not long after we'd finished the pavlova she'd brought for dessert. The mother, Alessandra, who was very quiet, immediately became "Alice" and then "Al" to Dad, although it appeared to me she wasn't thrilled by this, or didn't quite get it. She had so little English.

Umberto, the dad, could say whatever he pleased in English, though he was shy about his accent, which was thicker than most I'd heard. But he laughed when Dad took to calling him Bert. The kid, Fabrizia, was fascinated with Lucy's attempts to pick up a bit of Italian while conveying a bit of English, and Dad and Umberto got on like old mates, once it came out that Umberto was uncommonly well-informed on the Western Desert—his dad, it turned out, having gotten it in the neck at Alamein.

"Lucky bloke," Dad said after they'd left and I'd got back from running Lucy home to Paddo. "His wife looks just like what's her name, you know, the one with with the bonzer tits? Sophia Lolla-something-or-other?"

"Christ, Dad! You haven't been to a movie in ten years. The one to watch now is that Laura Antonelli. She's a goer. You get to see her completely naked in all her films."

"No!" Dad said, his eyes lighting up. "It ain't allowed, is it?"

"Yeah, it is. And Alice doesn't look a thing like her. But if you and Frank ever came closer to the beach at Bondi than the shark nets, you'd see every young girl there showing off her tits. They don't wear their bikini tops much anymore. Some don't wear anything you'd call a cossie at all."

"Harry," Dad said, shaking his head, "I was born too fucking late."

Nothing cracked or skewed about that observation, in my opinion.

Our new neighbors never complained, but I could tell they were bothered by a few things. That old house of Jack's was not in tip-top condition. Just glancing at the lay of the tiles on the roof, you could bet they had leaks in the kitchen and the main bedroom every time it rained. No wonder they looked depressed whenever the clouds gathered up and up in huge piles with dark bottoms, until you knew you were in for a drencher.

Jack's house was identical to all the rest on our street: red brick with a big bay window out front, a timber verandah (usually painted dark green or gold or brown) along one side, and the red tiled roof. The front gardens, excepting the old Clarke place, were neatly trimmed turf, with maybe one big plane tree, or a frangipani with fragrant creamy flowers, and lots of the ever-popular blue hydrangeas. Fences or hedging ran along the property lines between each house, and the back gardens opened to the alley.

Everyone but Jack had been serious about maintenance, repainting timber bleached and blistered by the sun every few years or so, replacing dry-rotted trim and posts and cracked roof tiles. Jack had let it all go for ages before he left. The rest of us had no leaks and fair drains and a sound set of windows and doors. The wind never howled in our place the way it must have over at Umberto's. I felt bad for them, with the little girl and all.

On Sundays they always put on their best, like North Shore Anglicans, but instead of going to church they'd head down to Circular Quay to watch the Harbour ferries dock, or take in some other sight in their new city, and give the kid an ice cream.

So one dry Sunday when they were gone I got a barrow-load of tiles from a mate of Dad's in the roofers' union, went up on their roof, ripped off all the bad ones and laid down a good new layer. I didn't tell them, of course.

Next time it rained—a great black bruiser that seemed to growl around the horizon for a long time before it made up its mind to dump on us—I saw Umberto come out his back door in the hard middle of it, mystified. Just staring up at the clouds getting soaked, as if he needed some proof it was really raining, since the usual evidence inside had gone missing. Big drops were splashing off his bald top.

"By Christ, he's demented!" Dad roared with laughter, the hole in his cheek sounding the way it does when you blow across the top of an empty bottle.

I believe Umberto may have spied us at the window laughing, which I was sorry for. But not long after, I arrived home from work to find a package all wrapped up in brown paper on the verandah. No name, no message, but inside there was a handknit jumper, good merino and just my size.

7

MOST EVENINGS AFTER THAT, as I strolled up the street from the bus stop, the kid would be swinging on my front garden gate like it was the best ride in a playground. She would leap off as soon as she spotted me and skip down to meet me, saying, "*Chow*, Harry" as she took my hand. Then she'd chatter happily on about what I supposed must have been her day's adventures, though I couldn't be sure since it was all in Italian. She seemed to take my smile for understanding and approval. She was such a little beaut.

It got to be so routine—an event I looked forward to—that I started carrying pieces of hard candy in my suit pocket. When we reached her gate, I'd take her under the arms and swing her giggling over into her garden, hand her the candy, and watch her scamper off to the verandah. Alice was usually there, or looking out the bay window. She'd give me a big smile and a wave.

Then one evening I was in the bottle shop of Loughlin's Hotel, fetching the usual beer ration for me and Dad, when who walked in but Umberto. He shook hands with me, then said hello to Loughlin, and ordered six bottles of red wine. All very easy, which I took to mean Bert had become a regular. Loughlin bagged the bottles, but never named the price. He wouldn't need to, with a regular. So I was surprised to see Umberto hand over about twice as much as that wine cost. And no change back to him.

"Scabbing off people, are you now, Bill? Believe I'll be keeping my hand deep in my pocket around here from now on," I said after Umberto had left. Dad and I had been buying our beer from Loughlin for dogs' years, so I figured I had the right. But he didn't seem to agree.

"What's it to you? Sticky beak," he snipped, meaning I could just mind my own business and piss off. "A bloody migrant."

Now I might have let the thing pass if Loughlin had been civil and shown a bit of shame, but the look he gave me along with the lip was too rancid for my taste. "Get fucked," I told him, and took my beer, deliberately leaving the door wide open behind me.

Nothing more might have come of it if I hadn't passed Umberto headed toward Loughlin's corner one evening a couple of weeks later. Without really thinking anything out, I said *chow*, reversed my direction and walked along with him.

Loughlin was no fool. His eyes were darting back and forth between Umberto and me as soon as we came into the shop together. Bert hadn't a clue anything was up. He said hello, asked for the usual. He was digging into his pocket for the money when I stepped in. It had come to me, what I might do.

I said, "I think I fancy a bit of a change."

Loughlin just looked at me.

I said, "I'll have six bottles of that plonk, too." I knew he wouldn't dare overcharge me.

"I'll just put it on your account," he said.

"Never mind, I'll pay." I put down the cash, which Loughlin scooped off the counter as quick as he could.

Then Umberto tried again to hand over his usual. "Hold on, that's much too much," I said to him. "You must be confused."

"But Harry, this I always pay, yes?"

"Then Loughlin here's been making huge errors," I said, turning back toward the man. "I'm bloody surprised at you, Bill. Your mind's not on your business. A bit of strife at home lately? The wife having a go with a trimmer man, maybe?"

"This I pay always," Umberto repeated, in that thick northern Italian accent that sounded almost German to my ear, no extra vowels at the end of any of his words. I could sense his uneasiness about the way Loughlin and I were facing off.

"Never mind, there's been a mistake," I said to Bert, keeping my eyes on Loughlin. "Hasn't there, Bill?"

Loughlin wasn't giving a thing away; he wanted to see how I'd play the rest of it. I took the money from Umberto's hand and counted out the right amount, putting each note and coin down on the counter slowly but pretty smartly so he'd get the idea. "That's the right tariff, isn't it?" I said to Loughlin, giving the rest of the money back to Bert. Loughlin handed over the bottles, but kept mum. Umberto and I walked home together.

"This is very strange, Harry," he said. "You get me, how do you say, the discount?"

I grinned at him. "You could call it that. The regular price for regular customers."

"Ah, I see," Umberto said. But his expression remained puzzled.

The next time I was buying my beer, Loughlin started whingeing. "I've known you since you were a kid, always been fair and you know it." His voice was pitched high for a man of his formidable mass. "Now you go and side with a wog over a couple of dollars. I'm disappointed in you, Harry, I truly am."

I had to laugh.

"First off," I said, "it deeply offends me to hear you call my friend a wog, you fat bastard. He's from Italy, but he's an Aussie now. Second, that plonk of yours is such rank piss you ought to be paying people to take it off your hands. Third, there's not a lot that's fair in the world, but the place where a man buys his drink ought to be.

"And fourth," I moved a bit closer to the counter, slapped my hands down on it and leaned my face as close to his as I could, "you're a fucking gutless spiv, and I'd be delighted if you'd care to step out here and have a go at proving me wrong."

"You're banned," Loughlin almost whispered, taking a step back to be sure he was beyond my reach.

"I wouldn't set foot in your rathole again if you guaranteed me free beer for life. Dad and I will be getting ours at Maffick's from now on."

I TOLD THE WHOLE STORY to Dad over supper. "Good on ya, Harry. Can't stand a cheat," he said. "But Jesus, I never reckoned Bill for one. That devious bugger."

Then he started laughing really hard in mid-chew, which caused a small eruption of sausage bits and potato from the hole in his cheek. "He's huge, but you know something? For years every time I looked at him, I couldn't help thinking of a giant pavlova! All puffed up! But flab only, just enough muscle to keep from collapsing. Christ, I'd have liked to see you give him a smart tap in the gut."

Two nights later, though, Dad came home red-wattled and tore into me. "Who the fuck do you think you are, threatening Bill Loughlin?" he shouted. "I've just been in there and heard all about it. Are you back on those drugs again, accusing a respectable man we've known for years of thievery? Or are you just a retard? Goddammit, Harry, I won't have this shit from you!"

"Dad," I began, baffled because I felt sure there was nothing Loughlin could have said to him to turn the incident around this way in his mind. But he wouldn't hear.

"Bugger off," he snapped. "And keep out of my bloody way or I'll take the belt to you." And after shoveling down supper without another word, he settled in to watch TV and fell asleep in his chair. I found him there in the morning, mouth hanging open and snoring. He shambled into the kitchen once the smell of frying bacon had pretty much filled the house, smiled at me and said, "Morning, Harry. Pile on that bacon, will you? I'm starved."

That's when the bulb finally flicked on for me. That's when I realized something very strange must be happening in Dad's head, though its nature and cause remained dark. "What were you raving about last night?" I asked, mildly as I could manage.

"Raving?" He laughed as he sat down. "No raving here as I recall. We had a bit of supper, watched the rugby match on TV. Must've fallen asleep."

"You gave me a flogging about Loughlin," I said.

"Bill Loughlin? What's he got to do with anything?"

"Seemed to send you into a fit. You yelled your bloody head off."

"Fucking did not," Dad said, looking almost astonished. Then he chuckled. "I don't mean to be crude, son, and please don't take offense, but I reckon our lovely Lucy is a bit too much for you. You're getting addled. Too much good rooting can do that to a man, you know. Seen it dozens of times. Blokes walking around in a dreamworld, imagining all sorts of shit. Get a grip, boy."

"DID YOU GET A WHIFF of his breath?" Lucy asked over lunch that afternoon as I explained my adventures of the previous few days. "No? Well Jesus, Harry, I'd think by now you'd still know very well when your dad was blotto."

"I don't believe he was drunk."

59

"Of course he was. He just managed to stay conscious long enough to eat, then passed out in his chair," she laughed. "And don't dare try to tell me you've never overdone it and failed to remember the night before on the morning after."

The clear peal of her laugh was always enough to shift any doubtful mood I might be in at least half-way right again, and what she said next completed the turn.

"The truth of it is, Harry," she lowered her voice and leaned across the cluttered little table toward me, her lucious mouth broadening into that smile I never could resist, "your dad's right. I am too much for you. Be a man and admit it. I turn you to jelly. You're too weak to walk when I'm finished with you in bed, and I've never heard a coherent word come out of your mouth until fifteen minutes after. Maybe we need to lengthen the intervals, before you go completely mental."

"Now hold hard there, miss."

"*That* is certainly not the solution, it's more likely part of the problem," she laughed, teasing up the cuff of one of my trouser legs with a foot that had somehow lost its shoe and stroking my calf. "I reckon it's starting to happen a bit now. It is, isn't it? And you're damning the fact that we both have to get back to work right about this instant and therefore can't possibly slip over to my place for an hour. Just as well, because it'd leave you incapable of any rational activity for the rest of the day."

"Forgetting one thing, aren't you?"

"Doubt it."

"Well, it seems to this trained reporter's observant eye that the woman in question here also tends toward the—I'll be kind and say 'languid' instead of 'ravished and sated to the point of semi-consciousness' after certain activities."

"Yeah! That's the whole bloody point of doing it, you ocker," Lucy laughed. "Why else would I keep you around?"

UMBERTO TOLD ME LATER THAT, being not entirely sure what had transpired the day I bought wine too (and naturally unaware of the private chat I'd had with Bill), he had tried to pay the inflated price next time he went back to Loughlin's. But Bill, surely thinking it was some kind of test or trap, gave him change back. At first hearing, I felt irritated with Bert, but once I had reasoned it through, I saw that I had put him in a fairly awkward place. He was no doubt glad of any good will he could find, even if it came from a cheating grog merchant. Because almost nobody was offering much of a welcome.

Bert and Alice had a different set of values from everyone else on our street. Though they worked very hard from what I could see of the hours they kept, they had to be finding things a bit tight; Bert was a tailor in a haberdashery and Alice was a restaurant hostess. So they lived simply, but with a touch of style that would have gone unremarked in the Eastern suburbs but stuck out in ours. Both of them were always well-dressed, and there was nothing too good for Fabrizia; not even her play clothes came off a Woolie's rack. Ever see someone in a good suit or a dress and then notice they're wearing cheap shoes? You know immediately they're putting on a show beyond their means, which don't stretch as far as their feet. The shoes always give it away. Well, even little Fabrizia had the best leather shoes. And not just for Sunday promenades.

That other corners might be cut to finance this was too complex a notion for the older folks on our street to grasp. So, for instance, when certain people saw Alessandra done up so nicely on Sundays, and Bert in a perfectly cut suit, and the little girl in a lovely white dress and a little navy blue montgomery if it was chilly, they'd cluck at one another about how the migrants were showing off, how the migrants were thinking they were better than the rest of us. They never considered that their own financial formula—take your income and spend one-third for drink and food, one-third for rent or mortgage and gamble away the rest with starting-price bookmakers—might be the reason they themselves looked so shabby.

PRETTY EARLY ONE EVENING, while Dad was down at a union meeting, I heard a scratching, not a knock, at the front door. It was Bert, looking apologetic but imploring me to come over to his house. It was Fabrizia's birthday; they were having a little party. I tried to beg off. Then Bert said Fabrizia kept asking why I wasn't there, she wouldn't leave it alone, she was that disappointed. The only way to ease her, he said, was to promise he'd fetch me.

You expect some light, some people, some chatter and laughter at a party. But all I saw when I walked in that evening was a teary little girl in her mother's arms. There was nobody else in the room. On a table I saw two packages wrapped up in colored paper and tied with ribbons. Fabrizia had on a blue dress and her mum had tied a bow of bright blue ribbon in her hair. Alice said something in Italian, which must have been "Here's Harry," for the little thing looked up and came scooting over to me with her arms held out, like she wanted to be picked up.

"G'day mate," she piped.

"G'day yourself," I replied, not even thinking. She giggled behind her hand.

Then it hit me that she'd done an exact mimic of Dad greeting the postman every day. She had Dad down dead. I laughed then, lifted her up and swung her around a bit.

Bert and Alice had made an effort with the wrapped presents and some ice cream, but I guess it hadn't seemed exactly festive to Fabrizia with only her parents there, no other kids at all since she'd not made any playmates yet—besides me, which was pretty pathetic. But she brightened now, and started digging into a bowl of ice cream with a spoon she could barely hold. When she'd finished she started circling the table, standing on her toes every now and then to sneak a peek at the presents.

"She grows up so fast, Harry," Umberto said, watching her lovingly. "How is this?"

"You've got me," I said, not quite catching his meaning.

"It goes very fast, the time," he said.

"Often seems so when it's past, but it can take forever when you're in the middle of something. Good or bad, almost always feels that way."

"Yes," he said. "It's very strange. It seems so long ago that we left Italy, and also it seems just a moment ago. Let me tell you, very confusing."

"That'll pass," I said. I'd felt like I'd been away for a lifetime when I got home from Fuck Toy, but it wore off pretty quick. Then it had seemed that Fuck Toy was just some very distant interval, a weird kind of holiday gone as wrong as it could go. "You lose the feeling soon enough."

"Just as well," Umberto said. "Some of those feelings you don't like to keep. You don't want to keep the feeling you had when you flew away."

All of a sudden I felt I did not want to hear these sorts of things just now. So I picked the kid up again and bounced her around a bit. I said, "Fabrizia, want to open your presents?"

"G'day, mate!" she said. I had nothing for the kid, so I reached in my pocket and gave her the shiniest coin I found there.

"No, Harry. It's not called for," Umberto protested.

"It's the creature's birthday," I said. "Ain't it, Fabrizia, you little bundle."

"Harry!" said Fabrizia, pointing at me and almost punching me in the nose when she did it. She had the coin grasped in her hand.

I set Fabrizia down and she climbed onto her mum's lap. I sat in the only other chair in the place, while Bert stood behind the one in which Alice was sitting. They had so little: the two chairs and the table and a couple of old lamps that gave off a kind of sad yellow light. They'd tried to make it nice, though. The place was impeccably clean, there was a pretty paisley shawl draped over the table, and on it a glass vase with some fresh flowers. It all looked fine. Leaning up in one corner was what I supposed was a well-used violin case, the leather scarred a bit here or there even though it was carefully polished.

"You play the violin then, Umberto?" I asked, nodding toward that case.

"A few notes, in the old days. No more now," he said.

"*Ma nonnay vero*," or something very like that came from Alice as she took one of the gifts off the table and handed it to Fabrizia. "Harry, Umberto, how you say, in Italia he is making the music for money?"

"A professional musician? That what you mean?"

"Is what she means, yes," Umberto said.

"Dance band, that sort of thing?"

"Only classical, Harry. In an orchestra. Also a string quartet," Bert said.

"So Mozart, Beethoven, all that lot?"

"Oh yes," Bert laughed. "All that lot, *sí*."

"Very much good, Umberto is. Best," Alice said, sounding fairly intense about it.

"That how you made your living, was it?" I asked Bert.

"Yes. In old days."

"Well, maybe I'll get some tickets next time there's something good on at the Opera House then, and we'll all go have a listen. Don't know much about classical music myself."

"Sure thing, Harry," Bert smiled. "We do that, for sure."

Fabrizia meanwhile had got the first package open, started chattering excitedly over a little wooden horse all trimmed and bridled like a circus animal. She tore the paper off the other and pulled out a puppet with a strange ugly face, like a Punch and Judy figure. She had one in one hand and one in the other and got the horse and the puppet talking rapidly to each other in Italian.

We sat up fairly late, drinking Loughlin's plonk. Fabrizia fell asleep on the floor with her new horse in one hand and her puppet in the other.

How easily kids are pleased, since they're able to make so much of their own imaginations. That's an advantage they have over us. The world constricts your imagination, your sense of possibility, the longer you live in it, I thought. And said so.

"True, absolutely. But I am not sure it's so peaceful being a child," Umberto replied. "She has bad dreams sometimes. We hear her crying in her sleep. You try to keep them safe, Harry, to make them always feel, what is word, secure? But they get scared, you don't know what. What to do? You don't know. They can't tell you."

Fabrizia, I learned that night, had taken very ill shortly before they were to leave Italy. Bert hadn't the English name for it, but it sounded like some kind of meningitis. They had spent all their days and nights in the hospital for a week, never leaving her side.

"I felt we are on our last hope then," he said. "She is thin and weak, she barely breathes. Harry, you should never feel what it is like to hold your child in your arms while she is dying. You become crazy, you would do anything, even murder someone, if that would save her. You would murder even God, for sure."

That sounded right enough. But Fabrizia had passed through the crisis and survived unscathed physically. What I didn't quite fathom was why Bert and Alice had left Italy, which seemed by all accounts a more prosperous—not to mention an infintely more civilized—place than Aussie. So I asked Umberto, straight out, what he was doing here in Oz, at the end of the earth. It didn't call for a long answer, he judged.

"To find a place that is getting better, to leave one that is getting worse and worse," he said. "For Fabrizia's future."

This seemed vaguely misguided to me. But later, when I did understand, my conclusion was he deserved a lot better than he got.

Like Dad, in that regard. Like too bloody many people.

8

G OT A REAL CRUSH on Fabrizia, don't you, cobber?" Lucy teased me late one night, after yet another of the tedious social functions we were professionally obliged to attend to keep up the connections and sources we needed. Her bed in Paddo was a welcome refuge from the blather of overgeared property developers, overambitious politicians, overdressed and overjeweled women, and the ceaseless flow of champagne that lubricated it all. We were snugged up like spoons in a drawer.

"Think I'd be keeping a very close eye on you, Hull," she said, molding her body even closer to mine. "If I didn't know the object of your affections for months now, you perve, is a preschooler."

"Caught me out, have you? Right. I confess. I'm head over heels," I said. "I'll even admit it's crossed my mind more than a few times that I might really love having one of my own just like her."

"Your own? Always thought it took two to make one."

"Always does. And that's been my general idea. You and me. Any interest?"

"I'll admit the concept's been entertained privately on occasion." She laughed lightly. "And dismissed."

"That a statement about you and me, or about having kids in general?"

"It's about timing," she said. I felt her lips on the back of my neck, her warm breath. "I'd love you to make me pregnant. One day. Just not now. Or in the near future. I need to get a bit further along in my career first."

"And then we'll see?"

"Then we will. Plenty of time for it, Harry," Lucy murmured. "All the time in the world."

So it seemed. As one season after another had its run and then skulked off to make way for the next, we worked and we played and we fell into inviting Bert and Alice and the kid on little jaunts and excursions. Sundays were the only days we all had free, and on one or two each month we'd take them out to do all the touristy things you generally give a miss in the place you've lived your whole life.

Postcards: Katoomba, The Three Sisters, Norman Lindsey's old house and studio in the Blue Mountains, the dunes of Cronulla, even Luna Park. It was fun. It was friendly. Then it stopped for a while. Lucy and I ran head on into a very heavy news cycle that kept us both putting in ridiculous hours in our newsrooms. A completely unremarkable state of affairs for journos. There were days and weeks when things were so quiet we worried how we'd ever manage to fill our pages, and yanked all sorts of lame feature stories with no time hook out of the files to do it, while there were other periods when news broke so fast and furious we could scarcely keep up. Dad and his pressroom blokes weren't exempt; they earned plenty in overtime when we were printing extra editions or putting the paper to bed late because we'd crammed in some late-breaking stories. It never was a regular nine-to-five trade, which is part of what attracted most of us to it in the first place.

Bert did work nine to five, and as a rule had to get straight home to watch Fabrizia so Alice could go off to the restaurant. But the restaurant was closed on Mondays as well as Sundays, and his store being very near the *Herald*, he'd tarried for a beer a few times when we'd run into each other on the street at the end of our workdays.

ON AN UNUSALLY FINE early winter Monday, we met just outside the *Herald*—by arrangement, not chance. Lucy had organized an evening out, even lining up a babysitter (one of the teenaged girls who lived on our street) so Alessandra could join us for dinner.

Bert and I walked down a few blocks and sat on a bench overlooking the Harbour to wait for the women. On crisp nights like this one, with the air clear as crystal, the lights reflecting in the black water looked almost too sharp to be real. The Coathanger arched above us, and you could see the docks down to Millers Point. Several large ships were berthed there, bright bulbs strung fore and aft like Christmas decorations, their funnels and flags illuminated by spotlights.

"You know, Harry," Bert said after looking at the ships for a time. "Sometimes I wonder if I done the right thing. You know about homesick, Harry? I believe I am homesick more or less. Alessandra has it very bad sometimes. What do you do for it?"

"Don't know the feeling at all. Never been away from home, really, except for a little army service."

"Often I think of going back. But then I think, how could we do it? What would be there for us? No job, Harry. No way to support a family."

"No work for tailors? Or musicians? You did that once, didn't you?"

"Those days? *Finito*."

"Yeah," I said. Seemed a bit evasive, Bert's answer, but I knew I shouldn't press for clarity just now. "Look on the bright side. What's to miss really? The food? Alessandra cooks it up here just as nice as she could back there, am I right? The weather or something? You couldn't ask for better than here, even if it does get a bit hot."

"It's my life I miss, Harry. Family, friends, the people who were part of my life. This is the homesick I think, knowing you have to live the rest of your life away from the people who care for you."

Nothing useful I could say to that. I hadn't much in the way of family and friends even here at home. Besides Dad, I realized, Bert was perhaps the only man in town I'd genuinely miss talking to if I never could again. That was a bloody bleak thought.

We sat there quietly again. I began thinking how he and I'd sometimes drop by Partridge's bookshop at lunch time. It wasn't far from his store or my paper. Bert was a born browser, and went in for anything with pictures of the Pyramids and King Tut's tomb and so forth, or the great cathedrals of Europe. I couldn't see how they'd built those things without power cranes and excavators and steel.

"With patience, stone by stone," Bert had said one day, going through some plates of Canterbury Cathredral. "Harry, have a look. A man would spend his entire life cutting stones, followed by his son and his grandson. Generations all building the same thing."

"Yeah, very nice," I'd said. "But damn frustrating I'd think, never getting it finished."

"They have patience, Harry. They don't need to see it finished. Enough to see only what they themselves do, to watch each stone they cut put into its place. World's too fast now. Nobody has this patience anymore."

"Have a look," he'd said, thrusting the big book in front of my face. It smelt a bit musty, and the photos had a sort of silvery tint. I saw Bert's point at once. The cathedral was astonishing and beautiful. The modern skyscrapers in the city center, just shoddy glass and steel boxes, seemed nothing more than gigantic aquariums next to this marvel. Who figured out how thick the cathedral walls had to be to bear the weight? How did they make groined vaults? How in the hell did they hold up all that stone while they put the keystones in the arches? Who dreamed up all the details and decorations? What made the builders so devoted?

Now, by the Harbour, I raised these questions about the Cathedral.

"Reckon we've lost something since those days," I said. "Nothing for us to be proud of that I can see."

"True, most likely, Harry," said Bert. "I think maybe the only ones who can be proud are some scientists, some chemists who invent the new medicines, this polio vaccine, things like that. Some doctors come up with new operations. They save some lives, no?"

"But mostly we're better at destroying things than making them," I said. "Proved that conclusively a few times. War. Every generation gets one."

"Very true. But always we're creating some little things at least," Bert said. "Here is one thing, Harry. Alessandra, she just gets pregnant."

I slapped him on the back. "Good on ya!"

Yet Bert went solemn.

"Not so good, Harry. For me, I'm happy, yes. I can say I am very happy, even though we don't plan this," he said. "But Alessandra? She is not so pleased."

"Whyever not?"

"Complicated, Harry. Hard to know for sure. She worry so much about money, I see that. She's afraid for her job."

"You'll manage all right. I'll help you out if you get short."

"That is kind of you, Harry. There is more, I think. She so scared she lose her place, is that how you say it? To lose her place in the work queue? She love her work, to be meeting so many people in the restaurant, talking with them, very friendly and so forth. But worst, I think, she hate to be at home with a baby again, nobody to drop by, as they did every day in Italy when Fabrizia was born. We had family, so many friends there, you see."

I figured Alessandra ought to be happy at home with a new kid. I didn't understand then how lonely that might seem to her, and how loneliness is the very hardest thing a migrant has to bear. Anyway I couldn't take it too seriously. Just female whingeing, I thought.

"Well, she can work a few more months until she starts to show," I said. "And then once the kid comes she'll most likely adore the whole thing."

"I don't know, Harry," Bert said. "Maybe you are right. That's my hope. But right now it take her in a very bad way. She don't want a child. Naturally she blames me. It is all my fault, she says."

"Better your fault than the milkman's," I said.

"What milkman?" Umberto asked. He didn't get it.

LUCY SHOWED UP about then, and within a few minutes Alice arrived. There was a restaurant nearby Lucy was keen on, a sort of nouvelle Aussie place with great seafood that would have been even better, in my view, if the chef gave the raspberry vinaigrette and other trendy sauces and condiments a miss.

The food was fine, the wine was fine, Lucy was her usual bright self, and Bert rose to that as he always did, even with the language handicap. Alice seemed pleased enough with the meal, too.

Bert and Alice didn't exchange a harsh word, which I was sort of prepared for, given what he'd told me, but then they hardly exchanged a word at all; it was all wrong between them. You could just feel it, like you could feel something odd in the air just before a big thunderstorm comes crashing down. Or maybe I only remember it that way. Lucy and Alice stopped in the ladies' room while I took care of the bill. Afterward, Bert and Alice caught a bus back to Ashfield, and Lucy and I flagged a cab for Paddo.

"Harry, she's knocked up," Lucy said as soon as we got to her room and began undressing. There was something in her tone I couldn't place.

"Don't I know it. And none too pleased, either," I said, relating my talk with Bert before dinner.

"Not pleased is mild. Not pleased is very bloody understated in this case. She hates everything about it. You should hear her complain. She says it's terrible, your stomach gets so heavy and your tits droop and ache and you feel gross and bloated and pukey for months on end. And then the birth itself hurts so much you want to die. So she says."

"I think there's a bit more at issue than some discomfort. According to Bert."

"Well, that's all she was on about."

"I thought women were supposed to enjoy being pregnant. Radiant, glowing, all that stuff?"

"Dream on. You may adore the kid once it's born, but you can probably hate the little thing in your belly that's making you feel so crook."

"And how would you know?" I said.

"That's retarded. I wouldn't have to actually kick you in the balls for you to have a fair idea what that'd feel like," Lucy grinned. "Or would I?"

She gazed out over the garden behind her house for a bit, holding my hand.

"Wonder if it's worth it?" she said eventually.

"Kicking me in the balls or getting pregnant?" I laughed. "If you give the kick a miss, I can handle the second, no worries. Ready to do my duty tonight if you like."

"You shouldn't try to be ironical, Harry," Lucy said softly. "You're no good at it. No good at all."

9

B EING A POOR EXCUSE for an ironist seems a small failing, compared with the truly terrible blunder I made not too long after our
dinner out. I told Bert and Alice about the auditions.

I'd spotted a small, boxed advertisement on the last page of the thin
little four-page fishwrap that was the *Herald*'s excuse for a culture sec-
tion. Not a part of the paper I generally read, unless Lucy and I were in
the mood for a movie, since film listings were by far the greater part of it.
I can't recall why I read the bloody ad, let alone remembered it. I'm not
much for music except for really good rock, and I'd been to exactly eight
classical concerts down at the Opera House in my entire life—each at
Lucy's insistence. She had that sort of background, a family circle (dis-
counting Bruce) keen on high culture of every sort, and she'd kept the
interest after the circle was destroyed. No matter that the Sydney Orchestra, word was, would have been hooted out of many European con-
cert halls, even those in smallish Austrian or even Polish cities.

Probably the sight one evening of that lovely leather violin case propped uselessly in a corner of Umberto's front room triggered it. As soon as I mentioned the Sydney Orchestra was holding open auditions for violinists, Alessandra got worked up in a way I'd never seen before.

"Umberto, this he can do! Eight years, he is first violinist. The best," she announced. That wasn't exactly news; it only brought up a thing I should have wondered about long before. Why, in all the time they'd lived there, hadn't I ever heard a single note come from that house? I found out later Bert hadn't so much as opened the instrument's case, let alone tuned it or bowed it a bit, since he'd got on the plane from Trieste.

Umberto had been first violin of the Orchestra of Udine, which Alice said—her English had improved dramatically in recent months—was a city of several hundred thousand people about midway between Venice and Trieste. With that job, and the engagements of a private string quartet he'd founded and led, he'd made a more than decent living.

But then the Italian government—if you could call the musical-chairs politics there a government—decided to drastically cut back subsidization of the smaller orchestras and operas, as well as almost everything related to the arts. And Umberto, first violin but not well-loved by a newish conductor (who deemed Bert's maestro-worship half-hearted) or by the orchestra's board (which didn't find him deferential and cravenly grateful enough), lost his place.

His family was far from well-to-do, the stepfather being a bricklayer. They'd supported his youthful musical ambitions, since lessons at the public school didn't cost anything. But when he left school at sixteen, that would have been that. Except, Alice explained, Bert apprenticed in the tailoring trade, and financed his further education himself; nightly lessons with a locally famous old professor.

His talent and persistence earned him a seat in the Udine Orchestra at twenty, and he was elevated to first violin at twenty-eight. The youngest first ever, Alice claimed.

Some very happy years they'd had after that. Then it ended. The quartet's bookings didn't bring in nearly enough to support a wife and baby. And he was much too proud, Alice said, to go back to tailoring in a place where he was so well-known. That's part of why, after a year of struggle and soul-searching, they applied to emigrate to Australia. Seemed a bit of a radical step to me; I didn't understand why they couldn't have tried somewhere else in their own country instead of moving all the way to Oz.

"Stop with all this nonsense, Alessandra!" Bert finally said, clearly exasperated. "All *storia*, ancient history, no? Harry, he don't care to hear you telling these things."

"It don't matter, not playing in years," Alice told me excitedly, ignoring Bert entirely. "He practice now a bit, pretty soon as good as ever."

"Sure, why not give it a go?" I said.

Bert just shook his head. He looked to me to be quite distressed, as well as pretty damned furious with Alice. But then he went over to the corner, opened the case, and removed his violin. Ignorant I may have been, but I could see right away the thing was really something special. The wood was handshaped into perfect, sinuous curves, all of it gleaming. When he handed it to me I felt awkward, like I was being offered someone's infant. I wasn't prepared for the extraordinary lightness, the glassy smoothness. And I was mortified to see my fingertips left smudges on the finish. I gingerly gave it back to Bert, only to be startled when he handled it casually as I might a cricket bat.

Alice started talking to Bert very seriously in Italian, her voice pitched low but insistent. As she spoke she never let her eyes stray from his. She clasped him by the arms for a long moment.

"Bert, have a go at least. Nothing to lose, is there?" I butted in. What did I know?

"Ah, Harry, you are as crazy as my wife. The music, it's finished for me. *Finito*."

Alice must have tightened the screws on him after I left, because next evening Bert came over and told me he would give it a try after all. I was pleased. Sat right down with my little Olivetti and typed the letter of application for him.

The night after, sitting quietly with Dad and Lucy on the verandah, we heard a few discordant screeches that must have been Bert tuning up.

"No hope," Dad laughed.

Suddenly the air was filled with some absolutely lovely tune that was also the most heartrending piece of music I'd ever heard. It was smooth and perfect.

"Tartini!" Lucy exclaimed. "One of the Sonate del Tasso. My God, I bet he's playing from memory, too, not from a sheet." She cocked her head, utterly rapt.

"You sure that's Bert and not a record or something?" Dad asked midway through the ten minutes or so the tune went on. Lucy shushed him instantly.

"Bloody amazing!" she said when the last note quavered away into the dark. "Better than anything I've heard live before. He's a first-rate artist, Bert is."

And this from a woman whom I witnessed on more than one occasion dancing wildy to the Stones blasting at about a hundred decibels. Naked. She was back on our verandah every night for a week and more after, just to listen to the beautiful sounds soaring from Bert's house.

A letter came back from the orchestra, the day of his audition was set. I took the morning off from work so I could drive Bert down to the Opera House. He and I sat up front, while Alice and Fabrizia rode in the back. The kid was excited, as she always seemed to be whenever she was in motion. She kept her face to the window the entire drive, pointing out and naming everything to her mother: Ford Falcon! Coppers! Cricket ground! An old lady with blue hair! "Why does your hair turn blue when you get old?" she asked. Bert was pensive, just held the violin case in his lap and drummed the fingers of his right hand on the dash.

"*Dío mío*, I don't know, I don't know," he kept saying. "This is maybe very stupid."

I parked as close to the Opera House as I could get, and Umberto headed inside. The Botanical Garden—a great manicured lawn made majestic by enormous English oaks, elms, chestnuts, and ancient Morton Bay figs with twisted, spreading crowns and thick trunks that sported flying buttresses—was only a skip away. We could hear some kids shouting somewhere in there. Fabrizia started tugging at her mum's skirt, wanting to go find them. Kids are like that, aren't they? Whenever they sense the presence of their own kind, they like to go get acquainted. Too bad we lose that instinct as adults.

There was no reason Alice shouldn't go over to the park and let Fabrizia have some fun with whatever little ones she might find. I'd wait by the car for Bert, who most likely would be some time, I thought. So I pointed her in the right direction and they were off.

It felt great to be outside on a fine day when I should have been working. Reminded me of the days I skipped school. I watched people going to and fro, wondering what they did for a living and why they weren't off doing it. Then it occured to me that most were tourists, drawn by the famous white curves of the Opera House, which were supposed to evoke a fan of scallop shells, or soaring seagulls' wings. Studying it for a while, I found myself thinking it looked remarkably like three white ducks in a line, buggering each other. I was on my third cigarette, cheerfully elaborating in my mind the resonances of this impression, when Umberto suddenly appeared beside me.

"How'd it go?" I asked. It seemed he'd been inside pretty briefly, and it was difficult to tell from his face whether he was confused about why they'd liked him, or surprised that they had.

"Harry, they ask where I got my diploma," he said.

"Yeah? So what else?"

"Nothing else. They ask where I got my diploma. I tell them I am once first violin in Udine, I play professionally in orchestra and chamber groups in Italy for maybe fifteen years. That I will play anything they want to hear. Bruckner, Mozart, Bach, Schubert, Rossini, Dvorák, Smetana, Corelli—anything they like. I'm very sorry, but I have no diploma, I tell them. I open my case and take out the instrument to play as much they want."

"And?" I asked.

"They say, no diploma? Ah, you must have a diploma from an accredited music school. I don't understand, this 'accredited.' But they don't want to hear anything. No, no. Not a little passage even. They don't let me play one note."

I cracked two knuckles punching the car door.

THAT'S THE SWEET LITTLE GIFT I gave those good people. And worse timing I could not imagine. Before I'd blabbed about the audition, I was damned worried about them anyway. I'd been watching Alice pretty closely. I thought if Lucy and I ever got around to having kids, it might not be a bad idea to have had a little preview of what women went through. And it troubled me, the way Alice seemed to be about her pregnancy. Nothing cheerful or expectant, even before the fucking audition. Alice seemed resigned at first, and then she declined into what looked like true depression.

It got much worse when she began showing at her hostess job at the restaurant, and was summarily sacked by the bloody Yugoslav bastard who owned what he promoted as a genuine Italian place. I'm sure there wasn't a lot of slack in the family budget even when she was working, so this must have shot it all to hell. They'd have to tighten up.

The standard drill, I reckoned: buying day-old bread instead of fresh, keeping a sharp eye for specials on every kind of food and drink, cutting meat almost completely out of your diet. No more restaurants at all. Mending clothes and darning socks instead of buying replacements. Walking or busing to places you'd once gone by taxi. Doing a clever juggling act with household bills, like making a small "error" between the numeral part of your cheque and the written-out sum. They have to send the cheque back if the sums don't match, so you gain an extra month or so of not paying. You also charge everything you can on credit cards, pay the minimum each month, and sometimes use the same cheque trick.

It's not so difficult (I'd seen Dad do it several times when his union went out on long strikes, except for the credit card business, since he never had one), but it does give you a bad sense of slipping back. And if the falling behind goes on long enough, you'll never make it up.

Dad came out with one thing during a strike when I was about twelve that I'll always remember, it being the most broody, soul-sick prediction I'd heard up to that point in life. He was bolting a plateful of cheese and crackers and pickles (got to watch those food dollars, right?), and he was leaking crumbs of it all through his cheek.

"We work to eat so we can live to work until we get old, get sick and die," Dad had said to the air, popping the last nugget of cheese into his mouth. "That's it."

That's it?

"Yeah, Harry. That's bloody it." Dad had nodded. "One day we'll all find ourselves in The Slough of Despond."

He couldn't explain precisely what that was, except that it was a bad fucking precinct. All his dad's officers in the Great War had been reading an old book called *Pilgrim's Progress* in the trenches and quoting that phrase from it as an acute metaphor for their dubitable existence. And his dad had gone on and on so often about this Slough place afterward that it attained mythic proportion in young Joe Hull's mind. And never left it.

I FELT DREADFUL for the longest while about the whole audition affair. Wished to God I had never even seen that ad, never blathered about it.

"Give it up, Harry," Lucy said. "Your motives were the best. You wanted to help a friend. And don't you see Umberto surely knew the sort of chance he was taking? After what happened to him in Italy? He had to know talent was unlikely to be the decisive factor in a thing like this. He gave it a go anyway. Because the man's a trier."

Bert did take it better than most would have. Not one word of complaint. Not even a hint of a whinge. I never had a hope or ambition or talent I loved so much that I'd studied and pursued it for years, as he had the violin. But only a retard wouldn't understand what a crusher that rubbish about a diploma must have been. I wanted him to get as angry as I was, to strike back. I wanted to hook him up with one of the *Herald*'s culture reporters who could wring a ton of pathos out of a story like Umberto's—and gleefully ram it up the bums of the orchestra taipans, a sort of public enema. The reporter was keen. Bert was not. He said there was no point, what was done was done.

"Hardly fair play, the way those shits treated you," I told him.

He said, "Fair? Oh Harry, you cannot expect fair. Forget fair and you will be a more content man in life. The *Signor*, He don't know fair. It's too small for Him."

"Your *Signor* is a gutless wonder, then," I said. "It wasn't right. And goddammit, sometimes things ought to come down on the side of right."

"For sure. But Harry, everybody has his own idea of right, no?"

"Some of it isn't open to opinion or interpretation, it's that bloody clear," I said. "You can't be saying you got properly judged?"

"No. But possibly it was a proper decision. According to how those people organize things."

"Hell, Bert, you're too fucking soft on the ratbags! They never even gave you a chance, just kicked you in the balls by way of saying hello and goodbye. This *Signor* can get stuffed if that's not worth his attention."

Umberto laughed. "Not so loudly, Harry, please. For your sake. He might start to pay attention to you. That, my friend, you do not want."

"Bollocks!"

"Please, Harry, go careful here," Bert said. "And listen, my friend. The *Signor*'s ways, they not for us to know. So never rule out even the most crazy thing you can imagine. For that may be exactly what the *Signor* will do."

1 0

I WASN'T YET IN Mr. *Signor*'s sights.
And whether He had any hand in it or not, Alessandra delivered—
right on schedule, to the very day in late December of '77—a lovely
eight-pound, four-ounce girl, who was called Camilla. Of course she
wasn't lovely, she was as mashed-faced and ugly as every newborn, but
nobody's ever crude enough to mention that fact, are they?

"Just in time. Alice was about to burst, and I don't mean her belly,
huge as it was," Dad chuckled to me at the little party Umberto gave to
celebrate the christening. "Poor bloody Bert, too. He's had a hard go
of it."

The party was just Dad and me and Lucy, Fabrizia poking and prodding at her sister as if Camilla was a curious new toy, a few folks Bert
knew from work, a few Alice knew from the restaurant business. And
the boarder, a funny little fellow who Dad said reminded him of a cane
toad. He'd turned up about midway through the pregnancy to live in

Umberto's and Alessandra's spare bedroom. An Italian migrant who called himself Alfredo, waited tables at Il Pelicano, a new and very up-market place in Double Bay.

I suppose Bert and Alice had needed the extra cash. Suppose as well Dad was right when he compared Alfredo to one of nature's biggest botched jobs. I'd tried talking to Alfredo on quite a few occasions, always allowing that a poor command of English was a legitimate excuse for brief, broken responses. But not for the listless, bugger-off attitude he carried.

I took two beers from a tin tub full of ice, handed one to Dad. Bert came over carrying a bottle of wine and refilled Lucy's glass.

"Good on ya, Bert," Dad said. "The kid's a real beaut."

"She is, for sure," Bert grinned, topping off his own wine glass. From the slight glaze in his eyes, I reckoned he'd downed quite a few glasses already. "Let me tell you one thing. A happy man, that's me."

"So you should be, cobber," Lucy said, kissing him on the cheek. Bert's grin widened.

"To hold your own child, brand new, she smile at you, *Dio mio*, the feeling you get," he said. "The words for this feeling, I don't have."

"I can imagine," Lucy said.

"Lucy, this is something you and Harry got to do sometime. Then you know what I'm saying, for sure," Bert said. "A happy man, that's me."

"I do believe you are," Lucy laughed.

A lot happier than Alice, it seemed to me. She was sitting about as far away from Camilla's cradle as you could be in that room, looking a bit washed out. She was saying something to Alfredo, who was close beside her chair. The cane toad's eyes were passive, cold. When some of her restaurant friends went up to her and started talking cheerfully, Alessandra's smile seemed lame and flat, placed against Bert's high spirits.

"Not a bad idea, Bert," Dad said. "About Harry and Lucy having a go."

"Don't you get started on that, Joe," Lucy said. "I'll make allowances for Bert today. Not for you."

"Hear that, Harry?" Dad laughed. "You're being rejected as father material."

"With fair reason," I said. "Any woman who got to know you should have her doubts about me."

"*Bo*," Bert said, chuckling. "Anybody sees how good Harry is with Fabrizia, he knows Harry okay."

"You're all cracked," Lucy said. "I'm going to go coo over Camilla again."

We trailed after her. Nobody but me seemed to notice Fabrizia had given up examining her new sister and was sitting on the floor, arms wrapped around her legs and chin resting on her raised knees, staring at her shoes. Dad and Bert and Lucy were too busy dandling the infant and agreeing she was a perfect specimen. Fabrizia just shook her head when I crouched down next to her and asked what was wrong. I tried to jolly her, but I wasn't any good at all that day. Pretty soon she just got up and went out on the verandah by herself. And her "So long, mate," when I left the party with Dad and Lucy maybe a hour later was purely rote.

I was worried about the kid. She'd often looked downhearted and bewildered before the birth, and the novelty of Camilla hadn't brought much improvement. Early one Sunday evening a few weeks after the christening, there was a scratching at our screen door. When Dad went over to see who was there, I heard Fabrizia pipe, "G'day mate. Can Harry come out?"

It wasn't the first time by any means, but Dad always had a laugh at that. "Why sure," he said. "Harry'll come out and play, but I want him home before dark, understand?"

Fabrizia and I sat on the verandah. Her legs didn't reach the ground from the chair, so she swung them back and forth, back and forth, looking sideways at me with a little gap-toothed smile.

"What's up, mate?" I said.

"*Niente*," she said. "Harry, you never shout, do you?"

"Like hell. He's a real roarer. Rants all the time," Dad called out from some dim recess inside the house where he was lurking.

"Bloody does not," Fabrizia said to the screen door. "Bugger off."

"Wash your mouth with soap," Dad called. "Where're you picking up words like that?"

"From you, who else?" Fabrizia giggled.

No reply from inside then.

"Listen, darls, everybody lets off once in a while," I said to the girl. "It doesn't mean anything's real wrong."

"Harry, it makes Camilla cry. She's a baby, Harry."

"That's what babies always do. Can't talk, can they? So they wail and wha-wha. And poop in their pants," I said. Fabrizia put her hand in front of her mouth.

"You said poop, Harry," she laughed, as if that were the funniest thing in the world. But she went quiet quick, more subdued than I liked to see.

"Tell you what, mate," I said to her. "Why don't I come over with you, so you can show me what you've been doing at school?"

"*Va bene*," she said. She was always mixing her English with Italian. I think she assumed everybody spoke both, if she realized at all that they were separate tongues and not just one big one.

We sat on the floor in the front room and Fabrizia showed me her drawings. She did them in chalk and crayons on a big pad of rough paper; art was her favorite subject, as I guess it is for most first-formers, since they can't yet write much more than their names, or read at all. There was one with my name under it. It was a stick figure like all of them, but this one was taller and thinner than average and instead of having a circle for a head it had a narrow rectangle. It was holding what I supposed was a beer tin in one hand. "That's you," the kid said, pretty pleased with herself. "Isn't it?"

I admitted she had the likeness.

"And that's me!" she said, pointing to another stick figure with a real round face, and a big smile, floating in the sky up above a house that actually was a fair if wobbly rendition of the one she lived in. There were a bunch of other stick people on the verandah. Frowning. Or at least with that smile half-circle drawn upside down on their faces.

She had to show me each and every picture, tell me the names of the colors she'd used, and which were her favorites. After a while she tuckered out. Alice, who'd been sitting silently with us the whole time, rose from her chair with a sigh and took her off to bed. Then Camilla got restless; I could hear her crying in the back. Bert got up to tend to her. Alice came back and flopped next to me on the old sofa Bert had rescued from a thrift shop and she'd covered with some white canvas.

"What's wrong with me, Harry?" she said, looking at me in a more open and honest way than she ever had before. "I'm falling apart. I getting cross always with Umberto, and the girl, too."

"Maybe you're a bit tired these days, that's all, having an infant. They're a handful, aren't they?" I said.

"Do I look tired?" she said, craning her neck so she could see her face in the mirror that hung over the mantel. "*Dío, Dío, Dío*. I do. Bags under the eyes. Everything falling apart."

"No, you're not. You look great," I said.

"Such a liar, Harry, I never believe. I see the mirror. Terrible. I am not used to a life like this. Hard work, yes. No problem. I am used to hard work. But to be trapped in a house all day, and then Umberto comes home tired and he just wants to play with the children, we don't talk hardly. Only argue sometimes. I starting to talk to myself, just to hear a voice."

Why not try the cane toad, I thought, then remembered he worked lunch and dinner shifts. Doubtful he'd trek all the way back to Ashfield from Double Bay in between for a chat. Doubtful he'd be a lively conversationalist even in Italian, either.

A crash came from the back. Alice started. "My nerves are so bad," she said. She stood up with a weary groan. "Clumsy man. He is trying to change a diaper, he think he is helping but he makes such a mess it's twice as much work later. *Dío mío.*" Then she left the room and I was sitting there by myself, about half my beer undrunk. Feeling sheepish and disconcerted as I might if I'd barged in on a couple I didn't know all that well and caught them in their underwear.

Reckoned I'd better go. I drained my beer, called out, "See ya" to the empty room, and quietly slipped out the front door.

FIRST CHANCE SHE GOT, with Camilla about five months old and off the breast, Alessandra went back to work. She dressed in her best one afternoon, went east, saw the man she needed to see, and started as a hostess the next night. At Il Pelicano. No coincidence there, of course. The boarder had to have known of the opening. And now he started trekking back between shifts. So he and Alice left the house together early every evening, and came home together late each night.

Right away, we stopped hearing any rows at all. Dad, the cynical bastard, said it was only because Bert and Alice now saw so little of each other, her going off to her job about the same time he came home from his, like they had before her pregnancy.

More likely, it seemed to me, she'd finally come out of her funk simply because she was feeling pretty again, and absolutely delighted to be out of the house talking to people and earning money instead of changing nappies night and day.

A SLY ONE when she wanted to be, my Lucy. "Wear your new Armani," she said when she rang me up early on my birthday. "I'm taking you someplace really chichi for dinner tonight. In Double Bay." I should have guessed by that alone it'd be Il Pelicano, but I felt stupidly startled when that's exactly where the taxi dropped us. Alessandra couldn't have had a clue we were coming, since Lucy'd had her assistant make the reservation under "Whitmoor," and she'd only ever been on a first-name basis with Alice. Yet Alessandra didn't miss a beat, behaving as if we were regulars, as if she were expecting us. She was all smiles and good grace as she took us to one of the best tables.

I'd seen Alice decked out many times, so I wasn't surprised by how fetching she looked: hair done but not too done, makeup slight and so perfect it was almost invisible, a very hip black sleeveless dress that ended a few inches above her knees, great crocodile flats an unusual olive color on her feet.

But as I watched her glide through her duties, her manner was so different from what I was used to that she seemed like another person. She called everyone "darling" without sounding phony. Her accent was alluring and sophisticated, her smile so intimate it was disturbing. She was flat-out flirting half the time, but just underneath, if she wasn't flirting directly with you and you weren't completely smitten, you could see it was all business.

The place was slick. The waiters wore white silk collarless shirts under black suits of a cut that made me fairly sure they were Versace or some really well-done local knockoffs. Even Alfredo, handling tables on the other side of the room, looked decent in the getup. The menus were handwritten with that day's date in burnt umber ink on thick parchment. The bottle of wine I ordered was at our side chilling in a silver bucket faster than a good publican could double-pour a schooner of Tooheys.

"Do you like all this, Harry?" Lucy grinned, glancing around. The walls had been painted to look like the faded and mellowed stucco of Italian renaissance rooms. There were church candles thick and long as your arm in black wrought-iron holders hanging everywhere, and shorter ones on every table. The tables and chairs themselves were ultramodern, brushed steel, while the floor was creamy stone blocks, really ancient or treated somehow to look like they'd come from an old palazzo. An odd mix, considered part by part, but it worked wonderfully as a whole.

"It'd be a perfect place to bring impressionable little girl-hacks," Lucy said.

"Oh, it is. Never a failure yet with the first half-dozen. Something magic in the atmosphere, I reckon, makes 'em incredibly eager to slip right out of their knickers," I said. She knew very well I'd never been there before.

While Lucy debated out loud whether pasta with wild boar sauce or grilled salmon with porcini should be her choice, I watched Alice at work, saw her exchange a few words with this waiter or that, nodding toward tables where she'd just seated customers. Saw too that whenever she spoke to Alfredo, she laid a hand on his arm.

"Anything to that, you think?" I asked Lucy after telling her what I'd noticed.

"Absurd thought, Harry," she said. "Well, wild boar wins."

I went for a grilled veal chop with rosemary. We were finishing up some very tasty Balmain bugs we'd ordered for starters when Alice seated a couple at the table next to us, which was the last empty one in the place. He was a broad fellow, his suit too tight across his shoulders and too short in the leg. But the suit was fine merino, and he had a big gold Rolex on his right wrist. His wife—and she was too worn to be anything but a wife—looked about his age, say mid-fifties, but she was probably a decade younger and had spent too much time in the sun. Her face wasn't wrinkled so much as it was incised. She was wearing some very flashy jewels around her neck, but Lucy thought she'd made a mistake; they only drew attention to her dewlaps.

Il Pelicano may have been young and hip, full of bright boomers in expensive suits with girls who were doing a great job of impersonating the models you saw in *Mode* or *Vogue*, even if their bone structures weren't quite up to carrying it off. It was also the sort of place where the cutlery weighed a ton, and I could see this bloke hefting his knife and fork and nodding with satisfaction at his wife.

Turned out good silver was about all he was prepared to be satisfied with. Not a Sydney-sider, I decided. Not a city man by nature. He ordered a bottle of a pretty dear Yarra Valley red, and sniffed the cork as suspiciously as a dog sniffing strange shit. He made quite a show of rolling the wine around in his mouth and actually chewing it, before he came out with "Christ, the plonk's corked."

Knew I was right about him, then. His accent was pure West Australia, he probably had a first name like Trevor or Nigel, and his money came from metals or minerals or opals, because that's about all there was to make it on out there.

The wine steward stiffened up immediately. He'd taken a quick sniff of the cork himself, and he had a look on his face like he was going to tell this ocker he could bugger off smartly if he thought the bottle was off. But Alessandra slipped up smoothly, murmured a few words in Italian into the steward's ear before saying more loudly, in English, "The gentleman, he knows his wine. Bring another bottle right away, Paolo."

Even I knew that was a crock, but Mr. Mineralmoney bought it. He hefted his knife and fork again with a pleased look, as if he'd just thought of a new and unique way to rook a friend out of a great mining lease.

That was all it took for Alice to size up her man. No, I'm wrong. She was too skilled. She surely had him marked the instant he walked in the door, and had her strategy quickly in place. When he complained about his Balmain bugs, Alice produced a fork and tasted one right off his plate, giving him a big smile as she did so. "You are right for sure, darling," she said. "A bit too much garlic. We'll bring new ones." She left with the plate and returned about a minute and half later with what I was sure was the same plate and the same bugs, because you couldn't cook them that fast. "Now please try these fresh ones, darling. I am certain they are just right, I watched the chef myself," she said. He munched and nodded, and she gave him a smile you'd expect from a woman you'd just charmed into coming home with you. Mr. Mineralmoney smacked his lips, he was feeling that spruce.

It went on that way through the main course and past dessert, him complaining and Alice charming him, while Mrs. Mineralmoney kept her head down and ate like a nag with a feedbag on.

"Jesus," Lucy breathed to me when the show was almost over. "Alice is brilliant! I wouldn't believe it if I didn't see it. Always thought she was so stiff and standoffish. Amazing performance. Imagine the huge tip that drongo's going to give her!"

THE MINERALMONEYS left bulging and pleased. I ordered grappa after our espressos. Alfredo hadn't waited our table, but he glided up with a second round. "*Buono sera*," he said, with what passed for him as a friendly smile. "Alessandra, she say to tell you this compliment of the house. We hope the food, it is okay for you, no?"

"Hi, Alfredo," Lucy said. "It was all lovely."

"*Bene, bene*," he almost bowed, then glided away.

Lucy's eyes seemed as richly green as Thai emeralds as she peered at me over that second glass, and even after all these years she was still unaware of—or at least utterly unselfconscious about—what her lips suggested. Yet as I sipped, I had the brief sensation that the woman across the table from me was someone I'd only recently met. Wasn't the first time this unsettling feeling had come over me. For a while now—when I'd see her at a party talking to someone on the other side of the room, or study her face in bed when I woke—I'd occasionally had the brief, uneasy sense of looking at someone I didn't know.

That some of the purely physical heat between us had cooled a bit, well, that was the natural way of it for everyone, after a certain amount of time together. But to me it had felt as though other warmths had moved in to compensate. A bit less urgency to the sex, a bit more intensity to emotional closeness, to words exchanged, the touch of hands, the comfort in one another's presence. Still, these flashes of Lucy as a woman unknown—though they never lasted more than an instant—troubled me. I couldn't understand the why of them.

Maybe it's an oblique sign, I thought, finishing the grappa, that it's time to take the next, natural step. Then I heard myself blurting straight into the middle of something or other Lucy was saying, "Why don't we get married?"

"What for?" she said, no change at all in the happily animated expression that'd been on her face when I interrupted. Trust Lucy to come up with the one response that'd leave me flat-footed. I was ready, I supposed, for a yes, a no, a maybe, or even just surprised silence. But not a bloody cool "What for?"

"Ah," feeling suddenly a complete wanker, "because it seems the right thing to do. The right time."

"Poor answer, Harry," she said, grinning and sparkling. "I'd rather do it if it was wrong."

"What?"

"Seems to me we've had it too easy, we're already too damned settled. We need to hit some rough going, battle through it a few times, and come out okay on the other side. We ought to be more flingy, let ourselves get hit by some emotional willie-willies. If we survive 'em, then we might talk marriage."

"I swear, Lucy," I said. "You're impossibly vague when you put your mind to it."

"Umberto'd understand what I'm about."

"What has he got to do with any of this?"

"Nothing at all. Except he'd know my meaning."

"I doubt anyone could understand your present line."

"You expressed, Harry, a probably sincere but awfully half-hearted interest in marriage. I said we were too settled already, you said 'What?' and I said Umberto'd understand. Clear as crystal."

"Why are you on about Bert, for Christ's sake?"

"Harry, you can be dim. I'm only saying I reckon he knows something about women's thinking, about what they want and do not want to hear. Not nearly all there is to know, but more than you."

"After all that warfare between him and Alice? You still think he's such a genius?"

"Kept it together, didn't he, though? With a woman as high-strung as Alice, that's quite an achievement."

"And I suppose you mean as well that I don't know enough to come close to managing something like that."

"No. Only that you've never had to try. Do you believe you could handle me through such a bad patch? I'm as chewed up as you are, Harry, but you can't see my scars because they're deep inside. You couldn't just stroke and kiss them as if they didn't matter."

"You got hit hard young, I know," I said. "That's not unique."

"Never said it was. Only said I don't know for sure if you could deal with some of it, if it ever came out under stress. I hide it from you, Harry."

"Then why all the doubts, if I've never seen it?"

"Oh, I have given you a glimpse or two," she grinned. "You just didn't notice."

I felt confounded. Lucy sailed right on in a rising breeze. She was lively and lovely when we got back to her house that night. What she'd said about me in the restaurant seemed to have little effect on her desires— except, oddly, to freshen them. She seemed, in fact, as excited and enthusiastic a lover as she'd been that very first time we'd had together.

But I didn't feel much like the Harry I'd started the evening being, let alone the Harry I'd been back then.

11

FOR A WHILE I FELT fazed and flurried by Lucy's words at Il Pelicano. Dreaded she might be going off me, for reasons I had neither sensed nor seen. Expected any day now she'd say it was all over. But it never happened.

We just swung along as we always had. Weeks flowed smoothly into months. Lucy seemed happy as she'd ever been. It was just a sharp tap to my ego, admitting she'd bagged me fairly. There was loads I didn't understand about women. Or, more precisely, about that woman, since she was the only one I had ever seriously devoted my attentions to.

But the Pelicano evening unnerved me enough that I stayed on guard against blurting out whatever popped into my head, and kept myself on high alert for any more of those glimpses of her inner self Lucy had claimed I'd missed. I'm sure she noticed my efforts. Maybe they even pleased her.

How to explain something none of us seemed to notice? Perhaps it was all the emotions and events that moiled round Lucy and me, Bert and Alice with their new kid. Perhaps all of us, including Dad, were too concentrated on daily cares and pleasures, too short-sighted. More likely it was the simple fact that we were all getting older. Whichever, the slouching seasons somehow seemed to pick up their pace 'til they were moving at a brisk march.

It took us all by surprise, how quickly years had passed when the summer of '79 roared in. A wicked number even by Sydney standards. The westerlies were remorseless, and Southern Busters came whirling violently out of nowhere, blowing sheets of rain sideways in defiance of gravity. In between, we steamed.

The trek to and from work each day was brutal; none of us wanted to leave our air-conditioned offices, even to grab a bit of lunch. And it must have been hellish for Alice and the kids at home most days. Alfredo had moved out a month or two after Alice returned to work, but she seemed to wilt visibly just walking from the house to Alf's rusty old Falcon when he picked her up each evening to go to the restaurant. We all spent our evenings on the verandah, hoping for any little breeze, fanning ourselves when none came by. It took an act of will to go to bed. In that humidity, the sheets you sweated through one night were still damp when you lay down on them the next. Even Fabrizia, who was always a bundle of energy, just lolled there, listless as a doll.

Since I was generally on the verandah 'til late with Lucy or Dad or both, I saw Alf's Falcon pull up most every night and Alice emerge from it. Bert and the kids had usually retired by then. It didn't register with me for the longest time that Alf was bringing Alice home close to one, even though Il Pelicano's kitchen closed, I knew, at ten.

"So what? Work's not over when the kitchen closes," Lucy said when I mentioned that. "People linger over their meals, Harry. And then the staff's got to clean up and get ready for tomorrow."

Seemed reasonable. Seemed a bit strange, though, that Alf also came calling during the day many Mondays, when the restaurant was closed. Or so my little friend reported.

"You like Alfredo, Harry?" Fabrizia asked one evening after she'd come scratching at the door to invite me outside and we'd taken a stroll down to the old ghost gum a rowdy mob of cockatoos had colonized.

"Hardly know him, darls," I said.

"Well, hope you don't. 'Cause I don't. He's always around on Mum's day off when Dad's at work. Having coffee in the kitchen with Mum. Gives me the shits," she said.

Dad's bad influence, her language. And mine. I wished there was a way to keep her from learning English on the fly from the likes of him and me.

"No way to talk, Fabrizia. There's lots of things you'll hear from men that oughtn't to be repeated by little girls. Isn't proper."

"Bloody hell!" she giggled. "I heard Lucy say exactly that to you once, and you laughed. Lucy's proper. Know she is."

"Yeah, we all ought to be more careful with our speech. People'll get the wrong impression."

"Then I'll invite them to bite their bums," she grinned. "Isn't that what you're supposed to say when people are rude?"

"Jesus," I said. "Listen, Fabrizia. Those are insults in English. Bad words. If you said anything like them in Italian, your mum and dad would be furious. Understand?"

"Too right," she replied. "I called Alfredo *sporco* and *cattivo* the other day. The bludger had told me to go to my room and play there when I came into the kitchen. Like he was my dad or something. So I called him that."

"And?"

"Mum spanked me straightaway. Then sent me to my room," she said. No giggling now.

"I'm going to spank you if you keep mimicking Dad and me in English then."

"No you won't, Harry." She seemed to brighten. "We're mates!"

ONE FRIDAY AFTERNOON later that summer as I was carting home the weekend beer, I ran into Bert getting off the bus from the center city. He looked beat and bushed, but he insisted on helping me carry the beer. He said he and Alessandra were going to take the kids to Bondi on Sunday, did we want to come along? Our Whale Beach refuge happened to be booked solid, so Lucy and I were at loose ends for the weekend.

"Sure thing," I said, forgetting how bad the heat at Bondi can be even in a normal summer, and no bloody shade anywhere. Bert seemed delighted. Said we'd meet at the Pavillion around ten in the morning.

"No worries, I'll drive," I said.

Now if Lucy's stubborness about her Paddo place was her way of giving the finger to boomer values, my ancient Holden was mine. It had a big rounded hood and a bulging grill and from the front, with the headlights staring at you, it looked like a cartoon face. I called it "Jacko," and though I used buses and taxis during the work week, nothing pleased me better than to take Jacko for spins and excursions. I couldn't count the times Lucy and Bert and Alice and the kids and I had done this.

But Umberto said, "No no no, you don't have to drive us."

"And why not?" I asked, thinking he'd somehow got re-infected with the guest-in-someone's-house mania that afflicted him and Alice for months after they had first arrived in Sydney.

"Ah, not enough room for so many," he said. "Alfredo, he is coming, too. So he drive us, and we meet Lucy and you at Bondi, no?"

"Sure," I said. I did not mention that Alf's inclusion put me off a bit.

Which it would have even if I hadn't been trained by my trade to be suspicious, and hadn't seen and heard what I'd seen and heard lately.

Sunday was a scorcher. Bondi was crawling with folks turning their skin to leather, sun-baking dark as they could get, completely ignoring the fact they were just begging for a real nice melanoma and a painful death. I set up a big umbrella. Umberto and Alessandra had brought a wicker basket full of the lovely things I'd often enjoyed at their house: perfectly fresh mozzarella balls drizzled with virgin olive oil and specked with pepper and salt, tangy black olives, long thin loaves of semolina bread, prosciutto sliced so thin it was almost transparent, ripe melons, sliced tomatoes with a bit of that oil and baby basil leaves, a great chunk of firm Parmesan. And, in an Esky, one of the lightest, freshest-tasting white wines I'd ever had, as well as tins of Toohey's.

Lucy was in heaven, since she adored good food and drink, and all you get at the beach concessions are lard-fried fish and chips or salad sandwiches with butter that's usually about a day past its prime.

It was pleasant under the umbrella at first. There was a smart, fresh breeze off the ocean. A mob of lifesavers strutted past wearing their skull caps. Alessandra laughed and nudged Alf, who said something very fast and low in Italian. When the lifesavers passed us, you could see they had the rear of their Speedos rolled up the cracks of their asses. Alice knew very well they did that to get a better grip, so to speak, on the varnished seats of their rescue boats, but the bum parade never failed to amuse her. Her personal sense of decorum was stricter; though she was certainly still well-structured enough to go topless, she never would.

It got much hotter after noon when the breeze died. Umberto had been down to his trunks since we'd arrived. Lucy, as sun-blocked as she could get, was toasting in just her thong. Alessandra finally removed her little tissue-thin linen jacket, revealing a modest white one-piece cossie, which looked nice against her black hair with its chestnut highlights. Alfredo, lounging beside her, began making limp fanning movements with one hand. I was overheating fast.

Bert noticed me hogging the umbrella's shrinking circle of shade but sweating to death anyway, and asked why I didn't shuck my shirt. We had been to a beach or two together many times before, of course, but never in heat like this. So the issue of my big hat and long-sleeved top had never come up. I said it was better not to, I wasn't real pretty underneath. I was fairly sure from the way he looked in my eyes that he had got the drift.

"Harry," Alessandra said. "Is too hot, no?"

Umberto said something to her in Italian, and she rattled back at him. "Harry," he said. "Take your shirt off. We don't mind."

I shook my head.

"Harry," Alice said. "I tell you one thing, Harry. We've seen worse, whatever you got. My father, you know, burned very bad in a tank in Libya. His face and body, they look like a melted white candle."

They made me feel I was being more than a little mental about my scars. Lucy just turned her face toward me, eyes invisible behind her sunglasses, smiled and went back to sun-baking. I took my shirt off.

"Damn dirty war you must have been in, no?" Bert said. Alf rolled onto his side to have a glance, flinched, rolled back. Alessandra didn't look away. What she did was reach out and try to trace one of my notches with a finger, saying something like *povero, povero*. I recoiled a fraction just before she was able to touch. I thought Christ, she's cheeky. But she kept her finger maybe an inch from my shoulder, until I looked up from the sand in which my feet were busy tunneling almost on their own will, and met her eyes. She looked real sharp into mine and she smiled. Then she reached into the Esky with the hand that had almost touched the scar and handed me a beer.

And then Fabrizia scurried over from the sandpile she'd been building and started tugging at my arm. "I think a shark took a bite of Harry, hated the taste and spit him out!" she cried.

"*Cattiva!*" Alice snapped. Fabrizia just made a face.

She tugged at my arm, pointed at the surf. "C'mon, Harry! Take me swimming. Please? You can't just sit here all day. Sharks don't like you anyway."

So I downed the beer and strolled hand in hand with Fabrizia to where the waves were turning into foam rushing up and back over the sand. Tossed her into the shallow water, fetched her, tossed her again. She was squealing with delight. A few people stared at me for a moment and then quickly looked away, but pretty soon I wasn't noticing anybody but the kid. I put her on my shoulders and waded out chest-deep, holding her skinny little legs. She shrieked each time a wave lifted and dropped us.

Then Bert came into the shallows with Camilla, who was just past two and still in nappies, and dipped her down so the foam would tickle her feet. The little thing flinched with fear instead of squealing happily like most kids her age. Bert kept trying, but Camilla was starting to wail when Lucy dashed past, so toned even her breasts didn't jiggle, and dove straight through a breaker, coming up on the far side spouting water and looking exalted. I glanced back toward our umbrella once, saw Alice and Alfredo, heads close together, apparently deep in some conversation that was causing him to flap both hands. I saw Bert cradle Camilla and turn away from the water. But Fabrizia reclaimed my attention smartly by yanking my ears. "Go out deeper, Harry," she urged. "Deeper."

We stayed past sundown. In the gray dusk, we saw the lights of a liner sailing north toward the Heads glow golden. Umberto watched its progress intently. Maybe he was thinking only about journeys. Maybe he was still unsure, or might forever remain unsure, if the one he'd made was a right one.

We packed it in when the liner vanished round the point. It was full dark as we walked back up the beach to the lot where the Holden was parked near Alf's Falcon. Camilla was asleep in Bert's arms, while Fabrizia was clutching my hand and rattling on endlessly about her teacher and her best friends in school and who she hated there, and how she couldn't wait to start school again in February. Alf and Alice and Lucy trailed behind carrying most of the gear except the umbrella, which I had tucked under my left arm.

When we got home, Dad was out. Smiling wickedly at each other, Lucy and I stripped and showered the sea salt and sand off together. It got more delightful when we moved on to the soaping, then the toweling off, then the bed.

"Tell me I'm going to live forever exactly like this. Tell me now and I'll believe it," Lucy whispered, bodies entwined, still joined in fact, after making love.

"You will," I said, kissing her on the vulnerable place just at the base of her throat, where I could see her skin move with each pulse of blood beneath it. "I promise."

Then I immediately began thinking of breaking it. In one particular way. Wondering how we'd be, Lucy and I, as a threesome, with a Fabrizia of our own. A place of our own. A family. My own kid tugging me toward the surf. Hearing "C'mon, Dad!"

Got so far into that pleasant prospect I even picked a name: Valentine, after a girl in that great novel *Parade's End* whom I'd sort of fallen in love with. I had that tendency, with certain characters in books and films. We'd send her to a fancy girls' school, not a public one. Nothing would be too good for her. She'd be gorgeous, I had no doubt about that.

Never said a word about this to Lucy, remembering too well my botched proposal. Reckoned she would let me know if and when she was ready.

WELL PAST MIDNIGHT, after running Lucy back to Paddo, I parked the Holden at the edge of our back garden and walked through the front door, musing pleasantly on my dream, on the little Valentine I imagined was hovering in the not so distant future.

"Who the hell are you, busting into my house," Dad growled, rising from his overstuffed chair. The TV screen was a glowing gray blank. He came shuffling toward me like a boxer, arms cocked and fists ready.

"Christ, Dad!" I said. Too late to stop a left jab that just brushed my shoulder, or the right cross that connected fair on my left cheekbone.

I spun away, kicking his legs out from under him so he tumbled to the floor. He seemed stunned. I ran around switching on every light in the room, saw him roll over on his back, and sat down fast on his chest.

"Bloody hell, Dad! What the fuck's with you?"

"Harry?" His voice was slow and slurry. "Bloody burglar, thought you were. Jesus, mate."

I remembered what Lucy had said once. I sniffed. No alcohol on his breath. I got up, took him under the arms, raised him to his feet. He made it to the chair under his own power.

"You all right, Dad? Are you crook or something?"

"Don't think so," he said, sounding near normal. "Just dozed off watching telly. Reckon it startled me, you banging through the door like that."

I'd come in quietly. "Nothing dozy about the way you came at me. Jesus, I've got to put some ice on my cheekbone. It's swelling way the hell up."

"Somebody hit you?"

"Yeah. You. Hell of right hand you've got, for an old fart." My brain felt jolted from its moorings, and not just because of the punch.

"Fuck me stupid! Christ, Harry, sorry about that."

"You sure you're not crook, Dad? Not feeling strange or anything? Where were you tonight?"

"Just down to Frank's, on the boat. Came home, turned on the telly. Like I said, just a bit of a shock when the door crashed open. Reckon I was still half asleep when I came at you. I'm real sorry. Never meant to hit you."

"No worries. Why don't you go on up to bed? Need a hand?"

" 'Course not," Dad grinned. "Believe I know the way."

I stood at the foot of the stairs, watched him climb. He walked straight and steady enough.

Straighter and steadier than me, when I went into the kitchen, took some ice from the fridge, wrapped it in a dish towel, and held it against my cheek. Then I sat down and rang Frank. Yeah, Dad and he had been out on the boat. One beer each. That was it, he told me. Dad had got on the bus for Ashfield after. Seemed perfectly fine.

So I called Lucy.

12

G'DAY!" DAD SAID, sauntering into the kitchen, where Lucy and I were sitting at the table sipping tea. "Best start to one I've had in a while, seeing your lovely face first thing, Luce. Instead of just Harry's ugly mug."

We'd been sitting there most of the night, in fact. She'd come over after I rang her, we had peeked in on Dad, who seemed to be sleeping peaceably, then gone downstairs and started talking things over.

"It's time he saw a doctor," Lucy had said.

"Doubt he'll go for that," I'd said.

"It's time. He has to, like it or not."

"Well, there were those other little mad minutes. But he always sprang back. And they've been few enough. Pretty far between, as well."

"Yeah, and I just wrote them off to drink. But it definitely wasn't drink this time, was it? Reckon I could have been wrong about the other times."

"You could've," I'd said. "But maybe it's still best to wait a bit, see how he goes for a while."

"Christ, Harry!" Lucy'd gone sharp and edgy. "Wait for what? It's as obvious as dog's balls *something's* not right. Let's just get him checked out. You'll not be doing him any favor, letting it slide."

"Maybe you're right," I'd conceded.

"Maybe up your bum, cobber. There could be something happening in your Dad's head that needs medical attention right now. Or not. Don't you think we should find out one way or the other? Why're you waffling? Why's a simple checkup got be a drama?"

Dad presently provided her with an answer to that.

"Christ, Harry, you do look crook," he said as he joined us at the table. "What'd you run into? Door or something?"

"Think you may've had something to do with Harry's face, Joe," Lucy smiled at him now. "Since your fist hit it. Have a cuppa?"

Dad laughed, poured himself one from the pot. "Now Lucy darls, who's been putting strange ideas into your head this morning?"

"You don't recall a bit of a punch-up last night? Late? In the front room?" she said.

He looked at me, taking in the purple weal on my cheek, then turned to her and grinned. "Well, Luce, if you had to smack the boy into line, my guess is he richly deserved it. For whatever it was he did. So good on ya, girl."

"Wasn't me, Joe," she said. "It was you."

"No!" He looked genuinely shocked. "Never did!"

Then he started laughing hard. "Just having you on, Luce," he said. "The bugger scared me shitless, bursting into the house in the middle of the night. I was half asleep, took a wild swing before I knew what I was doing. Young Harry was just too slow to get out of the way. Right, Harry?"

"Something like that, Dad," I said.

Lucy laid her hand on one of his. "Joe, how about a quick visit to a doctor? Bit of a checkup?"

"What on earth for? I'm fit and feeling fine, 'cept for this heat." He laughed again. "Fitter than Harry, it'd seem."

"Yeah, the heat's a crusher," Lucy said. "And everybody ought to get checked out once in a while anyway. Bet it's been ages since you've seen a doctor."

"Too bloody right! And it'll be ages 'til I waste my time at any quack's again. Drongos, the lot of them."

"Not the lot," Lucy said. "Know one I believe you'd like. Why not let him have a look at you?"

"What the bloody hell are you two on about?" Dad snappped. " 'Cause it's clear you're in this together."

"Just thinking that maybe, at your age, it'd be a good idea for you to visit a doctor, get a clean bill of health and all," I said. "I go in for a checkup every couple of years myself, let 'em take a reading on my blood pressure and so on."

"Yeah, well you can think again if you think you've a chance in hell of wheedling me into that. 'At my age,' my arse. I'll say it once more so it's real clear: NO QUACKS! I don't want another word about this garbage from either of you."

Lucy looked at me, lightly bit her lower lip. Then she stood up. "Well, gents, time for me to go to work. See you, Joe. Harry, shout me a beer this evening?"

"Sure. Your local?"

"Right," she said, and left.

THERE WAS ALMOST NOTHING, Lucy and I concluded that evening after close consideration of every scheme and scam we were able to imagine, that could be done. No way in the world a tough old union bat-tler like Joe Hull would be moved by either heavy pressure or any soft persuasions or deceptions she and I might bring to bear. He simply would not hear us; we knew him well enough to feel sure of that. So we went down to Bondi and had a word with Frank. I half expected he'd dismiss the whole thing, even while we gave him chapter and verse about each of Dad's episodes. He did not. He listened with concern, agreed absolutely that some sort of medical testing was necessary, promised he'd do his best to swing Joe around to that point of view.

I believe he did his best, but the call I got from him a few days later was brief. "Your Dad told me to get stuffed. Then he went further and invited me to bite my bum. Or use it as shark bait. Sorry, Harry," Frank said. "Reckon we'll just have to see how it plays out."

Only there was nothing playing out for the rest of that bone-busting summer and well into the autumn. Dad seemed fit and fine, just as he'd claimed to be. He was cheery most of the time, despite the sweats and some sleep trouble. His temper did flare now and then, but never beyond what we'd seen before. Never had more than a pint or two, except on an occasional night at the RSL, as usual. He complained about headaches from time to time, but who doesn't? Wash a couple of those large yellow Mersyndols down your throat with a glass of beer, and they take care of it all in a jiffy. I had more than the normal number myself, and just chalked them off to the weather.

I relaxed. I should have known better—hell, I did know better. Pit feelings against facts, and feelings win every time. Hopeful feelings that Dad was basically sound lured me into behaving as if he was. Even when Tito, the bloody cockatoo Bert had bought Fabrizia a couple of years back who turned out to be a brilliant talker, decided to take a hand—or a tongue—in matters.

Dad, like all of us, had a few habitual expressions and pet phrases, some filthy but most just banal shorthand he used in casual conversations with friends. One afternoon as I was coming in the front door, I heard, "Ahh, best and strongest beer in the world" from the back, and I thought Christ, hope Dad's left one for me. When I went into the kitchen, though, he was not there. Most likely he had stopped at the RSL to refuel before slogging the rest of the way home. Then I heard him again—"Ahh, best and strongest beer in the world"—and noticed Tito out back of Umberto's, sitting on his perch with his crest up and looking about as pleased with himself as a bird can be.

"Good on ya, mate," I called out, and back from the bird came, "Good on ya, mate," in Dad's exact voice, not mine. I'd only ever heard Tito imitate Bert and Fabrizia before. This was new, mimicking Dad. This was going to be really funny, I thought.

That evening at supper it was just Dad and me at the kitchen table, doors and windows open wide. He was describing a small confrontation his union committee had had with some ALP group about upcoming elections, and finished off with a typical "Greedy bloody spivs" about the politicals. In from the rear window came—in tones so precisely his it was uncanny— "Greedy bloody spivs." I gave no sign I'd heard a thing. But Dad's eyes went shifty, and he shook his head like a wet dog does.

Then he went on with other affairs of the day, dropping a familiar "whingeing buggers" into it. "Whingeing buggers" bounced back at us. Dad stuck a forefinger in his right ear and probed around a bit. Next up was "So I invited them to bite their bums." "Bite their bums" reverberated. I was having a real struggle keeping my face straight.

"You hear anything, Harry?" Dad asked uneasily.

"Sure. What you're telling me."

"No, I mean after I've stopped. Like my words being repeated. In my fucking voice!"

"Hell, no. There's just the two of us here. What are you on about?"

"An echo, sort of? Of what I say?" He looked truly worried now.

"You're dreaming, Dad."

"Well, fuck me stupid if I don't hear an echo."

At just the right interval came "Fuck me stupid."

"There it is again! Christ, Harry," Dad said, rubbing both his ears. "I must be losing it. There's this echo in my head. Do I seem all right to you? Am I talking sense, not babbling or repeating things twice or any-thing?"

"You seem fine. A bit boring in your conversation maybe, but there's nothing new in that," I grinned.

"Oh, thanks for your concern, you little prick."

"Little prick."

Dad stood up, his face flushing. "I am so losing it. I'm going mental. I keep hearing myself twice. Reckon I'll have to see a quack. This is bloody dreadful, Harry. Really."

I suddenly felt dreadful I'd let it go this far. Dad was very disturbed. So I yelled, in my best imitation of Umberto, "*Basta, idiota!*" Dad started in real alarm. I suppose he thought he'd begun to hallucinate. But through the window came "*Basta, idiota!*" as clear and recognizable as if Bert himself were lurking right outside.

Dad got cross then. He sat down, snatched my tin of beer, and started drinking it himself. "The bird," he said quietly but fiercely. "And you're a wretched bastard. You knew all the time, didn't you? That ain't fair play, Harry. I'll get you for it, no fear. And you can buy your own bloody beer in the meantime."

Couldn't help myself then. I started laughing so hard my ribs hurt.

"Think it's amusing?" Dad muttered. "You're a sicko, bagging me like that. I've raised a retarded perve."

After that, whenever he heard a peep out of Tito, in anybody's voice including Fabrizia's, Dad snarled, "I'm gonna poison that bastard," but real low. Within a short while, though, he forgot to keep his voice down, and a couple of weeks later whenever Tito heard Dad say anything at all, the bird shouted, "I'm going to poison that bastard!"

Drove Dad right up the wall. He began worrying the neighbors would think it was him yelling the threat. He started talking very softly around the house, which was a painful restraint because he couldn't hear as well as he used to—like most who've worked years in the din of a pressroom—and he did love the sound of his own voice, especially when he was boozed up a trifle.

Into the winter, something far more insidious and much more ominous than any of those short, sharp irruptions began a baleful corruption within Dad. It was impossible to pinpoint a beginning, or chart its slow, skulking course—for me, for Lucy, for Frank, for his pressmates and union brothers. Dad's fuse just got shorter and shorter, his memory bit by bit more erratic. Until it seemed that all at once, on one particular day, everybody began having a simultaneous thought: what the hell is happening to Joe Hull? He'd always had a temper, but mainly kept it confined to occasional sharp-witted rants about fairly important and legitimate issues. Reasoned reactions, if heated, to genuine provocations. And now suddenly he was angry almost all the time, unreasonably fractious at things nobody else could see. Even goaded old pals into a kind of contest to see whose cracked opinion backed up by no knowledge whatsoever of some truly trivial matter could come out on top by lung power alone.

If anyone mentioned one of these mad outbursts afterward, Dad would deny it had ever happened. And he'd be telling a sort of truth, for in his mind the incident hadn't got recorded.

One night we cornered him our kitchen—Frank, Lucy, me, and Bruce McKibbin, who had worked side by side with Dad for twenty-two years—and we begged him to let us get him to a doctor. He heard us out quite calmly. After we'd finished, he insisted, still calm, he'd have none of that.

Then we threatened him, and he only laughed. "Oh, I'll come along quite peaceably if the four of you want to shanghai me to some emergency room," he grinned. "Just for the pleasure of watching you make fools of yourselves. I can picture it clear: you lot floundering and fumbling when the medicos start asking exactly why you've rushed in with a perfectly healthy man. How do you plan to explain that? A bunch of tales they'll never credit? Am I ranting and drooling? Am I having violent fits?"

"Stop it, Joe!" Lucy said. "We're concerned for you. We're trying to help you."

"Odds are the quacks'll commit you all for insanity," Dad chuckled. He drained his beer. "Or simply boot you out for wasting their time. It'll be bloody hilarious, either way. Ready to go when you are."

"Bloody hell," Bruce murmured to me. "Old Joe's foxed us. Always was a clever bastard."

On a Tuesday afternoon in November of '79, maybe three or four weeks after our defeat, I got a call at my desk in the newsroom from Bruce. Dad had just passed out on the pressroom floor, he told me. His heart was beating and he was breathing well, but he was unconscious. They were loading him into an ambulance bound for the closest hospital even as we spoke.

SOUVENIRS. Everybody collects at least a few, don't they? When I was a kid, I used to think they had to be objects you could hold in your hands or display on a shelf or a wall. I've broadened my definition some since.

Here's one: fretting for hours in that damn hospital, the day I got the call from the pressroom about Dad. A doctor no older than me coming into the waiting room and sitting beside me, but perched really on the edge of the hard plastic chair.

"I'm Teddy Costas," he introduced himself.

"Harry Hull," I said, shaking the hand he extended.

"Glad to know you," he said. "Bloody sorry it's like this, but the news isn't all bad."

"What's up?"

"Ruin any faith you might have in modern medicine if I tell you we don't know?"

I just looked at him.

"No? Good enough. We *think* your dad's had a stroke. A slight one.

He's already conscious, he's got full movement, no paralysis at all, and he's lucid and very articulate about things."

"Let me guess. He's saying fuck all, I'm grand, and I want to get out of here now. Right?"

"That's the mild version," Dr. Costas grinned.

"But he can't go yet."

"That's it. We need to keep him here for the full battery of tests. Blood, urine, brain scan, the works. It'll take a few days."

"Oh, he's going to love that."

"My impression exactly. So I was wondering if you'd talk to him a bit, get him settled with the idea that it's absolutely necessary?"

"No worries."

"Great! Can't use any sedatives in a case like this, you see. And he's getting kind of worked up. But I've got a few questions for you first."

"Right."

"Has your dad been acting strangely in any way? Confusion, unusual irritability, some memory lapses, maybe some difficulty concentrating?"

I filled him in, all the way back to that day years ago when Dad woke up feeling the world had shifted somehow in the night and left him off-true, through to his mistaking me for a burglar last summer and the go-round with Tito. And finishing with the recent behavior everyone had noticed.

"Okay. Thanks. Now let's go see your dad," Dr. Costas said.

Here's another souvenir: In that waiting room again, seventy-two hours later, with Lucy holding my hand, and me wishing she wouldn't clasp it with such clear concern that I couldn't make a mental dodge around the frightening reality of the situation. I'd have rather been left alone. "It'll be right," she was saying for what seemed like the fifth or sixth time, when an older medico, half-glasses low on his nose and tiny tufts of white hair just peeking out of each nostril, walked up and said, "I'm Dr. Russell. You must be Mr. Hull."

Without waiting for a reply, he launched in. "Here's how it is, Mr.

Hull. Lesions on the frontal lobe of his brain, also the temporal lobe. Some necrosis in the liver. Very high dystolic pressure, evidence of arteriosclerosis. The lesions appear to be the result of a series of small infarcts. This last one was larger. We can prescribe medication to lower the blood pressure, but it's important that he cease drinking and smoking immediately, avoid stress as much as possible, and go on a low-fat diet."

"Anything else we should know?"

"Just be sure he follows the regimen I've prescribed. Bring him back about once a week for his treatment, it's all written down here. You can take him home in a half-hour or so. Goodbye," said Dr. Russell, handing me a typed sheet of paper and leaving the room.

"Did you make anything out of that nonsense?" Lucy said, releasing all her breath at once. "What a pompous ass!"

A couple of minutes later Costas strolled in. "Hello, Harry. And you're . . . ?" he asked Lucy.

"Lucy Whitmoor."

"I'm Teddy. You got Dr. Russell's report?"

"Don't know if it was a report. We got some blather, yeah," Lucy said.

"Clinical language," Costas smiled.

"Care to interpret, then?" I asked.

"You want the literal, or the soft version?"

"The straight one."

"Your dad's liver is fucked. Drink, and jungle stuff like malaria, dengue. Also tested positive for hepatitis. The liver's got about a third of the function it ought to have. Little bits are sloughing off from time to time and floating around his bloodstream. That's for starters."

"And?" Lucy said.

"Lots of his arteries and veins are clogged, narrower than they should be. 'Infarcts,' which Russell must have mentioned, just means blockage and leaking. Some of that dead liver tissue got stuck in vessels in his brain. Between that and the high blood pressure, some blood leaked out and did damage. All those episodes you told me about, Harry? Even that first little one? Silent strokes, we call them. Each one destroys some brain cells. New ones don't grow in their place."

"What's going to happen?" I asked.

"Nothing good, sad to say. He's likely to continue to have small infarcts, which means a gradual deterioration of his mental capacities. Unless he suffers a single mortal stroke, he's going to slip into dementia."

"Like Alzheimer's?"

"It isn't Alzheimer's, but the outward symptoms will be similar. A steady decline, starting with his memory. He'll become ever more irritable. He'll gradually lose touch with reality. Oh, he'll have his periods when you'd never guess there was a single thing wrong with him, but he'll also slip more and more into states in which he won't recognize his surroundings, or even you. Unless there's a fatal event, or his liver fails, near the end he'll resemble a baby. He'll have forgotten how to dress himself, how to eat, how to control certain bodily fuctions."

"Bodily functions?"

"He'll need the adult equivalent of diapers, Harry."

"How long?"

"Unless there's a killer stroke, he could go on for a year or two, even more. It would all depend on how many silent strokes he continues to have. Which we've no way of predicting."

"Bloody hell."

"Sorry, Harry." Costas paused. "Damn. I've got to tell you it might never get to that. There's another thing, you see. We found a melanoma very low on the back of his neck, below the collarbones. We cut it out, but this is one bloody aggressive cancer. There's a fairly high probability it's spread a bit. It usually heads for the nerves, especially around the right shoulder."

"Bloody fucking hell."

"Harry, your dad may die before the pain of the cancer really hits. If he doesn't, we can keep him comfortable with drugs. We can manage the pain, minimize it."

"Dad know all this?"

"He knows he's had a stroke. He knows to quit drinking, take the blood pressure medication. He knows we cut the melanoma out and he'll need radiation treatment—which Dr. Russell may not have told you, except on that paper he gave you. But your dad should even be able to go back to his job in a few weeks if he cares to. The rest? I'll tell him if you like, but I reckoned maybe you might want to. Or not, as you choose."

"What would you choose, if it was your dad?"

"I think I'd give the details about mental degeneration a complete miss."

"Thanks, Teddy. But when he starts losing his mind . . ."

"He's *already* demented, Harry," Costas said quietly. "Just doesn't realize it yet, because it's still early, still quite mild. But there's no going back, and no stopping. It'll only get worse. And at some point he might even feel it."

COSTAS WAS RIGHT.

"The hell of it, Harry, is I *know*," Dad said to me more than a year later when I was sitting up with him one night and he was in one of his increasingly rare lucid states. "I can see it happening. It's like watching a Christmas tree fucking loaded with little lights. Now and again one burns out—no worries, there are still so many shining on. But they keep burning out, and one night you're bloody surprised as hell to notice that brilliant tree has a fucking great lot of dead dark parts now. And it isn't a bloody Chrissie tree at all. It's fucking *me*!"

13

TEDDY WAS RIGHT as well about Dad and his job. He reported back to the *Herald* within a month—eagerly, relieved and grateful as hell. Feelings I shared, after watching what his enforced absence from the pressroom inflicted on him.

He'd spent his first day home in front of the TV, and when I came home that evening I found he'd lugged the thing into the back garden and left it where he'd slammed it down, a kind of post-modern sculpture with a shattered screen. Here's Dad completely mad already, I thought.

Until he spoke.

"Christ, Harry, I never realized 'til now that we're filling the world with rubbish, we're building one giant shitpile that's going to rot everybody's brains," he said when he saw the obviously troubled look on my face as I gazed at the garden's new decoration. "Never gave TV much thought before, just stared at it from time to time. But I started really

watching this morning and gave it a go the whole day. Tried every channel, back and forth.

"And aside from one tennis match, it was horrifying. Dramas that'd
be better acted by a school theater group, housewives who must have
been on drugs squealing and screaming to give the question back to
some host who's said the answer, some arrogant blokes calling each other
'professor' with every other breath seriously debating whether the fucking didgeridoo wasn't the precursor of symphonic bass brass and string
sections or some shit. Even the news! Morons looking fresh from the
hairdresser's, reciting stuff we wouldn't have run in this morning's paper
because it was too petty. Getting it wrong, as well!

"And Aussies go for this? They let their kids *watch* this garbage?" he
finished. "I'm bloody fucking shocked. I am. That's why the TV's out
here. I won't have one in the house."

I grabbed at that as a positive sign. Sure, I told myself, the gesture
he'd made was way over the top. But there was nothing mad about the
opinion. I held it myself, so did Lucy and lots of people we knew.

The second evening, though, I found him slumped in the overstuffed
chair in the front room surrounded by a berm of two dozen or so of our
books, most of them half-opened and spine-cracked from being thrown
down that way.

"The great fucking writers! Everybody says they are. And they can't
even tell a decent story," Dad fumed. "You read a few pages of this bloke
White, Noble Prize be damned, or *Across the River and into the Trees* by
Hemingway, and you wonder what possessed them to scribble such nonsense. And they put their real names on it, yet! Bloody embarrassing."

A negative turn, that. Alarming and dismaying. Dad had read for
pleasure all his life, not in any serious literary way but not just thrillers or
mysteries, either. He'd liked his Conrad, his Hemingway, his Dickens,
even Robert Graves and especially George Orwell. Shortened attention
span now, I thought. Or perhaps some of the little mental loops that a
story hooks on to were broken.

For the next couple of weeks, I imagine him wandering in some dismal, cheerless shadowland, feeling hopelessly trapped. I imagine him roaming from room to room anxious and agitated, not one damn thing to amuse him or claim his attention except whatever memories he could still dredge up. And the extent of that stockpile—as well as whether, on balance, the nice bits were vastly outnumbered by the nightmarish ones or vice versa—wasn't clear to me. Or to him either, I expect. He'd try for a calm demeanor whenever I was around, but the aimlessness and uselessness of his days were clearly paining him more than anything going wrong in his body.

Lucy agreed, though she saw it in more mundane terms. "The old story, Harry. Men fit as can be, delighted they've finally put in their required forty years of work so they can retire and really enjoy themselves, only to turn sour, bitter and sick, and then die within a few years? It's the boredom that kills them, the lack of purpose. The only ones who flourish when their working lives are over are those who have something else they're passionate about. Fishing. Building model planes. Going out to races and having a flutter. Hell, anything at all, so long as they love doing it.

"And it isn't as if your dad's off on holiday having fun. He's getting a forced preview of what he's got to look forward to, once he loses his trade and his union work for good. Can't be a pleasant prospect for him."

Too true.

So Dad was a mighty happy bloke when he was finally cleared to go back to work. Too happy, that first night after. His pressroom mates had shouted him a beer to welcome him home, and he'd been thrilled. Never mind alcohol being forbidden because it was exactly what his brain and liver needed no more of, and because the medication he was taking gave a single beer the effect of two or three.

I tore right into him when he staggered home, to no effect. He wouldn't be provoked. He just gave me this skewed, sly smile.

"Take 'er easy, Harry," he said. "You think I don't know what those quacks discovered? All the medicines they've got, and all the advice about avoiding beer and stress and the rest of it's pure garbage. We both know it. So I may as well enjoy myself as best I can before I croak."

"Yeah, Dad, that's really brilliant. If you're in a rush, you could just stick your head in the oven and turn on the gas."

"Maybe I'll do exactly that. But not just yet," Dad said. "Try to put yourself in my place. Would you want to have to wonder every day what I've got to wonder? You would not. Say different and I'll know you're the biggest bloody liar I've run across."

I said nothing.

"Garbage," he repeated. "We both know it. We both know exactly where I'm headed, that there's nothing to be done to stop it."

He suddenly grasped my mutilated arm, hard. His eyes went sharp and clear. "We know," he said. And behind that I swear I heard a plea: don't let it go too far. When the time comes, don't let me linger in agony. Put me down.

I just nodded.

Dad let go of my arm then, but still held my eyes with his, as if he were searching for something there. He must have found what he wanted. At last, he smiled. A smile neither sly nor skewed.

"Knew I could count on you, Harry."

And I knew then I would never badger him about his health, never utter a word of reproach if he strayed from his prescribed course, never speak of his illness unless he brought it up. I'd go on as if he hadn't a single thing wrong with him. Until the time came.

Then we'd go down hand in hand, Dad and I. Though no one else would ever know that, for we'd take our secret with us.

LUCY WENT MUTINOUS when I told her my plan—minus the why, for I could say nothing of my pact with Dad. From then on, it was her steely, unbending opinion that I was a bloody shirker, slithering out of my obligations by not subjecting Dad to military discipline regarding the ban on alcohol, cigarettes and most of the foods he liked, and military supervision over the medication schedule and the psychological therapy he was supposed to undergo.

"He's not entirely responsible for himself anymore, Harry," she argued. "At some level he's real depressed and giving up, but if he followed the regimen he's supposed to—if you forced him to follow it—he could have another few years, for all anyone knows. Years as good as he's ever had."

"As good? Picture him stripped of every scrap of dignity. Picture the Joe Hull you know hurting bad, no clue who or where he is. Helpless as a baby, wearing bloody diapers," I said.

"So refuse to fight at all, because it might turn that way? That's cowardly, Harry."

"And that's a pretty harsh indictment, for something you might not fully understand," I said.

"Got another word for sitting on your ass and letting your dad commit slow suicide because you're afraid it might get ugly later on?" she said. "Got some good excuses all lined up, too? 'He went the way he wanted to go' or 'He died in harness, like a man'? Some tough-guy bullshit like that you can say over his grave?"

"I'm doing no such thing. And Dad's not near dead yet."

"He will be sooner than later, if you go your way."

The ache on my mangled side was nearly unbearable. "What makes you so certain you've perfect insight into this?"

"Two dead parents," she said. "That good enough? That credential satisfy you?"

"Lucy, your folks drowned in a boating accident," I said gently, trying to dull the edge. "There was never anything you could have done to prevent it, or help them. It's hardly comparable."

"A genius, you are, Hull. Telling me something I knew ages before you even met me as if it's breaking news," she said. "But maybe it is news to you that the damage was permanent. That I was helpless, that I had no chance to try, that's haunted me all my life. Even now I sometimes wake up shivering with grief and guilt. Sure, it's irrational. Neurotic, too. But I can't stop myself from thinking I should have been out there with them that day! While they were fucking drowning, I was in some boy's room getting well fucked. I've loathed myself ever after.

"But you," she went on, "you bloody well *do* have a chance I didn't. Yeah, we know how it has to end, so don't give me that as a reason for just standing by watching, because it isn't one. We don't know how it has to be until then. You just might be able to make this awful thing a bit easier on your dad."

"Don't you see that's what I'm trying to do? That I'm thinking of what he wants?"

"No, I do not. What I see is a son who either doesn't care or can't be bothered, letting his dad run wild and ignore everything the doctors are recommending."

"The doctors themselves admit they don't know what's in store. The doctors themselves say we'll just have to see what happens."

"But they're still doing everything possible! Which is worth a bloody great deal more than your let-nature-take-its-course attitude," Lucy said. She stared at me in a way that made me feel suddenly childlike. No, childish. In the very worst sense. "You'll pay a heavy price for that. You'll keep paying all your life."

I reached out to take her hand. God, if I could only explain what Dad had silently asked of me, the weight I was already shouldering. She pulled back. And what she said next nearly broke me.

"I went for you because I thought you were a trier, Harry. Reckon I badly misjudged."

SO IT WAS LUCY who forced Dad into line. She started showing up in Ashfield every evening; my presence was tolerated but not required. And she was clever about it. No bashing, no lashing. She handled him as adroitly as Alessandra had handled that Mineralmoney ocker at Il Pelicano. In short order she'd manipulated Dad into taking his medication regularly and laying off the beer, allowing him one—just one glass—with his mates at The Drowned Man after Friday's pressrun. She cornered his best friends and bullied or charmed each as the case required into helping enforce the rule. She went so far as to drop by the pub for random spot-checks, just to see if she could catch him out.

The tremendous feat was getting him to join the psychological counseling program; she convinced Dad the group sessions would be an amusing sort of comedy review, that he could sit back and have a good laugh at the show. But she dropped persuasion and used pure rage finally when she discovered he'd been giving some of his radiation treatments a miss. To my surprise, Dad bent before the force of her anger on that one, and took it all—the whingers and sob-sisters at the psycho lounge, as he called the program, as well as the nausea and weariness from the radiation—without complaint. He couldn't have been exactly pleased and grateful. Yet his face did brighten and his spirits perked up every time Lucy came through our front door.

She was purely wonderful.

Me? God, I wish there was an Erase button, or that drugs or drink or the Dalai Lama weren't useless. I felt there was a spring in my head that was being compressed; I felt short of breath a lot. Many an evening I got wrapped so tight I'd flee to Umberto's and pester him, or get into little battles of wits with Fabrizia, which the kid would usually win. Or I'd have a go at coaxing Camilla, the shyest child I'd ever come across, to smile and play a bit. I met defeat again. One night, for instance, I tried acting out a kid's book called *Wombat Stew* as I read it to her, but when I pretended to be the evil dingo, Camilla started howling fearfully.

I even began to wonder, after a while, whether I'd only imagined what I believed had been Dad's plea. If maybe I'd dreamed up something that didn't exist to help me dodge past something I couldn't face.

Until late one evening, Lucy gone back to Paddo, I went into his room to say goodnight and he sat up, gripped my arm with surprising strength.

"We know, Harry," he said. "And I know what it's costing you, too. Thanks, mate."

There's no way to be sure, but Lucy bought Dad maybe as much as a year. At least that's how long he stayed well enough to hang on to his job. It couldn't have been easy for his mates—he was apparently getting more quarrelsome and more sloppy about his work week by week, his friends reported to Lucy. But the pressroom meant the world to Dad, and they all knew it. So they covered for him when they had to, and made special efforts to keep his short fuse from igniting, special efforts to damp it out when it did. And except for when the radiation made him really crook, they managed. They kept him generally cheerful and genial. Or as near those things as a man in Joe Hull's state could be expected to come.

Then I got another call one day I never wanted to get.

Dad had blacked out in the pressroom again, been ambulanced to the hospital. A second stroke. He was conscious and all systems were going after ten or twelve hours. But this time, he wasn't going back to his presses or the union. This time he was coming home and staying there. Teddy Costas said there was no choice, that Dad would be a danger to himself and others among the heavy machinery. The *Herald* put him on permanent disability.

14

I F THERE'S ANY SORT of accurate, absolute scale of misfortune, it
could have been worse.

Dad had no palsy or paralysis, no nerve damage, no balance difficul-
ties, no impairment of sight or hearing or the passage of words from his
mind to his mouth. No hint at all of raving lunacy. For quite some time
he could be safely left alone, no fear of him hurting himself or running
amok or anything.

But his life—or the rich essense of having lived—was slowly draining
away through the multiplying holes in his memory.

Frank stepped up then like the bloody little Dutch boy and plugged
as many as he could. He did it by some damn artful tale-spinning. He
seemed to have a sixth sense about when Dad was on the verge of falling
into one of the holes, of getting confused and then getting furious about
that. He'd head this off by interrupting whatever Dad was saying. "That's
the way it was, for sure, Joe," he'd say. And then Frank would continue

the story he felt Dad was about to go blank on. Dad would just nod happily as Frank led him back into clear reminiscence.

The first few times Frank pulled off this feat, I thought it was mainly by chance. The next few times I began to think that Frank was almost a miracle worker. And as he continued (he was at the house almost every evening after Dad lost his job), I was astonished how the lives of these two men had run so parallel, and how well they must have kept each other informed about the parts that weren't. Frank seemed to know scads about things he couldn't possibly have witnessed: the workings of the pressroom, the deals and scams and dirty tricks of ALP politics and union conflicts with the proprietors that Dad had been involved in, things even I'd never heard of.

And he countered the murderous boredom that had threatened to engulf Dad even during that short recuperation after his first major stroke—by taking him fishing several times a week and on little excursions other days, just to get him out of that hopeless house.

Frank stepped in. More and more it seemed all I was doing was shuffling through the daily maintenance of a household. Made breakfast, cleaned up after, put in my eight hours at the *Herald*, cooked dinner, washed those dishes, did some dusting and vacuuming as required, saw to it there were always clean linens and towels and clothes, wrote and mailed off checks for all the monthly bills, kept the fridge stocked with food and beer, changed a burned-out lightbulb now and again.

Emotions? Most of them must have sidled off to never-never when I wasn't paying attention. If anyone asked how I felt, I'd have had no answer beyond "Fine. And you?"

Dad may have been dying, his mind may have been holed like a sieve, but he saw my state clear enough.

"Fucking useless bludger! What's a bloke got to do to get clean sheets to sleep on around here!" he snapped one morning after mopping up a last yellow puddle of egg yolk on his plate with a piece of fried bread. I'd put on a set fresh from the laundry just the day before.

"Take a shower more than once a week," I muttered, unthinking.

"That's the spirit!" Dad said, laughing. "Well, almost. Decent come-back, but your delivery was a bit lame."

"What's with you?"

"Been getting away with bloody murder too long, I reckon," he said. "Frank's okay, but everybody else is acting like I'm some fucking invalid who's got to be handled with kid gloves. And I'm getting fed up with you moping about with a great dark cloud hovering over your head, too."

"You devious old bastard," I said. "Bagged me!"

"Fair go, Harry," he grinned. "And fair game. Just because I'm a bit forgetful and stuff don't mean you aren't entitled to a little give and take with your own dad."

"Am I?"

"We know," he said, that same clear sharpness in his eyes. "Remember, Harry? We both know."

I nodded, just as I had before.

"Now bugger off and go have some fun with Lucy, ya little drongo," Dad said. "And mind I get clean sheets, as well."

PULLED ME RIGHT BACK from never-never, Dad did. And pretty promptly I found it wasn't difficult to know when Dad was truly crook, when he really was a bit off his head and not up to much. And when he was only playing a role he believed people had come to expect of him. A role he even enjoyed, because bagging Lucy and Frank and Bert and everyone else who came around was the only way he had of proving to himself that he hadn't entirely lost his wits. It was part of our secret, though he told me he expected Frank'd catch on one of these days.

So when Dad went mean and fractious just for the hell of it, I'd give back as good as I'd got. It was like old times. We only chafed each other in private at first, but it seemed to cheer him so much I tried it on in public. I reckoned everyone would get what we were about, Dad and I.

They did not. Not even Frank.

Lucy saw me much too rough when I should have been sympathetic and soothing to a man who couldn't help his unreasonable outbursts. She saw as real the mock irritation I turned back on Dad when he complained the lamb I'd made for supper tasted more like his old army boots than food. She heard me snap that he was a bloody moron the time he called me the most useless bastard he'd ever known for not getting the TV repaired—the thing was still out in the back garden, where he'd tossed it. She missed the genuineness of the sly grins exchanged, wrote off Dad's laughter as another sign of encroaching dementia. And she dragged me onto the verandah more than once and flogged me for cruelty.

"Jesus Christ, Harry. Never reckoned you for a sadist," she laid into me one evening after some little back-and-forth with Dad.

"Can you truly not know what's going on?" I said. "You believe any of that was for real?"

"What I'm beginning to believe is your sense of reality is more erratic than that poor old man's. I'm beginning to believe you're the most cold-blooded, heartless bastard on earth."

"It's just a damn game, Lucy, he and I teasing each other."

"Game? Up your bum if that's any game. Mean, ugly and angry, that's what it is."

She didn't speak a single word to me for four days after that.

And if Frank was about when Dad insulted me and I said, "You bloody drongo" or "That's really retarded" in return, he'd simply give me a cool stare, the deep contempt in it more obvious with each occurrence, and either smooth over what he believed was Dad's delusionary outburst or pick up whatever Dad had apparently been trying and utterly failing to recall.

"Aw, you're a real no-hoper," I said to Dad once, giving him a wink, when he faltered in some tale.

"Right, Joe," Frank jumped in. "It was the sixty-six New South Wales election when you strolled up easy as you please to Pete McGlinchy's door and rang the bell. At midnight! And the exalted Labor candidate for prime minister almost shit in his pyjamas when you handed him those two big shopping bags full of cash and said, 'Found these by your front gate, Pete, reckoned you must have forgotten to bring 'em inside.' And you walked away without another word. There must have been fifteen thousand dollars in those bags."

"Exactly seventeen thousand six hundred dollars in smallish bills," Dad grinned, hole neatly plugged, and the rest of the tale now accessible to him. "Did shock the shit out of him. He knew damn well the trade unions were shoveling all sorts of illegal money his way. But fuck me if he ever expected to get his very own hands dirty with it. I think he dropped a small turd that night. The aroma! Unmistakable."

Frank laughed and laughed. I left the room.

Presently the worst happened: my judgment about Dad's state of mind proved fallible. One night, sitting by his bed, I tried to entertain him with some stories of Fuck Toy.

"What in bloody hell would you know about war?" he said harshly.

"Had my little taste in Nam, didn't I?" I replied.

"Hah!" he laughed. "Cut the bullshit. You never were a soldier; you were one of those damned hippie demonstrators."

"Was I, then?" Grinning, I pulled off my shirt, and was horrified at the look of total incomprehension that swept over Dad's face.

"Sweet Jesus, Harry, what a mess. How on earth did you get cut up so bad?" he said.

Full stop. I'd no idea what to do, no clue how to handle Dad after that. So I retreated again. Which, in the days that followed, seemed to convince Frank and Lucy that I was becoming as unpredictable as Dad, maybe as demented. Yet it wasn't more than a week or two later that Dad, lucid as could be, explained about the lights burning out on the Christmas tree. I wish he'd told it to all of us, not just in private to me.

IT WAS THE TAIL END of the autumn of '81 in Sydney but a good time to go up north to a warm place like Magnetic Island. Frank said I needed a break, that he'd look after things. What he really meant, I'm sure, was that I was a bloody pain and he'd do better without me around mucking everything up.

"Not sure I'm much in the mood," Lucy said when I asked her to go with me to a nice little resort, individual beachfront bungalows for the guests and a good restaurant overlooking a lagoon sheltered from the surging blue deep by a great curve of reef.

"C'mon, Luce," I pleaded. "I know it's been rocky. We need something like this. And I need you."

"Reckon you think you do. But I'm pretty bloody weary, Harry. I'm worn out."

"With reason. You've been trying so hard. That's why I thought of this place. Nothing to do but sun-bake, snorkel a bit if you like. It'll be good."

"Will it?" Lucy's small smile seemed tentative, and somehow as if it were intended only for her, not me.

Tranquility and quiet privacy, I thought, soothing us, healing us. I pressed her gently but persistently. And she finally did cave, agreed to fly up to Magnetic for two weeks.

The first night, she undressed with her back toward me, slipped quickly under a gauzy canopy of mosquito netting that flowed and wafted with the currents from the ceiling fan, curled on her side under the crisp linen sheet. I eased into bed beside her, kissed the back of her neck. "I'm bushed," she murmured, not stirring. So I kissed her neck softly once more, then rolled onto my back, with my hands behind my head on the pillow. Our bodies never touched.

I awoke to find her standing at the bungalow door, cossie, sarong and sunglasses already on, looking out at the sea. She didn't turn when I said, "G'day, mate."

"Think I'll have a bit of brekkie on the terrace by the pool," she said. "Come join me when you're ready."

I was there in less than five minutes. I found her sarong and glasses on the table. But she was gone. I looked all round, finally spotted a flash of red and the bright orange tip of a snorkel tube way out on the reef. I ordered a fruit salad and a pot of coffee, and watched her while I ate, then drank coffee and smoked. She was gliding along the smooth clear water above the reef, flippers scarcely making a splash. Every once in a while she'd dive, face and arms curving down out of sight and long legs high in the air for a moment before she disappeared entirely. She'd surface a minute or two later, maybe ten yards or so farther along. I could see spray sparkle in the early sun as she cleared her snorkel and glided on. When she got near the far end of the reef, she turned, and made the whole transit once more.

She was still in the water while I had grilled prawns and salad for lunch around noon. Then I went back to our bungalow, lay down in the rope hammock stretched between two palms outside, and napped. Late in the afternoon, I heard the screened door of our bungalow squeak open and quietly close, heard faintly the plash of the shower. I kept staring out at the changing hues of the lagoon as the sun lowered: celadon, turquoise, cerulean. The deep ocean beyond the reef remained a dark royal blue. Next thing I knew the hammock arced up wildly and swung back, almost tumbling me out.

"Lazy bludger," Lucy said, standing there in a batik shift, freshly washed hair pulled back into a ponytail, sunglasses hiding her eyes. "Drinks? Dinner?"

We had fresh mango daiquiris near the pool, watching the day swiftly dim down to night; there's no long, lingering twilight in the tropics. Waitresses scurried around lighting candles on every table, even though only two or three besides ours had anyone at them. We ordered up grilled grouper and a Hunter chardonnay.

"You were right, Harry," Lucy said as we ate. She still wore those sunglasses. "Lovely reef. Saw all sorts of interesting fish, and some beautiful coral. The grouper's great. Wine's not bad either. All said, very pleasant place."

"It'd be even more pleasant with some company."

"Don't, Harry. Just let things be," Lucy said. "Been strife enough, hasn't there?"

"Yeah, but it's not as if . . ."

"I'll ask again: please don't start in."

I didn't. But that night was a repeat of the first. Except that it was near dawn before I drifted into a tossed and troubled slumber. And next day I didn't see Lucy at all until drinks and dinner. She'd risen early and spent the day walking the island. She was quite chatty over the meal about what she'd seen on her wanderings, and when we went back to our bungalow and I kissed her, she kissed back. We made love, but it felt to me as if she were someone I'd never been with before and wasn't entirely sure I should or even wanted very much to be with. And it felt like my bedmate had the same impression. Afterward, I reached over once to touch her face, and felt tears on my fingertips. Lucy said nothing, just rolled over onto her side, back to me.

I slipped out at first light without a word to Lucy and snorkeled the reef until I was so exhausted it was a struggle to make it back to the beach. It was me, that night, who pretended exhaustion and lay with my back to her, never touching.

Probably we'd have cut the trip short and gone home if I hadn't downed near a full bottle of Bundaberg the next night as we wandered along the beach far from the lights and sounds of the resort after yet another day spent mainly avoiding each other. The beach curved away before us, a pale avenue between black jungle and black water. Junglee noise on one side, the swish of sea over sand on the other, and few words spoken. Suddenly I couldn't bear it any longer. Holding the bottle by its neck, I smashed it against a limestone outcrop. Sharp brown shards of glass sliced into my hand, but I scarcely felt the cuts and gave no attention to the streaming blood.

"Ah, Luce, fucking God's scabbing off me." The voice pitched high and quavery, not my own. "My bloody father! Love 'im, just like you said, ah shit, just like you said, and I mocked you for it. Now I'm being robbed of him. God can go bugger himself if that's the way He plays things."

"Don't know if it's God, Harry. I think we were left to get on with it all by ourselves a long time ago," Lucy said, taking my gashed hand in hers, instantly feeling the thick flow. "You're bleeding like hell!" she cried.

I tore away from her, stumbled a few yards into the sea, and stuck my wounded hand under water streaked palely here and there by phosphorescence. "Hey sharks! Sharks! Blood in the water, over here! You evil fucks never sleep, so come have a snack."

Lucy splashed up behind me, seized me round the waist, pulled me back to the fine white sand. I fell on my ass, then on my back. And I began to weep and sob in a way I never had before. Not even when Mum died. Not even when the RPG got me.

"Too soon. Too bloody soon!" I screamed up at the sky. "Show me your fucking face, you bastard. Show me!"

Lucy knelt behind me, cradling my head in her hands. "Harry, Harry," she was crooning. "Oh, Harry, I'm so sorry. So sorry."

I was drunk with more than rum. I swore up toward the face I knew I'd never see. "You think I'll beg? You think I'll plead? Get fucked!" I ranted and cursed and railed at the indifferent stars. I sent the entire cosmos to buggery.

"Harry, Harry," I heard Lucy whisper, and felt her smooth, cool hand stroking my forehead. My entire body spasmed as I rolled and puked onto the sand. Lucy never let go of my head. "Your hand's bad, Harry. We've got to get it looked at. You could bleed to death out here."

"Who gives a flying fuck?" I muttered, spitting out the remnants of vomit.

I think—no way I'll ever be certain—I heard Lucy say, "I do, dammit. I give the world!" as she tugged me upright, levered me onto my feet, and steered me back to the hotel. The night manager paled when we appeared. I must have wiped the sweat and puke off my face with my sliced hand and then run the hand through my hair. Once they'd got me cross island in a bouncing four-wheeler to the dispensary I shocked myself when I saw in a mirror the gory mess of a man Lucy was supporting.

"How many times was he stabbed? And where?" a young nurse asked.

"It's only a cut on his hand," I heard Lucy say.

The nurse wiped it down with gauze pads and water until she could see it properly, then manipulated my hand, told me to try to flex it. I could. "No nerves or tendons severed, I reckon. No major veins, either," she said. The gashes started at the tips of three fingers and ran down them to join into a single cut bisecting my palm almost to the wrist. But it was a shallow wound. She filled a stainless-steel bowl with alcohol and plunged my hand into it. I almost passed out, it hurt that much. I also sobered up a great deal. Then the nurse shot me up with a tetanus booster, put another hypo of local anesthethic into my hand, and started sewing as calmly as if she were mending a torn shirt.

About fifty neat stitches and three meters of gauze bandage later— plus a good scrubbing of my face and hair—we were in the four-wheeler, then back in our bungalow.

I was conscious that Lucy's hands had been on me in one place or another for hours, never once withdrawing. Now she undressed me and helped me into bed. I lay there flat on my back, the cut hand like a big white club resting on the pillow beside my head. I saw Lucy strip off and slip through the mossie netting. "Let's do it, cobber," she said, her voice clear as rain, her smile brighter than I'd seen in months. Then she fiddled around with certain things to make that possible, straddled me, and rode me off to a dreamless sleep.

No more snorkeling for me, that trip. But no more wariness, no more avoidance, no more anxious silences between us either. Whenever my grief leaked out—and it did quite often, tears forming at unexpected, embarrassing moments—Lucy sponged it away with her words and her touch. But there wasn't all that much of it left hidden inside; most had been purged that one raving night when I'd stained the white beach red. And so mainly, when she'd emerge from the sea with her perfect body glistening and lie beside the sand chair where I sat in my long-sleeved, zinc-oxided, straw-hatted splendor, she was my old Lucy. Mocking and teasing me affectionately, making sweetly indecent proposals for the night to come. And, always, blessing me with even her most casual touch.

"I think you saved us, Harry," she smiled as the plane lifted off and started climbing, the day we left for Sydney. "By showing me you're human after all."

BACK HOME, there was no question anymore of give and take with Dad, even in private. Couldn't be risked; I had to regard him as Frank and Lucy had all along. But I found I could face the tantrums over my cooking, the rages that broke sudden as a thunderstorm, the wildly pitching moods and the saddening lapses into near incoherence with more forebearance than I'd ever hoped for. I felt so near to being able to reach out to Dad, embrace his suffering, maybe even ease him as Lucy'd eased me.

But small things, simple things just cracked my heart wide open. And the strength Lucy'd transfused into my soul began flowing away.

Started with a conversation I wish I'd never overheard: Dad and Frank out on the verandah, Dad rambling about the night I was born, how he'd sat in the waiting room for six or seven hours, got restless, and gone out to the nearest pub.

"I only meant to have a quick one, but somehow there was another and another. Nerves, I reckon. By the time I got back, the little bastard'd popped out. I was looking in the baby room trying to see him, but fuck me if they all didn't look alike. I think . . . wait a moment . . . I think . . ."

Poor Dad, trying so hard to grasp a memory that was likely out of reach forever now.

" 'Got to be the ugliest creature here. Now which one's the most wombat-featured?' you said," Frank jumped in. "But when the nurse inside finally pointed out Harry, you said 'Christ, he's a beaut!' And you went down on your knees and started bawling."

"Fucking did not," Dad snorted.

"Hell, you were crying louder than any of the babies, Joe," Frank said. "Ought to know. After all, I shouted you those beers, and went back to the hospital with you."

I was in the front room reading. And every word stung like a hypodermic.

"Disgraceful!" Frank went on. "One of the nurses had to tell you to get a grip on yourself. And then she smelled the beer on you and threatened to have you kicked out."

"Ah, Frank. I must have been blotto."

"Hardly, mate. You'd only drunk enough to loosen you up a bit. You said it was the best day you'd ever had or ever would have, seeing little Harry in the world. We went out and got blotto *after* you finally finished crying and got up off your bloody knees."

I tried to dismiss it. Tried to believe Frank was skillfully fictionalizing Dad's life, but I couldn't manage. Knew Frank too well. Knew the bloody tale must have been true. I went up to bed. And wept the night through.

Such slight, simple things, those heart-crackers: the squeak and slap of Dad's cheap rubber thongs on the kitchen's lino floor, the sights of half-chewed bits of food dribbling out of the hole in his cheek, the long moments when his watery blue eyes seemed sightless or else focused on something only he could see, the skewed collar and front of a shirt buttoned wrong, an unzipped fly, the way he'd sometimes wander from room to room for hours or else simply sit with his hands on his knees in the big living room chair as if he expected someone to knock on our front door any moment.

It was nearly time, but Dad and I would not go down hand in hand after all, I began to feel. I couldn't hold up my side. Maybe, I think now, I went into a sort of deep mourning in advance. But all Frank and Lucy saw was Harry once again shuffling through the days and nights, taking care of necessary things but detached and struck almost dumb around Dad. Even a simple "What's for tucker?" from Dad gave me pause. I'd stare at him longer than it finally took to say, "Sausages and mashed potatos" in answer. If he was off his head and ranting, I'd flee to another part of the house so I wouldn't have to hear it, or deal with it.

Frank must have felt badly let down. I think now the crux of the matter was that Lucy was basically right: I was a fucking coward, and no trier at all.

Frank was strong and wise enough to handle it; poor Lucy, rightly, felt utterly betrayed.

15

AUTUMN TO AUTUMN—ALMOST. And Dad sliding, sliding down so deep into the Slough. Except when he slept, he couldn't be left alone for more than a few minutes. Holiday and sick time gone, I went on unpaid leave. Alice, unasked, came over each day, made lunch, watched over Dad for an hour or so. Bert arrived each evening. And Lucy, always.

But even with reinforcements, Frank and I stood to, day over night over day. Once a week, he'd take twenty-four hours off duty. Once a week I'd do the same.

Except for one hell week, around Christmas: three days straight of frantic, violent abuse, Dad screaming I was a fucking Jap primed to slice him bit by bit with my bayonet. Then two in which he lay semi-comotose, pissing and shitting himself. We bathed him as best we could, kept changing the sheets. And then a ghastly forty-eight hours on the Kokoda Track, Dad thigh-deep in mud and blood and blasted, stinking body parts. It took both Frank and me to restrain his thrashing and flailing as he tried to fight his way out of that horrific hallucination. The strength left in his wasted body amazed us.

Coming down the hall toward his room early on the eighth morning, I heard Dad's voice—weak, woozy, but his real voice. And it was clear after a few words he knew where he was again, knew it was Frank he was speaking to. I collapsed against the wall, leaning there with my eyes closed.

"Show me your hands," Frank said. He'd eased out of Dad's room, eased the door closed behind him.

I did, palms down. Twitches and tremors, though I was willing them steady with all my might.

"Bit of battle fatigue," Frank said softly. "Bound to happen. Get on out of here, Harry. Go off someplace nice and just rest. I can hold the line for a day."

There'd been a typhoon away in the east, around Samoa, but in Sydney it kept clear as a bell, the deepest blue sky unblemished by a single cloud. I rounded up Lucy, Bert, Alice and the kids and drove up to Whale Beach for a picnic. It was a lot farther than Bondi or Manly, but likely to be less mobbed. I felt a dread of being alone, but I was in no condition to be among crowds, smiling masses of perfectly normal people who appeared to be without a care in the world, even though I knew the odds were good a surprising number of those smiles would be masking some grief or burden. Fabrizia still had her childish habit of thrusting her stick-thin arm out the window to point at everything she saw, no matter how ordinary: "A mailbox! A postie! A church! A wombat, but he's all squashed!" Camilla huddled next to her, silent and indifferent.

I preferred Whale to Palm Beach, the next cove up, where the overly affluent managed somehow to spread an effluvia of snotty exclusionism, even though the sands were public domain. Thanks to Lucy's position at *The Bulletin* and mine at the *Herald*, we'd been party guests in their grand houses and on their boats often enough not to want to be near them if it wasn't necessary.

We spread out some blankets and opened beers. We had a beautiful day for it, but the surf was tremendous. Swells that had started building in Samoan winds came rolling in their fullest majesty into the cove. The red and yellow flags were crossed, which meant no swimming because of the surf and a rip. The waves were crashing into the rocky headlands at either end of the beach. Enormous plumes sprayed up a hundred feet or more. They looked like H.E. bursts from a 155mm howitzer, they were that mighty. A couple of dozen other picnic parties had scattered at more than decent intervals on the beach and under the raggedy Norfolk pines that backed it. Everyone was watching the surf as amazedly and excitedly as people watch fireworks. I heard the same sorts of oohs and aahs follow the deep boom as each big comber broke. And that was very unusual, for Sydney-siders by the time they're grown have seen just about every spectacular show the sea can put on.

We ate and drank and watched the display. We oohed and aahed.

"This is the life," Bert said, patting his stomach. "Food, as much you want. A bit of wine, that's even better. Now for a cigarette. And the force of nature shows itself. What more could you ask for?"

"You're easily pleased," Lucy said.

"No, all these things, they don't come so easy everywhere," Bert said, lighting up. "You can have big dreams for your life, okay. But even so the best is enough to eat, something to drink, and some hope for your children, that they will always have these things. Some places, you don't even have the hope."

"No worries here," Lucy said. "Yours are well taken care of."

"The Lucky Country, Australia, no?" Bert smiled.

"The author of that was being ironic," Lucy said.

"Maybe so, I don't know the book, only the phrase," Bert said. "But I hear it said so much, without this irony, by so many people, that it becomes true despite the writer's intention. Not perfect, sure. Problems, certainly. But still a place for a safe, decent life."

"So long as your *Signor Destino* doesn't snipe you," I said. "And if I got it right, that bastard has the range on everybody, wherever they may be."

Bert laughed. "Harry, I warn you again. Not so loud about the *Signor*."

"Who's he?" Lucy asked.

"The bloke in charge, according to Bert," I said. "Makes all the big decisions. Seems to micro-manage as well."

"Lucy, better you get Harry to shut up about this, I think," Bert said.

"Would if I could. But you know Harry . . ."

If there was an edge to her voice, I didn't catch it. And I'd been expecting one. There'd been times over the last—Christ, had it been six months or nine since Magnetic Island?—that tensions between us had built up so it seemed certain they'd break and crash as violently as the seas before us. Days when I thought I'd lose my mind hearing Dad drone over and over, "Where's Lucy? Where's my pretty Luce?" And me then being snippish and sullen toward her when she'd appear in the evenings after work.

She'd gone snippish and sullen right back at me.

It was the stress of it all, a friction natural to the situation. Even Frank, so laconic and easy, had gone testy once in a while lately. We'd been brushing and bumping each other, day after day and through many nights. We'd been in quarters much too close for much too long. Sometimes we were bound, I reckoned, to rub each other the wrong way.

Yet on this day Lucy had seemed so relaxed, so sweet with me from the moment we'd picked her up in Paddo. That breached my defenses properly. She'd just slipped easily through. I started looking at her in the old way, and she started looking back.

Even so, I was surprised late in the afternoon when she leaned across the remains of our picnic and whispered, "Want you to come play with me."

She had me on my feet and moving down the beach almost before I could call "Just having a bit of a stroll" to Bert and Alice. Bert paid no mind. He was busy with Fabrizia trying to determine the exact degree of dampness required in the sand to build crenellated towers at the corners of the castle they'd made, and then trying to keep Camilla from smashing the towers flat with her beach ball. The poor little thing had first tried to get her mum into a ball game, only to be impatiently shoo'd off toward the castle. Alessandra, languorous, was ignoring pretty much everything but the ceaseless waves.

Lucy and I went up into the rocks at the south end of the beach, past the concrete pool that was fed by the sea, and clambered around until we were sure nobody could see us unless they happened to have wings. And we made wonderful love, though poor Lucy got a bit of an abraded bum.

"Know something I reckon you don't, Harry," she said after.

"Wouldn't argue that," I said.

"It's our seventh anniversary, cobber. And that was fuck number one thousand one hundred!"

"Jesus! You've been counting?" I laughed.

"Not really," she grinned. "The figure's not exact. But real close. Huge variations over the years, but say it averages out to three times a week for three hundred sixty-four weeks, and eleven hundred's about right."

"Then I'll tell you something you can't know." I cradled her face with my palms, kissed her, then moved my lips up against her ear. "My one thousand, one hundreth encounter with lovely Lucy Whitmoor was as sweet and special as my first. And just about as big a surprise."

"Oh Christ, Harry." She was smiling, but a tear or two welled from her eyes. I thought it was the sentiment.

So I was feeling pleased when we strolled back, and then a bit embarrassed, for I saw right away that Alice knew what we'd been up to. She just sensed it, I suppose, and she couldn't be bothered to hide that or politely ignore it, the way most would. Instead she smiled a knowing smile at Lucy. Who did not smile back.

WE ONLY QUIT when the sun slipped behind the hills. Then south through Avalon and Newport and Mona Vale and Manly and eventually through Mosman and over the Coathanger. The sun was all the way down, the sky was that deep Prussian blue it gets at dusk, and a few high-flying clouds to the west were pink as a galah's wing feathers when we got home.

Frank was on the verandah, just a dim figure I could scarely make out, except for the regular arcs described by the glowing tip of his cigarette as it moved from his mouth to the arm of his chair and back again. "Your Dad's asleep," he said softly. "Why don't you and Lucy go have some supper someplace?"

"You sure, Frank?" I asked.

"Yeah. I like sitting by myself in the evening. Real peaceful. You two go on."

We drove down to the Blue Water Grill, a nice place perched up on the north heights of Bondi. The day'd been restful, but I suppose both of us were too careworn and weary for just one good day to restore. Lucy, after a glass of wine, geared way, way down, to about ten words a minute. And I was soon near to mute. I may have nodded or made some comment at appropriate intervals, for she never yanked my leash—which she'd always been quick to do when she saw I was drifting off someplace in my mind.

Or maybe this time she couldn't be bothered.

I'd ordered New Zealand rock lobster, a special the Grill had that night and generally a rare treat, but it wasn't up to standard. I began thinking about Camilla, whose mother wouldn't even toss a ball with her on a fine day at the beach. About the way, on other occasions lately, Camilla had sidled away from Alessandra until she was lightly leaning on my leg, looked up once quickly to see if I smiled down at her, then sort of settled in. Always silent, but at least it was something. Though why it was me she chose remained a mystery. And then somehow I was lost in my own childhood. That turned scary when I realized my vision of Mum was so much like seeing someone you think you might know through a thick, chill winter fog at some distance. Should you call out and risk making a mistake, or wait until you got closer and could be sure who that figure was? Why was she so shrouded, so damn unclear that I couldn't even call to mind the timbre of her voice, let alone anything she'd ever said to me?

Lucy wanted a walk after we'd finished eating, so I drove up to South Head. It was one of those breezeless nights when you'd swear you could touch the still air with your fingertips and find it silky as a cat's fur. To our left, as we strolled aimless through the cropped grass, the mild glow of the long twist of the Eastern Suburbs built into the glare of the center city, a compact cluster of skyscrapers that seemed unreasonably obtrusive, a gross affront to the gracefully scalloped coastline of the Harbour. To our right there was only blackness. The moon, if there was going to be one that night, hadn't yet cleared the horizon, and no ships were about. But the ocean insisted on not being regarded as a void; it slapped and crashed into the cliff.

"It's getting difficult again," Lucy said.

"Was there a bit when it wasn't? I must have missed it," I said.

"I'm not talking about your Dad's state."

"What, then?" I was wishing she'd quit, let the soft slow evening stay that way.

"Us. Our state. Me feeling close to you."

"Seemed, this afternoon, about as intimate as it could be."

"For as long as it lasted, yeah. It was lovely," Lucy sighed. "But day by day, Harry . . ."

"I've been the biggest bastard going." Christ, nobody'd let me forget that. Ever, it seemed. "And I'm sorry for it."

"The bastard part I can handle. Since I finally saw the why of it, up on Magnetic Island. What's hard, since then, is most times I can't find the rest of you. About three-quarters of you's gone missing."

I didn't reply. She was probably right. I'd disconnected. Trouble was, it wasn't a deliberate tactic I could change at will. I did not know anymore where the on-off switch was located. Probably couldn't have flicked it if I had.

"We should be facing this together, Harry," she said after a moment. "Bearing it as a couple, helping each other do what needs to be done."

"We are."

"No, Harry. I'm there with you every evening, but I'm operating alone, or with Frank. You just vanish, except when we tussle. You hide yourself from all of us somehow."

"I'm not meaning to," I said, taking her hand, which stayed cool and limp in mine. A sort of lie, of course. Now came a wave of hopelessness; I was damned if I did, damned if I didn't. My heart went racing. I was short of breath though we were walking easily on level turf. "What should I do?"

"Open up. Get drunk and rant like you did on the beach, if that's the only way you can manage."

"I could rave every day, but seems to me that's the last thing any of us needs more of."

"Then remember who I am, what we've had together. Show a bit of trust."

"Don't quite follow. You must know I trust you absolutely."

"Ah, Harry, you bloody wanker," she said with more sorrow than rancor. "You just won't hear, will you? Reckon even after seven years and eleven hundred times you still haven't bothered to learn me."

16

"FUCK IT ALL," Dad bellowed once during his last days. "Fuck Australia, fuck my mates, and fuck you, Harry. Fuck it all to hell."

"If you say so, Dad," I called out. Might just as well've shouted insults in Maori or Tuareg. Dad was veteran of too many roisterous labor rallies to let any sort of heckling disrupt a really good harangue.

"No point at all," he roared. "A complete bloody waste of time. Any bloody idiots who reckon there's some point or purpose to any of it, well they can buy their own fucking beer."

"Right, Dad," I said. It was well past midnight. Frank and I were sitting on opposite sides of his bed waiting for him to drift off, but Dad was having none of that just yet.

"As soon as I'm gone, all the gloating bastards who're glad it wasn't them will be telling you it was merciful it happened quick as it did. That I didn't suffer near as long as I might've. And that now I've gone to a better place. What a load of shit!"

Since Dad'd had the unlovely tendency—freely admitted—to laugh at those in trouble, I think some nominal part of him felt everyone was laughing at him. I think he'd been harboring a vain hope he'd have the last one. And he knew for certain now that he would not.

"There's no fucking mercy! I've been suffering my ass off for fucking ages, and there's no damn place to go besides a fucking narrow hole in the damp dark earth. You tell the scurvy bastards I said that, Harry," he concluded with a flourish, "and you tell them I'll see each and every one of 'em sent to buggery!"

"Do not go gentle into that good night," said Frank. "Rage, rage against the dying of the light."

"Oh right, Frank. A bloody poet now, are ya?" Dad said.

"Not me," Frank said. "A little drunken Welsh fellow, name of Thomas. He turns the stuff out by the barrelful. Or did, until he drank himself to death."

"Yeah, and it might be decent to keep it in the barrel. Good night, my ass," Dad said. "I'm a dead man."

I just looked at Dad taking it. Taking the clouting, taking the pain, taking the fear night and day. I doubt I ever admired anyone as much as I did this pathetic crumbling creature at that moment.

Damned if I could find any way at all to show it, though; to let him know it.

Dad was perfectly sound, knew precisely what he was about when he railed like that, lying there in his old iron-pipe bed, never moved in my memory from against the wall. There were cretonne curtains at the windows that had been left in place, unwashed, for what, sixteen or seventeen years now since Mum died? They were dingy. He was under a chenille bedspread that once had been white but now was a blotchy, faded yellow—same color as his face, his liver going out on him along with everything else. Except his tongue, as he was inclined to demonstrate from time to time.

For a while a nurse had been coming by each evening to give him a hypo against the racking torment in his shoulder, so he'd at least get a night's sleep. But now Teddy Costas had switched to brown glass bottles, unlabled but holding a quart of a liquid mixture of morphine and cocaine; the morphine masked agony, while the cocaine kept the morphine from making him stuporous or insensible. I had to store the bottles under lock and key, that was our contract. But Teddy told me to be generous whenever Dad asked for a swig. Frank and Lucy and I took a taste ourselves once after Dad had slipped deep into sleep. It sent us bouncing off the walls, we felt that good. Lucy cranked up a new band called Oingo Boingo and danced herself silly.

But we all felt dreadful next morning. Never had a worse hangover in his life, Frank said.

With Dad, who had developed quite a tolerance, it had a less dramatic but quite wonderful effect. The mixture calmed him, yet could sharpen his wits and ability to focus. It muted his dementia, damped down the hallucinations that had harrowed him. A heavy dose, and he seemed no more than a peaceful drunk well on the way to passing out.

"Ah, that's bonzer," he'd grin, only moments after a slug big enough to make his Adam's apple bob as it went down. "Wish I'd discovered this before. You can keep your 'best and strongest beer in the world.'"

He took to cheerful mischief, having a playful go, for instance, at grabbing Lucy's bum whenever she passed near enough, though she always managed to dodge his paw very neatly.

"Give it a rest," she'd say. "Next thing you know you'll be drooling and calling me 'girlie,' Joe."

"Aw, Lucy, I'm just an old man, and you remind me of my poor departed wife," the shameless bastard said one night, holding the saddest expression for at least fifteen seconds before he, Frank and I burst out laughing in near perfect sync.

"Like hell," Lucy grinned. "I've got four inches and fifteen pounds on her. Besides, she was a decent woman who wouldn't have put up with your groping for half a minute."

"She loved it, Luce. She went all sweet when I grabbed her," Dad said. I was thinking the cocaine had talked the morphine into slacking off in its duty.

"A regular Casanova, were you? Women swooning at your touch?" Lucy said.

"If I'm honest, yes," Dad said. "I should never have married. It broke so many hearts."

"I'm sure, a handsome man like you," Lucy said. "I bet your wife had to beat the other women off with a stick."

"She tried, Luce, she surely tried. You won't have to bother, though, if you stay with Harry. No females'll be trying to snatch him. It's a wonder to me that a lovely lady like yourself bothers with him," Dad said.

Then he went serious. "A lovely woman she was. But she needn't have ever worried. I was a faithful husband. I was faithful and I loved her with all my heart. Even at my worst, I never once raised voice or hand to her."

"Well hooray for you," Lucy said.

"I was a good husband, Luce. Given my limitations and faults, which I admit were many. Given how much I devoted to the union and politics. Maybe not much of a father after she passed on, but then Harry wasn't much of a son after that either. Were you, Harry?"

"Nah, Dad, I wasn't. A bloody failure as a son," I said.

And then all at once his eyelids were slowly fluttering. He resisted this like a real tired kid who did not want to fall asleep just yet.

"Hear that, Luce? I know what I'm talking about," Dad said.

"Of course you do, Joe," she said.

"Well . . . fuck me stupid," he murmured, drifting off.

Lucy and I went out to the verandah once we felt sure Dad was sound asleep. No stars to look at, though; a high haze reflecting the glow of the city lights blanked them out. Most of the houses on the street were already dark, their occupants sleeping like Dad, but almost certainly having a very different sort of experience in their night minds.

"It's clear who you take after, Harry," Lucy said.

"You've found out then?" I said.

"Yeah, it sure as hell isn't him, he's much too sweet," she said, gesturing toward the upstairs room where Dad lay. "Must have been a nasty postman."

"Truly? I've always wondered at my paternity, and now you've set me straight."

"Have I?"

"Yeah. For years I looked at Dad, then looked at myself in the mirror, and figured no way were we related. I believed it had to've been an immaculate conception and a virgin birth. Happens every now and again, you know. But now I see there's another possibility after all. The postie."

"And now I'm not so sure I'm right. The first might explain that persecution complex of yours."

"Everybody's always accusing me of that. Merciless, they are."

"Poor Harry. Come over here and let me ruffle your hair," Lucy said. And when I slid close enough for that, she said, "Getting a bit thin on top, aren't we, darls?"

Yeah, we were fighting the dying of the light, but not with rage for that one night at least. I was in her arms, heartsore and teary.

And tearful next day, when Dad woke up but not to the same world as any of us. He kept asking me who I was, and what the fuck did I think I was doing, confining him to barracks. He cursed me hard and heavy, demanding my name and unit, swore he'd get his own back on me one day when I least expected it. He cackled maniacally, promised he'd keep a bullet in reserve for me next time we went into combat.

He raged on and on, that flaming delirium racing like a bush fire. When at last it burned itself out, he seemed to wander aimlessly through a desolation of smokey wastelands for the longest time. He spoke to the unknown dead he saw there, inquiring about their condition.

Eventually he drifted in horrible regression to another hazy place I couldn't enter. He began murmuring to his mother, in her grave more than thirty years now, as if she were sitting right beside the bed looking after little Joe, who was down with the measles and feverish. "It's almost worth feeling so crook, not having to go to school," he whispered. "Any Aeroplane Jelly for me, ma? I'd love some Aeroplane Jelly."

I cracked.

I grabbed Dad by the shoulders and shook him, didn't stop even when I saw a rictus of pain on his face. Until a pair of strong arms yanked me off my feet. I went airborne, crashed hard against the wall.

"Stupid little bastard," Frank snarled over his shoulder at me while he eased Dad down on his pillows. "God, you're retarded. Losing it completely. As if he was doing all this to spite you. You can get stuffed."

"Watch it, Frank," I snapped. I was trembling, still half-mad and out of control.

"Oh do get fucked," Frank said, straightening up and turning toward me. He took a step forward. "Do bugger yourself. Or being thirty or so, give growing up a go. If you've got it in you. Which I doubt."

I did feel abashed as a schoolboy when I approached Frank some hours later. About as stupid and callow as well, hoping he'd understand what had driven me over the edge, how I'd never meant to hurt Dad, only pull him out of a dark place. When I knew full well there was no excuse, no possible apology for what he'd seen me do. He only gave me one of those cool, contemptuous stares, shrugged, and walked off without a word.

I'd fucked it. I stepped outside and punched brick 'til my knuckles were bloody.

FRANK WAS TRUE BLUE, truest I'd ever met or likely would. He seemed to sense Dad was very near the end of his run with the same perspicacity he'd displayed earlier when Joe had begun falling through those holes in his memory. Frank simply appeared at the house one morning in late January of '82, about three weeks before the finish, carrying a worn leather satchel of clothes, and moved into the spare room. No more back and forth between Bondi and Ashfield. I didn't call him, and he didn't ask. He knew.

As he nursed Dad, he never said or signaled a thing about the day I'd cracked. Dad may have deserved his generosity of spirit—I'd no idea of the debit and credit balance between them—but it was certain I didn't. I also realized that though I'd been shoulder to shoulder with Frank more times than I could count, in close company nearly every day for the past year, I knew almost nothing about him.

He naturally fascinated Umberto. Bert had been a regular visitor all along, but now he was there every evening after work. If Dad was awake and rational, Bert would talk with him as long as he could. Otherwise he'd sit on the verandah until Frank and I had seen the old man off to sleep, glasses of Scotch from the bottle he always brought already poured and waiting for us when we came out. His conversation was usually a guileless, innocent probing. Frank never cared to speak of himself, but Bert was so gentle in his questioning and so earnest in his curiosity that Frank spilled a lot almost without knowing it. Maybe he found it restful after dealing with Dad, who recognized him or me or anyone else less and less.

I never knew, for instance, that Frank had been a such a hero. I'd seen him at a dozen or more Anzac days. He wore the rosemary all right, but never a medal. It turned out he had a chestful—including a V.C.—earned first in North Africa and then through the New Guinea campaign and everywhere else Aussies engaged the Japs. Not only that, but he'd been commissioned and risen to major, though he was only a couple of years older than Dad, who'd started as a private and finished as a corporal.

"There was no particular credit in it," Frank said. "We were dropping like flies in forty, forty-one. They'd have made the company mule an officer if things had kept on much longer."

"Let me say one thing, Frank. Not true," Bert said.

"Right, mate. Whatever," Frank said.

"No, I mean about the officer part," Bert said. "They don't make majors just because everyone else is dead. I know this. My father, he's in the Italian Army four years until he got killed, a lieutenant the whole time, and he was not a stupid man."

"I'm sure he wasn't," Frank said. "Maybe the Italians were better organized than we were."

"I don't think so, Frank. We were very stupid to fight in the first place, and very stupidly got beat bad, no?" Bert said. "Frank, you must have been good at your trade."

"Wouldn't call it a trade. Be ashamed to. It was something we did for a while when we were young and then we stopped. What was left of us anyway," Frank said.

"I read about this Kokoda thing . . ." Bert said.

"Put a cork in it," Frank said evenly.

"If you say so, Frank," Bert said. "Still . . ."

"Any man who's proud of being good at that sort of work is a fool, or worse," Frank said.

"You could be proud of the skill, only the skill of it, and not be a fool," Bert said. "After all, you did not start any wars yourself, did you?"

"Point taken, mate. Let's just conclude the world went mad for a while and leave it at that, shall we?"

"Fair enough, Frank," Bert said.

"Pains me to admit I rather liked it," Frank said, a moment or two later.

"Liked it?" I said.

"Oh, you know," Frank said. "Shooting them."

"The Japs, Frank?" Bert said.

"Well, actually it was your dad's lot and Germans first, and then the Japs," Frank said. "But it could have been anybody. Would have made no difference to me."

"I knew a man, my uncle in fact, who was the same," Bert said.

"You mean who liked it?" Frank said, a hint of surprise in his voice.

"Oh yes. He like it so much he kept doing it after Italy surrenders. He joins the *partigiani,* just to shoot Germans," Bert said. "Then after the war, for many years he shoot Yugo partisans along the border."

"What happened to him?" Frank asked.

"Nothing. When it all ends, around fifty-five, he gets a job as janitor in an elementary school. There he stays, even now. He sweeps the corridors with a very wide brush, this type of thing," Bert said. "He wasn't mad. And people on our side were grateful to him for what he'd done. At first, anyway."

"Yeah, they would be at first, wouldn't they?" said Frank. "They want some men like that around when the chips are down, but they don't want to know ya afterwards. Offends their moral sense. Harry here got the worst taste of that, I reckon, with his war. All the Vietnam vets got treated like shit."

"Hypocrites, Frank," Bert agreed.

"Aren't we all, one way or another?" Frank said. "Right, Harry?"

The tone was so clear it startled me. The man wasn't taking a shot at me at all. He was allowing me back into the fold, including me despite everything.

"Not all of us, Frank," I said. "Not you and Bert for sure. Hoping I'll get there myself, too. One day, maybe."

Frank laughed. "Don't know about Bert, but if you're thinking my footsteps are worth taking a stroll in, best think again. Better yet, Harry, give the whole idea a miss. Not a pretty path, mine. You'll find much better."

I would not. And damned myself for never seeing that before.

"THE DEAD, they leave regret behind," I remember Alessandra saying once some years back when she'd got the news from Italy that her father had passed away. "You could have done this, you could have done that, that's what you tell yourself after they are gone. Dead people don't let you rest so easy."

Nor do the dying. Lucid, Dad remained that tough union battler. When at last it reached the point that somebody had to carry him to and from the loo, somebody had to wash him, somebody had to help him in and out of his pyjamas, he went stubborn as hell. It couldn't be just any-one, a hired nurse say, and it sure as hell couldn't be me. It had to be Frank, Dad was set on that, just as strongly as he'd been set against any hospital or hospice, where he'd have had considerably more care and comfort. He was determined to die where he'd lived.

So Frank took day shift. I took the nights.

Mostly it was guard duty, a watch to ensure the drugs kept him from waking suddenly all alone in agony or ghastly delusion, suffering or thrashing so wildly he'd hurt himself. Lucy was beside me almost always 'til midnight or so. We simply sat there in the dimmed light, chatting Dad to sleep if he wasn't already under and had any idea who was with him, or just looking at his face and then at each other's if he was out. We didn't talk. She'd kiss me on the cheek when she had to leave, wave a silent so long.

Then, on a night when a looming westerly unsettled the air, Dad didn't drift off after his swig of drugs. He kept shifting restlessly in his bed, plucking at the sheets with his hands.

"Got some pain? Want another sip?" I asked, after Lucy had gone downstairs for a break.

"Nah."

"Want anything else? Glass of water, anything at all?"

"You're Harry, my son, and I'm your dad, Joe Hull."

"I know, Dad."

"And you know that mostly I don't know any such thing. But right now I'm as clear in the head as I've ever been in my bloody life. Believe that?"

"Sure," I said. His voice was a bit slurred and his eyes were glittery as if he had a slight fever. But there was no doubt he was perfectly sound.

"If you're sure, will you stand a rant? A sane one?"

"Rant away," I smiled down at him.

"I've been drifting in and drifting out for a long time. Know that hasn't been easy for any of you," he said. "Remember that Christmas tree? Well, there are still a few lights left. Reckon you've all been thinking me daft, delerious, demented. Or etherized. But I've seen some things you'd be surprised I've seen. Heard some strife I'm likely the cause of, too."

"No worries, mate."

"Hate to think I'd left trouble in my wake."

"C'mon, Dad. Take 'er easy, won't you?"

"Just listen, Harry. You said you'd stand a rant."

"Right."

"Harry, how you are with me don't matter. We know, remember?" he said. "But don't fucking waste your life. Why in hell haven't you married Lucy and had a couple of kids? You're living in a bloody daze if you think you've got forever to get around to it."

I said I supposed that was true.

"You think you had it tough in Fuck Toy, and that gives you rights, don't you?" he said. "You've got no rights. Just as I don't for Kokoda. We had to stand on top of our own dead, and they outnumbered us. I'll never get the stink out of my nose. There's not a worse smell in the world than old corpses in jungle rains. And pretty soon I'm going to smell that way myself. I think I'm already a bit on the high side. Rotting inside, bloody hell. So don't say anything to me about how hard you had it."

"Hadn't planned on mentioning any such thing."

"Maybe not, but you're thinking it. You're feeling you're owed something. All of us who fought once feel that way. But we're not entitled to anything just 'cause we went to war. So get over it, Harry. Or you'll wind up like me and my mates."

"*Say la vee*, you old bugger," I said. And Dad laughed and laughed until I thought he might check out right then from lack of air. It had long been an expression of his, his little go at French.

Then he settled down. "Here's my real point, son. You're not owed Lucy. She's the best thing that ever happened to you, and if you don't change some of your ways you won't have her. You're not owed Frank and Umberto and Alessandra and the kids either, and they're as good as they make 'em. If you want them in your life, you've got some work to do to make them want to be there."

I nodded.

"Rant's finished," Dad said. "Now hand over that brown bottle, you selfish bugger. And then shut up and let a man get his sleep."

WHEN DAD HAD HAD a good slug and drifted off, I went down to the kitchen to fetch myself a quick cup of strong coffee. Frank and Lucy were huddling around the table. Soon as I walked in, Frank shoved his chair back and stood up. "Joe okay?" he demanded.

"Just fine. He's sleeping real easy," I said, wondering what'd provoked such a reaction. "Only came down for coffee. Then I'm going back up."

Frank untensed. "My God, Harry," Lucy said. "When you walked in just now I was sure . . . never seen you so pale. Are you alright?"

"Pale? Hell, I'm right as rain, darls."

"You sure?" she said, coming over and laying the back of her hand against my forehead. "No fever, anyway. Feel crook at all?"

"Not a bit."

Frank sat down. "Reckon we've all got a case of nerves about now. Ain't surprising, is it?"

"Be more surprising if we didn't," I said. "Had a good chat with Dad before he went out, though. He was quite himself, knew exactly who he was talking to, what his situation is."

"Standing straight even so, I'd guess," Frank said.

"Right. He even got himself laughing."

Frank chuckled, shook his head. "Yeah, that sounds about right," he said. "Why not have your coffee here, talk a bit, Harry?"

I hesitated. It was really only hitting me now, what Dad had said. And he'd actually understated things. Seemed to me the ground I'd lost with Frank and Lucy was vast, vast and hard as the dead red heart of this bloody country we dwelt in. Never mind what Frank had said that night on the verandah with Bert. I was doubtful I could recover that ground, ever really get back to them. And stupidly blundered right into losing more.

"Let me tell you something about your dad," Frank said when I sat down.

"No, let me guess. The crusty but lovable old bastard . . ."

"You get more boring every day, Harry," Frank cut me off. The look in his eye said a lot more, a lot rougher.

"I'm so sick of myself, Frank," I admitted. "I think sometimes I'm more fucked up in the head than Dad."

"All the more reason you ought to listen now. It's something you need to know. And it's time you knew about it," Frank said. "It's a hard thing to tell you, but your mother was not always an easy woman. She could bite, and she was very clever, so the bites sometimes drew blood. She knew just how to use a few choice words to make Joe feel all his devotion to the union and labor was pure dog-work. And besides you, that work was the most important thing in his life."

"I think you'd better drop this," I said. "About my mother."

"I reckon I won't. I owe it to Joe, if not to you. When you got out of the army, you saw your dad at his best. And these past two years seems you've often forgotten, seems you've sometimes slipped back into what-ever it was that made you an obnoxious little wretch when you were six-teen and seventeen and eighteen. You won't be clear about your dad's real worth unless you're clear on this: it was sad to see her go at him the way she did, him not understanding why. She'd a real quiet way of mak-ing him feel small and useless."

"Yeah, well, what's done is done."

"Harry," Frank said firmly, "your dad ain't done quite yet."

FRANK HAD A ROUGH watch next day. Dad was off his head, didn't know him, and combative through most of it. His mind cleared a bit as evening came on. He recognized Frank and had a friendly greeting for me when I came on duty. Even reminisced for a while about my cadet days, had a laugh over some of my early missteps. Laughed at himself too when he recalled that time I'd told him I was bringing a mate home for supper and it turned out to be Lucy. Then fell into what seemed a deep, untroubled sleep.

Middle of the night, lights dimmed, me dozing in the chair, then jerked awake by Dad when he ripped off a tremendous fart and said in the booming union-hall voice I hadn't heard in the longest time, "Yeah? And I'm the bloody King of Siam then, aren't I?"

I turned up the lights and looked at him, sure he was in the grip of another mad hallucination.

"Thought that'd get a rise out of you, ya lazy bastard," Dad said, wide awake and clear-eyed. "Sleeping on the bloody job."

"Christ, what's up?"

"You're Harry, my son, and I'm Joe Hull, your father."

"Yeah."

"Reckon we don't need to go through the rest of the drill then. Harry, it's time."

I sat there still and quiet as ever I'd been on an ambush in Phuoc Tuy. Scarcely breathed. Didn't dare blink. Dad's eyes stayed fixed on mine.

"It's time," he repeated softly.

I had the strangest sensation that I was still sitting motionless in the chair even as I got up, walked over to the bedside cabinet, took a little key from my pocket and unlocked the door. Still sitting even as I shook a brown bottle to be sure it was full, relocked the cabinet, found the cork on Dad's nighttable. Still sitting as I put that cork firmly into the hole in his cheek, unsealed the bottle. I took a little sip, then passed it to Dad as if it were a nice cold beer.

"Knew I could count on you, Harry," he said, taking a long, deep drink. "Good on ya, mate."

I went back to that chair it felt I'd never left, pulled it as close to the bed as I could. I watched him down another long, deep draught, then another and another and still one more. I caught the bottle as it slipped out of his grip, placed it on the nighttable. He turned his head to me, a slight smile flickering, and held my eyes with his. I reached out. He held my eyes until his own slowly closed. He was breathing so easy I never noticed each inhalation was just a bit shallower than the one before. Never looked at my watch, never felt the passage.

We did go down hand in hand, Dad and I. After all.

Frank found us like that when he came into the room, dawn light easing through those dingy cretonne curtains. So he said. I'd never noticed his arrival, only one departure.

17

WE PLANTED HIM IN the old cemetery atop Vaucluse next to Mum. That had been her bizarre inheritance from her father, who'd kicked off when I was still a small boy: two burial plots in one of the wealthiest sections of Sydney, a few square meters of turf in an area her dad knew very well his daughter could never hope to dwell in alive. Mum and Dad would have much preferred the considerable cash that bit of earth cost. But the will was firm, the plots couldn't be sold. From Ashfield in life to Vaucluse in death. What a hope.

There was a stiff breeze off the Tasman Sea that made the low gray clouds look smooth and polished as river stones. Lucy was having trouble walking through the cemetery. It had rained buckets the day before, and her high heels were sinking into the turf. She was clasping my left arm, leaning into it hard to keep her balance. I was having some trouble keeping my own, but for another reason entirely.

I'd envisioned a spare and lonely scene, just Frank and a few friends of mine from the *Herald*, a few young couples Lucy and I had socialized with, Umberto and his family, and maybe a dozen or so stragglers from the pressroom and the union and the RSL.

Instead, a great mob numbering in the hundreds parted to let Lucy and me approach the grave. We passed rank upon rank of probably every man in the city who'd ever worked presses, every trade union leader including the president and all the top officers of Dad's, ALP men so senior (including the mayor of Sydney, two members of Parliament, and four or five local elected officials) I could scarcely believe it. And the RSL blokes in almost battalion strength, most of them veterans of World War II but a contingent from Korea and even a small group from Nam, all formed up as a unit on parade.

"Never guessed your old man's reach, did you, Harry?" murmured Frank, when Lucy and I joined him at the foot of the coffin. Around it were more wreaths than I could count, a fragrant mountain of flowers that almost masked the powerful earthy odor of the freshly dug hole. Our deep blue flag draped the coffin. "Joe Hull touched more men's lives than you'll ever know."

"Never had a clue, Frank," I said.

"He wasn't one to crow about it," Frank replied.

There was a sort of freelance clergyman I'd hired to say a few words, since Dad and I weren't regulars—or even occasionals—at any church. He stood at the head of the coffin, a plump specimen with broken veins in his nose as if he'd attended too many Irish Catholic wakes, though I knew he'd done his drinking elsewhere because he was pure Anglican. He seemed to rest his little prayer book on the shelf formed by his well-upholstered stomach, but in a beautiful baritone voice he almost sang the graceful old words of comfort and reassurance that the departed loved one was now something far beyond a carcass. Hell, not a carcass; Dad'd been gutted and pumped full of some preserving fluid that must dry like poured concrete. I'd touched his face and gripped his hand once during the viewing; he was hard and chill as a marble statue. I wondered briefly how morticians disposed of the hearts, lungs, livers, stomachs and miles of intestines they sucked out of the dead. You couldn't just toss such stuff in the rubbish bin out back, even well-bagged; the garbos' union would go berserk.

So it wasn't Dad and it wasn't even Dad's corpse inside the coffin, but some man-made construction we were all in complicity to agree was the mortal remains of Joe Hull. Nobody had the faintest idea where old Joe was, including the plump bloke with the book on his belly and some professional claim to a connection with God the rest of us lacked. Except that Joe was no longer among us.

When the clergyman had finished leading the crowd in a chorus of the Lord's Prayer, there was a moment of absolute silence. Then from up on a little knoll above the gravesite, a familiar tune rose gently over us. One of the older RSL men had brought his bugle and had begun a weak-winded but full-hearted playing of "The Last Post." All the decrepit former warriors instantly squared their shoulders and stood at attention, hands aligned with their trouser seams. It seemed faintly comical at the start, a bit of movie melodrama. But then my heart lurched. They were paying tribute to a comrade the best way they knew.

I'd passed through the stages it's said we all do in the face of death—denial, anger, hope, depression, acceptance, even mourning—before Dad's last night, though maybe not in the prescribed order or at the appropriate time. So I'd gone into this funeral business coldly and calmly, and might have held that front even after the shock of the overwhelming turnout. But that damned "Last Post" and the mass salute at the quavering final note came close to breaking me down. I found myself fighting for composure then. It helped a bit when Dad's railing prophesy about his mates proved correct. As they filed by me after the coffin had been lowered, I heard a steady stream of "All his sufferings are over now" and the like.

Hundreds of hands shaking mine, hundreds of similar sentiments murmured. Grief palpable on so many of the faces. Probably on mine as well. Then I heard "Now Joe's gone to a better place" from a massive old brawler with faded blue tattoos on the backs of both his hands and torrents of tears pouring down either side of his badly broken nose. Felt the beginnings of a grin. But Frank caught my eye and held it. I sobered at once.

When at last everyone else had slipped away through the uneven rows of gray headstones, Umberto came up. His grip was firm and he did not murmur. "Harry, I am sorry, truly," he said in his normal growly voice. He was holding Camilla in his left arm. "We live, we die, who knows these things? It's not for us to know. We just keep on."

Alessandra kissed me on both cheeks. Fabrizia made a motion for me to bend over and kissed me too when I did. "Sorry about your dad, Harry," she whispered, her face real close to mine. "I reckon you miss him already. I do."

I did not, though I supposed I surely would later on. What I had at the moment was a sort of lifting sensation, this lightening, the feeling you have on that first day at winter's end warm enough to doff your overcoat.

"Yeah, it's a lot of bunk," Frank said quietly. Only he and I and Lucy were still by the grave, and two men with shovels were waiting patiently some yards away to finish their morning's work. "The poor bastard's dead. Everyone knows they're looking at their own future when they look down into a grave, and they don't know what to say so they say the same old phrases. Nobody's got words that'd mean anything. That these men came here to show respect for Joe—that's what has meaning, Harry."

It was only when Frank said, "See ya when I see ya" and turned brusquely away without shaking hands that a wrenching sense of abandonment hit me. I tried to stifle it, but the feeling intensified when I realized—no, admitted what I knew very well—that it was entirely my own fault, Frank parting like that.

It was Lucy who insisted I hold no wake at my house after the burial.

She knew better than me that I was too twisted, too unstable to deal with a crowd downing beer and rum. Probably I'd have drunk too much. Probably I'd have made a complete fool of myself, and a mockery of the good intentions of so many good people.

She had me down just about perfectly, I suppose.

LUCY HAD PLACED a wicker basket on the wide backseat of Jacko when I'd picked her up at Paddo before the funeral. After we left the cemetery and the director's limo had dropped us back at the funeral parlour, she took my hand and tugged me over to the Holden. She told me to drive, told me when to turn right and when to turn left repeatedly, until we wound up all the way down at Cronulla. There were a few surfies in the water—there always are, no matter the season or weather—but there was no one at all among the huge sand dunes. We roamed around them for nearly an hour, shoeless but never minding our clothes. Then she picked a spot at the peak of a high dune. She took a blanket out of the basket she'd been lugging the whole time and we sat on it. The ocean was gray as steel, but there was nothing solid or stable about it. We were sitting on grains of sand that shifted and slid, and the waves came and came and came and came. Watching them, I found myself almost hypnotized, and fairly soon there wasn't a thought in my head, not even a fading afterimage of a coffin or a grave or a crowd of old men wearing their medals.

I have no idea how long I stared at the ocean before Lucy silently placed a plate of sandwiches and a glass of Yarra chardonnay within my reach. I think it must have been quite a long time. My stomach started growling when I saw the food. I polished off my plate and drained my glass fast. Lucy refilled both. I went to work on the second round more slowly, savoring the salty sea tang of the fried oysters. When I finished, I lit two cigarettes and handed one to her.

"Thanks, cobber," she said. Those were her first words since we'd entered the dunes. I saw her plate, untouched, beside her.

"Feeling almost numb somehow, except a real crusher of a headache," I said, sucking in smoke. I was lying. My head was fine. But my chewed side had tightened up hard. The ache was bad. "Any Mersyndol in your purse?"

She placed four of the round yellow pills in my palm.

"Christ, I'll be wrecked. With the codeine in these, one or two's the maximum."

"Take 'em all, Harry," she said. "You're wrapped too tight. I can drive us home."

"One will do fine," I said, handing her back the others. "I don't think I need to get stoned or drunk, thank you very much. Don't think I'm wrapped too tight, either. Just a bit of headache, that's all it is."

"Feel sure it's not a bit more than that, love?"

"Yeah. Just the head."

"Don't feel up to talking about it, then?"

"It's not a matter of feeling *up* to anything."

"I didn't mean quite that. I was just wondering how you were going."

"Right enough. I'm handling it. I'm glad it's over."

"It isn't, Harry."

"What?"

"It isn't over just because Joseph Hull was buried today. That's not the end of it."

"Looked bloody final to me."

Lucy gazed keenly at my face, rightly concluded I wasn't worth talking to for the moment. She turned her green eyes toward the sea and kept them there. I did the same.

We finished off the wine slowly, smoked a few more cigarettes in silence.

"Sorry," I said at last. "Couldn't have made it through all this without you."

"Ah, you're incorrigible, Harry," she said, standing and taking my hand and pulling me up. She led me down from our perch to the deepest spot in the dunes. Then she took off her skirt, her fine black merino skirt, and spread it on the sand. She stepped out of her panties, tossed them to the winds, and lay down. "Love me now, Harry," she ordered. She wasn't smiling. And when we were just at that moment when everything flows together and you can't turn back, I could taste the salty tears when I kissed her cheeks.

IT WAS A LONG DRIVE back to town. Lucy talked of this or that, but failed to hide the effort it took to speak as if this were an ordinary day. I was beat, but she insisted we to go to a restaurant on Watson's Bay because she was sure a supper at my house would be misery. Through most of the meal she gave her best go at keeping away from the issue that still lingered despite our lovemaking in the Cronulla sands. She pulled it off, too.

When I drove her back to Paddo and was lucky enough to squeeze Jacko in among the gleaming English and Japanese and German wundermachines, she reached across, turned the engine off, and took the keys. "You're not going back to that house tonight. You're staying here with me."

We went straight to her room, stripped, and got into bed. "I want you to hold me all night, Hull," she said. "Don't dare let me go for even a minute." I think I was asleep as she finished that sentence.

We awoke next morning face to face, arms and legs entwined. "Righty-o, mate," she said, turning her back to me and stepping out of bed. She showered, then dressed for work. That was my intention, too, but I was going to go back home to do it, since my suit was pretty sandy despite a good brushing.

"Give you a lift to the office?" I asked when she was ready to face her day.

"No thanks. You go on home, I'll take a taxi. Ring you up later."

It took the longest time to get Jacko from Paddo to Ashfield in the morning rush hour. I parked out back, locked the car up properly, and went inside. If I'd expected to feel anything, if I'd thought some dammed up emotions would overflow, I was wrong. The house felt normal. I showered and shaved, dressed, had a quick cup of tea, then left to catch the bus downtown. I got a few odd looks when I strolled into the newsroom; I don't think anyone expected me back so soon. But what else was there for me to do but get on with my work?

Lucy rang in the afternoon to beg off seeing me that night. She said she felt a bit crook, like she was coming down with the flu. I went to The Drowned Man after work, endured a couple of expressions of condolences from colleagues who hadn't felt close enough to me to attend the funeral, but mostly chatted with Les Fallows, an old mate. Promoted to reporter about the same time I'd joined as a cadet, he'd sort of taken me under his wing then. His was one of the few faces I'd actually recognized at Vaucluse. I didn't stay long, didn't have more than three beers. Then I took the bus back to Ashfield, and for the first time in my life slept in that house entirely alone.

18

H AVING A BIT of a drama, are we?" Lucy said.
    We were. There at her kitchen table, drinking beer, the glasses leaving wet rings on the deeply varnished pine, and rain beating on the windows, and words somehow lingering in the air long after they'd been said and heard. Everything felt damp, and blame seemed to be falling all over me.

"I'm pregnant, cobber," Lucy'd announced with a crooked grin just minutes before. It was a few weeks since we'd buried Dad. We'd been to a film that night and had gone back to her place because I'd had my floors sanded and polyurethaned the day before, and in this damp they'd still be tacky. Bruce was out with his mates at the dog track.

We'd been talking about the movie, a lovely Italian comedy from the sixties called *Seduced and Abandoned*, starring a very young and sexy Stefania Sandrelli. We'd been laughing at the way the film had deftly satirized every prejudice about Sicilians: the women and girls dressed all in black despite the white, baking sun; the leering, lecherous men who were by turn absurdly jealous guardians of *their* women and their family honor. Then:

"I'm pregnant, cobber."

"How the bloody hell did that happen?" I blurted, thrown wildly off balance by news that, a year or two ago, would have made me whoop for joy. A worse reaction I couldn't imagine. Those were the first of the words that seemed to hover malignantly over us. I tried to make good.

"No worries, love!" I smiled, reaching for her hand. She drew hers back, and her grin went more crooked. "It's wonderful. I was just surprised for a sec. We'll get married right away. We can live at my place, the renovations are almost finished. Or we can put it on the market and get a great little apartment close to the Harbour. Whatever you'd like."

"It happened, Hull, on those damn rocks at Whale Beach, which I presume even you might recall," Lucy said peevishly. "The most foolish little interlude of my life, fucking on those rocks without a bloody condom. Jesus."

"Yeah, I remember it very clearly," I laughed. "Very foolish of you. Except I'm delighted with the result."

"Wrong answer, Harry," Lucy said.

I began to doubt anything I said would seem right just now, after my truly awful start. And then came the devastating feeling that everything I cared about was on the verge of slipping over some horizon and disappearing forever.

"Look, I'm sorry about what I first said. Just the shock, that's all it was. Can't blame a man for that. Not fairly."

"Oh fuck, Harry," Lucy said. "Take the bloody chip off your shoulder for half a moment, won't you? I'm not blaming you for anything."

"Then you're giving a good imitation of it." I reached for her hand again, and caught it this time. Her eyes flicked around for a moment, trying to evade mine, but I caught them, too. "Lucy, love, I'll marry you in a minute, if you say so."

"Oh, you will, will you?"

"Of course. Did you imagine I wouldn't? You need me. I'm here."

"Wrong again, Harry," she said. She was looking right through me, a kind of animal stare with nothing in it. I had to drop my gaze from her face. I picked up and put down my glass a couple of times to see the patterns of rings it made on the table. It came to me that I hadn't any idea what was passing through her mind at that moment, only a certainly that a few rogue words had gone extremely toxic.

Then she said, "Oh bugger off, Harry. Ever cross your mind that I might not want to marry you?"

"Well, no, not really." There was a sort of jump-cut in my head. I was sitting across a table from a woman I'd known for years and years, and a minute ago she had told me the happiest news of my life, and I'd been overflowing with love and a lovely anticipation. But all at once I had no idea who I was or who I was with. Fear filled me.

"We'll marry. Don't be dim, Luce," I said softly.

"I'm hardly that."

"Oh come on, Luce. You know what I meant."

"I doubt you yourself know what you mean, most of the time," she said.

"Right, old Harry's easily confused. But not about this. I love you. How can you not marry me?"

"Easy," said Lucy. "I just won't do it."

"But you've got to!"

And that's when a hard flash, cold and sharp as the glint off a diamond, came from Lucy's eyes. The flash that's on my shortlist for oblivion. That's when Lucy said, "Having a bit of a drama, are we?" That's when Lucy, who could brawl when she wanted to, who could put the boot in as well as anyone I knew in an argument, just stopped. That's when she said, "This is bloody boring. So I'm ending it."

And about a second after that she rose, picked up the phone, and called a taxi. Then she went to the front door, held it open, and told me to get out. It was raining hard, but I just stood in it until the taxi came. Then I realized I had the Holden parked right across the street. I went over to the taxi, stood there dripping while the driver wound down his window, and handed him ten dollars, which was way too much.

"Sorry, there's been a mistake," I said. He looked at the bill, wiped it on his shirt to get the damp off, and then put it in his pocket.

"No worries, mate," he said, his Turkish accent giving the familiar phrase a sinister undertone, and drove off. Then I got in the Holden. When I turned the key, the starter just whirred. "Oh fuck," I said, and drove the heel of my hand into the dashboard. The glass covering the speedometer cracked. I got out, popped the hood, and replaced the distributor cap. The engine turned over smoothly with the twist of the key, and I drove home.

FROM THE OUTSIDE, it appeared to be the same house I'd always lived in, but it was changing inside now. The first thing I undertook after Dad died was to clean out all his junk, scrub the house spotless, and begin to redecorate and repaint the rooms. I had in mind a sort of blue somewhere between sky and navy, but Alessandra had saved me from that disaster by talking me into a palette of whites that were really tones of cream or ivory, a slightly different one for each room, and a slightly darker shade of each tone for the trim. She and Bert also persuaded me to strip off the wallpaper first instead of doing the easier but clearly moronic thing of painting right over it. There wasn't much I could do about the furniture, cheap veneered stuff bought on hire-purchase in the early twenties, except get rid of almost all of it. I bought some modern Italian lights and junked the old heavily shaded lamps that for all my life had cast gloomy pools of yellowish light on the floor, and given the place its depressing atmosphere. The cretonne curtains and the heavy draperies were replaced by billowy white linen bedsheets hung with chrome Italian hardware. The place began to feel airier and brighter and lighter pretty quickly.

But not when I got home that rainy night and roamed the house for hours in dark confusion and self-reproach. Clarity of any sort—about Lucy, about me, about what'd just happened—kept eluding me. Lucy had to have meant only that she was ending a spat. She couldn't have meant anything beyond that. That's what I wound up concluding. That's why I decided to give her time to cool down, get over it. That's why I didn't ring her for a while.

It was a couple of days before I even noticed my shoe prints all over the fresh polyurethane, aimless and random as lizard tracks in the sand.

SINCE DAD HAD WORKED for the paper they'd run an obit on him, which ordinarily they didn't do for working men. Naturally I hadn't typed it up myself, but one of the newish girl-hacks—they seemed to pass through the *Herald* like migrating butterflies—managed. JOSEPH HULL, HERALD MAN FOR 36 YEARS, DEAD AT 63. That was the headline. She got his age wrong, he'd been born in 1921, died in early 1982. But the three paragraphs were accurate enough—mentioned his military service and his wounds, included a quote from the union chief. Noted he was survived by one son, Harry, a *Herald* reporter. A clipping on a couple of inches of paper that would turn yellow and crumble. That was it for him in the public domain.

What else did he have to show for his life? He had two suits, one at least fifteen years old and very shiny in the seat. He had six shirts, two ties, one hat, three pairs of trousers and two pairs of shoes. He had five sets of underwear, five pairs of socks, a trenchcoat and an umbrella. He had a box of newspapers, some of them dating back to his childhood, which I guess he'd saved because the lead stories on the front pages must have meant something to him at the time: HARBOUR BRIDGE OPENED BY LANG, March 19, 1932; PHAR LAP DEAD IN CALIFORNIA, April 5, 1932; MYSTERIOUS FIRE DESTROYS REICHSTAG, February 28, 1933; KIPLING,

FAMED FOR INDIA TALES, DIES, January 18, 1936; EARHART VANISHES ON ROUND-WORLD TRIP, July 18, 1937; ITALY, GERMANY SIGN PACT OF STEEL, May 22, 1939. Then a couple his dad must have saved for him, since he'd been off to the war: JAP FLEET BATTERED IN CORAL SEA, May 8, 1942; PM CURTIN DECLARES SEASON OF AUSTERITY, August 19, 1942; ATOMIC BOMB DESTROYS HIROSHIMA, August 8, 1945. And then some he'd had a hand in printing himself: TROOPS TO WORK OPEN-CUT MINES IN NSW, August 1, 1949; KING STREET RIOT PITS WHARFIES AGAINST PO-LICE, August 2, 1949; COMMIE PARTY OUTLAWED, October 20, 1950.

There must have been at least two dozen more of them, a real quirky history of the times in which he'd lived—including the fight between the Russian and Hungarian water polo teams at the '56 Olympics in Mel-bourne, the Sputnik launch, the Kennedy shooting in Dallas. Besides that pile, he had a tin box in which he kept his important papers: his dis-charge from the army, his combat citations, the paid-off mortgage on the house, his marriage certificate, my birth certificate, and a bankbook with a balance of $16,253.12.

He had a comb and a hairbrush, a shaving mug and a safety razor, and a pressboard box with some souvenirs: an Egyptian coin and a sepia photo of a fat belly dancer, two tickets on the Mosman ferry from 1939, a photograph of me and Mum at Luna Park when I was about seven and had a cowlick that made my hair, short as it was, stand up in front, a postcard I'd sent him from Saigon when I'd passed through there during the war, a clipping of Mum's death notice, one little wedding photo, the badge from his army wide-awake hat.

That was the sum of it. I know because I made a list, which I still have. Why? It just seemed like something that I ought to do since I was throwing everything out. The list at least was some record of him, and didn't seem half so meager as the actual possessions Dad had left behind. But Umberto thought of it differently.

"Harry, what are the chances you or I will leave much more? A little bit of paper and metal, a couple of photographs, that's usual," Bert said. He was over at the house helping me paint.

"Not a lot to show for being alive, is it?" I said.

"Wouldn't matter if it was mansions and big cars and stacks of shares. All junk, Harry, means nothing," he said. "What you have to show for being alive is the way people remember you, and maybe you have some kids who take after you a little."

"Well in Dad's case there's only me, and I'm not much to show," I said. My scarred side tightened, thinking of what was in Lucy's belly now.

"Cynical, Harry. You get ulcers if you are too cynical, I read this someplace. Your stomach burning you these days, Harry?"

Bert was shaking his head and wagging the brush he held in his right hand, which caused a little paint shower to hit the dropcloth on the floor and the front of his pants. He worked in an old pair of overalls and he'd tied a rag around his head, as if he were worried about getting paint on his bald dome.

"Look at yourself," I said. He was paint-dabbed from head to toe, except for his bald part. I had to laugh. "You look ridiculous."

"Harry, that is nothing new," he said. "A man gets used to appearing ridiculous at certain moments of his life. But I'll tell you one thing, Harry. The most ridiculous of all is what sometimes comes out of our mouths. Some of the things I have said! It makes me shake."

I reckoned Bert was right about shooting your mouth off. I'd been proof of that most of my life. A cocky man making a complete ass of himself and not even knowing it. Things I'd said to girls I wanted to get, to sources and colleagues, to mates, to Dad, to Frank, to Lucy. Oh Christ, especially to Lucy.

So it wasn't a line of conversation I was anxious to pursue. Too close to the bone, I reckoned, and sore as a bone bruise. There was Bert on the other side of the room, stroking on paint and just waiting for me to say something. I let him wait.

―――――――

WHAT I BEGAN to imagine and really long for after Lucy kicked me out came suddenly so clear and so simple: going home from work each evening to Lucy and our little girl. I was so sure it was going to be a girl. I'd already named her, remember? Valentine, after Tietjens' little Wannop love. I could see the three of us, happy and laughing in this newly brightened house. Or any goddamned house; it wouldn't be the place that mattered. It was a pleasant thing to dream on. It took on the complexion of a reality about to happen, something so certain that every time my phone rang I half-expected it to be Lucy.

She never called.

And when I finally rang her, she hung up on me without a word. She let the answering machine pick up when I phoned right back.

I hadn't even one contemporary, one mate, I could talk to about this—unless I was prepared to endure some bloody rough teasing in exchange, and probably no wisdom at the end of it. Bert only. So I dropped by his place one Saturday afternoon. Alessandra made me an espresso, then a second. Fabrizia was in the parlor doing her drawings while Camilla had her nap. Bert, to my dismay, was off running errands. It was Alice or nobody. I decided on nobody.

We sat chatting in the kitchen over our coffees. She was dressed and made-up for work, and she reminded me of Sophia Loren, young, in an old movie Lucy had dragged me to not long before, though Alice's features were finer, she didn't have such fleshy lips. My mind started to wander a bit until she said, "So, Harry, you having trouble with Lucy, no? You make her pregnant or something?"

That snapped me right back—in astonishment. I couldn't look at her, knowing her expression would be slightly mocking, slightly amused. I just stirred my coffee, never noticing the little spoon accelerating until black drops of the stuff splashed on the table.

"You may as well say, darling," she said in her restaurant voice. "I read it on your face anyway."

So I gave her the outline, harboring a fool's hope she'd be sympathetic. She was not.

"Harry, you are a stupid man," she said, looking disgusted. "You don't know nothing about women."

"I told her I'd marry her, Alessandra. What else was I supposed to say?"

"Harry, you stupid," she said. "All that time when your poor father sick, I'm watching. Lucy, she keep you from falling apart, always she is there for you. And you never showing her you love her. You, what's that they say, taking her for granite? You lose a lot of her respect, Harry."

"Reckon I lost a lot with everyone," I had to admit.

"With friends, doesn't matter. Everybody understand the hell you going through. With a lover, it's different naturally. A lover, she give you more. You got to give back. What you give Lucy all this time? *Niente.*"

"I told her after the funeral I couldn't have made it without her."

"*Idiota!* She is carrying your child, she tells you this, you don't even get up from your chair and wrap her in your arms. To say only 'we'll get married'? What is that? Just talk. Most likely you saying it rough, like maybe you do her a favor or something," Alice said. "You sending her flowers? You writing her love letters, words from your heart?"

"Well, no."

"Ah, hopeless. You are a stupid, stupid man."

I knew that was no insult. Just the truth.

So I reached out for the lifeboat once more when Bert got home and Alice left for the restaurant, giving him more details than I had her because she didn't seem to need many to understand the situation as clearly as a general understands a terrain map. But no ease came from him, either.

Bert shook his head. "I don't know. I don't know. One thing for sure, the women don't think like us. You wait too long, I believe maybe Lucy would see you in hell before she come back to you."

"Nah, you're all wet," I blustered. "She'll be round begging as soon as she shows. You can count on it."

"Not Lucy, I think," Bert said firmly. "Never Lucy."

I BROODED ON IT all for almost a week before Bert came over after dinner one evening, and we drank a bit, beer for me and Scotch for him. I'd rung Lucy each evening, and each time she'd hung up as soon as she heard my voice. So around ten I said I had to go over to *The Bulletin*. It was deadline night for the weekly, and I knew Lucy would be off-duty presently. A big smile spread across Bert's face.

"That's good, Harry, that's good," he said, no doubt thinking I'd patched it up.

When I asked him to ride along, he said no, he'd only be in the way. But when I insisted I'd be glad of the company, that Lucy'd be happy to see him, too, he agreed to come. We went out on the verandah and dashed through the rain to the Holden.

Old Jacko was good in the wet, heavy-footed enough to keep plenty of traction, though I generally drove pretty slow no matter what the weather. We parked across the street from *The Bulletin*'s entrance. I turned off the engine, let the windshield wipers die. I told Bert she'd be out in a jiff. The rain was beating hard on the roof, it sounded like pebbles thrown against sheet tin. We smoked and waited, my wing window cracked a bit to let the smoke out. We didn't talk much because of the noise.

Then the noise got huge. Everything lit up in a sudden glare of lightning, and the rolling bass boom of thunder shook the Holden.

"Tremendous," Bert said. "I love a good storm."

"Saw a man struck by lightning once," I said. "First dead man I ever saw."

I'd been nine or ten at the time. We'd gone on a picnic to the North Head with a bunch of Dad's mates and their families. There was the usual picnic fare, salad sandwiches and sausage rolls, and hardboiled eggs stained purple from floating in a big jar of beetroot and vinegar. After we'd eaten, the women sat under the trees talking about the latest in *Women's Week*, probably recipes or laundry hints or something, and how hard it was to raise children these days. The kids were scuttling here and there like ants, me and the other boys hoping to catch lizards so we could drop them on the girls to make them squeal. A boy named Rupert, who later got killed surfing at Cronulla, dared one of the girls, I think she was called Emma, into climbing a tree, and we all stood around beneath her trying to get a glimpse of her underpants. The men had thrown together a scratch cricket match. A big dark cloud was gathering overhead but the skies all around the horizon were blue, and the sun was glinting off the ocean. The air was perfectly still, there was no sense at all of a storm, just the one towering cloud right overhead.

The flash and the crash exploded all at once. We were shrieking under Emma's tree. Our ears were ringing and we had spots before our eyes, but we saw that all the men in the field had been knocked down. As some of us were running out there, the men began getting to their feet, all except one bloke, Emma's dad, who just lay there flat on his back, eyes and mouth open to the rain that was pouring down, a black smoking patch on the crown of his head, and a strange blue tinge to his skin.

"How did he look?" Bert asked.

"Amazed," I said. "He looked amazed."

Then I saw Lucy come out and stand for a moment frowning at the rain. No taxis in sight. She hunched her shoulders against it and started walking along the footpath. Bert saw her too.

"Well, why you waiting?" he said. "Go get her."

"The thing is, she doesn't know I'm here. She isn't talking to me these days."

"Now I'm confused, Harry. Why are we here?" Bert asked.

"Because I thought I might grab her, have a word. But I'm too scared."

"Oh, Harry," he said, looking at me with great disappointment in his eyes. "Harry, Harry, Harry. You sure you're feeling all right?"

I turned the key in the ignition. Jacko coughed once or twice and kicked over nicely. But then I saw that Bert was already out of the car. "You won't get her, I will go for you, my friend."

I thought that over for a moment, him standing out there in the rain all the while. I noticed that water was getting all over the Holden's front seat.

"Get back in," I said.

"You going to just give up?" Bert demanded, sticking his head in through the open door.

"Yeah," I said.

"You sure?"

"Yeah, yeah. I'm sure. Just get in and shut the damn door.

"Certain?"

"Christ, yes. Come on, the seat's getting rained on."

Bert slid inside. His pants made a squishy sound against the Holden's upholstery, and he smelled wet as anything.

"Harry, you making the biggest mistake of your life, you don't try harder to make this up with Lucy," he said.

"Sure thing," I said, and switched on the windshield wipers.

19

THE DROWNED MAN never had to be hosed out after closing, but it was no gentlemen's club either. During the couple of loud and smoky hours each evening when the place did most of its business, you needed to raise your voice smartly to be heard. You could drink beer or a Bundaberg. But you'd never dream of ordering a nice mango daiquiri. The Drowned Man had never heard of them.

Beer, and lately too much of it, was my choice every evening. The Drowned Man was just across the street from the *Herald*, but it drew a journo crowd from all over. The best thing about it was that it never changed in any way as the years went by, though you'd get fresh faces from time to time. And it was a purely nonpartisan, democratic place, the pressmen and truckers mixed in however you will with reporters and any editors who had no invitation to a chichi cocktail party on a particular night.

Most evenings I kept pretty much to myself, on the unlikely hope

Lucy might drop in. There were plenty of girl-hacks about, but no Ms. Whitmoor. Instead, it was Umberto, whose shop was just a few blocks away, who started appearing.

"So Harry," Bert said, rolling up to the bar on his fifth or sixth visit after that botched excursion to see Lucy as she left *The Bulletin*. "How does it go with her?"

"Doesn't go at all," I said. "She still rings off every time I ring up."

"Toohey's," Umberto said to the barman. Then he turned back to me. "No talking?"

"None," I said.

"You get the chance to say anything?" he asked.

"Not a thing. She slams down the receiver before I've even finished saying her name," I said.

"*Dio*," Bert said. He got absorbed for a moment in stroking beads of moisture off his glass with a forefinger. "Harry, listen to one thing. I'm thinking you go to her house one night before she comes home from work, you sit on the stoop, and you don't let her into the house until she listens a little to what you have to say."

"Oh fine. Except what do I have to say?"

"Say? Why, what you want to tell her, of course," he said.

"Christ, Bert, I don't know what that is anymore," I said.

"Sure you do, Harry," he said. "It is clear, no?"

"It seems plain to me. She can marry me and have the kid and we can make a good go of it. Or she can not marry me and start scrambling, because she's going to find life mighty hard."

"That's what you want to say? Oh, Harry," Bert said. "To the woman you love? You don't want to tell her something sweeter than that?"

"You're right. I'm such a bloody fool."

"Whinger, too. Never mind. Probably this child, she's not even yours. No doubt Sam Neill and Mel Gibson and Paul Hogan are the father," Bert said straightfaced. "One of them anyway, for sure. She probably don't know which."

"Put a cork in it, Umberto," I laughed, a rare event lately.

"Must be so. If it is your child, how come you are not sending Lucy flowers every day? Writing her loving letters? Like Alessandra say she tell you. Or waiting on her doorstop, like I say?"

"Wouldn't do any good."

That took him wrong, I could see the disapproval in his face. He got cross with me. He said, "No fair go? Heap of shit. You are not a trier then, Harry. I'm thinking even maybe you got some cracked idea Lucy, she should act grateful to you. *Idiota!*"

"So what?"

"You are the one that should be grateful, so good she's been these years. Like an angel, she's been, for sure. Maybe Lucy, she come around if she thought you felt these things. Maybe you'd deserve her if you really felt them."

Deserve her. That stung. I didn't, and knew it. I ordered another beer.

I was itching to keep talking about Lucy but I shut up, and Bert did the same when Les Fallows wandered over to join us. I liked Les well enough, but my travails in the women department weren't the sort of thing I wanted anyone at work to know about, and Les had a compulsion to tell everybody everything he heard. He wasn't malicious; he just had no ability to keep anything to himself, and didn't like to let anyone else do so either. Which is probably what made him both a good reporter and a dangerous man to confide in.

Bert liked Les because Les always had some fresh story that slagged and blackened the names of our more illustrious citizens and officials, and Les knew a receptive audience when he found one. As soon as we'd bought him a beer he began telling us about a property millionaire—an ethnic, naturally—big in construction and with some hard men on his payroll in case he had any union problems. This mogul had fallen for a sweet young thing—"absolutely luscious" was Les's phrase for her—and installed her in a Paddington terrace house for his private delectation.

Well and good, if you like them young enough to be your daughter or even your granddaughter. And the wife in Point Piper didn't suspect the property pasha was dipping his wick somewhere he shouldn't.

"All is idyllic for some time," Les said. "Surely you can picture it. The pasha in the autumn of his years is a happy man, for his willie hasn't let him down. What he does not know is that his lovely little friend is having it off most afternoons with a young man her own age.

"But he suspects, doesn't he?" Les went on. "Like any December in a May-December affair, our nabob begins to doubt he is loved for himself, he begins to imagine younger, more handsome rivals. He decides one afternoon to check up on the girl. He lets himself into the house. It's quiet. He prowls the place, every sense alert for signs of another man. He senses nothing. His heart throbs because he almost believes the girl is true. Then he opens the bedroom door and sees his dolly utterly and vulnerably naked, sleeping as peacefully as a child, in the arms of a drowsing young man."

"Oh Christ," I said. "Oh Jesus." Les was encouraged to continue, though he seemed annoyed at some loud talk nearby.

"The panjandrum roars, he leaps like a lion to the attack. The girl wakes and screams. It's high drama. It could well turn bloody," Les said.

"Mayhem, yes? Possibly murder?" Bert said.

"Neither mayhem nor murder, my friend. Worse." Les grinned, paused for a moment. He was always alert to timing when he told a tale. "Quick as a wink, the panjandrum finds himself in the local gaol, sharing a cell with a drunken boong. The young man is a police constable, off-duty at the moment. The terrace house just happens to be on his beat, which in fact is how he met the girl. And our lovelorn maharaja, our satrap of the property game, is charged, so help me this is true, with breaking and entering."

"No! That is too good," Bert said. "Will it be in the paper tomorrow?"

"It bloody well will not. Our panjandrum has powerful connections, you see," Les said. "The copper, however, will presently begin night duty on a different beat. And I reckon the popsy has already been pushed out of the love nest."

I was laughing so hard I sprayed the bar with beer. I wanted more details, the complete set of weights and measures on the girl, but Les was skimpy with them.

"But this one will be all over tomorrow," he grinned. "Our new Minister for Sport, Recreation and Tourism, Mr. John Brown, celebrated his appointment by rooting his wife silly right on the Ministerial desk!"

"No!" Bert said. "How can you know this is true?"

"Had it straight from the rootee's mouth. Mrs. Brown in the flesh told about a half-dozen reporters today at a Ministry event. She said it was bonzer, too."

We were howling.

WHILE I WAS WEAVING my beery way between work and pub and home and brooding darkly most nights, Lucy was all bright plans and organization. She was brisk, she was concentrated, she knew her own mind and gave no importance to what anyone else might think. When she arrived at a strategy she felt certain would work, she moved to implement it.

Or so I learned—after Bert revealed a few evenings later that he had gone himself to see her on my behalf—but only fully understood some years later.

He went to her because he felt I'd gotten too warped to manage anything myself. And I don't say he wasn't right. He'd done it very simply: he phoned her at work, inquired how she was doing, and asked if he could give her lunch. I assumed he turned on the charm, because Lucy had to know he wasn't coming free of motive, just for the pleasure of her company. She agreed anyway.

Bert had picked her up just outside her office. "The way she walked, it had purpose I would say," he told me. "Harry, listen to one thing. She is solid, she knows what she does. Not a false step."

"Why do you think that?" I asked.

"The way she behave, talk, everything," Bert said.

"Such as?"

"Harry, better you just let me tell you what happens, okay? Lucy, she comes right up to me and kisses me on the cheek, asks after my girls. I tell her they are fine, everything's fine. But, I tell her, Fabrizia asks always where Lucy has gone. Lucy laughs, says something like 'Gone nowhere but not forgotten,' I don't get it exactly. But I tell her she is gone, from us at least."

"As she well knows," I said.

"We go down the street to some trattoria, order a little bit to eat. Straightaway I say to her 'Okay, you are having trouble with Harry, he behave bad some way, I don't know. But I see how he is, and he's sorry for sure.' And she tells me, nice but firm, to slow down, have a care. She says she knows you are feeling sorry, but sorry is not the issue."

"Then what is the issue?" I said.

"Ah, that's no so clear, I think," Bert said. "Lucy, she says she's thought a lot and she don't want to do what you think she ought to do. She says how can she plan a future with a man who got no sense of future." Bert paused. "She says you are damned now-centered and self-centered."

"Like hell," I said.

"So I ask her, Lucy isn't your thing with Harry self-centered also? Hell yes, she tells me. She says I should ask who is Harry putting first. Naturally I say you believe you are thinking of her and the child first, nothing else."

"How did she take that?"

"Ah Harry," Bert sighed. "She grins at me. She says you probably do believe that. But then she asks me, do I think you are really capable of it? Catches me by surprise a little. I say Lucy, maybe Harry does not know what is best for you."

"Aw Jesus, Bert!" I said. "Lovely vote of confidence. Thanks very much."

"I don't know how it came out," he said sheepishly. "It just did."

"So what did she say to that?"

"She say 'Exactly.' She say that is why she could talk all night with you and it would not change how she is going to handle her problem. Then she laugh a little, says she make a mistake to call being pregnant a problem. It's not that, she says, it is a situation. So I ask her, Lucy, isn't it also Harry's situation? This child is his too, no?"

"Bloody right," I said.

Bert began looking very unhappy then. "Lucy says back—this I remember clearly—'In the making, yeah. But not in the raising, I think.' And maybe I seem worried or something to her then, because she says 'I'm up to this all on my own, no fear.' "

"That's it?"

"No. Then we eat our lunch, I walk her back to *The Bulletin*, she tells me not to forget to give her best to the girls and Alessandra."

"Oh, this lunch was a real help, Bert," I said.

"Wait. I'm not finished yet. Before I leave I say to Lucy can't she please talk with you? Have a word at least? She shakes her head. She says she don't hate you, she says she isn't even cross with you anymore, she says you still have one hell of a grip on her heart. Then she says this, these words exactly: 'Harry could turn me right off course, wreck me. I admit I am vulnerable now. So I have to keep him away until I've done what I have to do.' "

"What the hell does that mean?" I said when Bert related this. It sounded very ill-omened. "What does she have to do, except marry me so the kid'll have a father? And she'll have a partner?"

"I don't know," Bert said. "She didn't tell me her details."

"That's great. All this upset, strife and mystery just because my tone of voice wasn't quite right when she told me she was pregnant."

"Harry," Bert said. "I think there was maybe something more. Not just the voice, Harry."

"What else then?" I said.

"Everything else, Lucy said. She said you could not really be a husband, even less a father. She said you felt obliged to do what you are thinking is the right thing. But too beat up you are, after these last years. Your heart, too damaged. A good man, she called you, but not strong enough right now for this. Not—what was it?—'cut out' for this?"

"I wasn't cut out to be a soldier either, but I did all right as one."

"Sure you did, Harry. It's not me saying these things. It's what Lucy said. She said she knew you too good, she did not want to live by you and raise a kid. She said you could not do it."

"As if she gave me a chance."

"Maybe the women give us chances we don't know about. Tests, maybe. We pass, they stay. We fail, they go."

Bert said there was a time, just before they were married, when Alessandra would have nothing to do with him. He'd had no idea what he'd done wrong, and she wouldn't say. One day she was all in love with him again. Then he'd had no idea what he'd done right, and again she wouldn't say.

"I'll tell you one thing, Harry. It is strange how they do," Bert said, tapping his temple. "We will never know what goes on up there. I believe it is because they are more intelligent than us. They take, how to say, a longer view? They see farther then we're able."

20

WHAT BERT SAW AFTER that was ugly: Harry sulky, sullen and lost, growing worse by the day. Must have scared him a bit, I realized later, for he stuck real close to me. He'd pry me away from The Drowned Man before I got blotto, and he'd come by the house most weekends. Even invited me to purely family affairs, like a speech night at the St. Boniface School.

Speech nights, along with little plays and concerts and the like, were fixtures at good schools like St. Boniface. The drill was that all the kids, from the little ones up to the top formers, would recite some poem or song or speech they'd memorized. Alessandra even took a night off work so she could attend. Bert told me it was Fabrizia who really wanted me to be there.

St. Boniface was not the closest school to us. It was in a better suburb, and more expensive than most, but Umberto and Alessandra had that concept of rising. They'd no way to judge schools except by how much they cost, and whose kids went there. They'd concluded it was highly probable there was a direct relation between the tuition and the quality of the teaching, and so they had chosen the dearest one they could afford.

No doubt they were making much more of a stretch than most of the parents, though you wouldn't have known that looking at them; they were better-dressed than anyone else I saw at that speech night, and even Camilla was done up in quiet quality. Fabrizia wore the school uniform, naturally: tartan skirt, white blouse, fawn blazer with the school crest on the left breast, and a straw hat with a ribbon that matched the skirt. Little white socks and brown brogans, too.

The nuns had had arranged things so that the little ones and the big ones went on in no particular order, which made no sense to me but must have to them. It meant we had to sit through a babbling group of six-year-olds, a dramatic recitation of "Advance Australia Fair" by some sixth-form girls who were just budding, some of them, and no doubt hating every minute they had to spend on stage. There were more little ones, and there was the usual smirking version of "Waltzing Matilda" by some sixth-form boys who were already pimply and loutish, with prominent Adam's apples and cracked voices. God, what a bore.

Why was I there? Besides believing it might please Fabrizia, only for the company, and for something to do. I was spooked. Life had fallen into a bleak pattern, a Slough of Despond you might say if you felt like quoting my dad misquoting his dad. I'd been coming home after too many beers most evenings and sitting for too long in the dark, listening to the cicadas chorusing outside and the steady, irritating drip of a leaking toilet inside. Which, gripped by a growing inertia, I never seemed to get around to fixing. There in my freshly painted rooms, my newly bright and airy home, I felt utterly useless, utterly helpless.

It came to me, sitting there in the St. Boniface auditorium, that I wasn't missing Dad's presence about the house, only Lucy's. And not her actual presence so much as her good sense and support, from which I'd been cut off entirely. I realized this with as much dismay as I realized too that she and Frank had been right about me; I was very poorly informed about myself. But who can really help you with that? Some pastor or priest, who's probably twisted with a special set of frustrations and is almost certainly an accomplished liar from having to offer comfort to so many in a comfortless world? Not bloody likely. Some pyschiatrist or psychologist? The ones I'd met socially seemed to me to be as clueless and neurotic as all the rest of us.

Once when the thought of going back to those empty, creamy rooms was too much, I'd hopped a bus from The Drowned Man to Bondi Junction, and walked down to Frank's. He'd had the grace to seem pleased to see me. He lived in a bare little flat on the ground floor of a stucco building with peeling pale blue paint and rusty ironwork on the windows. There were odd touches about his place, like crocheted antimacassars on the backs of a pair of overstuffed chairs. He had no family he ever spoke of, and though everyone in Bondi knew him by sight, I never met one who considered himself Frank's mate. It seemed to me he had mastered being solitary, if anyone had.

"Hell, Harry, you're on the wrong track. Where'd you get the notion that growing old means growing wise?" he had said. He did not like to entertain in his flat, so we'd gone for a walk down past the pavilion and along the beach.

"Seems accumulated experience ought to add up to something," I'd said.

"Yeah, it would seem so. But experience, if you pay attention to the lessons of it, mainly warns you what to avoid, when to keep off. It doesn't really explain very much. Doesn't give you great insight, especially into yourself. And most especially into anyone else, or the way of the world."

"I don't need it all explained," I'd said. "Just enough to see why I wreck so many things, what it is about me that's so wrong, and what I can do to change."

"That's asking a great deal. Are you sure people can change very much? Sure we aren't all basically stuck with ourselves as is?"

"I'm hoping not."

"I reckon you are," Frank had said, "if you've come down here to talk to me about it. I do wish I had the answer for you."

"But you've been around, Frank. You've seen how things work. Are there some hoops I've got to go through, some hurdles I've got to clear? Is that it?"

"As many hoops as you want, if it pleases you. Give all the hurdles you can discover a go," Frank had said. "I think you'll find at the end of the day you'll wonder why you bothered."

"Right. Next you'll be telling me it's all up to fate and I may as well give up and make the best of whatever's put on my plate. That's Umberto's take on things."

"He's likely right," Frank had said. "Your basic problems, like that quick temper, Harry, are easy enough to damp down. No secret technique. Just pause a moment, have a thought, before you say a word. For the rest, to get through life with a minimum of fuss and without paining others, seems to me you've basically got to deny to yourself that you know certain things, not go hunting high and low for more to know."

That had been less than comforting to sleep on. I saw the sun come up the next morning for maybe the first time since I was in the army, not counting Anzac days and once at Whale Beach with Lucy.

And in the school auditorium now I only really snapped out of my brooding when Fabrizia scampered on stage and did the required little curtsy. Some of the littler kids just before her had recited bits of a Beatrix Potter story about rabbits, which didn't seem to me to be the best choice in a country where rabbits were never thought of as bunnies but about as adorable as rats or king browns. Now came Fabrizia, with her black hair clipped neatly in a sort of bowl cut that framed her round little face. You expected from the face she'd be plump, but she still hadn't filled out at all. She waited while the headmistress announced her name, made the smallest grimace when her last name was mispronounced, and launched into May Gibbs's famous old rhyme "The Willow":

> By the peaceful stream
> Or the shady pool
> I dip my leaves in the waters cool
> Over the water I lean all day
> Where the stickleback and minnows play
> I dance, I dance when the breezes blow
> And dip my toes in the stream below.

She sounded more English than Australian, though I doubt Bert and Alice could notice that, any more than I'd spot the difference between a Roman and a Venetian accent in Italian. I reckoned she'd got the Pom tone from the radio and TV; she had always been such a terrific mimic. Fabrizia curtsied like all the kids and ran off stage when she was done. Bert nudged me in the ribs and said, "She is a smart girl, Harry. Very well-spoken, no?" There was polite applause, and Bert grinned. Alice wore a vague smile, which vanished when she shook Camilla a bit too roughly for my taste to stop the kid whining.

We stood in the aisle after the show, Fabrizia clutching the loose fabric of one of Bert's trouser legs with one little hand. "I was great, wasn't I, mate?" she said, looking up at me. There were a lot of nuns about, waddling like fairy penguins but with none of the cuteness, and a coven of spinsterish lay teachers as well. My eye was held by one who was going up to people and chatting for a bit. She was no sister, though she'd dulled herself down with a black cardigan and long tweed skirt and sensible shoes so there would be no dissonance. Her face was plain, very young. From her manner you might have expected her to have a pseudo-English accent, not plummy but educated middle class. And she tried for it when she came to us, but right underneath was pure sheep-station Aussie, broad as a billabong in the wet.

"I'm Priscilla Moon, Fabrizia's teacher," she said, shaking hands with Umberto first and then Alessandra.

"Oh yes! Very pleased, very pleased to meet," Bert said. I supposed he was nervous, for his accent had thickened up considerably. "The girl, after some weeks only, she always talking all about you."

"Pardon?" Miss Moon said. "I didn't quite get that."

"He said Fabrizia's told them all about you," I said.

"That's Harry," Fabrizia piped.

"Harry Hull," I said. "I'm their neighbor, have been since the kid was real little."

"Really?" Miss Moon said. Then she lowered her voice a bit, and made one of the silliest moves I'd ever seen in polite company. I guessed she was fresh from teachers' college. "Ethnics, Fabrizia's parents are, right?"

"We are not from here of course. We are from Italy, where else?" Bert said, smiling but sounding like a German villain in a World War II movie. Miss Moon began to look very confused, as if she was mentally reviewing the geography part of her teachers' training course and failing to get a real clear picture of Europe.

"Really and truly? Very nice indeed, I'm sure," she said. "Fabrizia is a bright child, a good pupil."

"Thank you," Bert said.

"And her English is really, really good," Miss Moon said.

"Oh yes," Bert said amiably. "She's not speaking English with us, only Italian in the house. English she is speaking with Harry mainly, and in school, for sure."

"My word, a teacher as well, are you Mr. Hull?" she said.

"No fear!" I laughed. "I write for the *Herald*."

"Ah, a journalist," she said. I could see a little bit of the confusion go, now that she thought she had a category to put at least one of us in. She seemed the type who liked to do that. It made her more certain of her ground.

"Yeah."

"That's fair dinkum," she blurted. She caught herself at once, squelched the bush talk. "Well, Fabrizia, your poem went over really well."

"I was the best, wasn't I?" Fabrizia stood there smiling, waiting to hear just that. Until Alice reached behind Bert and pinched her on the arm. "Thank you, ma'am," the kid said quickly to Miss Moon.

"Well, I've got to go chat with some of the other parents now. It's been so nice meeting you and I trust we'll see each other soon," Miss Moon said.

"For sure," Bert said. He was still smiling as she looked at me once and then backed away a bit awkwardly. I noticed then that maybe she wasn't so plain after all, big bright eyes and small, delicate features, almost as if her face hadn't yet reached its adult form. But even with the dowdy clothes you could tell she had fine, full womanly lines.

Bert, Alice and the kid started having a discussion in Italian then, Fabrizia sort of hopping about on her toes while clutching her dad's trouser leg. Camilla had squeezed herself into a ball on the seat of a chair and seemed shivery. If Alessandra noticed—or cared—she gave no sign, standing with her back to the creature. I caught Camilla looking at me, a sort of hopeful expression on her face. So I gave her my best grin, which drew a small giggle from the girl. Then I watched Miss Moon moving here and there around the room. Her ankles looked pretty good, and so did what I could see of her calves, which was only the lower half. Fabrizia spotted me perving. "Great legs, right, Harry?" she said.

"Don't have a clue what you're talking about," I smiled.

"Bloody do," she tossed back. "I'm telling Lucy on you. When she comes around again. Where'd you put her, Harry?"

Alice scowled at her.

As we drove home in the Holden, I was having trouble concentrating on the conversation because I was so deep into dealing with the smart remark of a precocious kid. I did hear myself invited in for a drink when we pulled up to the house. "Sleep tight, don't let the bedbugs bite, Harry," Fabrizia said as her mother took her and Camilla off to bed. "But you're wicked, Harry. Maybe they ought to bite you."

"*Basta, cattiva*," Alice snapped. But that didn't stop Fabrizia from pulling a face at me as she disappeared.

Bert and I went into the kitchen, where he poured out three glasses of red wine, and pretty soon Alice joined us. "The girl don't want to sleep," she said. "She is too excited. She asks if Harry liked her poem."

"Sure did," I said.

"Maybe we have made a mistake," Bert said.

"How's that?" I said.

"You know, the girl have few friends there, and this is her second year already," he said. "She says they make jokes, tease her all the time."

"It's just kids," I said. "We always teased each other in school. They called me 'emu,' 'cause my neck was so long and skinny."

"A couple of the older ones, they always mocking her, Harry," Alice said. "Then she is asking me why we are speaking English so funny."

"Well," I said, thinking Fabrizia could handle just about anything any other kid could dish out and that it was the achingly shy and mostly mute Camilla they ought to be concerned about, but not daring to mention that. "It'd be worse most other places. As you know."

Fabrizia had spent her first couple of school years at the local public one, and had come home crying once—but only once—after some particularly nasty playground humiliation.

"That's a good school, St. Boniface," I went on. "She's better off there than she would be with the kids from around here."

"You're right no doubt, Harry," Bert said. "The education she gets, it's very good, I think. The teasing, it's not so rough."

That seemed to be that.

"These Australians, they don't know nothing," Alice suddenly burst out. "They have no manners, no culture, no nothing."

"She's got a point there, Bert," I grinned. "Have a look at me, for instance."

"Oh Harry, you I don't mean," Alice said. "But even the educated ones, the successful ones, sometimes they behave like peasants. I would say practically animals."

"That's a bit severe," I said.

"Ah, Alessandra, you take this too hard," Bert said

"Every night I am serving these people, watching them. The ones from the older money, they think this is still the nineteenth century and they are English lords. The ones with the new money, you wouldn't hire them to press olives, they are too crude."

"Very bitter," Bert said. "*Calma, cara.* You making your stomach bad, you keep this up."

"Sometimes we get discouraged, Harry," Bert said. "She don't mean nothing by what she says. We been here now what, five years? Six? Six at least. Every year we do a bit better. But she feels, what's that word, marooned here. It makes her cross sometimes."

"I reckon it might," I said. "Don't feel it myself of course. But I've got enough imagination to understand it."

"Sure you do, Harry," Bert said, patting me on the shoulder. "You know what I'm speaking. You prove that to me many times."

Right. Seemed to me that all I had proved to Bert and everyone else in all those years was that my mouth had a mind of its own, and a damned dim one at that. Too dim for this world.

21

LUCY WENT WALKABOUT.

She slipped off in almost the same shadowy way abos do when they reckon it's time to follow their songlines or consult with their ancestors or simply wander about in the bush. They're here one minute and gone the next, quick as a dream, without telling anyone where they're bound or when they'll be back. Most likely they don't know.

Lucy did tell some people she was going. She said where, too, and it was no traipse through the never-never, no journey to the back of beyond. But I wasn't one of the told, so it was walkabout to me. And especially maddening because I only found out about it from the person I least wished to learn anything from: Bruce.

I'd kept ringing Lucy at least four times a week. I hoped I might wear her down, that one day she'd get so tired of hanging up on me that she would talk a bit. I also had the thought that persistence might send her a signal she would recognize and respond to. But then, maybe a month

THOMAS MORAN

after the night she'd kicked me out, I suddenly stopped being hung up on. What I got instead, time after time, was Bruce, saying, "She isn't here, Harry."

"Where is she then?" I said.

"Out," he said.

"When will she be back?"

"Don't know," he said.

After a couple of weeks of this Bruce must have been feeling fatigued by so much effort, for finally he said, "Harry, stop wasting my time. Lucy isn't here for good."

"What the hell's that mean," I said.

"Means exactly that. She's gone."

"Gone where?"

"Ah Harry, can't tell you that, can I?"

"Why not?"

"Well, it'd ruin everything."

"Ruin what?"

"Her running away. She left so she wouldn't have to talk to you anymore."

"She wasn't talking to me anyway."

"Whatever."

"So why don't you tell me where she is?"

"Because she doesn't want you to know. Plain enough for you?"

"Now look, Bruce, I want you to think for a moment, and then tell me where Lucy's gone."

"Tough luck, Harry. I'm not saying. And you can get stuffed," Bruce said, putting the phone down more sharply than Lucy ever had.

That was too much, coming from him. I fumed over it. I grew furious with Lucy as well. She could have had the decency to tell me face to face. It wouldn't have cost her anything to say she was leaving and did not want to hear from me again. Did she imagine I'd lose it? Did she think I'd weep and wail and beg? I was turning all this over and over in my mind with the aid of a certain amount of beer the next evening at The Drowned Man, inventing things I could say that would hurt her as much as she'd hurt me. It came to me that instead of merely thinking, I ought to act. So I went outside, took a taxi over to Lucy's house, and banged on the door until Bruce opened it up.

"What're you doing here, Harry?" he said. The boy should have been stillborn. "Lucy's gone, I told you that."

"You did, mate," I said. "You told me, and I appreciate it. But her being away don't mean you and I can't have a beer together, does it?"

"Yeah, why not?" Bruce said. He was sounding way too cocky for my liking. I followed him back to the kitchen, and if I'd had any doubts about Lucy leaving, the conditions Bruce was living in put a stop to them immediately. She was definitely not in residence. There was a pile of plates in the sink streaked with congealed meat fat, there was a pyramid of beer tins on the counter, there were dirty clothes scattered over the chairs and on the floor, too, and the whole place seemed to have a thin layer of grease on most of the surfaces and a greasy stale smell. I handed Bruce a can of XXXX from the pack I was carrying. Then he sat down at the pine table, four slices of bread and a jar of Vegemite before him.

"Enjoying the bachelor life, are you, Bruce?" I said.

"Yeah, it's nice to have the place to myself," he said.

"Know just what you mean. Probably bringing girls home every night, you dog," I said. "But won't your sister be cross when she sees the way you're keeping things?"

"No worries, she won't be back for a long time," he said.

"How do you know she won't turn up unexpectedly? I'd worry about that, Bruce, if I were you."

"She rings up every now and again. She's not coming back anytime soon."

"So where's she ring from? Some holiday place on the coast or something?"

"What's it to you?" He was using his forefinger like a knife to scrape some Vegemite out of the jar and smear it on his bread.

"Don't be stupid, Bruce. Just tell me where she's gone."

"Bugger off, Harry."

He had his right forefinger in the Vegemite jar when I grabbed his left hand and bent his thumb back as far as it would go. "Holy Christ, Harry! That hurts. What the fuck are you doing?" he cried. He tried to twist out of my grip but I just forced his thumb back more toward his wrist until he stopped moving. He was breathing through his mouth now, clearly in what he considered to be severe pain, and I could see dark brown flecks of Vegemite on his teeth. His breath was disgusting.

"You can tell me where she's gone, and it'll be all right," I said. "Or you can not tell me, in which case I'll break your thumb and then I'll do the same to the other one."

"Quit fooling around, Harry," he whined. I put more pressure on, and he howled.

"Christ, Harry, leave off will you?" Tears were forming in his eyes. He was not sturdy, that lad.

"Now Bruce, I'm not asking you for her street address or phone number. Just tell me the city, and I'll let you go."

"Lucy'll kill me," Bruce said.

"She won't get the chance, because I'm going to do it any moment now. Just stop fucking whingeing and tell me the town, Bruce."

I forced that thumb back a bit more. I was standing over him and had good leverage, but I was hoping he'd talk soon, because even a bit more pressure might snap the bone. And he seemed close to fainting.

"Adelaide, oh Christ!" Bruce wailed. "Bloody hell, she's gone to Adelaide. Please, please Harry. Let off."

I did. He cradled his twisted thumb in the hand he'd been using to spread his Vegemite. "God damn you, Harry," he said, standing up. "Fuck off," he said. He had that edgy, wounded look you sometimes see in the eyes of a man who is about to try something way beyond his capabilities for the sake of pride. I decided to protect him from his own stupidity, since he was, after all, Lucy's brother. I kicked him in the right shin as hard as I could. He went down screeching. I was humming as I left the house and walked away. I was feeling great.

Lucy would have to get work, I was certain. She had only one trade. So next day, I confidently phoned the paper in Adelaide, got the newsroom, and then the surprising news that nobody there had ever heard of Lucy Whitmoor. I thought about going back to Bruce's, perhaps with a length of heavy rubber hose. It was an attractive prospect in principle, but probably a bad mistake in practice. So I broke one of my own rules and got Les involved. I didn't tell him Lucy was pregnant of course, but I did allow that she'd disappeared. Les rang a couple of his mates at *The Bulletin*, who told him Lucy had said she was moving to Adelaide when they'd shouted her drinks on her departure from the magazine. Next he tried some girl-hacks Lucy had been friendly with at other papers. They said Adelaide as well.

It seemed clear that Lucy had left a false trail, and never intended anyone to know where she'd gone. The rubber hose came to mind again, but I felt fairly sure that moron Bruce had no idea she wasn't where she told him she'd gone, even when she rang him up. Les poked around a bit more, but he could find no clue to where she might be in all that great brown country. I rang the papers in every decent-sized place in Australia, starting with Melbourne and working down through Canberra, Brisbane, Perth, Newcastle, Wollongong, Geelong, Kalgoorlie, Port Macquarie, Townsville, Darwin, even fucking Alice Springs, Wagga Wagga, Queanbeyan, Dubbo and Toowoomba. Not one of the rags in those places knew any Lucy Whitmoor. Drew a blank in Hobart, too.

Walkabout, all right. Couldn't file a missing persons with the police either, since Bruce claimed to know where she was. I was feeling desperate. But before I left the house one evening to pay Bruce another visit, a pair of coppers showed up at my front door. We had a polite discussion about an alleged assault, they listened to my lies about it, and in the end rather firmly suggested it would be in my best interest not to go calling at a particular house in Paddo. Ever.

Fucking Bruce! Never crossed my mind he'd get the police involved.

A COUPLE OF DAYS LATER I got home from work to find a letter from the Treasury Ministry. It was on heavy buff paper resplendent with official seals and signatures, though the typewriter that had been used badly needed a fresh ribbon. As soon as I read it, I went all hollow. I sat down, read it again. The feeling worsened.

"Imagine that, duty for death," Bert said when I told him about the malevolent thing. "You have to pay to die? I can understand paying to live, but they want you to pay to die as well? I think that is a bit much, no?"

What the government was announcing to its loyal rate-paying citizen Harry Hull was that the house he thought he owned free and clear was neither free, nor clear, and would no longer even be his unless he paid up an astonishing sum promptly. They judged the value at way beyond what I reckoned the place was worth, and set the tax at far more than the $16,000 Dad had left in the bank—which was also subject to a bloody tax.

Fuck me stupid, I thought. The government was about to rob me of most of my savings if I wanted to keep my home.

One blow too many. I felt as if I'd been smacked with a tire iron. The world didn't look right, it was wavery, and I was hard put to pay attention to anything for more than a minute or two. My head felt huge, and tender, and like I oughtn't to make any sudden movements or it might just come off and roll down the gutter with me inside it.

In this condition I had to go to work every day like every other man because I wasn't physically sick. But reporting is not a forgiving sort of trade, doesn't allow for bad days or bad moods. If you make a mistake and it gets past the editors and into print, the paper's nabobs take it damn personally and are all for summarily executing the culprit. Especially if they sniff a potential libel suit.

My mistakes weren't of the dangerous sort: 'bats' became 'rats' in one story, which made some snobs in Double Bay who saw them fly under the eaves of their houses look pretty silly. It was easy enough to call it a typo, blame the copy desk.

But the mistakes grew worse, impossible to pawn off on the desk. After about my seventh in five days, I was hauled into the glass-fronted office of the editor. Kennedy was a big fellow who always wore a skinny black tie with white short-sleeve shirts. He had the physical evidence of all my errors spread on the desk before him, and he wasn't looking glad to see me.

"Hull," he said, "you're fucking up."

No shit, I said to myself. Out loud I said, "A couple of slips. Could happen to anybody."

"Afraid it's more than a couple." He pointed to the papers on his desk. "It's beyond belief an experienced man like you could do so poorly. It can't go on like this."

I knew very well it couldn't. You could be fired, union or no union, if you screwed up enough. I was standing there in front of Kennedy and all of a sudden I saw myself out of work, owing all that bloody tax. I saw myself waking up each morning and staring at the ceiling, no reason to get out of bed because I had no job and no place to go. Then I saw the government evicting me for nonpayment of the death duty, and then how and where would I live? I saw just about everything in my battered, meager little existence taken away, and I saw myself swimming out to sea, straight out off Bondi one night, until I couldn't swim another stroke and the black slick water pulled me down.

So I did the right thing: Told the bastard my younger sister, who was pregnant and living with her American husband in Los Angeles, had got killed in a car wreck there just last week.

"Ah, Jesus, Harry," Kennedy said then. "Why the hell didn't you tell me? Or somebody? You should've taken some time off straightaway, not kept on working. Look, forget about all this. Take a holiday, long as you need to, starting right now. Terrible thing. First your dad, and then a bloody tragedy like this. Fuck! I'm really sorry, Harry."

HOLIDAY? The advice I'd once given Dad about putting his head in the oven seemed more appropriate. Felt near unhinged as I moped and even maundered darkly to myself that evening. And then, very late, I decided that maybe the custom of going walkabout was a damn fine thing. Maybe sometimes the only way to deal with events and happenstances that were beyond your powers was to walk away from them, put them far behind you in both time and space. It was a shiftless abo thing to do, or so I'd been led to believe. But right now I was feeling that maybe the black fellas were on to something quite basic.

So next morning before dawn, I threw a few things into Jacko's boot and bolted.

It was purely insane. I drove west for sixteen hours, crossing the Blue Mountains and entering drier, rougher country, then slept at a little hotel with six rooms in a town with an abo name and a population of less than a thousand. Started another twelve-hour drive very early the next day, heading in the general direction of Broken Hill, then turning off the main road into territory every fool knew should be traversed only in a four-wheel drive vehicle with twenty-gallon jerry cans of petrol and water and two spare tires up on a roof rack, not a thirty-five-year-old city car like Jacko. I stopped when I could no longer see any road, any town, any station homesteads, any cattle or sheep, any track, anything at all but red dirt, rocks, spinifex and the biggest sky in the world. I slept on the ground that night wrapped in a couple of old army blankets. If I died there, chances were fair my body would never be found.

I ate beans straight out of the can for breakfast. I loaded a couple of ten-round magazines for Dad's old .303 Enfield and spent most of the day in the shade of Jacko, having a slap at any kangaroo, wild pig or feral goat that wandered into range. Mostly I just heard the blast when I squeezed off, felt the steel buttplate slam into my shoulder, and saw puffs of dust where bullets hit ahead, behind, beyond or before whatever creature I was aiming at. Beans for lunch, beans for dinner, water to drink. In the dark, I turned on Jacko's headlights suddenly a couple of times and fired at the glowing eyes of dingos up on a ridge, but in the morning I didn't see any carcasses. There was a curious red-striped rock outcrop flat as a table about two hundred yards north of where I was camped. I took my empty bean cans and set them up there, and added a couple dozen stones about the same size. Then I spent much of the second day firing at them and missing, clip after clip, until my right shoulder was so sore I couldn't stand the recoil anymore. I held the Enfield by the barrel and slammed the stock as hard as I could against a rock. The wood splintered and broke right off.

Then there was no more sound at all, except a ringing in my ears that wouldn't go away.

The third day it seemed too much trouble to get up from my blankets, to even open a tin of beans. I just stared at Jacko, all dinged up and dusty, and felt nauseated by the sight. Not long before Mum got sick, Dad had picked up the thing—a '49 Red Top taxi with the sign removed from the roof—at a real bargain. The original bright red and yellow paint job had faded enough so that it no longer hurt your eyes. He had meant to restore it, but after Mum went he'd lost all interest.

It sat up on blocks in our back garden for years, was still sitting there when I got back from Fuck Toy. I had to look at that derelict every time I took my therapeutic strolls, finally got tired of its sad uselessness, and started in on it. Dad came home from work one evening and caught me deep in its innards, hood up and pieces of carburetor laid out on a sheet of newspaper on the grass.

"No hope," he laughed. "That bugger's older than you are."

But the next evening he came home with a thick, paper-bound

Holden repair manual, dog-eared and grease-stained. And over the next ten months or so, until I was fit and got my cadetship, working on the Holden with Dad was as regular an event as having a beer on the verandah. We had set out to do it properly, but we fucked up so many things so many times that two of Dad's union mates who were auto maniacs finally took pity on us and pitched in. Every worn-out part was replaced or rebuilt, from the piston rings to the brake drums to the differential gears to the inside sun visors. Every damned inch of it was scrubbed and polished and oiled or waxed. We even sprang for new paint. Dad was brilliant.

"We've got something special here, Harry," he said. "A real rare item. Let's keep it that way." So we had the painters use the original taxi red and yellow. Heads turned all over the city when we took it out for the first long road test. Heads did even now—which made me nervous since Sydney had become the car theft capital of the world. I'd had an elaborate alarm system installed. Still, I always removed the distributor cap whenever I parked it, even in my own back alley.

I'd fucked Jacko royally now, I saw. It looked worse than it had when it was rusting away up on blocks—dents here and there, one headlight broken and a spidery crack in the windshield from flying stones, the paint scratched deeply along the sides, a heavy chrome bumper bent half off. And God knows what I'd busted inside, slamming it through ruts and over rocks.

Toward day's end I spotted a plume of rusty dust spiralling quickly along the western limit of my vision. Some vehicle I couldn't see, with someone inside I didn't know, but no doubt heading somewhere specific with some specific purpose. The sun kept its lazy course for an hour or so after the plume had disappeared. But when it slid beneath the horizon that evening I was amazed and frightened by just how fast that huge bugger really traveled.

So very, very fast. No wonder the world seemed to be spinning out from under me.

Sleepless under a sky black as jewelers' velvet scattered with gleaming gems, I found myself talking out loud to the wheeling stars, crooning into the silence what I ought to have said to the woman of my life but never did. Too fucking late. I'd spent my life being too fucking late. For Lucy, for Dad, for Frank, for everyone and everything.

No more, I swore. I'd make good. With Dad, it would have to be the buggered thing we'd made so well together, side by side. Jacko would shine again. With Frank, whatever it took. With Bert and Alessandra, more care and caution. I'd catch up at the *Herald* with hard work; I'd deal with the taxmen.

Lucy? No hope there, I was sure. Lucy had left a hole in my life. But Dad had carried on with his cheek, and, goddammit, I'd carry on as well, even with a wound that would never entirely close.

Next morning I started the long drive back to Sydney, filthy and stinking after days in the bush without a wash or a change of clothes, weeping yet unaware of that most of the time. I was absolutely determined things would never come to this pass again.

22

Dio! HARRY, YOU OKAY? You look like to hell you been. Smell like it too." Bert was standing at my front door. It was after midnight. I'd not been home more than ten minutes, but he must have heard my car pull up and seen my house lights go on. And there he was, in his pyjamas. "We been worrying like crazy, Harry, the way you just disappear. You okay?"

"Yeah, no fear," I said. Would have given anyone a fright, the sight of me: hair matted, unshaven, coated with red dust from shoes to face, except where tears had made smudgy tracks on my cheeks. And a hollow, haunted look in my eyes I'd caught when I'd glanced at myself in the mirror.

Bert didn't seem real convinced by my reply, so I invited him into the kitchen and opened two beers.

"You sure you all right, Harry?" Bert asked after we'd taken a couple of swallows each. I was so tired I spewed out the whole story, even the humiliating bits about the Enfield and weeping. Bert's expression had changed from worried to relieved by the time I finished the tale.

"You done a good thing, I think. Crazy and dangerous, but good," he said, patting me on the shoulder as he rose to leave. "Now you need a shower and a good sleep. We talk more tomorrow, right?"

The world seemed perfectly normal next morning. Too normal, if you take my meaning; being home, everything exactly as I'd left it, felt somehow more dreamlike than real.

"You right to give it up for now with Lucy," Bert said. We were walking down Parramatta Road. For years, one Saturday every month, we'd been going down there together for a trim by Jimmy, a friendly but credulous old bloke who still had an ancient red and white striped barber's pole in front of his shop. It was always a bit of fun.

Bert got Jimmy snapping at his own tail like a mad rat terrier by telling him that the English weren't really English at all, but Germans interbred with Frenchified Vikings.

"Never was so," Jimmy snorted. I was glad it was Umberto in the chair and not me, because those scissors were clicking at an alarming rate. "What about Merrie Olde England, blokes like Robin Hood and so forth? We know that's true, it's in all the books."

"It's in the books, yes," Bert said. "But who were the Normans? Vikings who'd lived in France a long time. Who was Robin Hood? A *Saxon*. Saxons from Germany, Jimmy. Who was the king Robin Hood was loyal to, Jimmy?"

"Why, King Richard the Lionhearted, as every schoolboy knows," Jimmy said. "As English as the longbow and the Magna Carta."

"Oh, Jimmy, I have to tell you one thing," Bert said. "This King Richard, he was only in England twice in his life, for a few months only. The rest was all crusading, understand? And he spoke no English at all. French and German only."

"Ah, you're just having me on now, I know that," Jimmy said. "Otherwise, why would Richard have an English name?"

"Good point, Jimmy," Bert said, winking at me. "I guess you have got me there."

Baiting Jimmy always seemed to put Bert in an elevated mood, as if the survival of a man so gullible was proof that the world was basically benign. Jimmy had the opposite effect on me, I must say. But Bert's mind was concentrated after we left the barber shop. He was turning over my confessions so intently that we almost overshot Woolworth's before he remembered he had to pick up a few things Alice needed for the kitchen.

"I would say, Harry, when a man can do no more, he should give up and move on. I think you see this on your trip," he said as we pushed open the glass doors and entered the store. There was a kind of burnt caramel smell wafting over from the lunch counter, along with the familiar aroma of beans on toast.

"Yeah," I said. "The real difficult bit, though, is that it's my kid, too."

"Oh, so you're finally sure now it don't belong to Mel Gibson or someone?" he said. "You have become certain of this?"

"That joke was only funny once, Bert."

"Right. Sorry," he said. "The big thing, Lucy's going to have your child. For now, you got to give it up in your mind, much as you can. Don't hope for nothing."

He paused. "But Harry, don't forget, either. It's not certain you will never hear from her again."

"I've got to live as if it is certain."

"Yes, this is the best way. Lucy, she's not playing some kind of game. She's not saying 'chase me, chase me' like a little kid. My bet is that if you did find her, she would not be glad. She got to find you again—if she wants to."

We went up and down the aisles, threading our way between women armed with the red wire baskets the store provided for serious shoppers. When we reached the area Bert was hunting for, he picked up a gingham apron and held it before him as if he were trying it on. "That looks lovely, dear," said a chubby old thing whose basket was stuffed with cellophane bags of gummy bears and other candies, along with some twists of acrylic yarn in gaudy colors and several pairs of knitting needles.

"Do you think it will do?" Bert said to her.

"Oh yes, dear, I'm sure it will. It's lovely gingham, it is," she said.

Bert folded the apron and draped it over his arm. Then he picked up a bunch of terry dish towels and draped them, too. We moved over an aisle, where he selected a slotted serving spoon, an aluminum soup ladle, a vegetable peeler. Then we headed up front to the cashier stations. There was a narrow-faced, thin-lipped Scotch-Irish type behind the machine, her dirty blond hair in a pony tail. Bert gave her a big smile. "Just these things, miss," he said.

"Not married then, are ya?" the girl said. "Don't see too many men buying aprons and so on."

"I have a lovely wife, miss. I'm lucky there," Bert said. "These are for my friend here, who lives all by himself and is quite a good cook."

"Don't say?" She eyed me in a way that made me uncomfortable. Her top front teeth were edging out over her lower lip. "What's his specialty?"

"Rissoles. Oh yes, it's true," Bert said. "But I will tell you one thing, miss. He needs a wife. For all the other things."

"Bloody hell," I said.

"Don't get all bothered," the girl said, popping her gum at me and ringing up Bert's purchase. "Your friend here is kind of cute, but I don't reckon you're my type at all."

Bert started laughing as he paid and kept laughing when we were outside. I said I didn't think it was all that funny, putting me on the spot like that.

"It's not you, Harry. It is the gum, though really it is not such a humorous thing," Bert said. In his town after the war, when he was about five or six, the occupying troops were mainly young Americans. The people of the town had nothing, not enough to eat most of the time. The young girls started to go out with the soldiers, but most of them were shy about it and careful not to be too public with their affairs. Yet many gave themselves away by chewing gum, which along with canned foods and powdered milk the Americans had in abundance and handed out in quantities to their girlfriends and to any little children they encountered.

"You see a girl older than sixteen or so chewing gum, you knew straightaway she had taken a soldier for a lover," Bert said.

"Little sluts," I said.

"No, Harry, even good girls did this. They were very hungry. You will do a lot when you're very hungry that you never dream of doing when there is food," Bert said. "Many people in the town understand this. They don't hold it against the girls. But those who got pregnant, they had a hard time I would say, because then their soldier would not want to know them. And so all the food, the gum disappears for them."

And for a moment I saw Phong in her shabby hut, saying, "Au-see numbah one," as she slipped out of her pyjamas. I remembered sometimes hearing a baby crying on the other side of the beaded curtain that divided the hut into two rooms, and the high-pitched singsong of the old mama-san who must have been Phong's mother.

AS WE NEARED THE HOUSE, I saw Alice standing on the verandah with her arms folded under her bosom, looking up and down the street. She seemed agitated, shifting her weight from one leg to the other. When she spotted us she hurried down the steps and trotted over, launching some very fast Italian even before she reached us. Bert looked perplexed when she'd finished.

"Something very odd, Harry," he said, his voice about half an octave deeper than usual. "She says two men, big rough types even though they are wearing suits, come to the house asking for Alfredo. She tells them he don't live here, they push their way in, and one of them backs her against the wall, not touching her but standing very close, while the other goes quickly and looks in all the rooms of the house. Naturally they don't find Alfredo, so they leave."

Little Alf? Hadn't seen his face, or given the ratbag much thought, for ages. I knew he was still about, though. His Falcon made brief stops next door to pick Alice up or drop her off, early and late most evenings.

"Alf up to no good, is he?" I said. "But this doesn't sound like coppers to me."

"Here is the strange part, Harry," Umberto said, shaking his head. "They tell Alessandra to say to Alfredo that the Chinaman wants to see him, straightaway."

"Weren't cops, then," I said.

"Why Chinaman? Who is this Chinaman, Alessandra?" Bert said.

"Why you asking me?" she snapped. "I don't know, who ever heard of this before? I'm thinking at first, could they be some friends of Alfredo's?"

"Peculiar friends," I said. "None of my mates would come calling in quite that way."

All at once she started to cry, a powerful but silent gush of tears she seemed scarcely aware of. Her eyes just overflowed. "Can't be friends, I know this by the way they are," she said. "I'm scared a little bit. What do these people want?"

Bert put his arm around her and we began walking up to the house. "Most likely it's nothing, a mistake or something," Bert said. "Don't you worry."

"How not to worry? Umberto, you stupid," she said. "These men were not nice men. Like mafiosi. And just me here with the girls? I am frightened."

"Where's Alf call home these days?" I asked.

"He live down in Leichhardt. He work at this new place in Double Bay, Sabotino. Sometime we stop for drinks after work," Alessandra said.

That was news. I'd assumed he was still working with Alice at Il Pelicano. Bert's eyebrows moved a fraction. Might be news to him, too.

"I'll see what I can find out," I told her.

Umberto met me Monday after work at The Drowned Man, and when Les came in we took him aside and told him what had happened.

"The Chinaman?" he said. "Your Alf picks lovely company."

"Right, Les. What's the story?" I said.

"This Alf likes to have a flutter on the dogs and horses, does he?" Les said.

"Maybe he bet a little here, a little there. Just for the amusement," Bert said.

"Maybe he bet a lot here and a lot more there," Les said, mimicking Bert. "And maybe he lose it all, no? That's the only reason a cultivated sporting gentleman like the Chinaman would send his bruisers calling at your house, squire."

"Bookmaker, is he?" I said.

"Bookmaker?" Bert said.

"A bloke who takes bets, Bert," I said. "They're touchy, as a class, about being paid off promptly when you lose. Alfredo must owe this one a bit of money."

"A *lot* of money," Les said. "Otherwise, as noted before, you wouldn't have had your bruisers."

"*Dío*," Bert said.

Sydney wasn't New York, you weren't likely to wind up at the bottom of the Harbour with your feet encased in cement blocks. But you might earn a scar or two, maybe a limp that would stay with you ever after, and of course you would pay. What was before Alfredo was not a cheerful prospect, though I really didn't much care what happened to him except how it affected Bert and Alice and the kids.

That, I realized, concerned me a very, very great deal.

Turned out Alf had rung Alessandra while Les and Bert and I were at the pub. He told her he was hiding out for a while with a friend of his in Redfern, but that it would be better if she did not know exactly where.

214

No, he couldn't say when he'd be back. Yes, he had lost a wager or two on the greyhounds and the horses. He planned to raise the money from some friends.

"Not likely," Bert said on hearing all this when we got to his house that evening. "Alfredo, well, you have seen how he is with people, Harry. Who is going to give him money? I don't think many."

Alessandra glanced at me sideways quickly and then looked hard at her husband, as if she were judging him, weighing out the situation. She began tapping the table rapidly with the fingernails of her left hand while Bert poured us each a glass of wine.

"He needs the money, we will help too," she said finally. "That's the way of it, Umberto."

"Give money for something like this? Stupid idea, for sure. Yes, Harry?"

"Well," I said, sipping wine, not keen to be in the middle of what seemed to be shaping up as a battle. "Generally a man who gets himself into a mess like this doesn't drag his friends into it. He gets out of it on his own hook."

Alice glared at me, but said nothing.

"That should be the way of it," Bert said. "Anyway, this is not like a friend who gets ill or something. Then of course you do everything you can, not even thinking. Alfredo, he's our boarder, he drive Alessandra to work, once in a while we invite him for something. But more, how to say, an acquaintance? Not a close friend. No."

Alice's fingernails upped the tempo of the tattoo they were beating. I did not need to look at her; I could feel her glare still. I reckoned it was time for me to bow out.

"Might be best to just sit tight for a bit. I don't think anybody will come bothering you here again," I said.

I finished my wine in one long pull, said goodnight. And, soon as I was inside my house, promptly rang Les and asked him to check with his connections, see if he could get any details about Alf's problem with the Chinaman.

LES STROLLED OVER in the newsroom Wednesday morning and reported what he had learned. Ratbag Alf was in very deep indeed; he owed the Chinaman some $8,000 and change. The Chinaman was going to have that or Alf's balls. Soon, too. I phoned Bert at his shop, passed on the news.

Very late Friday evening, Bert and Alice came tapping at my door. It was a soft night, the house seemed close, so we sat out on the verandah. There was a hazy halo around the moon; it felt like rain was on the way. We couldn't see each other's faces.

"So, Harry. How do we do with this debt?" Alice started right in. She spoke quietly, but there was nothing the least bit tentative in her tone.

"Why, Alf's got to pay up quick, simple as that," I said. "If he wants to stay in one piece."

"We got the money, Harry," she said. That was a bit of a shock. "So how do we pay?"

"Fuck all!" Bert growled. He sounded disgusted, but resigned.

"Alfredo managed to raise it? His mates pitched in, did they?" I asked.

"Some, goddamn," Bert said. "And mainly someone who should not."

"Never mind him, Harry," Alice said, as if her husband was merely a pesky child she wished would shut up. "We got the money."

"From the biscuit tin, from under the mattress, however you call it," Bert snorted then.

"I tell you again, Umberto. It is my money. I earned it," Alice said sharply.

Oh shit, I thought. Here comes a buster.

"For sure it is yours," Bert said. "You slave for years, you save as much you can. But I am supposed to say nothing when you are throwing it away?"

"Not throwing away. Alfredo, he will pay back, I know this," Alice said.

"What a hope," I muttered, thinking of the rift Alice's decision had ripped open between her and Bert. But she took it another way.

"Harry, no offense, but you don't know Alfredo. He will give all of it back. Just tell me how to pay? Alfredo, he afraid to go himself."

"Yeah, Alf would be that," I said, liking the shitheap even less now than I had before. I was also wishing we could just mail the money or something, but I knew there was a certain protocol in these matters. Les could steer me in the right direction, but I was hoping maybe Frank might have some tips on how to behave during the handover. "I'll take care of it."

"Bah!" Bert said, standing up.

Alice passed me a bulging paper bag she must have been clutching the whole time. "Thank you, Harry," she said. Then she and Bert went back to their place. Inside, I opened the bag, which looked like it had carried somebody's lunch once or twice already. What I saw was a heap of crinkled, soiled and worn bills, all denominations from smallest to largest. I dumped the cash on my kitchen table, started counting. It took some time, but there it was: $8,275. Bloody hell.

23

CHINAMAN?" FRANK SAID when I went to see him in Bondi next day and explained my difficulty. "Gambling fella? Employs a few largish blokes to run errands? It would have to be the Chink, then."

"You know this Chinaman?" I asked.

"Oh, for maybe forty years off and on, I reckon," he grinned. "He ain't Chinese. He's a raw old Aussie who spent a lot of time in Hong Kong. Nasty piece of work when he wants to be."

"Oh shit," I said.

"No fear," Frank laughed. "C'mon, Harry. Drive me over to his place right now and we'll get this business settled in a jiff."

Old Frank. Still true blue. He stepped right in once more and took care of things. I was feeling damned relieved when I met Bert at The Drowned Man after work Monday and reported the deed done. Bert did not exactly seem pleased to know it. He was testy.

"To help a friend in trouble, yes, this you must do," he said, a bitter undertone in his voice. "But to risk so much what you work so hard for, to risk what you save for the future, for some man so stupid he lose all his money gambling?

"I tell you, Harry, this I don't understand," he went on. "This is not like Alessandra. She pinch every penny so we have something for the girls. She grudge every dollar we got to spend. And now she throws so much away?"

"So why did you let her?"

"Easy to say no to her. Not so easy to stop her, once she makes her mind up. She claim what she lends is only a little part of what she have anyway," Bert said, waving his hands about.

"How much did she chip in, if you don't mind my asking?"

"This tip money, Harry, is black money. Can't put it in a bank. No records, no taxes. So she keep it hidden someplace in the house, only she knows where. She put up about $2,000, maybe a little more. She say she still have four, five times that much. How could she get so much? Impossible, I think."

I did some quick reckoning in my head, knowing what a dinner tab at Il Pelicano could be, how long she'd worked there, how smooth she was with customers. "Well, Bert," I concluded, "it's more than possible. She could easily have tucked away that much, or more even. It'd depend on your budget and how you split it between you."

"To live, we are spending everything I make, all of Alessandra's salary, and some bit of her tips. She says one-quarter."

"Yeah, well she could very easily have $10,000 or $12,000 or even $15,000 under the mattress or wherever."

"You think that much?"

"Oh, for sure. Place like Il Pelicano? The customers are pretty generous with gratuities."

"Even so, this I don't like. Not one bit. Camilla, she got to start school soon. Costs a lot. Fabrizia, we are hoping she will go to university one day. Money saved, it should stay saved for these things."

"Since it's under the mattress and not earning bank interest anyway, reckon the only real question is will Alfredo make good?" I said. "Or is it money down the drain?"

"Ah, I don't know, Harry. Maybe, maybe not," he said. "Alessandra, she's not worried. She swears she knows Alfredo pay her back. But if he doesn't, what's she going to do, I ask her? She just smiles, says no worries."

"He doesn't pay, I'll handle that for you. You've got my promise." Probably an empty one, but I wanted to cheer Bert up a bit.

Alice's contribution and my go at being a bagman didn't save Alf entirely anyway. A broken nose and a broken right arm, that's what Alf got from the Chink's crushers, Alice told me tearfully a few weeks later. For late payment, I reckoned, and about what he deserved. But Alessandra weeping over that bruised cane toad? Not a performance I cared for. Not what Umberto deserved.

BUT I DID NOT DWELL on it. I was feeling much too battered myself about then. I had started my dealings with the taxmen over the house. It got pretty nasty right at the start, them talking to me as if I were some sort of criminal. Bert had a few wise words for me, though.

"Whatever you do, Harry, don't lose your temper," he warned. "They want you to lose your temper. They try so hard to make you do it, but if you do they punish you. They find every sort of diabolical way to make you suffer. And call it all 'regulations.' This I have seen in Italy. Same in every country I think, these bloody bureaucrats."

I did keep a leash on my temper, difficult as that was. I believe that saved me from a worse thumping, and any cash penalties. Didn't matter much, since in the end I had to pay up in fucking full.

And so did Bert, in another way and in endless installments. He took his own advice at home, you see. Bad mistake, I think, since a marriage isn't a negotiation with taxmen. Maybe one great explosion of rage, one huge angry rant, would have shaken up Alice severely and cleared Alf out of their lives for good. But Bert gave it a miss.

It wasn't long before Alf's Falcon started showing up again most evenings in front of Bert's house. And Alice, I noticed soon enough, was strutting around like a general who'd won a famous victory, snapping out orders and running the household just as she pleased, never minding Bert's wishes or sensibilities.

It was almost as if there were two families living in that house now: Bert and the kids being one, and Alice all to herself. There was a friction in the air when Alessandra was around, a clipped and gritty quality to necessary everyday exchanges. Not always, but too often, in my view. She'd tell Bert exactly what to buy at the grocery store, what to take to the dry cleaner's, which bills to pay in what order. If he erred in any little way, forgetting the eggs or something, she'd call him an idiot, even in front of the kids. And it got uglier sometimes.

"You so clumsy and stupid, like your papa," Alice snapped at poor Camilla once when the kid accidentally knocked over her glass of fruit juice.

Fabrizia especially felt and did not like the grating and strife. Any bit of contention at all, and she'd jump to Bert's side, pulling me along with her if I was present and ending every bit of lip she gave her mum with "Right, Harry?"

I was crazy about her, but this was awkward.

It got so I'd only stop over on evenings when Alice was off at work. Usually I'd find Bert in the kitchen making some little treat or other for the little ones to eat, or just playing with them. Fabrizia, as ever, was chatty as a budgie. She and her dad would have long conversations about the damnedest things, such as why a candle flame is mostly yellow while the flames on the gas rings are mostly blue. Bert would patiently go into the ratios between gas and air, insofar as he understood how they affected the colors, and the difference between that and the open burning of a waxed wick. Camilla had turned into a big kid for her age, with sturdy arms and legs and blond hair and tawny eyes. But she was still so quiet and withdrawn. At best, she would cast me those shy glances, laugh when I grinned at her.

Then, one night, she surprised the hell out of me by actually clambering up to sit on my lap, and asking to be cuddled. I was glad to do just that.

AND SOMEWHERE IN AUSTRALIA there was a woman who would pretty soon be bearing my own child. Thinking hard on that and what I was seeing next door, once in a while I'd feel myself on the verge of understanding how everything between people shifts and sways and changes. How the proximate causes are a sham, the true causes mostly as invisible as the wind. How there never seems to be any going back once a change has happened. I sometimes felt I was about to be enlightened.

Lucy was on my mind all the time. I wanted badly to comprehend the why of her going. I didn't notice when my thinking slipped more and more into pure reminiscence, or that most of the memories were from our first couple of years together, and almost none from the last. I suppose that's the way memory works. It's got its own filter, to protect you. Except it often breaks down at night, when you're really helpless and the dreams come. I've known men who haven't had an uninterrupted night's sleep in forty years. But if the conversation ever came around to the war, you'd find their memories sparse and arid, nothing to jerk you awake in the middle of the night, heart jumping.

A few weeks before Christmas, in '82, half a year or more since she'd flitted out of sight, Lucy surfaced in Cairns, a scrubby town on the north Queensland coast. I had a letter from her, with that postmark. I still have the thing, stashed away with a few important papers in a tin box not unlike the one Dad had, and maybe someday someone will puzzle over it and wonder if the stuff in the box is all there is to show I'd lived a life. It was pretty direct, Lucy's letter:

Harry,

It's a girl! Don't reckon you'd bother, but if you did fly up to see her you wouldn't see a thing, because we're moving on.

Except for a bit of a belly and some extra size to my tits, you'd never know I'm a new mother.

I'm certain you're cross, Harry, and you've some right to be, but don't be if you can help it. Put it away in a drawer, and get on with your life. You can have a good one. It doesn't matter that some of us aren't meant to marry and raise a family. I know I'm not. I don't think you are either.

I know if I'd let you, we'd have done it anyway. There's a pattern, you see, and almost nobody breaks it because it seems easier at the time of decision to just go along with the way things have always been done. It isn't easier later on, though. It's much more difficult, in the long run, trying to fit yourself into a situation which you don't fit and can't ever, really.

I still like you better than anyone else I know, but I don't see us living in the same house day and night, with little Harrys and Lucys running around. I don't see me able to cope, and I don't see you able to tolerate it.

I got a room in a boarding house here and a landlady who went real sweet and easy once I told her my husband was off mining uranium at Rum Jungle (and then paid her five months in advance!). Cairns is an odd sort of place, low mountains all around thick with rainforest. Sometimes the tops are up in the clouds, or maybe it's better to say the clouds are sometimes so low they cover the tops of the mountains. It's hot and it's damp, you get mildew in your shoes practically overnight if you're not careful.

There's lots of birds around too, big flocks of rosellas in the trees. And just at sunset every night this amazing horde of fruit bats come out of wherever they hide all day and fly over the town toward wherever they're going to feed all night.

The funny thing is the sea. It's not like it is around Sydney. At high tide you walk along the esplanade and the sea's right up to it but there are no waves at all, or nothing we'd call waves at Bondi or Whale. A few hours later when the tide's out, there's no sea at all, just mud flats almost to the horizon, except for the narrow little channel that leads to the wharves. Mobs of white pelicans stand around in the mud, preening themselves. I don't know how they stay so clean.

I've got enough left of my savings to last some months. After that I'll have to go back to work. Shouldn't be hard to find a post. But I guess I'll decide where when I have to. It doesn't seem such a difficult thing anymore.

I'm sad as hell about all this, Harry. Maybe you are, too. But we'll keep it to ourselves, won't we? And never let even a bit of misery touch this sunny little angel of ours. I'll stay strong. You stay strong.

See you when I see you, cobber.

your L.

I flew up to Cairns the next morning, and started searching. I took the local phone book, every tourist brochure in sight, the classified ad pages from the newspaper, and made a list of every hotel, boarding house, hostel and private home with rooms to let I could find. I spent four days going round to every place on my list, carrying a photo of Lucy. In between visits to places she might have lodged, I bought scads of things at the chemist's and other shops I reckoned she would have had to patronize, just to ingratiate myself with the help. Made myself very matey with a half-dozen newsagents and at least as many taxi drivers.

Hung around the hospital, noted a couple of pubs where the nurses seemed to congregate when they came off shift. Bought and drank too many beers trying to chat up a lot of them. Everywhere I used the story Lucy herself had provided: said I was just in from half a year working at Rum Jungle, expecting to meet my wife, who had stayed here, pregnant. And must have missed the telegram she'd sent out there after she'd had the baby and left Cairns.

"It's terrible," I'd tell anyone who'd listen. "She's probably shooting off wires to Rum Jungle, getting no response 'cause I'm here, and thinking I got killed in an accident or something. I'm wiring her folks and friends, hoping they've heard from her and know where she is. Yeah, it'll probably be right in a couple of days. But for the moment we've bloody lost each other! Pretty stupid, I know. And even a few days is too long when you're dying to see your new baby, right?"

Maybe I just didn't have the look of a uranium miner. The clerks and managers of the hotels brushed me right off, most of the boarding house owners seemed suspicious and were tight-lipped—although I felt sure I caught a glimpse of recognition in the narrowed eyes of one wiry old bird when I showed Lucy's photo, even as she denied ever renting her a room. A couple of taxi drivers and one news agent recognized her, but claimed they'd never got her name, had no idea where she might be. One of the nurses remembered there had been a Baby Whitmoor in the newborns' room, a girl. But she hadn't seen the mother.

Spent a day at the airport then, trying every stewardess from Ansett and Qantas who was coming or going. Nothing. I got desperate. Stupidly tried to bribe the ticket agents to let me see recent passenger lists. I wound up being taken back to town in the back of a police car and questioned at the station for an hour or so before the coppers turned me loose, with the clearest suggestion that I ought to leave off making a public nuisance of myself and leave Cairns damn smartly. Unless I enjoyed the prospect of spending more time with them.

So I flew back to Sydney without a single bloody clue.

But haunted. My little girl, heart beating and breathing the free air of the world, bunching her fists, wha-wha-wha-ing the way babies do. Then suddenly staring up with those enormous baby eyes that can't even focus yet, they're so new, and maybe smiling at me anyway.

My child. And not a chance in hell of me picking her up and cradling the tiny little bundle in my arms, studying her features to see if she looked at least a bit like me, or was all Lucy.

My baby. And I did not even know her name, let alone the smell of her, the amazing silky feel of her skin.

She was Valentine to me, no matter what Lucy was calling her. She was with me night and day, in the clearest part of my mind. And she never left me, not even in my deepest dreams.

24

FRANK WAS FIRM, refused to be moved. He told me to cork it, quit feeling sorry for myself, face that I'd made a bloody mess of my life, and get on with having another go at it. A more explicit form of what Lucy had suggested in her letter. Hard to hear, harder to do.

So all summer it was poor Bert who patiently endured torrents of woeful whingeing about my lost kid, my broken lonely heart, my despair. He never complained, seemed sympathetic for quite a while, and genuinely worried about my mental state. "Harry," he said, "I am thinking this Cairns business, it sucks out all your spirit."

But not very long after that he told me, in as soft a way as his command of English would allow, that I was acting like a bloody useless wanker. "Harry, I know you thinking 'hah, easy for Umberto to talk, he got his girls.'

"But Harry, I say this anyway. Most important thing a man can know is when to admit what's done is done, okay, now I got to get on with whatever's next."

But in my current sorry state, Bert felt sure, I'd never manage even a one-off root with a silly little girl-hack, let alone a worthwhile affair with a worthwhile woman.

And that, in his opinion, was what I most needed to get myself and my life moving again.

IT SEEMED ONLY FABRIZIA hadn't given up on me. Just after the start of the autumn term in February, she came scratching at my door and pleaded with me to come along to a speech night at St. Boniface.

"Think I'll give this one a miss," I told her. "Maybe another time."

"C'mon, Harry," she said, smile stretched all the way across her pie face, but looking on the verge of tears. "Please? You've got to come. Please? We're mates, aren't we?"

No-hoper that I was, I still couldn't let my little mate down, could I? And it would be Camilla's very first time on stage as well. But when Bert and I settled into our seats—amidst the mob of well-dressed parents who, I reckoned, would really rather have been anywhere else but were putting duty first, and congratulating themselves for it—I was furious and fuming.

Alessandra hadn't bothered to skip work for Camilla's debut.

Camilla's class put on some little play about the gum-nut kids. The wooden, awkward way she moved through her role was distressing. She looked down at her feet as she mumbled her few lines, while the other kids were chirpy and smiling in their turns. And when the group did a simple dance, Camilla was a beat or more behind all the rest. But she was first to run off the stage at the finish. Bert looked very solemn, though he said nothing.

Fabrizia and her cohorts gave speeches on the theme "What I Love About Australia." All I heard was jingo garbage cribbed from our enormous stock of songs and books that never let facts sully rousing patriotic sentiment. Made my eyes glaze.

I perked up when Fabrizia made the quite original and almost scandalous move of beginning with an outline of all the shameful things about Aussie history, starting with the shooting of abos out of hand and the floggings of convicts when the First Fleet arrived in Sydney Cove in 1788. Then she made what seemed to me an astonishing conceptual leap for a kid, positing the idea that a cruel beginning, provided we never forgot it, insured a better future for all Aussies, for freedoms hard-won would never be easily given up. And wasn't the fact that she, a New Australian, could stand up and say all this the proof of it?

The applause when she finished was kind of raggedy; she'd confused the hell out of the adults. The next girl droned on for her three minutes like a right-wing pol at election time. My eyes began to glaze again.

Then I noticed Miss Moon sitting just a couple of rows in front of me, and forgot all about the boring prattle. I started watching the back of her head, getting a glimpse of a partial profile every time she turned to say a word to the nun on her right. She had the best hair, thick and glossy auburn, cut blunt so it hung a couple of inches above her shoulders. It swung all together when she moved her head. I had a wicked thought or two, imagining what that hair must feel like. Not just to the hand, but brushing across some other expanses of skin.

After the show I watched her move around the room talking to the parents. She had such a small face, and small features. It was almost a child's face on a woman's body, and at first I couldn't decide whether it looked a bit odd or very erotic. My mind skittered from one to the other, afraid to come down firmly on the side of erotic, but always drawn back that way after a brief stay with odd. Then she came up to speak to Bert and the kids.

"Mr. Hull," she said, smiling at me and shaking my hand after greeting them. "You're becoming as regular as a parent here."

I'd only been three or four times last year, we'd done little more than nod hello to one another after each show, so right away I attached some extra meaning to the comment. Made it in my mind a sort of "Really glad to see you, mate." Then instantly dismissed the notion as an over-hopeful idiocy.

"You know, Miss Moon, if anything ever happened to me, I feel Harry would be like a father to my girls, for sure," Bert said, patting me on the shoulder.

"Nothing's going to happen to you," I said. Bloody embarrassing, Bert could be.

"I certainly hope not," Miss Moon said.

"Oh, I'm hoping the same of course. But you never know, after all," Bert said, beaming down at her, Fabrizia on one side with her hands on her hips, Camilla sort of hiding behind my legs.

"Camilla, what a fine gum nut you were," Miss Moon said. The kid ducked her head, so her hair screened her face. It was painful to watch.

"What about my speech?" Fabrizia demanded, her lower lip edging out toward what might develop into a mean pout if she didn't get the an-swer she wanted.

"Bold. Very original. A very good speech indeed," Miss Moon smiled. She did look like a kid herself, I concluded.

Then Bert, suddenly but so smoothly most of the surprise was muted, invited Miss Moon to come have tea one afternoon. She shied, her smile stiffening up a bit. He just glided on, saying it would be a great favor to him to have a quiet chat, he was interested in the girls' educa-tion, wanted to know the latest theories and methods, all the while look-ing as kind and sincere as could be. He said, why not Saturday?

Miss Moon hesitated. I believe she was weighing whether tea would be considered by her superiors a proper part of parent-teacher relations, especially now that Fabrizia was no longer in her class. But then she grinned, said she'd be delighted, and just for a moment looked right at me. Hold on, I thought, this has got nothing to do with you, Harry. It's all between Bert and Miss Moon. He's got his eye on her. She knows it, too, and isn't displeased by the attention, for he's a handsome man even if he is mostly bald. Bert, you old rogue, for shame, I thought. Your own daughter's former teacher.

Lying in bed that night, sleep elusive as always, I slipped into a little fantasy involving Miss Moon. It was much better than the usual painful brooding, even when it ended with Bert in the picture, not me. Must have been close to one when I heard a car pull up.

I peered out my window. Alf's Falcon, lights out. Then flicking on, and Alice walking carelessly from the car to her front door.

SATURDAY CAME. I slept in late. I ate a bit of lunch and had a beer, straightened up the kitchen afterward, did some fairly careless light cleaning and dusting around the house. Then I put on a pair of khakis and a T-shirt and brooded about the house for a while. None of the books I pulled off the shelves seemed worth going on with after I'd read the first couple of pages. None of my music tapes had any attraction. Finally I went out in the back garden and started hosing down Jacko, though I'd given the car the full treatment and a coat of wax just the weekend before. I got absorbed for a while in considering how the water seemed to leave the hose in a solid stream but pretty quickly formed an arc of distinct droplets, which gleamed with refracted sunlight. By directing the hose at a certain angle, I found I could create a small rainbow. Then I heard "G'day, Harry" piped at me, and saw Fabrizia's face peering over the fence.

"How ya going?" I called back.

"Going to tea in an hour or so with Miss Moon." She grimaced. "You better dry Jacko and put on a shirt."

"What for?"

"So we can go to tea, what else?" She grimaced again. Clearly tea with a teacher wasn't her idea of a great Saturday afternoon. "Are we taking Jacko or not?"

"Didn't know I was invited."

"Aw Harry, don't be a bludger."

"Well I didn't."

"Well, you were, you bloody well know that, and you better come. Papa's expecting you. You're not thinking of sticking me with him and Camilla and Miss Moon, are you? That'd be mean, Harry. You can't not come."

"Oh can't I not?" I grinned, turning the hose in her direction. The arc of water hit the base of the fence, but she ducked anyway.

"Bloody hell, Harry!" I heard. "Drongo!"

"Now miss, your mother hears you talking like that, and you're really in for it."

"Won't be! And don't care!" I heard. When I turned the hose back on the car, her face appeared again. "Drongo! Papa said we have to pick up Miss Moon at four-thirty. You better come or I won't forgive you."

So we drove Jacko—Fabrizia insisting on riding up front—down near Sydney University to pick up Miss Moon. She lived in a flat in a big old house with another young teacher. Then we went east to a teahouse just up the hill from Camp Cove, the first little beach on the Harbour side of South Head. It was a hot afternoon but we sat outside, where you could see a little sliver of the waters over the trees. We had Devonshire tea. In short order Camilla had a mustache of clotted cream on her upper lip, and Fabrizia had some jam stains down the front of her blouse that I knew Alice would raise hell about.

Miss Moon looked great in shorts and a cotton shell and sandals, perfectly fresh-faced except for the subtlest bit of makeup around her big dark eyes. I felt awkward, and superfluous. Bert, despite his growly accent, was fluent as a door-to-door salesman who was used to a lot of rejection. He manuevered Miss Moon into telling her whole story: where she'd grown up (Goolgowi, way the hell out on the middle of sheep country), how she'd got into teaching (on a government scholarship to teachers' college), what her theories were (plenty of hard work and praise only when it's earned), and so forth. They became so friendly he was soon teasing her gently, and I could tell she was stifling smart comebacks only because the kids were there.

Camilla wouldn't lift her eyes from some spot on the table where she'd fixed her gaze, and Fabrizia was bored, constantly shifting in her chair and fiddling with forks and empty plates. She began yammering away at me. "Why do they use pigs for money in New Guinea?" she asked.

"Why not?" I said. "They last longer than paper bills."

"How can they make enough of them?"

"They don't need many, since each one's very valuable. Like a hundred-dollar bill."

"So how do they make change?"

"Cowrie shells, I think. Or rocks."

"Kind of difficult, isn't it, carrying them around in your wallet?" she laughed.

"Who needs a wallet when your cash can walk alongside you? A handful of shells, that's no problem either."

We went back and forth that way for a while. Miss Moon would look over at me occasionally. I wasn't sure whether she was inviting me to join the conversation with her and Bert, or thinking I was just a prawn brought along to look after the kiddies while the adults had a natter. Not that it mattered; I had nothing much to say and it was Bert's show, I reckoned. So I just smiled at her. We took her home around six. Umberto went to the door with her, and the roommate was there. I saw him shake hands with both girls, then turn and come toward the car grinning from here to there.

"You look a bit smug, mate," I said. I don't think he noticed the edge in my voice, which was just as well. It had no right to be there.

"Nice girls, Harry, for sure. Very clever, too," he said. "You should see the other. Very pretty. But that Miss Moon, she's adorable, no? She likes you, Harry."

"Christ, Bert," I said. "You're cracked. I didn't exchange two words with her all day."

"Never mind then, Harry, you stubborn man. I told you what I know and you take it any way you want," he said, leaving me feeling like a schoolboy.

"Who's so pretty, Papa?" Fabrizia said.

"Why, Miss Moon's friend," he said. "She has red hair."

"Red? Yuck," Fabrizia said. "So Miss Moon likes Harry, Papa?"

"Oh yes, she does," he said.

"Wait 'til Lucy hears that," Fabrizia said.

"Hears what?" Bert said. "Lots of people like Harry. You do, don't you? Lucy does, but she's gone away. So does Miss Moon. Harry's a likable fellow, no? He's your mate, you always telling me."

"I guess so," Fabrizia said. "Even though he's kind of old. You're really old as the hills aren't you, Harry?"

"Old enough to know swagmen and abos who'll steal you in the night if I tell 'em to," I said. Fabrizia scowled at me in a way that said she was much too grown-up for that shit, but Camilla started crying, only stopped when I took her hand in mine and patted it, saying, "No fear, darls. Harry'll keep the swagmen well away from you."

A FEW MORE speech nights and play nights at the school. A few more words exchanged with Miss Moon, but a lot more looks, the appraising sort. Even I couldn't miss that. Bert just grinned as he gave me Miss Moon's number when I asked for it. I put the strip of paper he'd scrawled it on next to my phone and looked at it for a few days. Then I thought, fuck all, and rang to invite her to a movie. She said sure.

We saw *Breaker Morant*. I took her to an upmarket bar afterward for mango daiquiris or something like them, don't recall exactly. We slagged the Brits for a while, talked of this and that. We only shook hands when I dropped her at home that night.

I rang again a couple of nights later and made a date for dinner. And after about three movies and four dinners, she said straight out as soon as she got into the Holden one evening: "Not your type, then, am I, Harry? That why you haven't taken me to your place and fucked me?"

So we did that, for she definitely was.

Priscilla Moon was ten years younger than me. She had the most wonderful skin, fine-grained as a baby's and a curious pale gold color all over, as if she'd done some very judicious sun-baking in the nude. She was buffed and polished in all the right ways. Even flat on her back, her breasts stood right up and said hello. The contrast between her beautiful body and her features always gave me a jolt that bordered on the perverse. She had hesitated just a breath longer than Lucy had when she saw my scars, but asked right away how I had got them, heard "Vietnam," and then was bloody amazing in bed, lively and inexhaustible.

"Jesus, Priscilla," I panted afterward. "You're a lovely handful. Not quite what I imagined, seeing you at the school."

"Bloody good actress, I am. The nuns think I'm almost one of them," she laughed, sitting up in bed and bouncing a bit. She grabbed my left hand with both of hers and started running it all around her front contours. "If they only knew!"

"Knew what?" I grinned.

"I was the bloody town bike in Goolgowi! Started when I was thirteen." Her laughter was raucous and joyful. "That's why my dad, a champion bludger about as old-fashioned as they make 'em, got me out of there and into boarding school and teachers' college.

"'Course it wasn't that I gave a shit for most of the boys I went with, and mostly it wasn't even any fun. But I reckoned I'd have to do something pretty extreme to get Dad to let me out of that shitheap. You've spent all your life in Sydney, right? Then you can't know how bloody awful a place like Goolgowi can be."

She was pealing with laughter now. "Just say 'Goolgowi' three times, fast. That alone'll drive you fucking mad. Goolgowi! Goolgowi! Gool-gowi!"

She had me nearly convulsed. It was as if she were running her fingers lightly over all my most ticklish spots.

"I think," I gasped, "I'm getting the general picture. Gool-fucking-gowi!"

"And me the town bike! The pathetic young bastards there probably haven't found a replacement even after all these years. I know at least of a couple of them so horny I'd wager next month's wages they're creeping round at night and rooting the prettiest she-sheep they can nail! Gool-fucking-gowi! That's a beaut!"

Miss Moon, in private anyway, said and did everything with exclamation points at the end, laughing all the way. Never met a girl so pleased with herself. She'd set herself only one real rule: back at her shared flat by midnight, sharp. She apparently needed at least that interval to turn herself convincingly back into the dull little wren she had to seem each school day.

Weekends were another tale entirely. Once Priscilla had stripped off whatever she'd arrived in, she was damned reluctant to put a stitch back on until late Sunday night. Her attire for most of the winter consisted of a pair of my socks and a big cashmere throw she'd wrap loosely about herself. When it warmed up in the spring, she woke naked in the mornings, stayed naked all day even if she was doing some cooking, and loved to creep naked out on the verandah late at night, when the street was dark. We even did it out there a few times, Priscilla making a mighty effort to smother the cries she was accustomed to letting out whenever we made love, and if it wasn't for the fleas she'd have had us rolling around on the garden grass. One night, a full moon almost bright as day gilding her skin, she leaped off the verandah after a go and ran all the way around the house four times. Just for the hell of it.

Self-consciousness was simply not within her compass. She was just learning the world, she knew it, and didn't care a whit what anyone thought—at least in my half of the double life she was leading. It was all great fun to her, even public gaffes that would have made a more buttoned-up woman blush with embarrassment.

One evening, for instance, I drove us out toward Ku-ring-gai Chase, down a narrow road that ended in a single-car ferry across a stream south of Bobbin Head, and parked. We were on a splintery little dock thrust into the water, at our back a towering eucalypt forest thick with cicadas protesting our intrusion so vigorously we could hardly hear ourselves speak. Presently this little barge came chugging up out of the black and picked us and two other couples up. Then it chugged maybe a quarter-mile downstream to a building that looked like a Zen monastery. I thought I'd give her a treat by taking her here. It was the latest oh-so-chic restaurant around Sydney, called Berowra Waters. You had to book three weeks in advance to get a table.

Inside, the place seemed monastic, too. Waiters all in black glided around in those Japanese slippers, and the diners were bent over their food as if they were worshiping it. Heads snapped our way when Priscilla took a long look around and blurted, "Bugger me! We're in bean curd heaven, looks like!"

It was hardly that. The menu featured the rare, the strange, and the most costly: medallions of wild red stag from New Zealand; grilled barramundi flown fresh—not frozen as usual—from Queensland; rock lobster; milk-fed veal; Caspian Sea beluga; baby vegetables so delicate they appeared to have been born that very morning. After we'd made our selection, I chose a wine from the Russell Vineyards that was limited to 1,000 bottles a year. Priscilla was taking in everything as best she could in the dim, designer lighting, and laughing and grinning at me.

"Hey, Harry," she whispered. "Gool-fucking-gowi! Where's me bloody steak?"

And I was laughing, too. A few of the other diners, dead serious in their black Versace and Ferre and Krizia outfits, looked at us as if we were seriously disrupting their important meditations on cuisine.

When the waiter presented a plate of barramundi cross-hatched with black grill marks and somehow supported and surrounded by infant vegetables in such intricate structures that they must have had an architect back in the kitchen assisting the chef, Priscilla looked mildly up at him, grinned her never-never grin, and said in a perfectly clear voice: "Are we supposed to just gaze at this like a painting in a museum? Or are we allowed to actually tuck into our tucker, mate?"

I could feel the place freeze. I could see many eyes on us. And I didn't give a fuck. Priscilla snickered and started demolishing the hard-wrought construction on her plate before the waiter, who seemed brained for an instant, backed away soft as silk in his Japanese slippers.

It was more fun than I'd had in years, just watching that girl go. She was a wonder.

SHE WAS SUCH A WONDER that whenever I was in her presence, she managed to do what I'd thought would be impossible: completely clear any thought or image of Lucy and our kid from my mind. She gave me that tremendously exciting feeling of entering an entirely new territory, one where pasts no longer matter, or just vanish. We seemed to fit just right in every way; Priscilla even had a natural smell I loved to inhale. I could nestle my face right into the soft angle where her neck met her collarbone and sniff forever.

I'd see Bert smiling at me some mornings when I left the house. That Cilla and I were on was as open as any open secret could be; she and I just felt it wouldn't be quite right to present ourselves as a couple, because of the kids. And she did have to be careful of her reputation with the nuns at St. Boniface. But Bert was damned pleased for me, that was clear.

Around mid-spring, maybe October of '83, I got the notion I ought to somehow return the favor he'd done me. I was probably way offside, but it was clear that Alice wasn't bringing a whole lot of light into his life. Miss Moon had some unattached friends, but there was one special one that came to my mind: her roommate, the redhead, the one Bert thought was so pretty when he saw her after that first tea. So I did something about it. I arranged for the sixteen-year-old Copely girl who lived up the street to babysit, and got him to join us for dinner one night.

I PICKED THE BLUE WATER GRILL, for it was staffed by young Aussies who I felt sure had no connections with the Italian circles Alice and Alfredo moved in.

Umberto had no idea there'd be another woman with us. We drove together over near the Uni to pick up Miss Moon, and when the redhead came down the walk with her and climbed into the back of the car, he kept whatever surprise he may have felt well-hidden. It always amazed me how that man, who could be so self-effacing and downright timid, invariably rose to occasions that would have sent me into a deep funk. He shot me one grin, and then right away he was rattling on with Miss Moon and the redhead, whose name was Moira.

You'd have thought we'd gone to Italy and Bert was our uncle, intensely concerned with seeing that we had a great time. He discussed the pros and cons of everything on the menu with the girls. He had a way of offering compliments to them that held no hint of wicked intentions but were sure to please and arouse just the same. He kept just the right distance; the praise of their clothes and hair was personal, but not so obviously flirtatious that anyone could feel uncomfortable hearing it. Moira and Cilla were charmed. Even I could see in the way they responded that they thought he was very suave; they liked the way he was careful about his clothes, knew so much about food and wine, and was obviously cultured in a way only stuck-up Aussies were, without being at all stuck-up himself.

For form's sake we dropped both girls off at their home that night at a decent hour. Bert had a smile on his face that was maybe one part all the white wine he'd drunk at dinner and maybe two parts having had such an attractive audience for his talk. He did love to talk. My bet was that the redhead would have hopped into bed with him, married man or not, after one more dinner. I was hoping that's exactly what would happen. When we got home I mentioned casually as I could that I'd be glad to baby-sit the kids if ever he wanted a night out on his own.

He never did. After a week or two Miss Moon told me Moira kept asking why Bert didn't ring up, and couldn't we all do something together? When I put it to him over a beer one evening, he just laughed.

"Ah, Harry, she's a lovely girl for sure. But better for me if I stay away from temptation."

"Maybe giving into temptation'd be the ticket," I said.

"Not like that, Harry. Problems only."

"You wouldn't be the first married man to cut out in secret," I said.

"Where it might lead, that is the problem," Bert said. "Harry, I know you got eyes and ears, but you only guessing. The truth is rougher. Me and Alessandra, every year we lose a little something, not really knowing it goes. Now we got almost nothing between us anymore but some history. For me alone, I leave her tomorrow and never come back, no problem. But I'm afraid."

"Afraid?"

"For the girls," he said. "Not to say their mother is a bad woman. No, never to say that. But she don't know how to handle the girls. Sometimes I'm thinking she don't want to be bothered with them. But she fight like a tiger if I leave and try to take them with me. I love the girls so much, Harry. So I got to stay, for Fabrizia and Camilla."

"Yeah, but just a little fling? Might make life a bit sweeter, Bert."

"Harder only, Harry. Harder to stick it, with a young thing proving to me I'm not finished yet as a man. Takes almost all I got to stand by my little girls at home already. And that I have to do no matter what."

25

AUTUMN TO AUTUMN, then through another winter and into a second spring: all the while life with Cilla sweet and easy beyond my best hopes. We were a couple in her view, and that was that. She'd no interest at all in ever testing the strength of our attachment. Or in pointless probing of each others' psyches. Or in fretting about futures we couldn't know. Or any of the other rough patches lovers always seem to put themselves through. Cilla dwelt only in the now, and centered me firmly beside her there, too.

She made everything sweet and easy, it seemed. I got so firmly back on track at the paper that the nabobs promoted me. Frank stopped looking vaguely dismayed when I'd visit, once it came clear I was no longer coming to whinge or whine about anything. My mateship with Bert became the closest sort of brotherhood, and I loved Camilla and Fabrizia as if they were my own.

Only one bad incident the entire time: a humiliating encounter with Fabrizia, a few months after Cilla and I first got together.

I was sitting on the verandah having a smoke after dinner, feeling perfectly content and complacent in the warm spring air, when Fabrizia slipped through front gate, crossed the garden and took a seat beside me. Her habit, when she'd finished her homework early enough. Usually we'd have a pleasant little chat, but I could sense at once she was carrying a cloud with her this night. She wasn't about to just let it hover darkly there, either.

"Damned if you're my mate anymore, Harry," she'd blurted before I'd even had the chance to ask how she was.

"That's pretty severe, darls. What on earth's brought this on?"

"Rooting Miss Moon, you bastard!" she'd spat, with more true contempt in her tone than I'd thought a pubescent girl could muster.

"Nice bloody talk," I'd laughed. "Where'd you get such an idea, anyway?"

"Isn't funny, Harry. It's disgusting."

"Can't be disgusting if it isn't true."

"Is so true."

"Is not."

"Look, you. It was bad enough all winter, the two of you sneaking into your house Fridays and not leaving 'til Sundays. You're such a drongo if you think nobody noticed. Been hearing things for a long while some weeknights, too. And now I've seen it with my own eyes! Out my bedroom window! The two of you, here on the verandah, when you think everybody's asleep. And Miss Moon running starkers round your garden!"

That had knocked me back a bit. Shit, what a thing for a kid to have witnessed. "Now, hold on a minute, mate," I'd begun, rampaging through my brain for any path out of this I could find.

"Not your mate," she'd said. The lip was out, the mean pout full on.

"You've had sex education, haven't you? Well . . ."

"At St. Boniface? What a hope. But I don't need any, what with you and Miss Moon giving live demonstrations."

"Fabrizia, listen . . ."

"You shouldn't have done it. My own teacher!"

"Former teacher, Fabrizia. And a grown-up, a woman. Men and women get together sometimes. It's the way of the world. Miss Moon's not a kid or anything."

"What's that got to do with it? Two girls in the form just ahead of mine have already done it."

"A pair of fourteen-year-olds? Don't believe it. They're having you on."

"Yeah? Then how come what they described is exactly what I've seen you and that bitch Miss Moon up to?"

"Ah, you never saw a thing. In the middle of the night? On a verandah with a nice wide roof? You must have been dreaming."

"Come up to my bedroom, Harry, and have a look at the view. You'll be fucking shocked, what you can see."

What I'd seen, finally, was that poor little Fabrizia felt betrayed, with jealousy mixed in to make it more painful. She was just at that ungainly age when hormones start their disturbing work, and utterly impossible crushes suddenly seem not so far from the realm of possibility after all, if the years can just pass fast enough.

That she might have such a crush on me had made me smile a little, until I remembered how awful these things can be. I'd had one myself at thirteen, incredible fantasies about—who else?—my English teacher, who was twenty-three at the time. I'm not sure she was even very pretty, only fully developed. I used to lie in bed many a night with the clearest vision that when I got to be seventeen or eighteen she'd fall in love with me and take me to bed and reveal all the secrets I most wanted to know. But it was pure torment, thinking how slowly the years went.

Or maybe Fabrizia still liked Lucy enough to hate the idea that there'd be a new love in my life, even though Lucy had been gone so long. That my new love was someone she knew, taking the place of a woman she'd admired, maybe wished she'd grow to be like—bad either way, though I figured it would all pass pretty quickly. But that night she wouldn't be soothed by anything I could say. She just stood up and walked away, calling back over her shoulder: "I hate you, Harry. You're a shit. Hate Miss Moon as well. Hope she dies."

SEEMED A LIFETIME AGO, Fabrizia's snit. I was long back to being her best mate. And now the temperatures each day were marking the approach of another fine summer I'd every reason to think would be as lovely as last year's. Then one evening—a little westerly gone out to sea leaving a freshness in the air behind it, Priscilla lying belly down on my rumpled bed reading a magazine, me in my shorts content to simply admire for the two hundredth time the perfect ogive of her ass—there was a rap at the front door. Fuck.

"Yeah, yeah. I'm coming," I called, irritated by the intrusion, as I headed down the stairs. There in the fading light, slightly masked by the screened door, was Lucy.

"G'day, cobber," she said brightly, as if we'd just been together the night before instead of living in separate worlds for almost three years.

I found I couldn't move my arm, couldn't reach up to the handle and open the door. Couldn't move my jaw or my tongue to utter a reply. Couldn't muster a single thought. I even forgot the lovely naked girl in my bed.

"That shocking, is it?" Lucy grinned through the screen. Maybe that distorted it, but I seemed to recall a similar slightly crooked grin so far back—a bad night, bad words, then me standing stunned and stupid in the rain. I shuddered. "I should have phoned first, or written, is that what you're thinking? Maybe you'd be right. But you know how I am, Hull."

I stepped outside then, and Lucy's features sharpened. Her grin was a bit lopsided, as if it were costing her plenty to keep it in place, but she held herself tall and straight as she always had. She really hadn't changed in the face at all. Her body had thickened slightly. There was a bit of extra flesh at the backs of her arms, though her legs in the very short skirt she was wearing were as long and finely shaped as I remembered. And those green, green eyes: no hard glint in them now, but a sort of soft glow, almost like a cat's.

"So, what's new, Harry? Still at the *Herald*? I've just joined *The Australian*, couldn't face another go at *The Bulletin*. It's not bad at all," Lucy rattled, never letting go of that lame smile. "Moving back into Paddo was hell, though. Bruce had buggered the whole house. It was really disgusting. Jesus, the aroma hit me on the stoop, even before I opened the door."

Why is she going on as if nothing has happened, as if there wasn't a gulf between us with no bridge or ferry in sight? I thought. Is she so brave, or gone so mental, that she reckoned she could just pop by for a casual chat?

"How long have you been in Sydney?" I managed.

"Couple of weeks. Got the job, got a squad from Jiffy Cleaners to disinfect the Paddo garbage dump, settled in a little."

"And then thought you'd pay a social call on Harry. A bit overdue, maybe, but what the hell. Old friends and all that. No harm in just dropping by."

"Yeah. I wanted very much to see you again. Guess you know too well when I want to go, I go. And when I want to come . . . well, here I am."

"Our little girl? With a babysitter or something? Or over at Bert's? Or maybe you got married? I'd love to have a look at her. I really have to at least see her."

Lucy's grin gave up the ghost. Her eyes slid away from mine. Her body swiveled slightly toward the street, and her head moved more, so that I had her face only in profile.

"No, Harry. That's something I wanted to talk to you about." She'd been doing her best, doing it well, but unease and apprehension finally broke through in her voice when she said that. About bloody time, I thought.

"No, what?"

"She's not at Umberto's, she's not with a babysitter. I'm not married. And you can't see her." She was staring at that skeletal ghost gum with its regular evening crowd of cockatoos. I noticed her right leg was trembling. "She's not with me at all."

"What the hell's that mean?"

"I gave her up for adoption, Harry. Had to."

I'm not completely clear about the next few minutes, and expect I never will be. I heard more than felt my palm smack her cheek smartly. She took the blow and gave me back her full face in place of her profile, as if she were inviting me to hit her again. I believe I hissed something like you had no right to do that, you bloody cunt. You had no right. No right. She was mine, too. If you were too bloody selfish to be her mother, you should have given her to me. I'd have loved her. I'd have raised her. We would not have needed you at all. You had no bloody fucking right in the world to do what you did.

Lucy's eyes seemed to be moistening, but I had the strongest sense she would not cry, not then, not before me. "You haven't understood, Harry. I didn't have any choice. I *had* to give her up."

"Bullshit! There can't be a single reason in this fucking world for that. You didn't even bother to *ask* me about it. I'd have grabbed her up in a minute, if you couldn't care for her. Don't give me a heap of shit about how it broke your heart to do it, either."

"There was a reason, Harry! I'm not lying. There was a powerful reason. I *did* have to. There wasn't any choice."

"There was me. I was a choice. You wouldn't have had to marry me or anything. You could have stayed wherever the fuck you were, never seen me again. All you had to do was dial my number and tell me where I could collect my child."

"You couldn't have kept her either, Harry. No matter how much you think you wanted her, you couldn't have done it."

"Fuck your arrogance, Lucy. Who the hell do you think you are, making a judgment on me like that? Judge yourself, you heartless bitch."

"Harry, if you'll just listen . . ."

"Where is she? Who's got her?" I grabbed her arm and squeezed it until she winced. "Tell me, Lucy. Where the fuck's my kid?"

"I can't, Harry. The law, the adoption law . . ."

"Hell with the law. You tell me or I'll beat it out of you right here, right now."

"But there was a reason, you've got to believe that. Just give me a chance to explain."

"Stop the nonsense and tell me where she is." I felt my right hand clench into a fist, my muscles tense to strike. Her face blurred, everything went blurry. And not because of the deepening dusk.

"If you'd just let me explain . . ."

"Hey, you old bugger," Priscilla's voice came floating down from upstairs. "When you're finished scrappin' with the Hoover saleslady or Jehovah's Witness or whoever she is, c'mon back up. Got something neat to show you."

I just imploded. The rage rushed out of me like air from a ballon that's been pricked by a pin. I felt I was standing on will alone, every muscle in my body limp, my hand falling away from Lucy's arm. She glanced through the doorway, her eyes moving up the stairs as far as the doorframe allowed, then back at my face. She took half a step toward me.

"Get away. Get out of my sight," I said listlessly.

And that broke Lucy. Huge sobs shook her, tears gushed, and her legs seemed to go right out from under her. She was suddenly sitting on the floor of the verandah, words slurred and muffled by her weeping.

"Oh God, Harry, it's been such a hell I've wanted to die," she snuffled, head down as if in prayer. "Please, Harry. I'm begging you. Please try even a little to understand. I need that so badly."

"I have to see my girl," I whispered.

She looked up at me with such anguish as I'd never seen in anyone's face before. "If I could show her to you, don't you know I would?"

"I don't know any such thing. But I know where you live, know where you work. I'm going to haunt you until I find out what you've done with my daughter." But there was no force at all behind my words.

That crooked grin crept across Lucy's tear-streaked face, once her shoulders stopped heaving and she got to her feet. God, the woman had guts. The muscles at her throat were taut, but she said, "Righty-o, mate," as she stepped off the verandah. "See ya when I see ya."

"NASTY BIT OF A row, that," Cilla said when I went back upstairs. "You look knackered. Reckon it wasn't a Jehovah's Witness after all. Sounded more like some poor sheila you knocked up and abandoned."

"No such thing. It's a great deal more complicated than that," I said, wondering how much she'd actually overheard, or if she'd just caught the general tone and made a flip remark.

"Yeah?"

"Yeah."

"Well?"

"Too long a story."

"Bloody hell, then you better get started right now. Because don't even think for one moment I'm going to let you off until I get every detail."

"Aw Cilla, it was just an old girlfriend. She left me years ago."

"Really and truly?" she laughed. "Reckon it wasn't exactly a clean break, judging from all the drama just now. Reckon if you didn't knock her up, something fairly disgusting happened. What'd you do to the pathetic creature, Harry?"

"You might ask what she did to me."

"No point to that. Men always twist things around so it looks like they're innocent victims." She sat up, waving a forefinger at me like a bloody magistrate. "Now, under oath, who the hell is she, what'd you do to her, and why'd she start wailing? Answer, Mr. Hull."

So I gave her a thumbnail of the Harry-Lucy saga, not even excluding some of the awful bits about Dad's decline and death, my bad behavior during that time. But definitely giving a very wide miss to the salient fact: Lucy'd borne my child, whom I'd never seen and maybe never would.

"Jesus, I feel sorry as hell for the both of you. Fucking tragic, all that," Cilla said. "Really strange, though."

"What is?"

"Her showing up at all. If I was this Lucy, the only reason I'd ever come back is to shoot you with my dad's shotgun," she grinned. "Assuming you've told something near the truth, you ratbag, that's what you'd deserve. Love to hear her side of things one day."

"Doubt you will. Doubt she'll be coming round here anymore."

"Wouldn't bet my knickers on that, Harry."

26

I DID HAUNT LUCY. She seemed—I know this is odd—almost glad of it. She never slammed down the phone even when I ranted viciously. In fact she always tried to prolong the conversation when I'd cut it off the moment she'd refuse to tell me what I wanted to know about my little girl.

For a long time it was only phone calls. I didn't trust myself anywhere near Lucy, for fear I'd crack and go violent. Eventually I must have got to some point of dumb resignation, for I agreed to meet her for a beer when she asked for that. I knocked over my chair and bolted, glass still half-full, the first time. Just couldn't bear her presence. We tried again, at her urging, managed semi-civilized conversation, clipped and awkward though it was. And again. And again. It never got much easier or more pleasant, even after I stopped pressing on the whereabouts issue. But then, when I went after the reason, the one she'd said she wanted to tell me that awful evening on my verandah, she cracked much as she had then, only worse. Everyone in the pub was staring as I helped her out of the place.

That terrible spasm had eased by the time I got her to the door of her place in Paddo. She thanked me, invited me in. I shook my head no, repeated the question I'd asked in the pub. And now, pretty damn calmly, Lucy fucking refused. Rage again. I bolted before I lost control.

"Well, I was about half-right," Cilla said that night, lying with her head on my chest after we'd made love. "Your sheila hasn't turned up here in person. But I reckon she doesn't have to."

"Whatever are you on about, love?"

"Nothing much. Except that she's on your mind an awful lot, Harry."

"Not really. We talk on the phone sometimes."

"Must be lovely chats then," she laughed. "I can tell every time you've had one, 'cause your eyes are sort of skewed and unfocused. Like you'd just been romper-stomped, taken a few kicks to the head."

Yeah, really lovely. It was months before I felt in control enough to meet Lucy face to face again, though she'd called often and even written that she wanted to see me.

"I'll tell you that why, Harry," she said when we did get together at a little Paddo pub one day in the early summer of '86 "only when I feel sure you'll believe me. When I feel you truly understand that I didn't just toss my own child away."

"You've got nerve, setting conditions," I muttered.

"When you trust me again, Harry, I'll explain it all, every detail. I swear it. But I'm not going to relive in the telling the worst pain I've ever known as long as you're convinced I'm a lying cunt. Which you still are."

I'D THOUGHT, early on, to have a talk with Frank about things. But that would've been going back to old ways. Decided I should just handle whatever came my way, which is all Frank would have told me anyway. Bert, naturally, got the blow-by-blow account, though I wasn't expecting anything in the way of aid or advice. Even though old Bert, my best mate, was trying his damnedest to broker a truce between Lucy and me. He thought I didn't know, but I did, from the way he'd sometimes gently speak to me about her, and from the time or two I spotted him having lunch with Lucy in one of those little trattorias on the side streets around the *Herald*.

Some Sundays that year, when I was weary of skirmishing with Lucy—and Cilla most always being perfectly content to sleep in past noon—it was a great comfort to rise before dawn, collect Bert, and spend the morning fishing with Frank. Troubles of my sort were never on our conversational agenda.

Generally we'd skip the boat and just heave our lines off the rocks. Often we didn't catch a thing, but it didn't matter much. The casting and jigging and reeling in cleared the head.

You face more or less into the rising sun from the rocks at Bondi. The sea's silvered, you have to squint it's so bright, and you talk without looking at who you're talking to. You scan seaward, half an eye on the ever-shifting, rising and falling point where your line disappears into the water, but most of your attention is on the motionless horizon, which seems a fixed place you might reach. Though I knew if you tried, it would constantly recede. There's a journey for the imagination: always approaching, never arriving.

"But you'd get there eventually, barring wreck and ruin," Frank replied when I'd mentioned that notion. "If you sailed dead east from here, never turning, always at the same latitude, you'd just miss the North Cape of New Zealand, and then there'd be nothing but the bleak ocean fore and aft for a long, long time. But one day you'd spy the coast of Chile, almost right at Santiago. Then you'd reach your horizon, and you'd be damned glad of it by then."

"For sure," Bert said. "Imagine Columbus, Magellan, those fellows sailing off never knowing if they see land again. Think how they felt when they found it."

"I expect they were pretty confident they'd hit something, or they'd never have gone," I said. "Wasn't the whole point to find some lands they thought were out there?"

"The point was riches," Frank said. "Spices, gold, slaves and so forth. Not that Columbus got any. But that's what made all of them take the risk. Bit of greed. They didn't go just to see what they could see."

"What I would like to see," Bert said, in one of those antic leaps he was always liable to make, "is the Pyramids. I would like to see them once before I die."

"I've seen 'em," Frank said. "A bit skanky. You get to the top and what catches your eye is names scratched and carved into the stones. They say Flaubert's is on one of them, but I never saw it. Soldiers' names I saw plenty of. Some of Bonaparte's, some of Kitchener's, some Aussie Light Horse."

"A terrible thing to deface something so ancient," Bert said. "But what can you do?"

"You can carve your own name on," Frank said. "I did. It was irresistible."

"You're exactly right!" Bert laughed. Once years ago he had gone to visit a tenth-century church famous for its mosaic floors in a ruined Roman town not far from his home, he said. He called the church paleo-Christian, and said the town was Aquilèia and had been sacked by the Huns, the real slant-eyed Huns of Attila mind you, not the square-heads of the Great War. Down in a sort of cellar beneath the part of the church where the altar is, down there where they kept the finger bones of obscure saints who were probably scrofulous in life, and other holy-roller talismans, there was a beautifully fading fresco on the wall. He'd spotted some graffiti scratched into it, one line ending with a date: 1623.

"I thought, what can this be? I expected it was something high-flown, being in Latin," he said. "Until the girl I was with, a very pretty girl with some education who knew Latin, read it out loud. Can you guess what this man of 1623 scratches in Latin into a priceless fresco?"

"Got me," Frank said.

"Guido loves Paola?" I said.

"He say: 'I, Francesco Revedin, have the most enormous cock in all of the Veneto!'"

"Common delusion," I laughed.

"Right. And that's what those blokes there were likely believing about themselves when they started out this morning," Frank said, pointing to a little boat that wasn't being handled properly. It was pitching around in the swell most awkwardly. It looked like it was going to go over any minute, get smashed up in the surf, and the lifesavers on the beach thought so too, for they were whistling and waving their flags very vigorously. "Reckon their willies have shrunk a bit now, though."

"Stupid buggers," I said. "Suppose we'll get to watch a rescue."

"Tell me something: why do people yell 'Help! Help!' when they're in trouble?" Bert said.

"What're they going to yell? 'Free beer'?" I said.

"No Harry, I meant why do we expect anyone to listen?" Bert said. He was serious, I could see that, and Frank decided to take it that way.

"Because someone always does," Frank said.

"That some stranger will put himself in danger to help you?" Bert said. "It seems too much to expect."

"It is. But people always try anyway. Sometimes to their great regret, for they go down themselves in the attempt," Frank said. "It'd take a very hard man to just let it pass. I'd guess every time you've seen anyone in big trouble, you've responded, Umberto. Reckon you couldn't just stand by."

"This I'm not sure of," Bert said. "A serious cry for help, I have never heard."

I thought that was honest, about not being sure. You just never know. I'd come so close to getting my ass blown off splashing through a paddy to get to a screaming gut-shot mate I'd pissed my pants. I was never put to the test in any way like that again, but I'm sure how you acted once is never any sort of indicator of how you'll behave another time. Another time, I might decide it would be stupid to take the risk.

255

It never occurred to me then that what I was hearing from behind the bold, brave front of a certain woman was a call for help. A pretty desperate plea—near to a scream, in fact—that I was too literal-minded to recognize for what it was.

UMBERTO FINALLY MADE ME hear her.

"Ah, Harry, you ever recall that mad walkabout you took to never-never?" he said one evening when we were having a beer on my verandah, talking things over.

"Don't I, though! Unforgettable little jaunt, that was."

"You such a fucking mess, Jacko such a fucking mess. *Dío mío.* Me, I'm thinking you had gone truly mental when I saw this."

"S'pose I was. At the time."

"But then you talked sense, remember? You told me you have got a hole in your life, it's never going to heal. But, goddamn, you are going to live with it, like your Dad lived with the hole in his cheek."

"Yeah. Felt that way then. A wound that wouldn't close."

"Harry, one question. You ever consider Lucy, she's got a hole in her life also?"

"Doubt she does. Aren't you forgetting she's the one that cut me open, running off like she did?"

"Oh, you think she was just taking some sort of pleasure trip when she does that? You think she has just been on holiday these last three years? Harry, Harry. A wound is a wound, never mind how it happens. Lucy's? Very real. Very deep. Very slow to heal."

"Well, that'd make us just about even."

"Enough pain all around then, no? More than enough of suffering, for sure. So why are you trying to make more?"

"I'm not." The accusation surprised me. "I was doing just fine until she came back around."

"*Exactamente.* A good life you got. You got Cilla, you got no problems at work, you got the chance to be happy. Why hurt anybody?"

"You're talking gibberish, Bert."

"Harry, you are very thick sometimes, no offense. Lucy, she's very strong, she bears this pain all on her own as long as she's able. She don't come around now because she wants to torture you."

"Then why'd she come at all?"

"She don't want to, for sure. But I think finally she has to. This thing with the baby, it's killing her. Some help, that is what she needs badly."

"From me? What a hope. She owes me some answers, dammit."

"Nothing, that's what Lucy owes you," Bert declared. "She's already given you everything she got to give. You forgetting those years when your father is dying?"

Direct hit on my most vulnerable spot, those words.

"With every question about your kid, you are ripping Lucy apart," Bert went on. "And for what? What kind of answer will make your life any better? You can't get your daughter, she's gone. Lucy don't tell me why, but she says she had no choice and I believe her. She don't say this either, but I see she will never heal until she makes some peace with you."

"Forgive and forget, that it? Bloody hell!"

"Yes. Forgive. Forget. Okay, the child, she's gone. Terrible thing, and nothing anyone can do. But you can save the mother of your child. A very simple thing. Be a friend to Lucy again."

"Listen, Bert . . ."

"No, you got nothing to say worth hearing, Harry," Umberto snapped. "I tell you this, then I'm finished with you. You got this one chance to do good. One chance to do something to be proud of all your life. Only a fool would walk away from this."

And that, once it sank into my disordered mind, ended my war with Lucy. Not by some fragile armistice laced with resentment and hostility, but a double, unconditional surrender to the knowledge that whatever had gone wrong between us was done, couldn't be undone, and couldn't destroy a certain bond. In fact, once the fighting stopped (and I shut up about our girl), we managed bit by bit to gain comfort in each other's presence instead of remembrance of a terrible, permanent fissure in our lives. We were battered, scarred and flawed for sure. But connected, like survivors of some disaster.

Cilla noticed the change even as it was still in the process of happening.

"That Lucy vanish back to wherever the hell she sprang? Or have you guys kissed and made up?" she said one night over dinner in my kitchen. "You're still carrying her around, but you don't seem half-cracked so much anymore."

"Made up, I suppose. Skipped the kiss, it would've felt bloody incestuous. Don't know how exactly, but she seems like a sister or something now."

Cilla rocked with laughter. "That's the most amazingly fucking original evasion it's ever been my privilege to hear. You're a bloody wonder, mate. Tell true now. You invent that all by yourself? Or did you get a little help?"

"Cilla, I swear," I grinned. "Know it sounds really strange. Hell, it feels really strange. But it's true."

"How many fingers am I holding up? Three? Right, you can see fine." She was still chuckling. "Reckon you haven't just been punched silly again. Still a bit concussed from previous bouts, maybe. Time'll tell."

"Now Cilla . . ."

"Relax, mate." Cilla smiled, leaned over the table and gave me a deep kiss. "I've got way too many ex-boyfriends floating around to get my knickers in a knot over one ex-girlfriend. Though I doubt I'd ever feel like one of 'em was my bloody *brother*. Whoops! Take that back. Do feel like they were my brothers. Hated those bastards almost as much as I hated me dad!"

WHAT HARRY SAW

IT WAS NOT EASY to achieve the right balance with Lucy. It might
never have happened except for one thing, one part of our mutual past:
we'd built a friendship over those two years before we became lovers. So
we had a model of sorts to rebuild a fresh one, and this time with no goal
or hope beyond that, which took all the tension out of the process.

But not all the awkwardness, in the beginning anyway.

"So tell me about Cilla, Harry. Think she's the one? Marriage and
all?" Lucy had asked the first time either one of us had pushed past the
dailiness of our lives in conversation. It was well over a year now since
she'd appeared out of nowhere at my door.

I instantly felt shy and hesitant. No words would come. Lucy's look
was completely benign, but it seemed to me too loaded a question to be
entirely free of motive. She must have sensed my suspicion.

"Just a mate asking a mate, that's all, Harry," she said. "Just wanting to
know how you're going, if you're happy and content with that part of
your life. Spare me the gory details. Truly."

"I don't know," I said, pretty much believing her but still harboring
some doubt about the matter.

"You don't know about Cilla, or you don't know if I'm a close enough
friend to talk to?"

"Bit of both," I grinned.

"I had to work hard to even ask, I confess," Lucy smiled back. "I've
this sort of residue still of our time together. Together in the way you
and Cilla are, I mean. I know that we've moved on to another plane entirely. Know there's no going back, wouldn't want to anyway. Even so . . .
maybe you feel it too?"

"I do. Once in a while I even find myself wondering why it's Cilla I'm
with and not Lucy."

"Same for me. But we'll get past it or we won't. I hope we do. We
should be able, since we both know we weren't meant to be. And if we

259

don't, we're going to have a hard time being as matey as I'd like. I so want one man in my life who's a true and genuine friend. With no sex getting in the way."

"I hear Charlie McGuire's still alive. Retired now of course. In every way, so I'm told," I smiled. McGuire, who had been a *Herald* editor when I was a cadet, was absolutely notorious for seducing every young, naive hackette who ever joined the paper. Talked about converting to Islam so he could have a regular harem of 'em. "Maybe he's your man."

Lucy had just taken a sip of beer, and now she laughed so violently a bit of it shot out of her nostrils. "Christ!" she managed after a moment. "If it was anyone else but you across the table I'd have to run out of here right now in terminal embarrassment. Anyway, I think your sources are wrong. What I hear is that McGuire is preternaturally un-retired in his preferred sphere. Except that now instead of girl-hacks, he's reduced to hiring teenage hookers off Williams Street."

"Somehow this doesn't surprise me. Wonder if he ever did turn Muslim?"

"Now that we're back to houris, care to try my original question on again?"

"Not if you're thinking of Cilla like that," I said.

"Sorry. I wasn't, really. Awkward transition." That crooked grin was back on her face.

"Make those myself from time to time. Anyway, the answer's the same. I don't know," I said, and it was a truth I'd only just realized. "The pheromones are just right. We like each other tremendously at lots of levels. There's a real love there. I can see myself spending my life with her. But . . . Cilla's a kid, really. Don't know if she's all that interested in a permanent connection anyway. It never comes up."

"You can't tell from that. Her not bringing it up doesn't mean she isn't dreaming real hard that you will."

"Now I'm getting a slight flashback here," I said.

"Oh, don't, Harry." Lucy gave me a rueful smile. "You did ask me.

Twice. First time it was too soon, the second time it was too late. But that wasn't your fault. There was one little window of opportunity there in the middle. I saw it, I could have gone through it and asked you. You know I'm not shy when I want something. But I didn't. Don't know why exactly."

"You think I'm about to miss my window with Cilla?"

"Don't even know if there is one. I'd have to be around the two of you together for a while to get any sense of that."

"Not sure I'm quite ready to handle the two of you in the same room. Though she's curious as hell, has been since that little surprise scene on the verandah. Hell, Cilla'd probably enjoy meeting you. But truth is, I'm scared to death of any little change in my very pleasant little situation."

"Found your natural place, have you?" Lucy grinned. "About bloody fucking time, pardon my French."

MAYBE LUCY HAD FOUND hers as well. I was sure she wasn't living like a nun. But she never offered and I never cared to inquire about who, let alone the what, when and where. The "gory details," as she'd once put it, seemed utterly unimportant, utterly meaningless.

So, careful never to cut into my time with Cilla, I began to see Lucy quite regularly. We weren't out and about much; I'd ditched our social network during Dad's last year, never had bothered to get back into it after she went walkabout. But we did slide back into something like our old pattern with Bert and Alice and the kids, though their configuration had altered a lot, and evenings at Bert's house were more frequent than Sunday excursions. Alice only occasionally joined us either way, which was fine by me. If it bothered Bert and Fabrizia, they never showed it. They seemed so truly pleased have Lucy with us again. Camilla, the pitiful creature, was indifferent to almost everything.

And there was a rule to it: the better it went with Lucy as a friend, the better it went with Cilla as my love. For a long time.

27

"BLOODY HELL, HARRY," Cilla said one night in the very midst of a great canter. It was past the end of the hot, more than two years since Lucy had returned. Cicadas outside the screened windows cheering us on, sheets rumpling and the bed dancing, sweat glistening on my chest and Cilla slick—it's an article of faith here that women never perspire, they glow—Cilla glowing in the moonlight.

"It feels like that old sheila of yours is standing right behind the bed, watching me," she panted.

"And she's fucking smiling at me in approval when I do this or that," she hissed, shifting her hips and leaning way back from the waist. "It's like she's urging me to give you a really bonzer root!"

"You're doing a lovely job of it," I managed, though she had jerked my bit violently with those words. Nothing had existed except Cilla's body. Not a single thought or image of anything but the here and now of her had been in my mind. Suddenly all sorts of memories came jostling and shoving for my attention, and me shoving back, desperate not to slide away from the perfect girl astride me. "Forget Lucy. I never so much as touch her hand. We only talk."

"Rather you kept your damned mouths shut," Cilla moaned, her back arching amazingly and her long neck extending the curve until her hair swung like heavy silk against my legs, close to bringing herself off even as she was leaving me behind, "and just fucked once in a while. Then she wouldn't be in the bloody bed with *us!*

"Goddammit, Harry. Oh! Oh! Oh, Christ!" she shuddered, holding that Chinese acrobat's posture longer than I'd have believed possible. "That was bloody good enough, I reckon. All right by you, Lucy? Now bugger off, ya nosey bitch. Show's over."

I couldn't see her face, only her belly and heaving chest curving away from me. But I could see her point.

With one difference. If Cilla had been spending as much time with a former lover as I was with Lucy, I wouldn't for a moment believe they were just good friends who liked to natter. I'd be sure they were screwing each other silly. And I'd be really pissed about that bit, not the talking.

Some sex therapist or marriage counselor ought to write a paper about this sort of balls-up. They could title it "Hull's Fallacy: A Dysfunctional Perception of Intimacy."

It'd begin with the premise that men almost universally place more value on the physical than the emotional. If their wives and lovers have a fling, they feel they've been robbed—of something they never actually *possessed* in the first place. Yet they seldom feel they're stealing anything from their partners if they go off for a casual root.

Second, men generally have trouble accepting the notion that women—unless they've had a rough or unsavory initiation to the act— are probably more intensely sexual than they are, but still crave an emotional connection men don't require in a pleasant root.

Finally, men seldom understand a concept most women recognize clearly: that what drives a true wedge between a couple isn't that bit on the side, especially if it's kept well to the side. What's far more dangerous is a closeness of heart and mind. It's deep emotional intimacy with a third party that's the true threat. Not the short, strange and faintly ridiculous ceremony of bodies joining.

If I'd only been casually and quietly fucking Lucy once in a while, Cilla need never have known. But it's a great deal more difficult to keep that other sort of unfaithfulness, the perfectly chaste kind, in the dark. You carry home the scent of those encounters no matter what; it doesn't wash off in the shower afterward.

Cilla had interrogated me, the first time she'd caught it—maybe a few months after that night in my kitchen when I'd told her Lucy felt like a sister. She'd let me off as easy as she had after the sister bit. But when she kept catching it again and again and again, she pressed me harder. And I—feeling utterly innocent since neither Lucy nor I had even a trace of physical interest in each other anymore—blithely blabbed everything.

"Shit, you're like a bloody swagman, lugging her around with you. Didn't matter at first, but it's not like it was at first anymore. It's gone bloody serious between the two of you," Cilla said. "And I'm not liking that one bit, Harry."

"Cilla, you know I only love you."

"I know you love fucking me," she said. "But dammit, Harry, I do wish sometimes you'd talk to me the way I know you talk to her. There's got to be more for us than bed. I feel like I've only got half of you these days. That bitch's snatched away the other half."

"All she's got is a bit of my past, because I've known her longer. And that's not exactly a treat," I said, too aware that Cilla was closer to the truth than I wanted her to be.

"Your past? Bugger that. Don't care about history. What concerns me is the now and the future. She claiming half of those, as well? Bloody feels like it."

"Lucy's not making any claims at all."

"Fucking is. And you're letting her take whatever she wants. I reckon whenever I'm not in fondling distance, you don't give me a thought. And whenever I am in reach, a good grope's all you're interested in. No reason to talk about your fears or feelings or dreams. If you have any. I certainly wouldn't know. I reckon if you do, you don't see any point in repeating yourself since you've already discussed everything with her."

"She's like a mate, for Christ's sake."

"That's the bloody problem, bludger! Used to be a woman only had to compete for attention with a man's male mates. Now I've got the shit luck to be with maybe the only man around who's got 'em in both genders."

"You don't have to compete for anything, Cilla."

"Yeah? If I stopped rooting with you, how long would you hang around just for the pleasure of my company and conversation?"

I was silent for just half a beat too long.

"I'll tell you," Cilla snapped. "About a minute. Just like the boys who enjoyed a nice ride with Goolgowi's town bike. You prick."

FAIR WARNING. And fairly shocking, the prospect it raised. Made me real deteremined to give my all with Cilla, to do whatever it might take to keep her happily with me.

First I tried to shift our relations up the spectrum from a love affair toward a genuine union. Cilla and I were private, kept almost completely to ourselves. She'd felt that was necessary when we started, and it had become a firm habit. Whatever social life she needed she seemed to find through nights out with her girlfriends, mainly going dancing at clubs.

I broke the habit. We went public. As a couple. Very public.

Lots of people want to know you when your byline's in the newspaper every day, and I started accepting again those invitations to the chic Darling Point parties, the gallery shows, the new restaurant and club openings, the premiers of dance and theater at the Opera House and other venues. Sydney was booming, there was always something going on, and Cilla was by my side at the best of it. She looked smashing with her great hair and perfect little features, whether she was dressed up in some Italian designer number I'd got for her in an Oxford Street boutique or half-naked in a cossie lounging on a yacht. She drew so much attention and created so much lustful envy among the men that I showed her off more and more.

Until I realized I was beginning to resemble those newly rich asses whose biggest delight besides making more money and spending it as visibly as possible was parading their second, much younger trophy wives. And then Cilla made it clear the social whirl had lost its appeal to her.

"Right, Harry," she said eventually. "Now that you've taken me places, now that you've flashed me around Sydney, now that all your really stuck-up connections and acquaintances have perved my tits and bum— a couple of these 'friends' of yours actually asked me if I was game for a root on the side, did you know that?—wherever do we go from here?"

So I toned things down a bit.

I angled some overnight sails in Pittwater, for instance, from youngish proto-moguls eager for a good press connection and not yet too obnoxious, with just another couple or two on board. I took her to small dinner parties when I thought there'd be a couple of people she'd enjoy meeting. Took her dancing at her favorite clubs, too.

Then, in mid-winter of '87 a long weekender on Hayman Island. Being a sheep station brat and knowing only Sydney's surf beaches, she leaped and scampered more like an excited Fabrizia than a grown woman when she got her first sight of a lagoon and coral reefs. I taught her to snorkel, though that proved more difficult than I'd expected with a girl so gracefully physical.

"Yaahh!" she shouted, spouting and coughing when she foundered for maybe the sixth time. "Bloody hopeless, I am."

She could barely swim, so in the shallows I held her level with both my hands on her toned belly. "The secret's to relax, let the water hold you, darls. It will if you let it," I explained, walking her along the reef's edge. "Don't need to flail your arms. Let 'em trail down along your sides. Yeah, like that. Give a gentle flick with the flippers every now and then. Keep your face down, just the tip of the tube above the water. Relax. Know it feels unnatural at first. Just relax, though. You'll see. That's it, darls. Imagine you're flying in a dream."

"Oh, Harry, it is like a dream," she said, almost bursting with delight when she finally got the knack of it. "The most beautiful feeling! Really and truly."

She pulled off the T-shirt she'd been wearing against the sun and stood there bare-breasted and beautiful. "Now I'm a mermaid," she laughed, and slid out over the reef on her own.

She loved it so much that I took her back twice more. We spent a little time sun-baking, a little more gossiping wickedly about everyone else there, but most of the daylight hours out in the waters. She even bought a book on reef life and studied it, so she'd know the names of the brilliantly hued fishes and the vast arrays of corals she gazed so raptly at, this unlikely mermaid from Goolgowi.

When I felt she was water-competent enough, I organized a week at Byron Bay, including Moira and her boyfriend, a decent enough bloke in his late twenties who was rising pretty rapidly at the Bank of New South Wales. The main agenda was scuba lessons. Cilla showed something then I'd never seen in her before: fear. But only during the first short training dive, when the weird sensation of breathing through the aqualung must have panicked her a little. After that she was game to go as deep as the instructor would let us.

"I'm a bit cross with you, Harry," she murmured in my ear the last night at Byron. We'd just made love in what lately had become our new way: not less passionate, but less like a rambunctious tussle and altogether more tender, more deliberate, more gently rhythmic.

"Been bad in some way, have I?"

"No, darling. Much worse. Selfish," Cilla said. "You've known all about this water world and kept it from me for ages. I'm finding it hard to forgive you."

"Are you?"

"Yeah. But I'll manage, no worries. Love you too much."

AND THROUGH ALL OF IT I tried to talk, really talk to her. And listen seriously to all she might have to say.

Instead of simply retailing daily office goings-on that might amuse her, I began to tell her deeper truths about my trade. And about my life, for work took up the larger part of it. I told her how bloody boring most of it actually was, because even the hottest story was only a variation of one you'd handled a dozen times before. Basically the only things that changed were names, places, times. We usually supplied whys for form's sake, but made them up, because no journo alive ever really learned the true why of any story.

Which meant, to me, that the whole exercise was pointless. A regular paycheck was the only reason to keep on with it.

That surprised Cilla; she'd assumed, like most who aren't in the media, that knowing the inside dirt and news of the day before anyone else and writing it up must be damned exciting.

"Good reporters and editors have one great talent," I explained to her. "They're bloody brilliant at forgetting it's always the same story, absolute geniuses in deluding themselves that the stories have some meaning and importance."

She had claimed she didn't care about history, but she got all that, too. As detailed accounts as I could manage (and had always only sketched before if I spoke of them at all) about my early days, my time in Fuck Toy, my affair with Lucy, Dad's decline and death. Found a lot of that surprising, too, Cilla did. Found some of it hilarious.

"What a drongo! Had no idea you were a druggie and no more clever than Goolgowi ockers," she laughed when I told her about stealing the clapped-out Toyota and trying to outrun the coppers in that pitiful excuse for a car.

But she burst into tears when I described the evening Tito repeated everything Dad said. "That's the saddest tale I've ever heard. The poor man. Imagine what must have been going on in his mind. It breaks my heart to think of it."

"It's no wonder you're so badly scarred," she said softly when I described all those days and nights of Dad's last year. "Your heart and soul, I mean. I hate my geezer like anything, but if he went like that and I had to watch it all ... doubt I could bear it."

Cilla seemed to draw nearer and nearer, to forget for some months about her Lucy grievances. I was so pleased, so relieved, that I never even considered the main reason might be that our newly busy life as a couple was sharply reducing time spent with Lucy, so Cilla was catching her scent much less. And so, though the brightest, tightest bond we had was being centered side by side in the now, I risked a wild leap toward a future.

I took her to a wonderfully intimate little restaurant called Jour et Nuit, the most romantic one I knew anywhere in Sydney. We ate New Zealand mussels and sole meuniere, drank a bottle of Puligny-Montrachet and finished with one of vintage Moët. Afterward, Cilla giggling, we hopped the fence around the closed Botanical Gardens and strolled hip to hip across the green under a midnight moon the color of old gold. I leaned her up against a huge old Morton fig, kissed her tenderly but deeply, then cupped her little face in my hands. There was a ring in my pocket, a band of gold set with the most beautiful fire opal I could find.

"Cilla, you're the love of my life," I murmured. "Will you marry me? Will you have kids with me?"

"Oh God, Harry." She started crying. "I can't. Not yet."

"You don't love me?"

"I do," she snuffled. "But Harry, I feel I barely know you, years on now. It's true you've told me all you think you have to tell about yourself.

Fooled me for a while with that. But you know they were just bedtime stories, Harry."

"Told you things I've never dared tell another soul," I said, feeling that old tetanus tightening on my scarred side for the first time in years.

"The events, sure. But not one word about how you *felt*, Harry," she said. "Must've big emotions raging round. Had to've been. But nobody'd even guess you were there through most of it. It's like you're telling some other bloke's tale."

"Cilla . . ."

"I know some stuff's too painful to speak of," Cilla said. "But Christ, Harry, you never let on about even the smallest things. To me, anyway. Sometimes I ask myself what Harry'd think about some little nothing—shit, a new pair of shoes I fancy, a skirt, a different haircut that might please you—and I realize I don't have any fucking idea.

"You know what I think, Harry?" she said next, all the softness slipping away. "I think your special dream is a threesome. I think you want your dick inside me, or some girl like me who loves to fuck and doesn't ask for much else, and your heart beating next to Lucy's. The two of you, sharing, secretive as spies. And your lovers can just piss off if they don't like it.

"If you ever wake up from that dream—and it'll only ever be a dream, you'll find that out one day—ask me again. Maybe you'll get the answer you think you wanted tonight."

28

SHE'S GOT A POINT, cobber, except for the bit about sharing with me," Lucy said when I mustered the courage to tell of my disaster. "You've never done that, besides that one night on Magnetic Island, until right this minute."

"Jesus, that's cold comfort," I said.

"Truths about ourselves usually are. You don't want to lose Cilla, do you?"

"No. I did mean what I said to her."

"You're sure? And she just turned down the proposal? She's not leaving you right away or anything?"

"Seems not. We spent the next night together. She was sweet as could be about it all. She's coming over again this evening, too."

"Then," Lucy said, "all we've got to do is figure a way to prove to her that you aren't trapped in that dream she described."

"Lucy, one thing. What if Cilla's right? What if I am dreaming exactly what she said?"

"Then we'll wake you out of it, Harry. I might have to give you a good shaking to do it, though. You up to that?"

"No fear," I said. I was so bloody shaken already I'd stand anything and do anything Lucy told me to do to make things right with Cilla again.

THAT SATURDAY AFTERNOON, when the sun was low enough that some trees just across the alley shaded the entire car, I was waxing Jacko—always good occupational therapy for troubled minds—and I heard Fabrizia's familiar "Hey, mate!"

She and a boy I'd never seen before were coming through my back garden. He was a tall lad, perhaps sixteen, with blond hair and pleasant features, and he moved with less of the gawkiness you usually see in adolescents who've recently shot up a couple of inches in height. Fabrizia looked up at him, said something I didn't catch, and he smiled agreeably.

"This is my mate Harry," she said when they'd got within handshake distance. "Harry, this is Colin."

"G'day. Great car!" Colin said. "Never seen a real Holden before, just pictures."

"There aren't many around anymore," I said. "It sat up on blocks for ages before my dad and I restored it in the early seventies."

"It is so cool," the boy said, wandering around to look at the front end.

"Got a name, too," Fabrizia said. "It's Jacko, right, Harry?"

"Well, g'day Jacko," the boy said. "I'm getting my license next week, and sure wish I had something like this to drive. I'll have to borrow my old man's Mazda. Get it once in a while, if I'm lucky."

"Ah, these days there's so much bloody traffic in Sydney it's not much fun to drive at all," I said. "And the Coathanger's a real death trap. Watch close when you first head over that bastard."

We chatted about this and that for about five minutes. Then Fabrizia said they'd better get down the street to the bus stop if they were going to make the movie they planned to see. It wasn't until they were out of sight that I wondered what in the hell was going on. Fabrizia had a date?

Cilla was going out that night clubbing with Moira and a couple of their girlfriends (I didn't feel bad about not being invited, since Moira's banker wasn't either), so Lucy came over for dinner. We'd just finished the osso bucco I'd had simmering most of the afternoon and gone out to the verandah when Fabrizia came through the front gate, seeming on the verge of skipping but suppressing it. She perched on the railing facing Lucy and me and said, "What'd you think, Harry?"

I missed the hopefulness in her tone. Thought I'd tease her a bit.

"About what?"

"You know. Him. Colin."

"You mean that little bloke you brought around this afternoon who's about to get his driver's license?"

"He's not little. He's your height at least."

"Do your dad and mum know you're sneaking around with boys?"

"Yeah, and it isn't sneaking. I met Colin a month ago. He's taken me to a couple of movies."

"You're too young to be starting that off," I grinned.

"And you're too old to be doing that business with Miss Moon. Isn't he, Lucy?" Fabrizia flashed back.

"You're putting me in an awkward spot here, Fabrizia," Lucy said, chuckling.

"He is, though, isn't he?" she said.

"Well, considering that Cilla's almost young enough to be his daughter . . ." Lucy'd started lightly but froze under the weight of that last word. I tried to help her shuck it.

"Ten years only. That's not much of an age difference between adults. Of course it'd be huge between a little thing like you and a young man. Umberto'd probably have to kill him."

"C'mon, you fossil," Fabrizia said. "What did you think? Nice, right?"

"You could do a lot better," I said, mock-serious.

"What's wrong with him?" There was a strange expression on Fabrizia's face. I felt a blow from Lucy's elbow on my ribs.

"Sort of the school dag, isn't he?" I blundered on anyway. "Reckon he'd rather scribble verses in a little mauve notebook than play rugby. A real girl, isn't he?"

"He is not! He's got his brown belt in karate already," Fabrizia said, hopping off the railing. "Reckon he could knock you on your ancient bum. Lucy, you know what this old bugger used to do late at night when he thought everyone was alseep? He chased that lard-ass Miss Moon around the house naked. Don't mean in the house. I mean around the outside. They say the senile get childish. Reckon Harry's the proof of that!"

She stormed off. Soon as Fabrizia slammed her front door, Lucy let her laughter roll at me. "Christ! Nude moonlight romps? At your age, cobber?"

"It was ages ago," I said, "and that little minx spied on us."

"Harry, Harry, Harry. What on earth are we going to do with you?"

"Isn't Fabrizia a bit young to be fooling around with boys?"

"No. Just the right age. In case you somehow missed how much she's grown up. But much too tender to be teased the way you teased her. You really hurt her feelings."

"Oh fuck."

"She brought the boy around because she wanted your approval of him. You told me at dinner he seemed a decent kid. You should have told her that. It would have sent her over the moon."

I felt like some species of filthy felon. Not to mention a total moron. My stupidities stung all the more when a cause came clear to me: I had developed a pure dread of time's passage. Dread of any more change at all. I desperately wanted all the people, at whatever remove from me, to stay precisely where they were, as orderly and dependable an arrangement as the stars in the sky. I wanted Umberto as my best friend, and Cilla as my lover, and Lucy as my soul mate, and Fabrizia as my bright little pal who always turned to Harry with whatever questions or troubles came to her.

And yet Lucy seemed determined to remind me that the stars kept moving because the world kept turning, that change was natural law.

The one person who should have been changing, the one I kept hoping would, wasn't. And that was a heartbreaker. We'd all thought Camilla would outgrow that timid, withdrawn and nearly mute stage, but as the years went by it had only gotten worse. No one could really talk to her for more than a sentence or two, because something said was bound to drive her catatonic with embarrassment or fear, or something she said would fill her so full of shame she'd turn red as beetroot.

Sometimes with me she seemed almost okay. She would seek that grin I'd always given her since she was little, and when she got it you could see the tension leave her muscles. She'd turned lean and lanky as she'd grown, and moved so gracefully when she thought no one was looking at her. No doubt that was from the ballet lessons Bert had started her on when she was six—just after her awkward debut as a gum nut at St. Boniface. Once or twice, when no one else was around, she even showed me some pliés and en pointes. Had to coax her, of course, but she did it.

When she got real upset, though, she'd start to tremble. Recently she'd developed some sort of asthma. Pitiful, her gasping and only coming around if Umberto held her and murmured to her in Italian. Or if I took her hands in mine and stroked them. She was sometimes so nervous she'd wet her pants even though she was already, what, ten? A few clipped words from Alice were usually enough to send her scurrying under the table or into a closet, where she'd hide until her dad came to get her.

"Bugger all, Harry," Fabrizia complained one day. "My bloody mother's always criticizing every little thing about the kid. All the while using that 'Darling' nonsense of hers. 'Darling, you not washing your hair? It looks so greasy.' Or 'Darling, this skirt with that color jumper? Everybody laughing at you if you wear them.' Makes me want to chunder, Harry."

Sounded about right, considering Alice.

FOR A WHILE it seemed as if I'd get my wish about nothing changing anymore. Cilla and I'd been carrying on for weeks as if that scene in the Botanical Gardens had been imaginary only. And we were lying pretty peacefully in bed late one night, smoking, Cilla sketching comet trails in the dark with the glowing coal of her cigarette.

Then she made the world slide sideways a bit.

"It's all your fault, Harry," she said.

"Which particular thing on your growing list?" I asked. I feared we were heading into some of the same choppy waters we'd encountered a few times ever since Lucy had become the ghost behind the bed.

"This filthy habit. Smoking. Why'd you make me start?"

That was it? I rolled toward her, kissed the tip of her little nose, and then laughed with relief.

"That's right, bludger, have a good laugh," she said, sending her red comet on one final orbit before stubbing it out. "Laugh all you want. I mean, I'm just part of your schedule of amusements anyway, right?"

Another little slide then.

"Cilla, that's no way to look at what we have together. I want to marry you, if you'll ever have me. You're the center of my world."

"Hardly," she said. "You see, I've finally figured out how you arrange things, Harry. You put everything in compartments. There's me in one. There's your work in another. There's Bert and Alice and the kids and bloody Lucy crammed like sardines into yet another. I'm never allowed out of mine. I'm never included in anything you do with your friends, even though Bert likes me a lot. He'd be glad to have me along, I'm sure.

And I've still never met Lucy. Why is that, Harry? I reckon she knows all about me. I reckon you tell her every personal detail. That's not fair play."

"I do not do that. So let's you and I drive over to Lucy's house right now and I'll introduce you."

"It's two in the morning, Harry. You'll say anything at two in the morning because you know you won't have to live up to it."

"I'll wake the bitch up, I swear it. I'll hold her while you interrogate her."

"Not amusing, Harry. Let's just sleep."

I ran my hand lightly up her flank to that soft place between her breast and her armpit. She flinched a bit, but settled down when I did it again.

"I don't like being in a fucking box," she said suddenly. "I'm either with you or I'm not. If I am, then why do you bloody exclude me from about three-quarters of your life?"

"Is this excluding you?" I said, snuggling her up as close to me as I could.

"Yeah, it is, actually, you bloody lecher. It's just the usual playing around in my box. Not what I want, Harry. Fuckin' getting tired of it."

Clever girl. Cleverer than me about me, anyway. But she gave me an idea how to prove to her I wasn't trapped in any dream. It seemed so obvious I couldn't fathom why Lucy and I hadn't hit on it straightaway. I'd just make Cilla part of the family, bring her right in with Bert and the kids and Lucy.

Told Lucy the next day, and then told Bert. They were encouraging. "Could be perfect," Lucy said. "Solid proof." It was Bert, I think, who suggested the dinner.

I WAS IN THE KITCHEN, devotedly stirring the risotto with porcini that would precede the main dish—baked salmon and fresh peas—but feeling really anxious about the voices wafting in from the front room: Lucy's to Cilla, Cilla's back to Lucy and then to Alice, Alice's to Lucy and Cilla, and Bert's to all of them. I could only pick up a word or a phrase here and there, disconnected and meaningless, but the tone seemed easy and light enough. There were soft bursts of laughter from time to time, and a cheerfulness in the rumble of Bert's bass.

The table was properly set, the wine was open and breathing, the candles were lit and I'd dimmed my fancy Italian lighting. I was ladling the risotto into a serving bowl when Bert wandered back, several glasses of wine to the good and smiling about it, as he always did.

"Christ, Bert," I said softly. "How's it going? Any troubles?"

"Beautiful, it goes. Cilla, she's a little shy for sure. But Lucy is trying so hard. Like an older sister, she's acting. Beautiful."

I found Bert wasn't too far off in some ways when we all sat down to eat. I'd given a lot of thought to the arrangement: me in between Alice and Cilla on one side, Bert facing Cilla and Lucy facing Alice on the other. Cilla seemed only a trifle nervous now compared to the way she'd been when she arrived. After Lucy told a few stories about life in Cairns, Bert made some dry jokes about them. Then he gently questioned Cilla about Goolgowi, and she took off, bush-girl style. Brash and hilarious tales came rushing merrily from her, including some things I'd never heard before. She did give the part about being the town bike a miss, though.

"What was really and truly disgusting was gelding the bloody rams," Cilla laughed heartily in response to a question from Bert. "Spoil any-body's dinner if I say? Well, you slice the ball bag off with a knife—whish, one stroke unless you've fucked it.

"But there's a tricky bit," she giggled. "There's this long stringy thing still coming out of them after the balls are off. And you've got to *bite* it through, 'cause your hands are full."

"This I have to see someday," Bert was near convulsed with laughter.

"Bloody won't be me who takes you out to the show," Cilla grinned.

Lucy was laughing as hard as Bert. "And I thought things the Queensland banana boys got up to were weird. Some of the young blokes used to go out and catch these huge, hideous cane toads. Then they'd all get together somewhere, maybe out on the beach, and *lick* the horrible creatures."

"My word!" Cilla made a face. "That's disgusting, really and truly. Were they cracked or what?"

"Nah, they wanted to *get* cracked. Or out of their minds, actually," Lucy laughed. "These toads have some kind of chemical on their slimy skins that's poison to predators. But the banana boys claim a good lick is just like blotter acid."

"What's blotter acid?" Cilla asked.

"LSD. Reckon the rage for that died out when you were little, but all the hippies used to love the stuff. Gives you incredible hallucinations."

"You *tried* LSD?" Cilla said. "God, Lucy, I'd be terrified to do that. Seeing all sorts of things that don't exist. What if you saw really horrid things, monsters and corpses and stuff?"

"A few had bad trips. I never did. But some of my friends lost it entirely. Had to to take them to the hospital for a shot of Thorazine," Lucy grinned. "Reckon that's why the rage for it cooled off."

Back and forth it went like that through the meal. Very lively. I couldn't feel a bit of tension. Lucy caught my eye once or twice and told me with hers it was all okay, no worries. But the worry stayed in place. A fair warning? That thought got me apprehensive as hell.

The ladies retired to the verandah with glasses of grappa when dinner was over, leaving Bert and me to tidy up. He was humming some opera or other and somehow managing to dry the dishes I washed in rhythm.

"Christ, I'm a wreck," I said.

"Harry, she's a young woman," Bert said, as if that made everything as clear as crystal.

"Oh, I didn't know. Thanks for letting me in on it," I said.

"Harry, she needs a lot of reassurance, that's all. So young, they're always insecure. Hard to see that with Cilla, so full of life. But she's the kid among us, she knows that."

"But is it working, including her?"

"For sure. Lucy, she takes good care to see to that. After tonight, I think Cilla will think of Lucy as your sister. And maybe a good sister-in-law to have," Bert said as we headed out to the verandah ourselves, the grappa bottle and two more glasses in his hands.

After an hour or so out there, watching Lucy sitting next to Cilla and from time to time abandoning the general chat to have a few low words with the girl that left her smiling, I began to believe Bert might be right.

VERY LATE. A thin shimmer of moonlight entering through the windows. We were both a bit unsteady on our feet, and I fumbled undoing the buttons of Cilla's blouse and slipping it off her. She'd already stepped out of her skirt and panties. I scooped her up, laid her gently on the bed, and eased myself down on top of her. Her eyes were closed as she wrapped her arms and legs around me. And the moment my lips found hers, Cilla began to weep.

"Whatever is it, darling?" I whispered in her ear.

"Oh fuck all!" she sobbed. "Lucy was so sweet with me, she tried really hard to be a friend. And I like her so much. It's horrible."

"That sounds nice, not horrible."

"It bloody is bad. And sad, so sad. It'd be so much easier if I could hate her, don't you see? It'd be better if she'd been a real bitch. Because she's got you, Harry. She's my natural enemy."

"She hasn't got anything but my friendship, and a bit of shared past."

"So you've always told me," Cilla snuffled. She was still crying and her nose was running. "You just don't see it, do you, Harry? I reckon you truly are blind to it. I wasn't sure before. I am now, though."

"Sure of what?"

"Harry, she *owns* you. And you her, as well. It's fucking tragic. I don't have a hope. No girl'd have a hope with you."

"That's rubbish. Lucy and I scarcely exchanged words. You saw how it is with us."

"I saw the bloody pair of you so close you don't need words! Your eyes meet, you understand exactly what you're both thinking. And I could fucking *feel* that connection. Shit! Why'd she have to be so nice? It's hard to hate someone so nice."

"But it's good you got on. No more boxes now. Isn't that what you wanted? To be included? Now you are. You're part of every part of my life, Cilla."

"Yeah, a part. Like the spare tire in Jacko's trunk."

Then she was sobbing violently. I held her close, I rocked her gently as I would a child. I murmured words I'd meant before: marriage, having kids.

"What a hope! Don't say such things, Harry. I'm begging you," she said, then spasmed with sobs once more. So I just held her, watching the faint moonlight ease around the room on its unalterable circuit. After a while Cilla went still and silent. Then she began to make love to me. No acrobatics, just slow and smooth and silent. She held on to me when it was over.

"That's one for my memory," she murmured. "That's one for what won't ever be, because of Lucy."

"She's not taking anything away from us, Cilla," I said, still hopeful we might slip past this crisis.

But Cilla said, "Nothing to take. She's already got it all."

PEOPLE MAKE whatever adjustments required to get along, don't they? I made mine, Lucy made hers, Bert made his with his wreck of a marriage for the sake of his kids. Hell, Miss Moon turned around one day and made hers as well. And so she should have, though my reaction was hardly so reasonable at the time. It doesn't do to inquire too closely into the details. They aren't important, because if I've learned one thing in my scuffed and raggedy life, it's that no one can really understand anyone else's compromises or arrangements. The best you can do is be satisfied if you've managed to make your own situation tolerable, and behave as if the other fellow's content with his. And if you have higher longings and unnamed desires, if you yearn for anything transporting, it's generally advisable to keep it to yourself.

Cilla collected herself perfectly after that bad night. Cilla shone bright and full for quite a while after that dinner. There were more evenings with Lucy, Bert and Alice, at their place or mine or out on the town. Cilla gave every sign of liking it all. But near the end of '87 she began to wane anyway. I scarcely noticed at the start.

"Have to give tonight a miss, Harry. Teachers' conference," she said first.

"Don't mind if I have a night out with Moira and the girls, do you?" she said the second time she cancelled an evening with me.

The excuses very gradually became more frequent, more transparent. Miss Moon went gibbous, then half, then slimming still until she was only a thin crescent, low on the horizon. I was lucky to have a night or two a week with her. When I complained, she jollied me through it. "Just a phase," she said, and made love with me in her old wild way.

And then she was gone from my sky entirely, with a simple "It's over, Harry. All the best" as she left my house for the last time, close to midnight on a Sunday.

AUTUMN TO AUTUMN, and round again a few more times. Every circuit more rapid than the last. Yet the hole Cilla left in my life did not diminish at all. One more wound that would never completely close.

Autumn to autumn, and round again.

29

SOUTH HEAD. A huge buttress between the open ocean and the Harbour, topped by grassy parkland and low, wind-twisted trees. From its green height, it falls away sudden and sheer for at least a hundred feet to the sea below. There's a derelict lighthouse there, sealed and whitewashed and fitted out with a bronze plaque recording its age and service.

We were there on a Sunday, having a picnic. The usual good things to eat, the usual rambling talk. The usual Camilla, hiding as much as she could of what had become an absolutely beautiful face behind her thick blond hair. Coltish as you'd expect, ill at ease; she never seemed to know what to do with her lovely form, her graceful hands and small feet. Except when she danced. Dancing, she seemed to forget herself.

Otherwise she couldn't bear anyone looking at her (and so many did, she was that striking), and she tended to peer at everyone out of the corners of her eyes rather than face them directly. She seemed genuinely pained when addressed. No one could know the thoughts abroad in her mind, or what most anything she heard or saw might mean to her, for she volunteered nothing but the minimum: "Yes, thanks"; "No, thanks"; "Maybe later"; "Yeah I'm fine"; "Yeah, I see it. Not impressed." Fabrizia had tried for years, in a big-sisterly way, to coax her from whatever shell she'd withdrawn into, but without success. Bert was loving but baffled by her, near his wit's end. Alice bore down hard, almost mercilessly. Doing far more harm than good, judging from the result.

By the time all that was left of our meal was a litter of crusts and soiled plates and half-empty glasses, Camilla was edgy, wanting to move. She mumbled something that probably was "Excuse me" but may have been "I hate you all," and wandered off. I stood up, my right knee sore and stiff from sitting cross-legged on the ground, lit a cigarette and limped over to the waist-high whitewashed plank fence right at the edge of the cliff. I was looking at the surging sea so far below hurling itself again and again as high up that rock wall as it could. Quite a drama.

Camilla began using the fence like the bar in a dance studio, only spinning her way along it, pushing off with her hands and then turning to raise one leg to the top. It was a careless sort of practice, more a restless repetition, bored and aimless. I paid her scant attention. She wasn't three feet from me when she leaned into the top plank and it gave way.

There was only an instant before she'd be lost, irrevocably, to the fall. I reached for her in that instant, just managed to catch one of her bony wrists, and yanked her toward me, away from the edge. I saw a piece of the plank go down to the surf below, fluttering like a feather as the wind of its own descent caught it.

That's the tale I would have liked to tell. That's what should have happened. But it did not. Camilla was there, and then she was gone.

WHEN CAMILLA FELL, our world was soaring, all of us borne up at least in some ways by the energy and wealth pulsating through Sydney.

The big bicentennial in 1988 had been a huge success, property values were sky-high, new money was being minted in all sorts of business ventures, times were the best they'd ever been in anyone's memory.

Bert's career had taken a tremendous turn for the better. He and another Italian had set up in a little space off Macquarie Street as custom tailors. They'd targeted their market perfectly. No Savile Row imitations for the old moguls and bank presidents and corporate directors. They'd gone after the really successful boomers, the fast-moving blokes in their mid- to late thirties who were hoovering up cash in the financial markets and the property bubble and had already been through their Armani phase. They'd leave Italian designers to those a few rungs below them, Bert and his partner had reckoned, and move on to really classic Italian custom tailoring, at a price none of the younger or less successful ones could afford. Their clientele wanted the finest fabrics, the details like suit sleeves with buttons that really worked instead of simply being sewn on for decoration. They loved going through four or five fittings, loved announcing after a midday squash match or a power lunch that they were due at their tailor's for one.

"Not stupid, these men. Only very vain. They know Agnelli and de Benedetti of Olivetti and Berlusconi wear only custom, from Caraceni in Milan. So we make ourselves the Caraceni of Sydney," Bert explained. "Harry, it makes me laugh sometimes. They don't blink when I say the suit will cost $4,000 if we use the best Australian merino, but $5,000 if we use the superfine wool from Zegna in Italy. They smile, they say the Italian fabric of course."

He grinned. "They don't understand the Italian fabric is woven with Aussie wool!"

I remembered how worried about the risk he had been at the start, how within a few weeks after opening his worries had vanished. "Seven clients already, Harry," he said happily. "Seven! And just one who orders one suit. The others, they want three or four to start. This season, they say. Three or four more for next season. Fantastic, no? Already we got to hire two tailors to help us."

When Camilla fell, Alice had already made a giant leap in her trade as well. A few of the regulars she'd charmed for years at Il Pelicano, more flush than they'd ever been before, had backed her in opening her own place. She had only a small percentage of ownership, but she was no longer a hired employee. She called her restaurant Do Forni, and she located it downtown. It was the sort of place businessmen with hefty expense accounts ate lunch, where they came back for dinner with their mistresses or their wives or their clients. Solid luxury that would last, that's what she was after, not something hip and cool that drew mobs of foodies for a few months and then faded away. The average tab was more than a day's pay for a cadet at the *Herald* or any of the other papers.

Alice loved it, loved the theatrics of it. You could see that all over her, in her voice and face and the way she carried herself. It must have felt to her as if she were on stage and at the same time directing a drama in which the actors were the restaurant's patrons.

She had her favorite characters. One was a young comer in the advertising business who liked to bring clients to Do Forni because Alice would make a great fuss over him, and tell him specials in a tone and timbre that implied the chef had made these delicacies only for him and his guests, who were presumed to be men of impeccable taste in food and drink. He'd try any dish, Alice said, and always pronounced the food "Super, Alessandra! Really fabulous! I say, *fabuloso,* no? *Stupendo!* Have I got that right, *cara?*"

They'd tested him once by overcooking the pasta, but he never noticed. After that they knew they need take no special trouble over him. He always let Alice choose the courses for him. But he was so enthusiastic about anything he was served—even the stuff that wasn't moving well that day and she wanted to get rid of—that Alice always gave him the best table she had, always called it "your table" to him.

"What a ponce," I said.

"Oh no, Harry. A regular fellow. Many times he bringing a girl in for dinner, usually very pretty and young." Alice was as close to giggling as I ever saw her when she added, "But you know I imagine him, after he has just made love to this girl or that, saying 'Super! Really fantastic! *Fabuloso!* Right, *cara?*'"

When Camilla fell, Fabrizia was approaching her final year at Sydney University with a perfect record. She'd led her class at St. Boniface, been jumped a grade, and had won a Queen's Scholarship to go on with her schooling. From then on we talked often about Fabrizia's bright future, whether she'd study architecture or Italian literature or biology. Umberto favored architecture.

She'd chosen architecture, and Umberto was proud, stayed so proud that even now he could scarcely speak of Fabrizia's achievement. He wanted to praise her but fumbled the words.

"Let me tell you just one thing, Harry," he said. "Now, for sure, Fabrizia will do whatever she likes, she earned this by work, so hard and smart, always quick in the mind she is, so anything can be hers. *Dío*, have a look at the grades. When she finish, any job she want? She get it, no problem. She's not scared of nothing. She design the most beautiful buildings in Sydney. Buildings to last two hundred, maybe three hundred years."

"Tell him he's cracked, Harry," Fabrizia said. "Doesn't quite go that way anymore, *pappacci*. I reckon nothing built in Sydney now will stand more than twenty years, tops. Then some property bloke will claim it's obsolete, want something taller, more modern. So boom! A heap of rubble gets cleared away and something new goes up."

"Who cares, anyway? So what if you're a smartie?" Camilla muttered. Fabrizia smiled indulgently at her, then turned back to her father.

"Bah. So it is not the Renaissance, I understand this. Doesn't matter. You'll make beautiful buildings, *puppa*," Bert said. "Never would this thing have happened in Italy, these chances she have. I'm telling you, Alessandra, we make the right choice to come here."

Fabrizia had neatly dodged the only little obstacle in her happy path. Alice would interrogate any boy she brought around. With a few choice words, with her famous "Darling" in a certain tone, she left the poor lads feeling small and humiliated. Fabrizia stood it maybe three or four times, then stopped bringing anyone home at all. She left the house early and came home late. She had a flawless excuse: study at the library.

"Bugger the library, Harry," she told me, laughing. "The work's not that difficult. If there isn't a party to go to somewhere, there's always the clubs! Uni life's bonzer, mate."

If Fabrizia was well on her way, Camilla surely wasn't. She had another three years to go before she'd graduate from St. Boniface, but she was barely keeping up with her class so the issue was in doubt. Alice was beginning what seemed to me a bizarre—no, make that sickening—strategy to insure the girl's future. She'd started scouting out and registering a very carefully chosen group of sons and nephews and cousins of prosperous Italians she knew, of other friends and customers—boys five to ten years older than Camilla with family money or university educations behind them. Her Filofax was thick with names and addresses, and after each barbecue or dinner party she threw, some names would be crossed out and maybe a new name or two would be added.

Fabrizia was disgusted. "Mum's completely out of her tree," she told me. "She's trying to bloody *market* my retarded baby sister! A sick woman, Harry. Wish Dad'd get her committed or something."

Seemed like a fair idea to me.

"Only three, four years, Camilla will be ready," Alice said one night as she and I were cleaning up in the kitchen after a dinner at my place, not long before the accident. Everyone else was out on the verandah, watching the stars come out and arguing about where that Southern Cross might be.

"She's only a kid, Alice! Jesus, she's barely got any tits yet and you're making plans to marry her off?" I said.

"Four years, Harry. Goes like nothing. She'll be eighteen, a beautiful tall girl, like me when I was young, no? With tits, too," she said, digging her knuckles into my ribs. "Ten years older be best, I think. That is not too much difference. He have some money by then, his business will be better established. I get the best one to want Camilla, no problem. He won't be able to think of anything else but taking her to bed. You'll see."

"Don't think I care to witness any such thing," I snapped.

When Camilla fell, Lucy's circumstances were great. Bruce had got some sort of job with Ansett up in Brisbane, so she finally had Paddo to herself. She was in line to be named deputy editor of her paper. And she'd weathered well; she looked a great deal younger than she was with a bit of help from Shiseido products, her legs were still perfect. It'd be a rare man indeed who'd turn her down if she asked him to come home with her.

Frank? Still out and about in his boat, though he was pushing eighty. He creaked and wobbled accordingly, but was still the same Frank inside. Many a time Bert and I would fish with him. Or I'd drive down to Bondi just to have a chat, usually more for my own benefit than to see how the geezer was going; he seemed indestructable.

And my story? Not ideal. Nothing to celebrate. Oh, I'd prospered in my trade as well; I was now city editor, but that was almost more depressing than pleasing, since I wasn't especially young for the post, and I was fairly sure it was my ceiling at the *Herald*, or anyplace else. Nobody even close to Cilla had turned up in my life, and I did still miss my bush girl turned schoolteacher.

Actually, it was worse than that. Ever since Cilla, there was no point or purpose or use to me that I could see. And, at first, when I wasn't missing her, I began brooding again about my lost daughter, though I was pretty successful in keeping that bit of soul-sickness hidden, even from Lucy.

So on the sleepless nights, thigh muscles twitching, I often felt I should have been a casualty of evolution. A buried fossil of some species long extinct because it failed to adapt.

I was a bit dazed after Cilla left me, as you'd imagine. Fuck all, I was shattered, just didn't know it. Like a bush boxer who's taken a knockout punch, but is still standing on pure adrenaline. Lucy had allowed a decent interval to pass, then swept up most of the shards of me and very gracefully presented them first to one and then another and still a few more young women she knew. Girls too inexperienced to recognize the man in their hands wasn't whole. They were always pretty enough, lively enough so that it took me quite some time to figure out why those affairs ended up feeling so unsavory, so near to incestuous, instead of exhilarating and great fun.

"Looks like you're stuck with me, Harry," Lucy said after the last one fizzled, not too long before the South Head picnic. I heard disappointment in her voice. Distinctly. "Reckon I'm the only one who can put up with you."

Only then did I begin to puzzle over what she'd tried to do. I didn't like my first conclusion one bit: Lucy had set me up with replacements for Miss Moon to keep control, to guard against me falling in love and maybe marrying some woman—maybe making babies with her—who might have cut her out of my life. She wanted me to have another Cilla, only a hand-picked Cilla who liked her, liked having her around.

So I worked my way around to thinking I was foolishly flattering myself by imagining Lucy needed my friendship so much she'd stoop to such a thing. I worked my way around to thinking her motives pure, her concern only what anyone would feel for a good friend who's taken a blow. I was pretty bloody brilliant, convincing myself of this.

SO, BEFORE CAMILLA FELL, we had our closed circle, our peculiar, cobbled-up family: Lucy and Umberto and Fabrizia and Camilla and me. Alessandra, too. We were sharing lives, whether we thought of it that way or not. Most likely we didn't. What we had together was the dailiness, a sympathy, a time-tested affection, so many memories in common. If we needed any drama, Alice was always willing to drum some up, seizing upon something one of us said or did—or had once said or done—

and making a production of it, which we all could laugh about after it was over. It wasn't a bad little clan we'd made together, we'd convinced ourselves. Seemed well-set. Seemed pretty unshakable, the bonds strong and stable as any ever are.

And time had done it's job on the one bit that should have been integral but never would be: the daughter Lucy and I had made. The idea of her had become more and more indistinct, to the point that weeks or more might pass without a thought of her, to the point that when I did recall and wonder, she seemed unreal, an imaginary child, no more than a fantasy I'd once held.

WHEN CAMILLA FELL, it was late in the summer of 1990, around the end of February I think, actually February 18th at 1:47 P.M. A cloudless day, almost breezeless. The sailors crowding the Harbour had to tack and haul and really work to keep underway at all. A familiar phenomenon: far to the east the wild winds of a typhoon drove the massy ocean against our shores. Out to sea even the biggest ships would be pitching and rolling in the great swells. But we were safe, the Heads an insuperable bulwark against which the enormous waves smashed themselves to pieces.

Then Camilla goes off, bored. I walk over to smoke and watch the heaving sea. Bert and Alice and Lucy and Fabrizia stay around the blanket. Camilla pirouettes, she spins and pushes. The fucking board breaks with a sharp, ragged crack.

Don't know whether I cried out or Camilla did, it all went silent for me. But suddenly they were all right there, gaping at the busted fence and the empty space where Camilla had been.

What happened—privately, just between Camilla and me—was this: when the railing snapped, there was a moment before she was lost to the fall when I might have been able to do something. I reached for her. She pulled her arms to her sides, refusing my hand. And as she did I felt the pull of her imminent plunge and a great fear that I'd go over too and I stepped back from the edge. I swear she smiled at me then. I'd never seen a smile quite like that. It was not peaceful, but it was not frightened either. And with that smile, a young girl's life was ending before my eyes.

30

A BROKEN COLLARBONE. That was the extent of the damage. The gash on her forehead was nothing, a couple of stitches. There'd be no scar to speak of.

Camilla had not fallen all the way to the surging sea, which would have crushed her body against the rocks. She'd only tumbled a few yards to a narrow, turfed ledge. She'd the presence of mind to heed our calls not to stir, not to move a muscle on that precarious perch. When the rescue squad came, two men rappelled down, eased her onto a stretcher, had her up and into an ambulance within minutes. She didn't appear to be in much pain. She even smiled at me, though it was an altogether different sort now.

"Jesus Christ, a bloody miracle," Lucy said, trembling, awe in her voice. Bert was crying as he clambered into the ambulance to ride with Camilla to the hospital. Alice was pale, but her face was set hard and she didn't make a sound. Fabrizia hung on to one of the posts and peered out and down at the ledge. "Amazing," she said, pushing lightly on the jagged stub of the plank, which broke away from the post easily and feathered down, down.

Bert brought Camilla home from the hospital no more than four or five hours after we'd arrived back there from South Head.

A shocking experience, a chillingly close call, but so little harm done that it's hard to fathom the way it rolled and resonated and realigned everything for all of us. I believe the fundamental force started the instant we all stared down at Camilla on the ledge, but the changes after were so subtle and gradual that none of us saw them as they were occurring, only after they'd happened.

Over at Bert's, the family wasn't drawn together the way you might expect after they'd been passed over by as great a tragedy as Camilla's fall could have been. Instead, they began spinning off away from one another, as if the gravity that had kept them in close orbit all these years had mysteriously vanished. Yet it was some months before I realized that I almost never saw the four of them together anymore. Fabrizia would stay "at the library" 'til all hours, or allegedly sleep over at one or another of her girlfriends' flats near the Uni. Bert seemed to have so much business he could never get home until some hours after Alice had gone to Do Forni, even started working some Saturdays and Sundays. Alice never returned from the restaurant before two A.M., even though the kitchen closed at eleven. And, oddest of all, Camilla, alone in the lengthening intervals between Alice's departures and Bert's arrivals, started coming over to sit with me in the evenings when she spotted me out on the verandah having a beer. She never, ever mentioned South Head—didn't speak much at all, in fact, though for the first time in all the years I'd known her she would answer direct questions pretty straight.

And every once in a while she'd look cooly and directly into my eyes, that heart-cracking shyness replaced for a moment by self-possession beyond her years, and give me a smile so loaded with secret complicity it actually made the short hairs on the back of my neck rise the first few times she did it.

I began getting a strange new type of smile from Lucy as well: mournful, fragile, almost tremulous now and again. No more saucy, playfully mocking grins and rough teasing, or at least not nearly the usual quota. Instead, she fell into a lot of reminiscing about our early days. Some of it seemed just a bit too wistful. Not like her at all. But she still kept well clear of one chapter of our history: from about the time she conceived on the rocks at Whale Beach to the time a few years later when we made our final truce and became mates again. Never a word, never an allusion or hint. Easy enough to understand; that interval felt like Dreamtime now.

"God, Harry, I truly do wish it had worked out with you and Cilla," was the closest Lucy ventured. "You'd likely be a dad by now. She was sweet, so good for you. And I hate to see you alone."

That wasn't it at all. Later the same evening she buried her face in my chest, went teary, and murmured, "I feel so old, Harry. I feel ancient. It's scaring me. What's it all been about? What's any of it meant? Harry, please tell me life hasn't left me behind."

You know my casual attitude toward truth. I told her of course it hadn't, it never would.

FABRIZIA GRADUATED with honors from Sydney University the following November. We all went to the ceremony. I have a snapshot of her in her cap and gown, on tiptoe to kiss a beaming Umberto on the cheek, flanked on one side by Alessandra and on the other by Camilla, me and Lucy behind her. One of Fabrizia's mates took it with Lucy's little Olympus.

A more witless gift is hard to imagine, but I gave Fabrizia a watch, a Seiko copy of the classic Cartier tank. Useless thing, good only for marking the passage of what I truly wanted to give her: all the time in the world. Yet it might have been made of gold and diamonds in Switzerland from the warm way she threw her arms around me and said, "Harry! Thanks, mate!" just like she had when she was a kid and I gave her any little thing.

Within three months she was gone. Soon I had a postcard from her. She was in Japan. Said she was teaching English, a sort of transient job to finance her travels. Six months later, another card came from Vancouver, a rainy but incredibly beautiful place, she said, where she'd got involved with some theater group. Six months after that, got one from New York. She was working as a waitress, making scads of money from tips, and was saving for a trip to Italy. Finally a card from Venice. She said she'd found where she belonged. But later I heard from Bert that she'd gone back to New York after a couple of months, persuaded a gay man she'd got friendly with to marry her so she could get a green card, the talisman of permanent U.S. resident status. Bert didn't care to say how she was making her living, except that she wasn't practicing architecture. Never a beautiful building designed by his daughter would rise in Sydney, he said sadly.

"Give her time, mate," I said. "Every kid in Aussie who can manage it makes a long jaunt to have a look at the world, and then comes back in a year or two and settles into a regular life here."

That was true enough, but poor comfort. Knowing Fabrizia, no comfort at all, really. Exceptional as she was, her jaunt might well be permanent, I reckoned. Though I hoped like hell I'd be proved wrong.

With every card I'd badly wanted to write her back, to tell her we missed her and needed her here. But I reckon my clever little Fabrizia knew that well enough already and didn't want to hear it from me, for she never included her own address on anything she sent me.

I knew why Fabrizia had left. I never was certain of how or why Bert kept on with Alessandra. In the end I suppose it was only his concept of honor and loyalty, words people laugh at today and don't understand or think are quaint. Honor and loyalty to Camilla anyway. The last thin strands of what had bound Alice and him frayed through after Camilla's fall. Alice lived only for her restaurant; she spent so much more time there, day and night, than she ever did at home. Christ, I used to wish Bert would put Camilla in boarding school and find himself a Miss Moon and run off to Port Douglas or Perth or even back to Italy, and get some joy in his life. But he never would do a thing like that. He wasn't the sort.

Neither was I, I suppose. I could have left and tried to find a bit of joy somewhere else as well, since Sydney had gone so off. But I was just too worn out to give it a go, and maybe Bert was too.

"Harry, lately I'm thinking life is like some mad long-distance race, no finish line," he said one evening at The Drowned Man. We were a party of two there many nights. Les had moved to Melbourne, a lot of other familiar faces had vanished and been replaced by younger, fresher spirits.

"Everyone just run until they drop," he said. "Are you a winner if you run longer than anyone else you know? I don't think so. I think you are only exhausted and lonely and very stupid. And wondering why you tried so hard when there's nothing to be won, when you end up nowhere."

THE FUNNY BIT IS that only Alice seemed to think it was odd how Camilla sought out my company, talked to me in ways she did not with her parents or anyone else. She had to sit up front with me whenever we would all go on an outing in Jacko, which wasn't nearly as often as we used to, and she would always stick close to me at the beach or in the mountains or wherever we'd gone. She whispered a lot in my ear. Normal chatter, banal things there was no need to hush up, but she whispered anyway. And Alice kept her mouth shut about it, which was odder still. I'd only see this deeply suspicious uncertainty in her eyes from time to time, when I caught her looking at me with Camilla.

Lucy and I would get together pretty regularly for an espresso, or lunch, or dinner, as well as on those outings. She'd found herself a lover, apparently a decent bloke some years younger than her. I never met him. She'd hinted she needed to invent tales about where she was going whenever she was going to see me. Don't know why—unless she believed her man had resentful tendencies even beyond Cilla's. I couldn't have given a flying fuck that she was getting some good rooting. I was honestly pleased for her, in fact. It gave me some hope for myself. It couldn't be too late, just the wrong side of forty, to fall in love, fall still further, maybe start a family. I've met a lot of nice women. I have one or two especially in mind. All I'd need to do is make a bit of an effort.

Maybe I'll get around to it one of these days, when I have more time. Right now, though, apart from work and talks with Lucy and drinking with Umberto and visits from Camilla, I spend the little that's left—and a bloody fortune—keeping old Jacko running. That's getting more and more difficult; there'll come a day when I'll scavange every junkyard in New South Wales and still won't find some crucial part for a '49 Holden. And that will be it for poor Jacko.

THERE ARE WORSE THINGS to live with. I'd stepped back, up there on South Head. Nobody saw me except Camilla, nobody ever blamed me, nobody suggested I could have caught her. But the scene invades my mind so often, usually in the early evening, when the darkness is coming on and the cicadas grate the nerves unbearably. Neither of us knew there was a ledge. Neither of us knew there'd be a miracle. We both thought it was a death plunge. I can't decide if she meant it to be one.

Could I have reached her, could I have pulled her away in time? I don't think so. I think when she tucked in her arms I lost all chance, and she was lost to her own intention.

But I stepped back, afraid.

So I'll never be sure, will I?

31

S HE COULDN'T SEE, HARRY." Lucy's voice was flat, mechanical. "Something didn't develop properly in her brain and optic nerves. Never showed in the sonograms. Never a warning or a clue. But her eyes were dead the moment her life began, the moment she took her first breath."

That's the truth of it, and the very long time it took to learn it did nothing to lessen the blow. My daughter was born blind.

This burst sudden and scorching as that RPG in Fuck Toy, out of a past that we'd made black and spooky as the jungle at night, a place we never willingly ventured. It had been at least two years since Camilla fell—Lucy must have been between lovers for she'd begun spending almost all her time with me, and I was between no one so I welcomed that, was glad of it. We'd been larking, having whatever fun we could. On that particular evening we were dining at Kinsela's, a former funeral parlor in Darlinghurst. An unlikely place of the moment, with a club upstairs and an ambitiously hip restaurant in what had been the embalming room. God knows why the room's past use didn't put off anyone who knew of it from eating there.

And God knows why—besides the bottle of Veuve Clicquot we polished off even before we ordered, and the bottle of Hunter red we drank with the meal, and the cognacs I had after to dull the ache of all those holes in my life—I dared ask that old, moldering question. The one I'd thought had become unaskable. The one Lucy once promised she'd answer when she felt sure she could trust me to believe her, but never had.

"It couldn't have been . . ." I felt concussed. "I mean, not permanent. Not final."

"It was. I took her to specialists."

"Yeah," I said, a temper rising unbidden and unwanted. "I'm sure there were real experts in fucking Cairns."

Lucy ignored my anger. Maybe her sorrow had built over the years a sort of bunkered perimeter far too strong for any sort of assault to breach.

"I flew with her to Brisbane, and then Melbourne. I did my research. The doctors were the best, as good as any in the world," she replied calmly. "Not a single word of hope."

"So bloody what? She was *alive*. She'd have been loved and cared for, blind or crippled or brain-damaged."

"She has been loved and cared for, Harry. I spent a month in Brisbane with the couple who wanted to adopt her. I never met two better people in my life. They were *good*, Harry. The wife was only twenty-seven then. She'd had four late-term miscarriages, there was no chance for them at all. The doctors had to perform a hysterectomy after that last one.

"The baby needed an especially devoted and patient mother. I didn't reckon I could go the limit," she said, tears coming on now. "I had a living to earn, remember? She'd need so much attention, so much help always. Who'd have provided it? A fucking careless teenage au pair? This man was doing very well as a lawyer, and his wife wanted nothing more in the world than to mother a child. This child. She fell in love with our baby the instant she first held her. I could feel it."

Lucy's softly spoken words registered all right, even in the loud buzz of animated conversations all around us. But there was such a din, such a riot of confusion in my mind.

"Fuck that," I heard myself saying, as if from some distance. "We could have managed. We could have made it here, on my salary."

"But there never was any 'we,' Harry," Lucy said. "There was you and there was me. Our own separate selves. We had a lovely connection once, but never a true union. We missed our window, if there was a real one and not just a hope, even before I got pregnant, remember? You seemed to understand that well enough all those years ago, after I'd come back to Sydney and showed up at your door and we got past the battling."

"Reckon I thought so, yeah. But now, hearing this . . . Jesus, we did something unbelievably selfish. We could have sacrificed whatever the hell we were seeking and couldn't find together for the kid's sake. That we didn't is damned ironic, isn't it? Since it seems neither of us has found much happiness anyway."

"Don't you think that torments me, too? Do you imagine I sleep easy and peaceful many nights?"

"Hell, Lucy. An imperfect couple we'd have been, but we could have dedicated ourselves to our own child. We could have given her everything."

"Without real love, a real union? That's what those Brisbane folks had. We would have been linked only by a fragile child. Think about that. And think how couples joined at the hip but not the heart hobble through life on three legs."

"Seems to me we're both a bit gimpy all on our own."

"Exactly. But at least when we stumble, we hurt nobody but ourselves. If we'd tried to raise her the way we were, we'd have surely scuffed and bruised her. Maybe wrecked her. So I made a different sort of sacrifice than the one you mean. Not a lesser one, either."

"We've paid for it."

"Haven't we, though?" she laughed edgily through those tears. "Aren't we still paying? Won't we always be?"

"Did it have to go that way? People do marry, have kids, make a decent try at being a family."

"Look at Fabrizia, and your new little pal Camilla. Truly sweet. Truly damaged. Both Bert and Alice, on their own, have good hearts. Yet what they've done as a couple must appall them. Should we have inflicted anything like that on a child of our own?"

I felt all at once as if Lucy and I were in a cone of pure silence, as if everyone else in the restaurant had vanished, along with everything we should or might say to each other.

"I can't accept . . ." I started in again. And then felt as helpless as I did that bad junglee night, when I could hear the private I'd abused saying, 'Smarts a bit, does it, Corporal Hull?' as I lay flayed and bleeding in the mud.

"You ought to've told me," I said weakly. "You ought to have allowed me that."

"Too dangerous, Harry," she said, seizing my good hand. "Couldn't risk you managing to turn me round. If I'd believed in my heart there'd been even half a chance with the normal kid I expected I'd be having, I wouldn't have run off, would I?"

"So I was too much of a bastard to be a husband. Couldn't we have gone on being mates? I'd have paid for all the kid's needs, I'd have loved her and been a decent father to her, and you could have kept working and lived your life any way you wanted."

"Harry, I only wanted to raise my baby. Christ, I never wanted anything so much in my life. But I couldn't do it, not the way she was. And I was terrified I'd muck it up even if I had a man by my side to help me. Can't you grasp that?"

I could. I did. But not strongly enough to prevent an almost forgotten reflex. "How could you have abandoned that poor little creature without even talking to me about her, letting me at least see her? Christ, I've never even known her name, you heartless bitch."

Suddenly I recalled a baby, groping its sightless way along a packed earth floor. A grub. I'd laughed. But then I went to pick up the poor little bludger and Phong exploded. She threw herself between me and the kid, shouldered me hard. She screeched something at her mother that caused the woman to scoop the tiny thing off the floor and scuttle out the back door.

"No baby!" Phong had snarled, all the bogus whore-charm in her voice replaced by a desperate anger. I'd backed well away. Phong had calmed then, resumed her usual act. "Numbah one fuck, Au-see, okay? You no see bloody baby, you see Phong."

I'd slipped double the usual wad of piastres under her pillow when I left that night. Never saw the kid again. Never wanted to.

"Heartless bitch," I murmured unconsciously, when I was really badly wanting to erase my wicked, wretched insults to Lucy, and maybe to Phong as well. But Lucy heard only the hateful words again.

And so she shut me up forever, made me loathe myself and all that I'd ever said.

"I fed her from my breasts for three months, Harry. You will never in your life, no matter what happens to you, no matter how bad it is for you, come anywhere near the pain I bore—and still know every day."

SOMETIMES I THINK OF a pretty girl, she'd be about fourteen now, tall for her age and lean. I think of her most often when I muse on those green girls you see on the beach at the beginning of every summer, the kids who've grown breasts from last year to this. They're pleased of course, but even more they're embarrassed by the way boys and men are looking at them now. The little things so shy, with both arms folded in front of their tender chests, so self-conscious. But when they think they're unobserved, they gaze down with a sort of wonderment, adjust their posture to make them stand out, then go all bashful and blushing. They don't know how to live in their bodies at that age, thirteen or fourteen; they feel so strange to themselves. I see my daughter, face and name unknown, among them.

Except she wouldn't be like the green girls. She'd feel the sun, and the sea breeze, and the changes in her body. But she'd never know the swift appraising gazes, the sordid thoughts she was inspiring. She'd be spared the discomfort, the embarrassment. If she was lucky, if she'd been loved enough by her father and mother, she might not even feel sorry for herself, or depressed about her handicap. She might be a laughing, cheerful girl, in love with the life before her. She might be at peace. She might have that special innocence, that state of grace, and never feel unreal to herself at all.

I think sometimes of going to Brisbane. Not to claim her, not to intrude in her life, not to wreck whatever equilibrium she's reached. Just to have a look at her. Just to hear her voice.

From a distance. I'd be so discreet. She and the couple who raised her would never even know I'd come, touched her with my eyes, and slipped away again with a stolen image they'd never miss, but would mean the world to me.

But I never will. It's just a dream I allow myself every now and again. A dream against heavy casualties. A dream against all the regret and remorse over so many things done, so many undone.

And somehow Lucy and I go on, best mates, never speaking anymore of what we have lost, what we might have had, never admitting our separate, secret despairs. Never a "we" as she once put it. But still as one, in our one odd way.

So we'll remain, until our unknown ends.

Thomas Moran, a former journalist, is the author of *The Man in the Box*, winner of Book-of-the-Month Club's Stephen Crane Award for First Fiction; *The World I Made for Her*; and *Water, Carry Me*. His novels have been translated into seven languages.